Cat's Whisker

by Robert Steven Goldstein

ISBN 978-1-64663-463-7

REVIEW COPY: This is an advanced printing subject to corrections and revisions.

Published by

köehlerbooks™

3705 Shore Drive
Virginia Beach, Va 23455
800–435–4811
www.koehlerbooks.com

Cat's Whisker

Robert Steven Goldstein

VIRGINIA BEACH
CAPE CHARLES

For Sapphire. In her final years, she taught me more about dignity, grace, and courage than had any other being I have known.

1.
An Old Dog

WALKING AN OLD DOG teaches me a great deal.

Sapphire is seventeen, a mixed breed. Her size, coat, and head structure are those of an Australian cattle dog. Her barrel-like torso and short legs are unmistakably Welsh corgi.

I found her in a shelter when she was about two. The staff had already named her Sapphire—not a name I would have chosen, but it was her name and she recognized it. It seemed wrong to force her to adopt a new one.

Her hair is grey now, but when the shelter found her she was young, and like many Australian cattle dogs had striking blue hairs jutting out from her merle coat on the sides of her head below her ears. Cattle dogs are also sometimes called blue heelers because of those blue hairs, coupled with the fact that the dogs herd cattle by nipping at the bovines' heels. But to the woman performing intake for the shelter, the hairs resembled bright sapphire earrings. So she named the dog Sapphire.

Cattle dogs are remarkably intelligent. Sapphire has always been bright, but now she processes thoughts much more deliberately. Her hearing has deteriorated. Cataracts have blurred her vision. Her limbs are arthritic; she moves slowly.

When we walk now, she stops repeatedly to intensively sniff whatever she has encountered, be it the base of a tree, the lower edge of a bush, or a barely discernable pool of moisture on the road. She used to give objects a brief sniff, decide immediately whether to mark the spot with a squirt of urine, and then move on. Now she lingers interminably. Sometimes I think she is tired and uses the opportunity to rest. But more often it seems that she does this because her sense of smell is the only sense she can now fully trust and rely upon. She can no longer utilize hearing and eyesight to assess the situation she is exploring, but her need to know and understand is as strong as ever.

My veterinarian once explained to me that a dog's walk is the equivalent of a human reading that morning's newspaper. It is Sapphire's opportunity to assess the condition of her territory, and piece together recent goings-on. My personal theory on why dogs and mail carriers have such turbulent relationships is based upon this. Mail carriers convey on their shoes and clothing the collective scents of the entire neighborhood, which to a dog must be a confusing and overwhelming gestalt.

Sapphire's need to ingest and process this sort of information seems eminently more critical to her now than ever before.

Many owners, I am sure, would grow impatient and pull her along. She can make a walk go quite slowly. I never do so. Every time I am tempted, I remind myself that this may be her last opportunity to engage in this ritual that she loves so much. She still displays the excitement of a puppy when she sees me lace up my walking shoes.

———◡———

Not long ago, I had a chance meeting at a farmers market in Berkeley with a fellow I hadn't seen in over twenty years. He is middle-aged now, but when I first met him he was a promising young psychoanalyst candidate at San Francisco's C. G. Jung Institute. I was engaged by the institute then as a consultant, to help enable video presentations. He was one of my main contacts for the project.

When I greeted him at the Berkeley farmers market he gazed at me oddly, as though he was not pleased to see me. But I quickly realized that he didn't recognize who I was. It was almost as if we had traded veneers. As a young, aspiring psychoanalyst, he was shaggy and a bit unkempt—he now was immaculately groomed with closely cropped hair and a well-trimmed beard. I, on the other hand, am a good deal greyer and far more bohemian than when he knew me. I may also be a few pounds thinner—I no longer work out with weights.

But when I identified myself to him, his demeanor immediately lightened. We conversed briefly. I was happy to hear that he was now a full-fledged Jungian analyst with a thriving practice in Berkeley. I was quite surprised, however, to learn that among the various lines of counseling in which he specialized, one was geared exclusively toward people who had experienced the state of mystical transcendence.

He said it had first occurred to him to open this line when he met me, decades ago.

It may seem to some a strange, esoteric sort of therapeutic offering, but episodes of mystical transcendence are far more common than is generally imagined. When I first met him, I recognized immediately that he had experienced spiritual illumination. I confided in him that I had as well. He seemed relieved to have someone with whom to share his secret.

In his practice now, he helps clients who have had such experiences to integrate that spiritual sensibility back into their day-to-day lives through Jungian psychoanalysis. It is a brilliant notion.

No such psychotherapeutic services were offered decades ago. Had they been, I certainly would have availed myself of them. It might have made my journey far easier.

In the mornings now, Sapphire and I hike on trails where she can roam off leash. We walk unhurriedly.

I have taken to practicing walking meditation while Sapphire scrupulously sniffs the terrain. The trails we choose are long loops that slope uphill first and then descend back to the trailhead.

Sapphire teaches me that I too can make a slow walk meaningful.

The walking meditation I practice is a modified version of the Buddhist meditation technique known as mindfulness. Some years ago, I worked briefly with a yoga teacher who stressed a traditional and intensive approach to postures and meditation. I suspect he would disapprove strongly of my walking meditation practice. It was his adamant belief that the sensibility of illumination evoked in the meditative state derived exclusively from complete stillness of both body and mind.

I am now far less rigid on this matter. I find meditation while hiking to be both more enjoyable and more fruitful than my previously established practice of meditating motionlessly while seated cross-legged following a ninety-minute session of yoga.

Classically, mindfulness consists of trying to still the mind by briefly and calmly acknowledging any thought that intrudes, and letting it dissipate. But I recently developed a slightly different approach.

The psychoanalyst I ran into at the farmers market mentioned that he and several of his colleagues had become avid meditators. They are, in fact, researching new approaches to meditation. The most promising new techniques involve easygoing variations on the classical practice of mindfulness. Interestingly, some of these approaches do not require that thoughts be forced away at the outset of a session. Meditators are instead encouraged to examine and ponder thoughts that arise early in the session if the ideas seem important or interesting.

During our impromptu conversation at the farmers market, he had very little time to outline these approaches in detail. He had to rush to an appointment.

But I found the concept most intriguing. Over the next few months, I worked out, through trial and error during my morning hikes with Sapphire, an efficacious application of the theory. I now employ the method daily.

I set aside substantial time at the beginning of each hike to think through issues of importance. But even as I do, I simultaneously anticipate that my brain will at some point acknowledge that nothing of pressing significance remains to be considered. When I reach that juncture, the background process asserts itself over my foreground deliberations, and emptying my mind becomes almost effortless and instantaneous.

It took a while, of course, to train my mind to execute this dance seamlessly on a daily basis. At first, after pondering my issues, I would become aware of a general sense of conclusion, accompanied by a desire to relax and meditate. But conscious effort was still required to track down random notions and escort them away. After a few months, though, the entire process automated itself.

This approach, which would be heresy to most meditation teachers, appealed to me immediately because of my inherent love for methodical examination of ideas. But I also understand the importance of periodically stilling my mind to enable the replenishment of my spiritual coffers. I find now that I am comforted in having ample time to ruminate on anything I wish. Allowing my brain to decide for itself at what point it is ready to empty itself of thought, and become a vessel for universal consciousness, makes the whole experience quite joyful.

I would have been afraid to adopt such a radical approach to meditation on my own, fearing that it was somehow spurious or fraudulent. For whatever reason, knowing that this Jungian psychoanalyst and his colleagues are investigating these sorts of variants allows me to embrace this technique without qualm.

Sapphire's leisurely pace guides me. It enables me to resist any urge to rush through in a perfunctory manner.

Sapphire also appears to appreciate this state of nonjudgmental attentiveness, as it frees her to amble on the trails without feeling pestered.

2.
Mastery of Life

THERE WERE TWO MAGAZINES. One featured science and the other mechanics, but once inside them, they were essentially indistinguishable. They featured glossy, book-sized pages portraying advances and products from labs around the world, ideas for inventions submitted by readers, and many articles depicting futuristic possibilities.

When I was eleven years old, my father purchased subscriptions for both.

He put the subscriptions in my name. He very much wanted me to feel the journals were mine. I loved science and mathematics and excelled at those subjects in school. My father, who shared those interests, read the magazines as well; they provided the two of us with fodder for many discussions during the long hours my mother spent helping my younger brother, David, with his homework.

But for me, the magazines' advertisements soon became my secret indulgence. Interspersed sparsely throughout the initial pages of text, drawings, and diagrams, the ad density increased further into the magazine. Finally, the only feature text that appeared was relegated to a few narrow columns containing the final paragraphs of long articles from the front of the journal. The rest were ads.

The advertisements that captured and fascinated me were those that touched upon a different sort of reality. It seemed curious to me that in journals devoted to science and mechanics there would be so many ads featuring things mystical and otherworldly. "Otherworldly" not in the extraterrestrial sense, but in the sense of a spiritual or mystical reality coexisting with the corporeal world of mathematics and physics—equally palpable to the initiated, but subject to an entirely different set of rules and principles. Precepts so different from those of science that they were ultimately not measurable, not documentable, not subject to traditional systematic inquiry. *Why*, I wondered, *would people reading magazines grounded in science and mechanics be drawn to such ads?* Yet clearly, many of us were.

The advertisements that most consistently enticed me were from an organization called the Rosicrucians. My family lived in a small apartment in the Bronx. The Rosicrucian Order was housed in a seemingly mysterious complex in a place called San Jose, California. That alone seemed exotic to me. But the ads promised transcendent powers far more impressive:

"Mastery of Life."

An irresistible claim. What greater capability could be promised?

The ads themselves were alluringly rendered. My favorite featured beautiful pen-and-ink portraits of Benjamin Franklin, Isaac Newton, and Francis Bacon. "These great minds were Rosicrucians," it announced. "What secret power did they possess?"

By filling out and mailing a coupon, you could receive a free book, *The Mastery of Life*. The ads further stated that "the Rosicrucians (NOT a religious organization)" had "been in existence for centuries" and today, their headquarters in San Jose sent "over seven million pieces of mail annually to all parts of the world."

I pondered all this for months, but with the utmost secrecy. I intuitively realized that my preoccupation with this area of inquiry would be viewed as subversive and dangerous by my family, though rationally I was not certain why that would be.

Sometimes it seemed possible to lay out the facts to my father in a logically defensible manner: The book was free. The Rosicrucian organization was, by their own description, *not* a religious order; my father couldn't reasonably accuse me of jeopardizing our semi-practicing allegiance to the neighborhood's Conservative Jewish temple. The Rosicrucians were arguably legitimate, having existed for centuries and distributing millions of pieces of mail.

But I was never convinced viscerally that these plausible contentions would prove in any way persuasive to my family. In any event, those concerns soon became moot. The allure grew irrepressible. I filled out the coupon and sent for the book, ignoring the consequences I knew would ensue.

———

I had not consciously planned on maintaining secrecy. I was aware that eventually my family would discover I was investigating the Rosicrucian Order, especially if I decided to pursue any sort of long-term interaction. Perhaps I thought that if I had time to examine the initial material and make sense of it, I could better explain its contents and the reasons for my interest. Regardless of any focused intent, however, I found myself checking our mailbox promptly each afternoon when I returned home from school so that I could intercept *The Mastery of Life* before my parents saw it.

But I failed to take into account Saturday delivery.

I spent that entire Saturday constructing a small-scale working steam engine and the truck-like vehicle it powered. The components of the miniature apparatus were from a kit my father had purchased for me. In the morning, following the instructions meticulously, I assembled the small truck, paying special attention to assure that the wheel axles were positioned with precision, bolted tightly to the frame, and that all four wheels could spin freely. Then, after lunch, I anchored a squat alcohol lamp onto the flatbed rear of the vehicle, and mounted a tin bottle just above it, followed by a piston assembly with a series of gears that reached down to the wheel axles. When I was sure the assembly was sturdy, I carefully filled the tin bottle with water and lit the alcohol lamp. As the water came to a hard boil, steam shot from the bottle's narrow spout. The force of the vapor raised and lowered a mechanism hovering just above the bottle's lip, which rotated the piston rod, and in turn transferred that energy to the wheel axles.

I watched with excitement as the little truck started moving. It was proceeding slowly down the long linoleum foyer of my family's two-bedroom apartment when I heard the front door's deadbolt engage and saw my father, Emmanuel, enter. The neighborhood TV repair shop he owned stayed open well into the evening Monday through Friday, but he always closed the store in the late afternoon on Saturday to begin his abbreviated weekend.

The truck moved toward him as he came in, a pile of mail in his hands. Generally, his seeing one of my mechanical projects come to life would bring a great smile to his face and animation to his body language. But for some reason his jaw was set. The steam-powered vehicle heading his way did nothing to soften his stern demeanor. I noticed that one of the pieces of mail in his hand was a large white envelope with a prominent symbol above the address label. The envelope's contents were bulky, as if it contained a thick pamphlet and accompanying papers.

I knew exactly what had happened before he said a word.

The Rosicrucians are a rather scholarly lot. For centuries, they have thoroughly investigated and chronicled various documents, practices, and symbols of mysticism and spiritual illumination, wherever such might be found. They have done so with sincere and unbiased intellectual curiosity. So, whereas ancient Rosicrucians may have immersed themselves in the study of such things as alchemy and Egyptian mummification, the Rosicrucian lodge just a mile from my home in San Francisco has, in the past year alone, presented lectures on topics as varied as psychological visualization, the power of silence in Zen Buddhism, masculine and feminine symbolism in the Kabbalah, and how congruent vowel sounds have formed the core of mystical chants in a variety of religious and spiritual practices across the globe.

The Rosicrucians are open and receptive to mystical ideas and artifacts garnered from a wide variety of sources, including traditional faith-based religions, experientially based Eastern meditative practices, scientific research, archeological and anthropological finds, and many other venues. Their lectures in the lodge near my home are presented by articulate individuals with notable credentials, and are open to the public. Although I am not and have never been a practicing Rosicrucian, I have attended and enjoyed a number of these presentations in the years since I retired from work.

The Rosicrucians have chronicled, and often display, various mystical symbols from throughout the ages. The order's central symbol, from which the name "Rosicrucian" is derived, is the Rosy Cross. Officially, the organization's full name is Antiquus Mysticusque Ordo Rosæ Crucis (Ancient and Mystic Order of the Rosy Cross), often abbreviated as AMORC.

Today, those in charge of Rosicrucian marketing (as evinced by the layout of the order's modern website) have relegated the Rosy Cross to an almost imperceptible presence, most likely so as not to offend potential enrollees who are not Christian.

That nod to religious inclusivity was evidently not yet appreciated by the Rosicrucian leaders of the early 1950s.

Included among their mailings was a bulky white envelope sent to the small apartment of a family in the Bronx, whose patriarch, Emmanuel Baron, despite being only nominally religiously observant, was ethnically and culturally both fiercely and stubbornly Jewish. The envelope was addressed to me, his eleven-year-old son, Samuel. The logo on that envelope was a large, imposing, colorful Rosy Cross.

There are varying theories as to the Rosy Cross's origin and meaning. The Rosicrucians assert that it predates Christianity and represents the human body—the red rose at its center symbolizing an individual's expansive consciousness.

Regardless of any such interpretation, to my father, it was clearly a Christian crucifix.

When my father became angry, he did not simply lose his temper—he temporarily transformed into a different being. As a young boy, this change seemed to me akin to the metamorphosis scenes in the werewolf films from the 1930s and 1940s that I watched in reruns at our neighborhood movie theater's weekend matinees. But whereas those cinematic transmutations occurred slowly, and were traced in minute detail by the camera, my father's metamorphosis was instantaneous.

My father was a short, slight man—five foot, four inches tall—with a growing paunch around his middle. He generally displayed a calm and gentle demeanor. Socially he was reticent and did not have many friends, but on those occasions that I observed him working in his television repair shop, he was different: fully engaged with his patrons, conversing with them comfortably in English or Yiddish, whichever the customer preferred. When he and I discussed or collaborated on anything scientific or mathematical, he was animated and absorbed.

But several times a week, always at home, something would provoke him, and he would fly into a frightening rage. When he did, his body leaned menacingly, and his torso distended. His lower jaw jutted forward, his face reddened, his eyes widened and glared. His entire being took on a fearsome, apelike guise. He screamed uncontrollably in piercing, guttural eruptions. If he was near me, he lashed out and slapped me without warning across the face or neck.

The envelope from the Rosicrucians propelled him into such a frenzy.

He hit me twice across the face. He kicked the slowly moving steam truck aside, overturning it against a wall and sending a small puddle of boiling water onto the linoleum, the burning alcohol lamp poised dangerously on its side. My mother slipped silently behind him—she mopped up the hot water with a kitchen towel, blew out the flame on the alcohol lamp, and set the apparatus quietly back into an upright position on the floor, all without his noticing.

I instinctively drew back. My father stepped closer to me and dropped all the mail other than the large white envelope. My mother watched us from the corner of the foyer, making no effort to intervene.

My father hit me again, screaming vehemently about the envelope and the cross. "What the hell is this? What's the matter with you? Why did you send for this? You want to be a Christian?"

My younger brother, David, appeared in the doorway of our bedroom to observe the altercation, but came no closer and said nothing.

"It's not Christian," I said, cowering against a closet door.

My father slapped me again—this one hit my lower cheek and neck. "What are you, an idiot?" he yelled. "It's a cross! It's a Christian cross!"

I said nothing. My father's outstretched hand trembled slightly, a familiar indication that he was beginning to calm down. In a few minutes we'd be able to talk it through rationally. I just needed to not provoke him again while we waited.

He tore open the envelope and found the booklet. He thumbed through some of the pages, at first violently, but soon more methodically and thoughtfully. His face and body slowly retracted back into their normal configuration. He grew calm.

He now seemed engrossed by the booklet. "What is this?" he asked. "Where did you get it?"

"It's from a group called the Rosicrucians. They have ads in the magazines we read. They're not a religious organization. The ads say so."

"I've seen those ads. They say it here too: 'not a religious organization.' But I don't believe them, not for a minute. Their symbol is a cross!" He lifted his head from the book and looked at me. "Sammy, they're just trying to trick you. The Goyim are always trying to convert Jews. Don't fall for it, Sammy. They tried to kill us all. More than once. That didn't work. Now they try to do it this way. Don't fall for their schemes."

He rifled through the accompanying letter and membership offer. "Now you gave them our name and address," he muttered, shaking his head, "who knows what these lunatics will do with it."

It didn't seem likely to me that the Rosicrucians would send armed intruders to our Bronx apartment, but I refrained from saying so.

"You didn't pay any money for this, did you?" he asked.

"No," I said. "It was free."

"All right, I'm going to throw all this *dreck* into the garbage. Don't send for anything else without my permission, Sammy. *Farshtey?*"

"OK," I said.

Derisive humor held a strong appeal for my father. For months after the Rosicrucian incident, he made jokes to my younger brother, but always within my own earshot, about how "Sammy was duped by a bunch of Christians." Emmanuel's favorite ploy was to surreptitiously draw and snip out a Christian cross from a piece of paper, attach a small ring of cellophane tape to it, and, in the guise of slapping me approvingly on the back, affix it to the rear of my shirt. Then he and David would laugh and snicker until I figured out what they had done.

3.
White Jasmine Rice

SAPPHIRE AND I returned to San Francisco two nights ago, after several weeks in New York City. We make such trips to New York every spring and fall. I own an apartment there overlooking Manhattan's Central Park.

Most of my evenings in New York are spent with my good friend Professor Wayne Jakob Kenneman, whom I've known for many years. As young men, he and I worked together in the field of electronics. We both lived in New York then. Jake went on to become an esteemed professor and research scientist.

Jake is quite cynical regarding spiritual enlightenment. We shared a deep friendship for over a decade before I even mentioned this aspect of my life to him. I only did so because I had written an article on the topic, which to my great surprise had been published by a reputable journal. I wanted him to read it.

Jake imagines the experience of mystical transcendence to be simply a chemical manipulation of one's brain state. He sees nothing inherently wrong with manipulating one's mind in that manner, but equates it more to downing several martinis than to anything more significant.

Jake and I have enjoyed many martinis together, engaged in discussions on topics of this sort. He prefers gin martinis over vodka. That preference is adamant, but his curiosity with respect to examining a wide variety of other alcoholic reagents and amalgams has not diminished with age.

For as long as I can remember, he has referred to me as "Doc," out of admiration for the technical prowess in electronic engineering I displayed when we first met. I am not a doctor, and do not have an advanced degree of any sort. Jake, who possesses such credentials, has often told me that my scientific wizardry far exceeded many who earned such honors.

Jake is a pure and confirmed atheist. He does not just reject the biblical portrayal of an anthropomorphic God. (Were that my definition of a pure atheist, I would certainly categorize myself as one as well.) Jake's atheism is far more encompassing and fundamental. He believes that humans are no more than a fortuitous permutation of chemicals and DNA. He does not envision us as part of anything greater than ourselves. He is quite certain that we erode no differently than inert matter when we die.

He respects my opinions but finds it hard to understand how I, as a fellow scientist and engineer, continue to adhere to them.

I am greatly impressed by his ability to proceed with relative happiness through an existence he has delineated as unattached to anything greater than himself. Yet I remain somewhat saddened that he can't or won't recognize the mystical aspects of our cosmos, the experience of which brings me such joy.

On the last night of my most recent visit to New York City, Jake and I shared a farewell dinner out. We started with a few drinks at a favorite bar in Greenwich Village, the neighborhood where Jake has lived since I met him. We then took the subway to Midtown, where we dined on the outdoor patio of an excellent Thai restaurant we've visited many times. They are very good about omitting fish sauce from the vegetable curries I order. Or at least they assure me they are.

It was a beautiful spring evening. From the patio, we had an arresting view of the Empire State Building just a few blocks away. In honor of some occasion, the famous skyscraper had been swaddled with immense arrays of colored lights, now flashing on and off in a dazzling display.

Jake gulped down half a glass of Thai beer, looked up, and in keeping with his intellectually contentious nature, seized upon an aspect of my behavior he wished to probe.

"Doc," he said as he licked his lips to savor a lingering droplet, "you have expressed to me on a number of occasions an awareness that your material incarnation is not ultimately who you are. You claim that your fear of death is now long gone. Is that not true?

I could tell he was readying a salvo. "Yes, Jake," I said. "That's true."

"Yet it occurs to me, Doc, that the spiritual disciplines you currently practice, tai chi and yoga, are designed precisely to prolong life and impart vitality to your corporeal being. That seems to me a contradiction."

"Really?" I chuckled. "A contradiction?"

"Yes! And your vegan diet—I'll grant you that in one sense it's a spiritual statement, being non-injurious to living beings and nurturing our planet's fragile ecosystem, and all that folderol. But, Doc, you're not simply a vegan. You're a fanatic about eating only organic fruits and vegetables, whole grains, monounsaturated fats, and balanced nutrients. You eschew all refined and processed foods. You swallow a baby aspirin and a vitamin capsule the size of a wine cork every night. All that is designed to maximize your longevity and well-being."

He paused a moment. "Thank goodness you loosen up a bit when we're out, Dockles," he said, and punctuated that statement by spooning an additional dollop of white jasmine rice onto my plate, seeing that my vegetable and tofu curry had exhausted its accompanying starch.

"And, Doc, your obsessive handwashing and avoidance of germs exposes you completely. You clearly have no immediate interest in dying and moving on to the next life, no matter how much you claim to know your soul has a place to go. If that's not a blatant contradiction, it's at least a paradox, worthy of exploration. Don't you think?"

He seemed quite pleased with himself.

"I don't see it as a paradox, Jake." I smiled. "But then again, the mystical experience tends to obliterate such annoying dualities."

That made him chuckle.

I continued: "Why is loving life and wanting to prolong it contradictory to understanding that a part of us is immutable and moves on when we die?"

"It's *absolutely* contradictory, Dockles. Our human organism is programmed to prolong life because we fear death as the end of life. If we embrace death, our survival programming fails."

"If humans have evolved sufficiently to embrace physics and mathematics, Jakles," I said, "we've probably also reached a point where we can cherish life without fearing death. However, you do raise an interesting question. Is living a sacred duty? Is clinging to life at any cost a moral obligation, as espoused by traditional organized religions? What do you think, Jake?"

"It's biology, Doc. Our genes are programmed to propagate the species at all costs, which demands that we stay alive. It's quite clear to me that it's not a moral question. It's pure chemistry. This chemical programming just happens to persist after we're past childbearing age because there's no evolutionary imperative for it to disappear. But I'm curious to know, what are *your* conclusions, Dockles, as a self-described spiritually enlightened but firmly nonreligious man?"

"To some extent ambivalent, Jake. For example, I heartily approve of assisted suicide in appropriate cases. It's absurd to me that people will, with utmost compassion, put an end to the suffering of a dog or a cat but deny that same consideration to a much-loved human relative or friend. Nonetheless, the idea of suicide as an escape from a bevy of problems that could be overcome with self-discipline, focus, and patience is, to me, sad and appalling."

"I'm in full agreement there, Doc."

"The key, Jakles, I've come to believe, is to love life, embrace it, use it to the extent possible to know oneself and to help others, but to simultaneously be poised to depart when the time is appropriate, and to do so with grace and detachment. Sometimes I believe I'm prepared to do exactly that, at a moment's notice if summoned. At other times, though, the thought of leaving renders me so sad that I will cry just pondering it.

Not frightened, Jake, just very sad. I'm usually tripped up by the people I'll miss—friends like you, and good talk like this. Because I'm convinced that *this* part doesn't move on. The part that moves on is stripped of our individual identity. It's like when we sleep: we're alive, but we're not aware of it." I took a long swig of beer. "I love being here. I'll miss it. I'll miss you, Jakles."

Jake poured the remainder of the bottle of Thai beer we were sharing into my glass, and gestured to the waitress to bring us another.

───────〜───────

There is a dream state I find wondrous. It occurs only on mornings when I am lucky enough to be unhurried, with no deadline for arising, no alarm set, no distractions. I awaken briefly but decide I am not quite ready to get up, and relax instead into an additional half hour or so of sleep. Some mornings I am unable to fall back asleep at all, and other times I resume my normal pattern of deep sleep. But on rare occasions, I find myself in a mesmerizing in-between state of light dream sleep—so light that I am aware of my dream, consciously watching it unfold as I would a movie, perceiving every image and snippet of dialogue as it manifests. Yet I exercise no volitional control whatsoever upon the dream's progress or outcome.

I enjoyed such a dream state this morning. The dream's visual images were especially evocative. It carried an emotional immediacy that made it poignant and memorable. It also seemed to harbor unresolved issues.

The dream demanded to be examined.

───────〜───────

It was over twenty years ago that I did consulting work at the C. G. Jung Institute of San Francisco, where I met the psychotherapist I recently ran into at the Berkeley farmers market. All the other analysts with whom I worked at the institute were women, older, and fully established with respect to their therapeutic credentials.

I was at a transitional point in my life. I had not yet fully retired, but

I had divested myself of all my major business interests. It was a period of exploration, during which I took consulting engagements on a part-time basis, as they suited me.

I worked the first twenty hours for the institute at a discounted rate. Even so, that stint exhausted their paltry consulting budget for the year. It was obvious that they needed far more of my time to accomplish their goals. So I gave them several more months pro bono, donating ten hours of my time each week.

It was a most enjoyable experience.

Jung's thinking had always fascinated me. I had done a good deal of reading on his theories prior to consulting at the institute. Whereas Freud put sex at the center of his psychological perspective, and Adler seized upon power for his, Carl Jung insisted that a nonrational spiritual sensibility was truly at the core of every human's psyche. That resonated with me.

Perhaps because they weren't paying me, or perhaps because they found me an eager and intellectually curious seeker, the analysts at the institute would often ask me if I'd had any dreams, and would take the time to walk me through a thorough Jungian analysis of any I offered. From those informal sessions, I learned the principles of Jungian dream interpretation.

The most provocative tenet of Jungian dream analysis for me was the notion that you never dream about anyone other than yourself. Every person who appears in your dreams is an aspect of your own psyche.

Because I am male, any other male character appearing in my dream is some part of my "shadow." The shadow represents those aspects of my personality that are suppressed, parts of me that I am uncomfortable in displaying or recognizing.

I found the concept of the shadow rather easy to comprehend.

Much more difficult for me to fathom, though, was the concept of the "anima." According to Jung, for males, the anima is always represented by female characters in dreams, and is the gateway to one's soul or spirit.

Over the years, when I've tried to analyze a dream, determining the personality traits of a male shadow character and relating them back to aspects of my psyche seemed relatively straightforward. But comprehending how specific attributes in a female character tie back to my spiritual quest has often proven elusive.

I don't find this odd. I've always had difficulty relating to women without pretense. Throughout my life, I've resorted inevitably to role-playing, and to psychodramas based around power and sexuality.

I believe I'm finally past all that now. But at my age, the significance of that achievement is most likely moot.

———⌣———

Sapphire and I followed the steep trail to the top of Strawberry Hill, a small, tree-packed island in San Francisco's Golden Gate Park. Accessible by footbridge, it is surrounded by a sizable lake, whose waters support thriving families of ducks, geese, gulls, and turtles.

I took Sapphire off leash after we crossed the footbridge. While allowing dogs off leash is technically against the law in San Francisco, Strawberry Hill is one of those secluded areas of the park where the rule is routinely ignored and dogs frolic freely, running from their owners to greet and play with approaching pooches, somehow fully understanding that exercising any sort of aggressiveness or turf sovereignty would be wholly inappropriate on these quiet trails. Once every year or two, the same friendly old park police officer fulfills his obligation and drives his patrol car up the narrow road, stopping to request of each dog owner he encounters that they please leash their pet. The officer smiles and winks as if to acknowledge that he realizes the dogs will be back off leash within moments of his departure.

We climbed the steep grade. Sapphire walked slowly, stopping frequently to probe aromas that fascinated her, myriad scents I could not begin to discern.

I strolled ahead. I paused briefly to locate a particular tree on a tiny island across the water, to see if any great blue herons were yet active in its nest—the birds returned each year and were due soon. I also stopped alongside a familiar bush and peered through a naturally occurring peephole in the otherwise dense foliage at a snippet of the waterfall a quarter mile away.

The dream I had that morning, which I had watched unfold like a movie, reemerged in my thoughts. It had been emotionally moving. I realized at once that in order to clear my mind to achieve the meditative state, I needed to first examine and unravel the meaning of this dream. It was not something I could simply dismiss unresolved.

I tried now to recall precisely the dream's images and storyline:

I am on a spacecraft for a short but especially memorable trip. The views from the windows of the craft are beautiful. I am aware that we travelers are making history of some sort. There are only a few of us in the passenger compartment, which is laid out more like a small, informal dining room than a commercial cabin. The pilot and navigator are housed elsewhere, unseen by us.

I am seated at a large table. Across from me is a lovely girl, perhaps twelve or thirteen, just entering her womanhood, alluring with that mix of child and adult attributes. Next to her sits a paunchy bald man who clearly dislikes me.

I say to the girl, "This experience is going to make you famous. You'll receive lots of attention. I would love to stay in touch with you. May we exchange email addresses?"

The bald man is incensed, reading some sort of iniquity or lechery into my request. "Everyone is entitled to privacy," he says to me bluntly, his voice raised in anger. "Leave her—"

The girl, however, interrupts him. "We should all stay in touch," she says. "I'll create a group mailbox so we all can post emails that every one of us can see."

"Oh look, we're descending," I exclaim. "You can see the lights of New York City below us." It is night—the lights of the city are dazzling and beautiful. The pilot skirts the edge of the Empire State Building at high speed and buzzes a number of nearby skyscrapers before heading for the landing pad at the heliport on the East River. I am aware that his maneuvers are solely for the benefit of passengers and onlookers.

The dream ends as the spacecraft approaches for landing.

My first conclusion regarding the dream was that its venue of Midtown Manhattan and the Empire State Building was a fond recollection of the dinner Jake and I shared on my last night in New York. After dinner, Jake and I had moved a few doors down for a farewell toast of sweet Moscato wine on the outdoor patio of a small Italian café, to watch the light show on the Empire State Building before bidding each other goodnight. The following morning Sapphire and I flew home to San Francisco on a small chartered jet piloted by an old friend who always permitted Sapphire to sit with us in the main cabin.

I now subjected the haunting dream to my best effort at Jungian interpretation:

All the characters in the dream were contained on the spaceship with me. I surmised that the ship symbolized my psyche in its daily foray to reunite with the spiritual aspect of the cosmos—the time I empty my mind in meditation and experience the mystical state.

The young girl is my anima, my gateway to the spiritual realm. I do not want to lose contact with her, or with the mystical aspect of the cosmos. That is why I request of her that we remain in touch.

The bald man must be an aspect of my shadow, a part of my personality that remains suppressed and untapped. But what is he actually saying? Why is he so vehement about not wanting me to keep in touch with the girl?

I explored many approaches to explain the bald man's intent, but none seemed right. I moved instead, for a moment, to the fact that he was completely bald—it was clearly how I identified and labeled him. I knew that hair or fur in a dream often reflected warmth of character, so I deduced the bald man must represent a side of me that is cold, calculating, empirically scientific.

Perhaps the bald man was afraid that if I became too engrossed in my spiritual immersion, I would lose touch with reality, become incapable of acting logically or even sanely in the corporeal world. I experienced a visceral sense of having snapped into place the crucial puzzle piece the moment I conceptualized his role in this manner.

But the young woman in the dream, my anima and spiritual guide, advised both my shadow and myself that no such fears were necessary, as long as I shared my spiritual immersion with all the others, all the facets of my persona and subconscious. As long as I integrated it into my corporeal being.

This interpretation felt irrefutable, and instantly freed me of any need to further pursue the dream's meaning. It was at that moment that Sapphire and I arrived at the summit of Strawberry Hill and commenced our leisurely descent. Sapphire loped past me after having lagged behind the entire way up.

My mind then effortlessly emptied of all thought. I was drawn into the meditative state as we walked, suffused with an overwhelming feeling of love and joy. All sense of duality dissipated. I experienced profound peace. An abiding conviction of belonging intimately to everything that existed in the cosmos occupied my being, expressed in the moment by a palpable oneness with the trees, hills, shrubs, grasses, and wildlife that surrounded Sapphire and me as we walked.

4.
Contagion

HAD IT NOT BEEN for Virginia Ferguson, I would never have begun attending presentations at the small Rosicrucian lodge near my home in San Francisco. I would most likely have remained unaware that the lodge even existed.

The meetings are held in a large old Victorian house across the street from Golden Gate Park. The house is used by many local organizations for gatherings and church services. The sizable main meeting quarters in the front of the house are frequently occupied by other groups. But the Rosicrucians utilize a modest room in the rear for their monthly meetings. It has its own inconspicuous entrance around the side of the house and is accessed through a narrow gate.

The Rosicrucian lodge's following is loyal, but quite small.

When we first met, Virginia Ferguson was walking her tiny dog a few doors down from the Victorian. Holding her dog's leash in one hand, with her other hand she dragged behind her a small hand truck bearing a tall, cylindrical tank of oxygen. A clear plastic tube conveyed the oxygen to a nosepiece with a narrow strip that encircled Virginia's head.

My meeting Virginia that day was a most unlikely coincidence.

Sapphire and I had just left Golden Gate Park through an exit we almost never used. It was much further from my home, at least a quarter mile out of our way. But there was a rowdy horde of young children screaming and in constant pointless motion adjacent to the park exit Sapphire and I generally employ after our morning hike—some sort of elementary school or summer camp outing. There were a couple of young teachers or counselors ostensibly overseeing the children. But little control was being asserted.

A bevy of disorderly children of this sort, aside from being extraordinarily disruptive to the calm meditative state I so fastidiously work to achieve, is also a prime breeding ground for infectious microorganisms. Personal hygiene and simple courtesies such as covering one's face when sneezing are sadly absent from the innate behavior patterns of children this age.

My dear friend Wayne Jakob Kenneman would cite my avoiding such gaggles as an aspect of the obsessive-compulsive disorder from which he insists I suffer. But I have explained to Jake dozens of times that true victims of OCD exhibit irrational behaviors, such as needing to let a phone ring precisely four times before picking it up, or tapping a table exactly six times before sitting down. I exhibit no such quirks. My recognition that a mob of screaming children is much like a massive petri dish can be construed as rational, and my desire to avoid wading into such a throng eminently logical.

So I eluded the swarm by crossing the road. Sapphire and I took a series of alternate trails, which caused us to exit the park a good deal farther east.

That morning, I certainly would have tried to avoid Virginia as well, as soon as I saw the oxygen tank she was lugging. But I had already exited the park and crossed the boulevard running along it. I was halfway down that block when she turned the corner and was suddenly coming toward me. Even though we had never met and I had no idea who she was, it would have been obvious and embarrassing to cross and evade her at that point.

And rationally, I was aware that she was probably not contagious.

But if pressed by Jake as to whether my reaction to the oxygen tank was indeed purely rational, I would have been forced to acknowledge that something more was at play.

───────⌣───────

Some years ago, I was driving down the old Pacific Coast Highway with Sapphire, to hike on trails we visited occasionally in Butano State Park, about an hour south of San Francisco. The car was slowly negotiating a sloping curve when the public radio station began playing an interview with a psychologist who had written a book about individuals raised with damaged siblings.

The topic caught my attention. My late brother, David, certainly qualified as damaged.

The interview contained a good deal of seeming psychobabble and the usual marketing ploys of an author pushing a book. But when the author listed the four indelible psychological characteristics she had determined to be commonly shared among individuals raised with damaged siblings, I was so bowled over I considered pulling off the road to compose myself:

Driven to excel.

Survivor's guilt.

The need to convince others that everything is OK, whether or not it truly is.

Fear of contagion.

It was "fear of contagion" that rattled me. The other three assertions rang true but far less viscerally, and in any case, they were relatively common personality traits and seemed to derive logically from the dynamic being examined.

But my fear of contagion had always seemed extraordinarily idiosyncratic and unquestionably hardwired.

───────⌣───────

My father rarely yelled at David or hit him. It wasn't that Emmanuel saw David's behavior as acceptable. Sadly, it was more that my father saw little point in investing time or energy in my younger brother. Emmanuel, for better or worse, had transferred his focus almost entirely to me, leaving David to my mother.

Four years younger than I, David was small for his age and not especially adept at athletics. My mother, Rachel, tried to teach David to read prior to kindergarten as she had done with me, but David's attention span was short, and he grew frazzled after brief periods of attempting to focus. Now in second grade, David was experiencing academic problems in school, and his teacher had suggested that my parents spend time with him each day after class, reviewing his lessons. That responsibility fell to my mother.

I grew accustomed to watching David spend hours each evening in the living room on my mother's lap, doing schoolwork with her. It seemed incredible that Rachel's lap could support him for such long durations. My mother was anorexic and bulimic long before such words entered the common lexicon. Even though David was small, he seemed too heavy for her tiny thighs.

My mother concluded early on that the study sessions went much better if she gave David frequent breaks: perhaps a cookie with a glass of milk, or a few minutes to rearrange his endless brigades of tiny, dark-green rubber soldiers.

David's needs were extensive and commanded hours of my mother's attention. Her remaining time was consumed with cooking, housework, sewing, and the like. My dealings with my mother, as a result, grew brief and perfunctory.

My father sometimes filled that gap by engaging me in after-dinner chats about science and mechanics, or by working with me on engineering projects. Often, though, he sat alone in the kitchen, reading the paper or a technology-related magazine, leaving me to my own devices.

I had no problem spending time by myself.

I never discussed with my parents, or with anyone else, a conversation that I secretly overheard one Sunday in the early-morning hours. My mother and father were talking in hushed tones in their bedroom. They must have assumed I was still asleep; their door was left ajar. But I was awake, next door to them, in the small bedroom I shared with David, who was sound asleep. My parents were talking with great concern about my brother. I attended to every word.

My father referenced David's birth and how my mother's blood pressure had at one point during David's delivery dropped precipitously. He fixated upon that brief period of oxygen deprivation and insisted that it must have had a lasting effect of some sort.

That intimation upset my mother severely. She was generally compliant and dutiful around my father, but here she exhibited unaccustomed agitation. She reminded my father that the doctor had assured them that David would be fine. It was irrational, she insisted, to imagine that David suffered from some sort of brain damage. She pointed out that in her years as an elementary school teacher, she had seen many boys with issues similar to David's, which almost always resolved themselves as the boys matured.

My father seemed unconvinced and not at all optimistic with respect to David's future prospects.

———————⌣———————

It is generally safe to assume that a middle-aged woman dependent upon oxygen does *not* suffer from a disorder that is contagious.

Nonetheless, it is not entirely irrational to attempt to avoid such a person, and thus shield oneself from the statistically unlikely but still plausible risk of contracting a lung infection.

So, whether or not my fear of contagion was in this case wholly rational, my intent was to quickly race by this woman dragging an oxygen tank behind her as she walked her tiny dog, and to inconspicuously hold my breath while doing so.

Sapphire had completely different designs.

Sapphire is strong, and with so much cattle dog in her personality, she can be willful and stubborn, more so as she ages. Squat and with a low center of gravity from her corgi side, when Sapphire decides to stop and hold her ground, there is little I can do short of violently dragging her, which I'd never consider. Even today in her frail and weakened state, if she stops abruptly, her leash snaps taut, my walking cadence is violently dismantled, and my only choice is to turn and join her in examining the source of her fascination.

In this case it was Virginia Ferguson's tiny dog.

This was most unexpected, given that even when Sapphire is curious about other dogs, she is rarely affectionate or interested in prolonged play. In this case, she was intent upon both.

Virginia smiled and said hello to me.

I was still holding my breath, but as I stood facing Virginia, with our dogs frolicking joyfully between our feet, it was clear that a polite conversation with her was about to ensue.

"Hi," I said.

We exchanged the expected niceties centered around our dogs' names, ages, and genders. It is oddly common, I have found, to learn the names of people's dogs but never become privy to the names of the owners themselves, despite running into them and chatting with them daily in the park.

I thought the encounter was nearing its end. Then Virginia flabbergasted me.

In her gentle, conversational, slightly upbeat manner, she said, "I can see your aura. I see it clearly. It's very powerful. You are a spiritual seeker. We have that in common."

I looked at her speechlessly, completely taken aback.

"My name is Virginia," she said. She held out her hand.

I had no choice but to shake it. "Hi, I'm Sammy," I said, making a mental note to ablute my palms with hand sanitizer the moment I was out of her field of vision.

Although I wasn't exactly sure what to make of her assertion about my "aura," I found myself feeling extraordinarily flattered. Nevertheless, a softly muttered thank-you was the best I could conjure in way of a delayed response.

"My disease is terminal," Virginia blurted out, devoid of any particular emotion. "If you don't feel comfortable befriending someone who is going to die soon, I'd understand."

What came out of me in response utterly surprised me: "That makes it all the more important that we become friends *now*," I said.

I sensed in her an energy and verve that I had not anticipated. She was tall for a woman, perhaps a bit taller than I, and despite being racked with disease, her frame displayed an underlying power. We chatted a bit as our dogs played, exchanged information. She lived around the corner with her husband, who sold insurance. She had been a nurse and over time drifted into medical informatics. She told me she now coordinated the events at the local Rosicrucian lodge.

"Really," I said, "a Rosicrucian lodge? I had no idea there was one in this neighborhood. I've been fascinated with the Rosicrucians since I was a boy."

She gave me a folded handbill from her purse, the paper worn and stained with some sort of beverage. It listed upcoming presentations at the Rosicrucian lodge that were open to the public. The topics seemed surprisingly sophisticated. One interested me in particular.

"I'll definitely see you at the meeting on the third of next month," I said.

Then I felt a tug. Virginia's small dog, Kata, had been dancing about furiously, accentuating his movements with periodic yelps. In doing so, his leash now tangled with Sapphire's, and the intertwined cords were about to knock over Virginia's oxygen tank.

I initiated a dipping lunge to prevent the tank from toppling. I successfully caught it and set the hand truck back upright before it fell. But in the instant it took me to do so, I noticed Virginia's body instinctively curl in response to my sudden movement, and gird itself into a pose I found unmistakable.

"You've studied martial arts," I said, as I slowly returned to an upright posture.

"Yes, for many years," she replied. She glanced down and pointed at the oxygen tank and smiled. "The lung issue is fairly recent. But before that it was karate, primarily. And you?"

"Jiu-jitsu," I said. "For many years as well."

"Now I understand your choosing the lodge presentation on the third of next month," she said. "Tai chi and qigong. Shaolin mystical pathways and artifacts. It took a bit of doing to get that speaker to commit."

"It sounds quite fascinating," I said.

"I look forward to seeing you on the third then, Sammy," she said. "We'll have lots to talk about after the presentation."

She smiled and bowed slightly, suggestive of the more exaggerated bow martial arts opponents offer each other after sparring. I returned the courtesy.

I waited until I was around the corner and well out of sight before I gave the handbill one last glance to commit the date to memory. Then I threw the soiled flyer in a trashcan and abluted my hands thoroughly with the alcohol-based hand sanitizer I always carried in my fanny pack.

Then, with clean hands, I entered the presentation date for the Rosicrucian lecture on my smart phone's calendar.

5.
Kotegaeshi

THE PROBLEM MANIFESTED when I was twelve years old.

I realized I had stopped growing.

In some respects, I had already far exceeded reasonable size expectations. I was almost five foot seven, a good deal taller than my father, who was five foot four, and my mother, who was five foot one. My poor, growth-stunted brother was significantly shorter than both of them.

But I had become accustomed to being one of the biggest boys my age, having shot up to adult height so quickly. I was still husky with baby fat and had always been very strong. That combination of height, size, and strength made me physically imposing on the gritty streets where I grew up. Fights broke out frequently in the South Bronx.

Some of those fights erupted spontaneously. But for me, the bulk of my violent encounters involved defending David. He was a perennial target of neighborhood bullies. New oppressors would periodically appear, and David would seek me out for help.

I never refused him. In retrospect, I enjoyed my triumphs in the resulting skirmishes as much as those bullies enjoyed victimizing their own prey. I navigated those clashes adeptly, and generally emerged unscathed other than a few bloody lips and black eyes. Battle scars such as those were so common among neighborhood boys that even our teachers didn't take notice or make mention of them unless the wounds were egregious or became habitual.

But just after my twelfth birthday, the change in my growth pattern became obvious. It was palpable as I walked among my fellow students in the schoolyard each day. My size advantage was slowly eroding. Boys whom I had towered over my entire life were now catching up and surpassing me. I hadn't grown at all in well over a year.

My father had warned me repeatedly. Over and over he scolded and reminded me that he and many of his brothers and cousins had shared a similar early growth spurt, only to stop abruptly around age eleven or twelve. None of them ever grew another inch, and all were relatively short and unimposing as adults.

"All these boys you're fighting with, Sammy," he'd enjoin me, "they'll all be bigger than you. Maybe very soon. Watch what you're doing, Sammy. Watch who you're making enemies with. Pretty soon they'll *all* be able to beat the hell out of you."

———————

Sapphire was sprawled out across the doorway that separated my office from the foyer in the rear of my home. It is a familiar spot for her now, but Sapphire began frequenting it only recently.

When I adopted her and brought her home fifteen years ago, Sapphire immediately appropriated the walk-in closet in my back office as her private sanctuary. The closet is of modest size. When it is packed with my shirts, pants, outerwear, and shoes, there is little floor space remaining. Even so, Sapphire found enough room to plop down and stake her claim.

I assume the small area and the walls surrounding her so closely made her feel secure. She spent many hours in that closet. I laid mats and small rugs over the wooden floor to make it more comfortable for her, though she never seemed to mind the hardwood as long as she could be in her closet.

But recently she stopped visiting the closet entirely. I have now figured out why.

Sapphire used to sleep there while I spent hours in my office, reading and using the computer. When she heard me get up to leave, she always followed me out to check where I was off to. I finally realized that as Sapphire lost her hearing, more and more often she'd fail to awaken when I abandoned the office for another part of the house. She'd find me hours later, but always seemed distressed to have awakened in a deserted room, uncertain of where I was, or if I was even still in the house with her.

It is hard to say exactly how she formulated her solution to the problem, but it required her to forsake her beloved closet, which must have been painful for her. She had obviously in some fashion weighed the alternatives and concluded that as much as she adored her closet, keeping tabs on my whereabouts was more important.

So when I work in the office now, Sapphire positions herself carefully across the threshold between my office and the foyer so that I am forced to step over her if I decide to leave the room. She can no longer hear me, but she can detect the vibrations caused by my feet, no matter how gingerly I step. That awakens her, and enables her to follow me wherever I go in the house.

My ill-fated exploration of the magazine advertisements for the Rosicrucian Order had destroyed for me the secret appeal of the back pages of my science magazines. Although my curiosity still lured me into perusing those pages, I did so now with a sense of resignation and sadness. I knew that even if I discovered something fascinating, I would most likely be constrained from pursuing it.

One evening, with my father reading in the kitchen and my mother doing homework with David, I reclined alone on my bed, thumbing listlessly through the pages of advertisements. A series of them, however, began to perk my interest. They all featured methods of unarmed self-defense: karate, jiu-jitsu, savate, aikido, and similar fighting arts. Each ad presented its combat method in a series of drawings with accompanying text, promising that purchase of the course would reveal secrets enabling a small man to defeat opponents bigger and stronger than himself.

These advertisements had not been of particular interest to me before. But now that I was losing my size advantage over neighborhood rivals, I became convinced that these ads held the solution to that dilemma. Some of the ads even suggested that their style of fighting was grounded in a tradition of spirituality—their students became virtuous and peaceful warriors. That intriguing aspect seemed reminiscent of the mystical sensibility promised by the Rosicrucians.

But these ruminations only caused me to grow more despondent. I was convinced that I had squandered any opportunity I might have had to send for one of these martial arts training courses. Had I been more patient, had I resisted my desire to probe the teachings of the Rosicrucians, I might now be able to seek permission from my father to purchase one of these courses. But I had cashed that chit—my chance was now gone, and there was no point even asking about it. My father would just use the request to point out how foolish I had been the last time, and how I had obviously not learned from that incident because I now wanted to do the same thing again.

I spent one entire Saturday afternoon staring at the magazines' self-defense advertisements, closely studying the drawings that accompanied them, hoping desperately to decipher from them some tiny nugget of the esoteric knowledge I had been denied. However, there was nothing more there to be garnered.

I pondered my dilemma at length, and was profoundly dejected for several days. But to my great surprise, when I at last emerged from this emotionally depressed state, certain new insights made themselves known:

First, I realized it was erroneous to imagine that had I resisted the exploration of the Rosicrucians, Emmanuel would have been any more likely to approve my delving into some foreign fighting art. He would have seen the purchase of any such course as a scam to steal our money, and perhaps to lure me away from Judaism. The Rosicrucian debacle was not a factor here at all, even if my father might pretend it was. It was simply part of a predictable pattern.

Second, my father's bouts of anger were often irrational. I recalled many episodes where he had become enraged over behavior on my part that had been no different from modes of behavior I had exhibited many times prior while eliciting no emotional reaction from him whatsoever. Therefore, my taking to heart anything that he criticized was pointless. His irritability was far more likely a result of his having had a bad day than attributable to any action on my part.

And third, with respect to self-defense teachings, why would critical reservoirs of knowledge be available only through small advertisements in the back pages of a science magazine? If these secrets were truly thousands of years old and important, wouldn't someone in all that time have written a book about them or disseminated that information in some other way?

These insights were emancipating. The only question still unanswered for me was this: were these advertised systems of martial arts legitimate collections of effective fighting techniques, or were they simply commercial hyperbole that had been used to defraud people for centuries?

I began my investigation with jiu-jitsu. The fighting techniques that involved the striking of blows, such as the Japanese art of karate or the French kick-fighting art of savate, lost their appeal to me after further conjecture. Punching and kicking could be dangerous. Were I to master these arts and seriously injure a classmate or other neighborhood boy, the consequences for me could be damaging and long-lasting. Also, such techniques seemed to me undignified—it was difficult to imagine how such practices could encompass enduring spiritual aspects.

But the many advertisements featuring jiu-jitsu, judo, aikido, and other grappling arts resonated strongly with me. The knowledge of how to exploit an arm joint's range of motion or overload a muscle's vulnerable pressure points required precision and focus to execute. Such approaches could be extremely useful in turning a larger opponent's speed and strength against him, and could be calibrated to control the degree of damage inflicted.

Of these grappling techniques, the sound of the syllables comprising the phrase "jiu-jitsu" appealed to me most. There was something about the two words that suggested a potentially mystical quality.

I went first to the big dictionary on a shelf in our living room.

Prior to marrying Emmanuel, Rachel had been an elementary school teacher. Now she cooked and kept house, and spent hours trying to rectify David's educational deficiencies. But before David was born, she had devoted a great deal of time to me, and had taught me to read before I reached the age of three. She had also taught me that the first place I should go when seeking knowledge about something new was the dictionary, so I could understand how the unknown entity was defined. From there I could try the encyclopedia for a more in-depth summary of the topic being investigated. And if I wished, I could eventually find more detailed knowledge in books devoted solely to the topic I was exploring.

I turned the book's large, delicate pages slowly, in part not to tear them but more so out of fear that a term so foreign in origin and shrouded in secrecy would not appear at all in an ordinary American dictionary. But to my surprise and great joy, I found the following entry for jiu-jitsu: "An art of weaponless self-defense developed in China and Japan that uses throws, holds, and blows and derives added power from the attacker's own weight and strength."

So, jiu-jitsu was real! Being defined in the dictionary made it legitimate, not just some fraudulent hoax created by criminals trying to steal money through magazine advertisements. The dictionary also pointed out etymologically that in Japanese *jiu* meant "gentle or yielding," and *jitsu* meant "art or technique." That too was consistent with the text in the magazines.

My family did not own a set of encyclopedias. I generally used the ones at the library, but that was blocks away, and I was impatient to learn more immediately. My best friend Michael owned a set, however, and lived in the apartment just above ours. It was a Sunday morning, so he was probably home.

I ran into the living room where my mother was sewing and asked,

"Can I play with Michael?"—a request she heard me blurt out dozens of times each week. She nodded without even looking up.

I scampered out of our apartment, up a flight of stairs, and rang Michael's doorbell. "Can I play with Michael?" I asked again when the door opened, this time of Michael's mother, who also nodded silently and stepped aside as I flew by her and back into Michael's bedroom. The encyclopedias were stored there along with Michael's toys. He was sitting on the floor, piecing together a puzzle.

"Do you want to learn about jiu-jitsu?" I asked as I reached for the encyclopedia volume covering words starting with *I*, *J*, and *K*. Michael smiled. He was accustomed to me inquiring into strange new ideas. He was not by nature likely to pursue such things himself but very much enjoyed accompanying me on these expeditions.

His set of encyclopedias was for children, with easy-to-read text and abundant illustrations. I preferred the more adult encyclopedias at the library, but this was a sufficient place to start. I impatiently thumbed to the listing for jiu-jitsu and found an entry that took up an entire page, with a column and a half of text and a couple of drawings showing men in robes executing holds and throws. This was extremely exciting.

One of the illustrations showed a man on his back tossing his adversary into the air by holding on to his lapels while thrusting a foot into his abdomen. That seemed a bit complicated and scary, but the other drawing showed a simple wristlock, called "kotegaeshi." Observing the picture closely, I asked Michael to stand facing me, and to hold his right hand out in my direction. I situated his hand so that Michael was looking at his palm, with his fingers facing up toward the ceiling. I gently positioned both of my thumbs together against the back of his hand while my fingers grasped Michael's palm. Then, very slowly and carefully, I pressed Michael's wrist back toward him and rotated it away from Michael's body as the illustration suggested. Although I exerted only the barest pressure, Michael screamed, "Ow!" and fell sideways to the floor.

We gazed at each other with our mouths agape.

"I'm sorry, Michael, did I hurt you?" I asked.

"Just for a second," said Michael. "I'm OK now. This stuff is amazing."

"Yes it is," I whispered. "It's absolutely amazing."

My impromptu encounter with Virginia Ferguson piqued my curiosity and prompted me to conduct a bit of informal reconnaissance.

Virginia Ferguson was easy to locate on the internet. Her current affiliation with the local Rosicrucian lodge was posted prominently. She had also published an impressive string of articles during her years as a consultant. I established an email connection with her, and confirmed my attendance at the upcoming lecture on mystical artifacts associated with Shaolin tai chi and qigong.

As I delved further, my findings suggested that Virginia had enjoyed a rather impressive career prior to her lung problem. After years as an emergency room nurse, she had joined the healthcare division of a major consulting firm. It was during her tenure there that she produced her collection of articles.

One article she had authored was particularly interesting to me—it likened earning a black belt in karate to acquiring a nursing degree. All the other articles concerned medical informatics. From what I could garner, her personal focus was on "proactive medicine." Virginia characterized the type of doctor–patient interaction to which we all were familiar as "reactive," in that caregivers "reacted" to information provided by patients. She advocated for a shift to more "proactive medicine," where aggregated medical data from millions of patients would be analyzed to provide patterns and projections. The resulting findings would then be applied to identify individual patients at risk of future illness. These patients could be contacted proactively, enabling early intervention, affording better patient outcomes, and lowering medical costs.

It seemed from my reading, though, that not much in the way of application of such theories was extant in the current practice of medicine either in the United States or elsewhere in the world.

As I thought more about Virginia, I recalled that the soiled flyer she had handed me contained information about another lecture, a few months in the future, on Rosicrucian meditation approaches. I decided that if I found the lecture on Shaolin mysticism informative and well researched, I'd attend the presentation on meditation as well. I had an insatiable curiosity about different meditation techniques. Despite my having learned and employed so many over the years, I still wondered if alternative methods existed that might be more efficacious for me personally.

That decision impelled me to do a bit of research on Rosicrucian meditation. I had read a good deal on the meditation paths advocated by Yoga and by Buddhism, as well as on new techniques such as the variant of mindfulness advocated by the psychoanalyst I knew in Berkeley. I was curious if Rosicrucian meditation had borrowed substantially from any of those traditions.

As a rule, inquiry into Rosicrucian teachings of any sort is not easily accomplished. I tried many times in the past to learn about different aspects of Rosicrucianism. The internet now is a somewhat richer source than the books I used to find in the library, but even the internet has relatively little substantive or reliable information. This is not accidental. The Rosicrucians, for whatever reason, remain a *secret* society, and work very hard at maintaining the extreme level of impermeability they've cultivated for hundreds of years.

I did find an interesting tract by an occultist and Rosicrucian named Joseph J. Weed, who was active in the early to mid-twentieth century, and whose writings were somewhat more forthcoming and open than those of most other Rosicrucians.

After reading it, I rose from the computer and stepped over Sapphire, who was still asleep in the doorway. Although I moved gently, Sapphire opened her eyes and watched me walk away, barely moving her head as she did. When she ascertained that I was merely using the bathroom and was probably returning, she deemed it unnecessary to stir, and drifted immediately back to sleep.

6.
Ju Yoku Go O Seisu
Gentleness Controls Strength

IN THE EAST TREMONT neighborhood of the South Bronx where I grew up, I loved the small local branch of the New York Public Library. Built in 1905, the two-story brick building still stands and serves as a library today. I spent hours there, mostly in the children's reading room on the second floor, studying books on a variety of subjects and sneaking glimpses of the beautiful librarian at the children's checkout desk. She was a tall African American woman with lush, shoulder-length hair, large round breasts, and a tiny waist invariably cinched with a wide belt. Her dark eyes mesmerized me. She seemed to me a goddess.

Occasionally, I worked up the courage to walk over to her desk and ask her to help me find books on a given subject. She would always say, "I think you know how to use the card catalog, don't you, young man? I've seen you use it many times."

I would stare into her eyes and nod compliantly, then linger just another moment until with a knowing smile she said, "Go ahead, be on your way."

I'd walk over to the card catalog and pretend to peruse a series of cards while imagining the beautiful librarian taking me to her office to punish me for disturbing her. In my fantasy, she'd bind my wrists with ropes attached to a ceiling beam. She'd fasten a scarf around my mouth to keep me silent, then hoist me up and leave me there suspended, my feet dangling high above the ground.

The librarian would then turn and walk slowly away, her lower torso undulating hypnotically in her snug skirt. I would watch helplessly as she exited the office and locked the door behind her. She would not be back for hours as she completed her shift at her desk outside my prison, no one but the bewitching librarian knowing where I could be found.

***

The lecture at the Rosicrucian lodge was far more engrossing than I anticipated. The speaker, a professor of anthropology at a local junior college, was a practitioner of Shaolin tai chi and qigong. Virginia Ferguson met him three years ago at the martial arts academy where she was then studying karate. It had taken her this long to persuade him to lecture on the topic.

The half dozen people in the room applauded politely when the professor completed his remarks. Virginia and a couple of others engaged with him warmly during the small, informal post-lecture reception.

Virginia had requested that I stay after the presentation until she could chat. When she mentioned to me via email a week earlier that all Rosicrucian functions were catered with vegetarian and vegan fare, my hopes were buoyed, but the sweet punch and sugary pastries laid out were not the sort of food I habitually consumed. So I waited in the back of the room for her.

Sapphire was with me. Virginia said it was fine to bring her as long as she was quiet. I assured her that Sapphire had never barked much even when she was younger. Given the sedate nature of the lecture, and the fact that Sapphire's hearing had deteriorated to the point where only the loudest possible sounds from outside the house could alarm her, I knew there would be no issue.

A few minutes after the presentation ended, Virginia located Sapphire and me in the back of the room and joined us, lugging her mobile oxygen supply behind her. Sapphire sniffed her briefly and licked the knuckles of her hand in recognition and greeting.

"Did you enjoy the talk?" she asked me.

"Yes. He's an articulate fellow," I said.

"Not the most scintillating speaker, but his subject matter was well researched and most apropos, don't you think?"

"I agree completely, Virginia. And he was absolutely right about tai chi being 'full-body mediation.' I find that with yoga too. I practice both now. But it made me think back on all the years I studied jiu-jitsu. The practice itself and the meditation techniques we learned were supposed to combine to form a spiritual discipline. But for me they never really did, not fully. How many years did you study karate, Virginia?"

"Close to thirty years. It was mostly karate, but some other martial arts as well."

"Did you find that martial arts on their own got you to a spiritually enlightened state?" I asked.

"The meditation focused me, but into the warrior sphere, not the spiritual. For me, it wasn't until my lungs started failing and I couldn't practice anymore that I started meditating differently. I discovered Rosicrucian meditation. That changed it for me. But honestly, during the whole time I practiced martial arts, I had no idea that there was so much more to experience. I guess I wasn't looking for it then." She paused. "You've always been looking for it though, haven't you, Sammy?"

"Yes."

"How long has it been for you? Since you had your first breakthrough experience?"

"Many years, Virginia. What about you?"

"Oh, it's still rather new for me. It was just about a year and a half ago that I first experienced cosmic consciousness."

From my reading, I knew that "cosmic consciousness" was the Rosicrucian term for the archetypal mystical experience.

"So, is it still fresh for you?" I asked. "Vibrant and ascendant as it was at that first moment?"

"Oh, God no," she laughed. "That first experience was wonderful, and the sensation lasted for over a month. But it faded. They told me it would—the more experienced members here. I can recapture it, though, when I meditate. Isn't that how it is for you, Sammy?"

"Most definitely. But I didn't know that at first. I couldn't understand how it could come and then leave."

"Didn't you have anyone to help you?"

I chuckled. "Virginia, I've never been much of a joiner. I tend to do things alone. It makes it harder for me, but it's who I am. It took me a long time to learn that no matter how overwhelming the initial experience of spiritual illumination was, how much it felt as if it had transformed me into a completely new person, I had to keep practicing or it was gone."

"It's just like karate or jiu-jitsu in that way," she said. "You know, Sammy, I love talking to other people who have experienced the breakthrough into cosmic consciousness. If people haven't, they just can't understand."

I nodded affirmatively. "I remember reading the novels by Hermann Hesse when I was young," I said. "The climax, the moment of spiritual illumination, always came at the very end, which implied that it represented a final, immutable state. The character is transformed into some perfect demigod. I loved reading Hesse, but it's not like that at all."

"It's actually a new beginning," Virginia said.

"And we remain flawed beings, don't we?"

"Absolutely. Look at me. I'm toting an oxygen tank around."

"People somehow think that spiritual illumination should render you a perfect being," I said, "and if it doesn't, it can't be real. It's ridiculous. We remain human beings, flawed and imperfect."

"I'd have it no other way," said Virginia. "And how are you flawed, Sammy? You seem pretty together to me."

I smiled. "Thank you, Virginia. But I'm flawed in so many ways."

"Tell me."

I hesitated. "Sexually, for one," I finally blurted out.

"You can't perform sexually?"

"Oh, it's not a matter of performing physiologically, Virginia. In fact I'm quite robust in that area for a man my age," I said with a shy grin. "No. It's my psychological preferences with respect to what arouses me. Some would call them deviant or perverted."

"Oh God, you're not a pedophile, are you?"

"No, I would never do that. No. What I want is to surrender completely to a woman, worship her, become submissive to her and have her assume the dominant role."

"That doesn't sound terribly scary, Sammy. Actually it sounds somewhat appealing."

"Well, I suppose. But once you introduce ropes and handcuffs and paddles and nipple clamps into the equation, it become more difficult for most people to fathom. I've just always been hardwired that way, Virginia—psychologically. Spiritual enlightenment has changed me profoundly. But it can't rewire me sexually."

"Have you found women who want to do this?"

"A few. Most just for play. One became a good friend." I paused for a moment. "But there was one woman I had a real relationship with, a long intimate relationship. I almost married her. Stephanie. She would do the SM, and did it well. I don't think she would have been driven to do it otherwise, but she did it for me." I paused, and took a slow breath. "Losing her was a huge mistake."

"A reparable one, Sammy?"

"Not at all. I burned that bridge."

"It sounds complicated."

"She worked for me too, in the business I owned. It was quite a mess."

As a boy, I spent many hours secretly fantasizing about the beautiful African American librarian. In those reveries I was always enslaved to her in some manner. She treated me as her property. I worshipped her. My life was devoted to serving her. I reveled in the ecstasy of any sort of bondage or punishment she devised for me.

Yet even then, in the comparative innocence of those childhood fantasies, I'd occasionally stumble upon a grand contradiction, the same incompatibility that would haunt me in later years and destroy my relationship with Stephanie. Most often, though, it didn't enter the fantasies at all. I'd just be lost in the rhapsody of surrender. I'd imagine my helplessness, my complete acquiescence to her beauty and regality. I'd climax in that euphoria.

But sometimes, for reasons I could not understand, the fantasy demanded more explicit rules and prerequisites before it took on its life. I had to somehow provide a logical framework to explain away the grand contradiction that my infatuation with submission and enslavement presented.

The contradiction was this: I did not, outside of my sexual fantasies, have any desire whatever to prostrate myself before anyone, or to limit myself to tasks assigned to me by others. I secretly saw myself as someone destined to be a leader, who would ply his ideas without encumbrance.

My fantasies sometimes needed to take that into account, yet still feel real.

I was not a huge fan of science fiction. But I did read a bit of it, and sometimes watched movies or television shows that used it as a premise. So I borrowed from its common themes a motif that could be applied to my fantasies whenever the grand contradiction asserted itself.

When I did so, the African American librarian morphed into an alien from outer space. Her appearance was unchanged—she was still ravishing and provocatively dressed. She still spoke in the same measured, confident tones. But she was now part of a superior race. She had infiltrated the population here on Earth temporarily, to identify a slave to take back with her to her planet.

Aside from possessing advanced technology, this alien race was also compassionate. They wanted slaves but sought to procure only those who possessed a secret yearning to be enslaved.

Moreover, the aliens knew that no one wanted to be entirely a slave. They also appreciated that families and loved ones would be devastated and saddened if a boy they loved suddenly and inexplicably disappeared.

So the aliens utilized an advanced cloning capability. It could duplicate an individual, creating an exact replica the same age as the original. It could also fine-tune the psychological propensities of the clone, in this case intensifying the subject's submissive predilections, while curtailing other aspirations.

The librarian took the clone back with her to her home planet, to serve her. I was left here on Earth but had been somehow imbued with the ability to psychically observe my clone as he tended to his mistress light-years away.

———

After reading about jiu-jitsu in my friend Michael's encyclopedia, I seized the first opportunity available to investigate my local library's card catalog for any books on the subject. As I entered the reading room, my eyes met those of the regal librarian sitting behind her desk. She nodded hello. I smiled and waved briefly in greeting. She was wearing a satiny brown blouse, cinched snugly about her torso, its top two buttons unfastened and revealing an enticing hint of cleavage. Her posture, as always, was effortlessly erect. As I passed her and headed toward the card files, I felt her eyes on my back, and endeavored to display my most manly posture and athletic gait for her visual consumption.

To my great surprise, I found the local library branch stocked with a good number of books about jiu-jitsu, on the shelves housing Dewey Decimal subclass 796. This discovery was especially interesting: the magazine advertisements had characterized jiu-jitsu's secrets as well guarded and little known. And while none of my friends to whom I had mentioned jiu-jitsu in an offhanded way seemed to know anything about it, here on the shelf were a dozen books, available to anyone who wanted to learn jiu-jitsu's mysteries.

I checked out four books, the library's limit for children. Each was full of photographs and instructions for learning throws, arm and leg locks, and counters to various sorts of attacks.

The librarian methodically recorded each volume and tucked a card with the book's mandated return date into the cardboard pocket inside each of the front covers. She said to me, "I see you have a new interest, young man."

"Yes ma'am," I said softly.

"Be careful now; don't hurt yourself," she said. She smiled—her huge brown eyes gazed momentarily into mine.

"Yes ma'am, I'll be careful," I said, lowering my head sheepishly.

From the books, I discovered that jiu-jitsu and related grappling arts first manifested in early Japan as a means of defense against attackers wearing armor and carrying weapons. Attempting to strike such assailants would be fruitless. But the ability to throw such opponents to the ground and inflict injury on vulnerable bones and joints proved an effective stratagem for survival.

The codification and enhancement of such techniques, by Jigoro Kano in Japan's late 1800s, led to an official standard eventually adopted by the Japanese government for military training and other purposes.

All the books I brought home referenced and extolled the work of Jigoro Kano, citing him as the founder of modern jiu-jitsu. One particular quote from Mr. Kano, repeated in several of the books, etched itself powerfully in my psyche:

"In short, resisting a more powerful opponent will result in your defeat, whilst adjusting to and evading your opponent's attack will cause him to lose his balance, his power will be reduced, and you will defeat him. This can apply whatever the relative values of power, thus making it possible for weaker opponents to beat significantly stronger ones. This is the theory of *ju yoku go o seisu.*"

Gentleness controls strength.

Or, as another book so directly put it, "Pull when pushed, and push when pulled."

I gathered Michael and my younger brother, and had them agree to a daily jiu-jitsu practice session, led by myself, during which we'd practice moves I carefully chose from the library books. I insisted upon only two conditions: that attendance was mandatory unless an emergency intervened, and that the sessions were to be our special secret, shared with no one else in the neighborhood. Both Michael and David were eager to begin.

Balance and momentum are pivotal elements of jiu-jitsu. Not just your own balance and momentum—more so those of your opponent. At any level, training essentially consists of becoming attuned to your attackers' movements and positions, and learning to react instantaneously to the vulnerabilities you perceive.

The magazine ads promised secrets. And the books did indeed contain secrets. But those secrets formed only one end of a continuum where the other was the practice and repetition required to execute upon those secrets. Mastery of both was necessary.

My innate response, when I first viewed those ads and searched for books in the library, was to imagine those secrets to be insular and self-contained: as long as I knew what to do, I would be able to defeat my attackers regardless of their actions. What quickly became evident was that my fighting success hinged not nearly as much on what I did at any given moment as on what my opponent did and how I was able to read those actions and seize upon the opportunities they created.

I could perform exactly the same movements with completely different outcomes, depending solely upon what my opponent was doing at that same instant.

If my opponent stepped toward me and momentarily placed all his weight on his front leg, I could kick that leg out from under him just as his foot touched down, and easily upend him and throw him to the ground. But should I execute exactly that same leg kick while he was securely balanced with both feet planted, the kick would have little effect.

A large attacker leaping toward me could be thrown to the ground over my back if I turned, leaned, and redirected his momentum. Attempting to throw that same person using sheer strength would be fruitless.

The movements of an assailant could be influenced through stealth and skill. Much of the magic of jiu-jitsu occurs subtly, prior to a throw or takedown, in what appears to be haphazard grappling and shoving but in truth is a precisely calculated set of salvos designed to render an attacker susceptible to your next strike.

Such skill comes only with extensive practice.

7.
Transistors and Diodes

I HAVE NOTICED SOMETHING surprising during my morning hikes with Sapphire. I expected that my ability to empty my mind of thought and achieve a mystical sensibility would be relatively constant no matter where I was walking, if the area was relatively free of distractions and presented no dangers for Sapphire.

But that is not the case.

I habitually do not achieve the state I seek until I am in an area surrounded by dense foliage. In fact, when I walk in these areas of bountiful plant life and experience samadhi, I feel as if I am somehow sharing in a spiritual consciousness that already abundantly fills the space around me, emanating directly from the trees, bushes, and plants. I merely need to become an empty vessel and allow that consciousness to stream into my being.

For years, I was convinced that this syndrome was a product of my imagination, some sort of learned response to specific environmental cues. I no longer think so.

My repressed suspicion that plants exude consciousness is now, remarkably, fodder for scientific inquiry. I recently came across several articles addressing an emerging area of scientific inquiry termed "plant neurobiology." I have since done a good deal of research on current thinking on this topic.

Many scientists are still appalled by any suggestion of plant intelligence, much less plant consciousness. These individuals particularly despise the term "plant neurobiology," calling it oxymoronic because plants have no neurons, and certainly no brains.

However, scientists defending the concept of plant neurobiology counter that it would be evolutionarily unwise for plants to have developed brains. Plants, as stationary beings, are designed so that parts of them can be eaten or destroyed without compromising the essence of the being. In some cases, plants multiply most effectively when animals eat their fruit and later excrete seeds in distant areas, so it makes sense that any sort of intelligence in plants would be distributed throughout the organism, perhaps on the cellular level. Even humans and animals have certain behaviors and responses that are triggered on the cellular rather than the neurological level.

The array of experiments demonstrating plant consciousness is compelling. It has long been known that in a forest, if a single tree is attacked by some sort of disease and begins to produce antibodies to ward off the invader, other trees in the forest will begin producing similar antibodies in anticipation of a similar strike. Researchers have affectionately termed the communication network of trees the "wood-wide web."

But recent experiments suggest that plants employ the same senses possessed by humans and animals, and may even have sensory capabilities beyond those. Moreover, plants can process and respond intelligently to sensory input.

Plants can hear. A scientist identified a plant that produced a specific antibody when caterpillars began chewing upon its leaves. That same species of plant produced identical antibodies when the researcher played for it an audio recording of a caterpillar chomping its leaves, even when no caterpillar was present.

Plants can see or otherwise sense objects around them. Close observation shows that when tree roots change their growth direction to circumvent rocks under the ground, the roots make the decision to alter their course quite a ways prior to coming in contact with the rock.

And researchers have observed that bean plants seeking a pole to climb as they grow do not just wait until they happen to bump into one—they identify and move toward one in the distance. But how do they see it? Some scientists believe that a form of echolocation, based upon tiny "grunts" made by expanding cells, is the means they use, much in the way that bats and dolphins, and even some blind humans, have been known to navigate.

Perhaps most compelling was an experiment proving that plants can "remember." There is a plant sometimes referred to as a "sensitive mimosa" because surrounding leaves curl up if a single leaf is touched. This appears to be a defense mechanism to protect the delicate foliage from predators. The leaves react similarly if a potted version of the plant is dropped— apparently the plant can sense that it is falling, because the leaves contract prior to the plant hitting the ground.

A researcher created a device that allowed potted sensitive mimosa plants to begin to fall but caught them prior to impact, so the plants never hit the ground. The machine repeated this motion every five seconds.

It did not take the plants long to realize that the falls were always aborted. In response, the plants stopped curling their leaves in anticipation of impact with the ground. This in itself is quite remarkable because one of the classic measurements of animal intelligence is a creature's ability to override its instinctual programming when doing so makes sense. Here, a plant demonstrated that precise ability.

But even more remarkable was the fact that these plants "remembered" that curling their leaves in anticipation of falling was not necessary, as much as a month later! That is a longer period of time than was noted in some animals whose memories were tested in similar situations. The leaves of these plants still recoiled when the sensitive mimosas were touched, or shaken, or threatened in other ways. Somehow, these plants could differentiate the sensation of falling from other potentially injurious stimuli and react accordingly.

Do plants feel compassion or a responsibility to care for their young? It is well known that plants ingest sunlight and need it to survive. It has recently been discovered that baby trees shaded from needed sunlight in areas of dense foliage are nourished by nearby "mother trees" through their adjoining root systems, until the babies are tall enough to collect sunlight on their own. The term "mother trees" is not gratuitous. Further studies indicated that the mature trees accurately differentiated between nearby baby trees that were direct relatives and those that weren't—they fed their own progeny more robustly.

Even among scientists willing to ascribe some degree of intelligence to plants, many still bristle at the thought of referring to plants as "conscious." Yet these experiments clearly demonstrate that while perhaps not "self-conscious," plants appear to be conscious of things around them and of their own existence within their immediate space. There are varying definitions of consciousness. According to some of those definitions, plants most definitely qualify.

The older I grow, the more baffled and saddened I am by the increasing hostility toward science exhibited by so many Americans, often based on their religious beliefs. In many parts of our country, the percentage of people who reject even a scientific principle so basic as evolution is persistently expanding.

The more I learn about new scientific discoveries, the more it seems to me that science and spirituality are perfectly compatible aspects of the same truth. And when I meditate now in the mornings on my hikes with Sapphire, I gratefully share the consciousness of the flora among which I walk.

———⌣———

My father and I had worked together on occasional electronics projects over the years, but his interest in doing so had piqued significantly in recent days.

It was clear to me why.

Emmanuel was now sorely bothered by my preoccupation with books on jiu-jitsu. He had grown accustomed to my reading volumes on science: biographies of luminaries like Thomas Edison and Alexander Graham Bell, collections presenting scientific and mathematical conundrums throughout history and their eventual solutions. He recently tried to dissuade me from spending so much time with my jiu-jitsu books, characterizing them as a waste of my time. But I told him that I found them interesting, and continued reading them.

I secretly enjoyed the leverage over him they now afforded me. His enthusiasm for electronics projects upon which we could work together was firmly reinvigorated. Such pursuits could at least lure me away from jiu-jitsu for a couple hours each evening.

At the core of all these projects was radio.

My father had always found radio intrinsically magical. Growing up, he and his parents listened together for hours each evening to the console radio that commanded a prominent location in their small living room. The radio offered news and every conceivable form of entertainment. Music, comedy, mysteries, sports, and adventure could all be had. And as Emmanuel constantly reminded me, unlike television, which imposed upon you the pictures it wanted you to see, radio beguiled you into creating those images yourself: images tailored to your unique personal fantasies and caprices.

But from the beginning, as much as he loved listening to radio, my father was fascinated even more with its inner workings. Electromagnetic radio waves, dispatched by a transmitter in some distant location, traveled for miles in the atmosphere, only to be captured by an antenna and converted back into the precise sounds that engendered the waves initially. That metamorphic odyssey seemed miraculous to me as well.

Unwilling to experience the miracle of radio without understanding the science behind it, my father became obsessively curious about the engineering and technology involved. He fiddled with components on his own throughout high school. During his two-year stint in the Army, he garnered some bona fide training and hands-on experience.

That knowledge enabled Emmanuel to open a small radio repair shop upon his discharge from the military. As televisions became popular, incorporating their repair into the store's repertoire was a natural progression.

The signs posted in the shop in the late 1950s still stated that the store repaired radios as well as televisions. But in practice, that was really no longer the case. Only my father's elderly customers, many of whom spoke only Yiddish, brought radios in for repair. These were people who had been brought up on radio—most hadn't yet made the transition to television. When they presented their malfunctioning radios for examination, Emmanuel always took a few minutes to fiddle with the machine's innards. Sometimes he did so out of politeness, though occasionally he was able to replace a relatively inexpensive vacuum tube and render the machine operational.

But far more frequently Emmanuel had to announce to his client, in either English or Yiddish, that it would cost them far more to fix the radio than to buy one of the new transistor-operated models that he stocked in the shop.

"It's sad for me," he'd say, "because I like fixing radios. But that's the way things work these days. If you leave the old radio with me as a trade-in, I'll give you a discount on the new one. I can salvage some of the parts for projects I build with my son."

It always made me smile when he said that.

***

The traditional technology of radio is two sided: a transmitter on one end and a receiver on the other. The uses of radio technology continue to be abundant. Even the now ubiquitous cell phone is, in reality, a miniature radio transmitter and receiver in a single package, capable of transmitting and receiving simultaneously on different frequencies. (Which explains why you can sometimes lose one direction of a cell phone conversation but retain the other.)

The core technology of radio is surprisingly simple, especially on the receiving end. When the somewhat more complex task of converting sound into electromagnetic waves and transmitting those waves into the atmosphere through an antenna has been effected, the components needed to convert those waves back to discernable sound in a receiver, or what we commonly call a "radio," can on the most basic level be absurdly minimal.

The first AM radio that I built with Emmanuel was comprised of only four items: an antenna, a ground, a pair of headphones, and a magical little trinket known as a crystal diode. Yet it unambiguously demonstrated how electromagnetic radio waves could be converted back to sound.

The antenna was simply a long length of wire that my father and I had strung horizontally in a vacant area on the roof of our apartment house.

Gaining access to the roof was not a problem. While each individual apartment in our building sported at least two deadbolt locks on the inside of its thick, metal entry door, security of the building itself was virtually nonexistent. The ornate front doors to the apartment house were unlocked and unattended, as were various side doors easily reachable by scaling the low wall surrounding the building's rear courtyard. The courtyard also led to an intriguing labyrinth of underground cellars, which Michael and I explored and played in without impediment. The apartment house consisted of five stories. Simply walking up an additional flight led to the roof, the door to which was always ajar. This level of security was completely normal for the South Bronx in the 1950s.

Emmanuel and I strung up that long antenna wire on a sunny summer afternoon, placing small fiberglass insulators on each end, one of which we attached to an unused screw eye protruding from the mortar between layers of the roof wall's red brick, and the other to an exhaust pipe. We affixed to the antenna a long wire we allowed to dangle down the brick wall in the courtyard, such that its terminus hung directly alongside our second-story kitchen window. We used this antenna for years on a variety of receivers, just pulling the wire in through the window when we needed it, making sure it was placed back outside during rain or thunderstorms, as it could theoretically become a conductor of lightning.

The ground connection, the electronic yin to the antenna's celestial yang, guarded against power surges and kept the electron flow fluid. It was simply a wire, its end stripped of a couple feet of insulation and wrapped securely around the cold-water pipe of our kitchen sink. Such pipes were invariably metal in those days, and reached deep into the earth.

So, by opening the kitchen window and pulling in the antenna wire, and accessing the cabinet under the kitchen sink and spooling out the ground wire, we provided ourselves with two key components for various radio projects whenever needed. Both wires reached easily to the small Formica-topped kitchen table, our regular workspace for electronic experiments.

The third component was a pair of sensitive headphones, purchased by mail from a catalog shop on the eastern edge of Long Island. Basic radio work on this level entailed no amplification of signal strength through batteries or electrical current. The small amount of electricity residual in the electromagnetic radio wave itself powered the device. Only sensitive headphones could pick up the faint sounds generated by this sparse equipment.

The final element was the crystal diode. This tiny nodule encompassed simultaneously the magic and the astounding simplicity of radio technology.

Electronically, only one obstacle stands in the way of capturing a radio signal on an antenna and feeding it directly into headphones: oscillation. Electromagnetic radio waves are an oscillating phenomenon, which is why they are generally diagrammed as half circles alternating above and below a horizontal line along which they travel. Their oscillation produces an alternating current in the antenna. Were that alternating current permitted to reach the headphones unaltered, it would shove electrons through the phones and then immediately pull them back. Radio waves cannot be reconstituted into sound in that manner.

What is needed is a sort of one-way electronic valve, permitting current to flow in one direction but not back in the other. Vacuum tubes and transistors were eventually developed to do exactly that, but the earliest and simplest contrivance to accomplish this was called a crystal detector, later miniaturized into a device known as a crystal diode. It was a tiny glass capsule with a short, stiff wire protruding from each end.

By adding the crystal diode to the configuration of an antenna, ground, and headphones, radio signals could immediately be detected in the headphones. I recall vividly first hearing these signals—it seemed miraculous. The mysterious, seemingly unfathomable workings hidden within the walls of a radio receiver had been unmasked and simplified down to their most basic components. And the thing worked!

However, all sorts of undifferentiated signals from various stations poured into the headphones simultaneously, creating a cacophony of radio sounds from assorted programs. This problem was quickly mitigated with the inclusion of one additional component: a variable capacitor. This simple element consisted of a small set of semicircular, parallel metal plates, each mounted a fixed distance from the next. A second set of similar plates, each of which fit precisely halfway between the plates of the first set, was affixed to a handle that could be rotated by hand, thus varying the amount the plates overlapped. By feeding the signal through this variable capacitor, individual stations could be tuned in simply by turning the handle.

Although Emmanuel and I went on to build many increasingly complex and powerful radios using transistors, vacuum tubes, and power sources to amplify the signal to the point where it could be heard through a speaker rather than headphones, our most memorable project was constructed one Sunday afternoon when I asked my father this question:

"What exactly is inside the crystal diode that makes it do what it does?"

At my father's urging we immediately pulled out a piece of pegboard and quickly assembled that same four-piece receiver: antenna, ground, headphones, and a crystal diode. Then Emmanuel said to me, "OK, Sammy, remove the crystal diode. We're going to build our own."

My eyes grew wide with anticipation. Duplicating the sorcery sealed in the tiny glass body of the diode seemed profoundly daunting.

My father opened our silverware drawer and rummaged through the knives, causing lots of clinging and rattling as he spoke. "The very first types of diodes, Sammy, were called cat's whiskers, or cat's whisker detectors. They were really just big, open-air versions of what's now miniaturized inside the crystal diode. They all start with some sort of naturally semiconducting mineral. Originally they used a crystal of galena, which is a lead sulfide—now they use mostly silicon, but there are other minerals that work too, selenium or germanium."

As he spoke, he retrieved an old silver butter knife that we never used because it had developed severely discolored blotches. "We're going to use a tarnished kitchen knife, Sammy. The tarnish is an oxidation, like rust—it's actually a semiconductor. Not a great one, but it will work."

Emmanuel glanced around the table and countertop but didn't seem to find what he was looking for. "Sammy, get a pencil and a single-edged razor blade from the toolbox."

I did so, and as my father guided me, I carefully shaved off enough yellow pencil wood to expose an inch of graphite, which we broke off and grafted onto the end of a very stiff piece of copper wire by wrapping the two with hair-thin magnet wire, leaving the point of the graphite just barely protruding from the end of the copper.

We attached the copper wire to the antenna side of the circuit where the diode had been, and the tarnished silver knife to the ground side.

"Put the headphones on, Sammy. Then bend the copper wire so the graphite point just barely touches the tarnished part of the knife. Do you hear anything?"

"No," I said.

"Move the wire slowly so the graphite point touches different parts of the knife blade. Also try playing with it so the point rests heavier or lighter on the knife. Keep playing with it."

I spent several minutes manipulating the wire and the knife as my father watched. Suddenly my mouth opened wide in astonishment. Radio signals were coming through the headphones. They were faint and discordant, an amalgam of random music and human speech. I took off the headphones and gave them to Emmanuel. He put them on and smiled broadly.

"You built a cat's whisker, Sammy! It's essentially the same mechanism that's miniaturized in the diode and sealed in glass."

He gave me back the headphones. I put them on and listened alone for twenty minutes with my eyes closed.

I had assembled far more complex devices with sophisticated components. But never had I felt so viscerally that I had built a radio.

Some months after the cat's-whisker experiment, I constructed a rather impressive amplified receiver of my own design that employed vacuum tubes, batteries, and a small loudspeaker. I accomplished it over several weekends, and was especially gratified by the fact that it incorporated capacitors and resistors at various points along the signal's path to regulate and refine the quality of sound.

I left the contraption in place on the kitchen table so that my father would see it and sample its performance when he came home from work. It seemed to operate as well as many of the commercial sets we had owned.

While waiting for him to come home, I returned to the kitchen every few minutes to gaze at the project and wallow in the pride of my successful handiwork. On one such visit, as I stood in our narrow kitchen, I rested one hand on the kitchen sink and casually reached out to lean on the old white refrigerator with the other. The moment my hand made contact with the refrigerator, I was jolted by an electrical shock that passed from one arm to the other and caused a powerful rumbling vibration through my chest. I released my hold on the appliances and staggered backward a couple of steps.

I was stunned. The sensation, though, was curiously alluring.

I waited about thirty seconds, then walked back to the same spot and duplicated my movements. The shock passed through me again.

I knew this was dangerous. I understood that repeatedly exposing myself to this current might cause me harm. Yet the feeling it imparted was hypnotic and, for me, clearly addictive.

I returned to that spot in the kitchen the next evening, and the next, waiting for a moment when no one was nearby. I touched the sink and refrigerator simultaneously and shocked myself again. I began to repeat the act nightly.

It took me several months to summon up the willpower to abandon the ritual permanently.

8.
Sending and Receiving

BY THE EIGHTH GRADE, tedious hours of teacher babble had begun to try my patience sorely. Basic concepts I found easily comprehensible within a couple of minutes were reiterated, with only the slightest variation, for the entire forty-five-minute class period. My mother admonished me to display patience and pay attention in class, even if the teachers' instruction appeared redundant.

"Not everyone gets concepts as quickly as you do, Sammy," she said. "Don't be rude to your teachers or condescending to your classmates." That warning proved far more difficult for me to negotiate than she imagined.

Still, I tried to be fair. Some teachers were genuinely nice people, and in their classes I did my best to feign interest. I'd watch them intently for a moment, then periodically lower my head to write in my binder. Ostensibly I was taking notes, though in reality I was either designing my next personal electronics project or mapping out a set of throws and parries to include in my next jiu-jitsu session with Michael and David.

But there were teachers who were needlessly strident. Some were even willfully cruel and sadistic. Interestingly, these harsh teachers generally struck me as less innately intelligent and knowledgeable than the nice ones. I reasoned that they were therefore trying to compensate with a show of iron will, at the expense of innocent students. For these teachers, I plotted special stratagems.

My favorite ploy, which I unsheathed whenever one of these teachers behaved in an especially odious manner, seized upon the propensity of these instructors to pose a question and then ignore students who raised their hands, calling instead upon a student not likely to know the answer. Their intent was to engender embarrassment and peer ridicule. Their favorite targets were students whose attention had seemingly drifted.

A principle of jiu-jitsu resonated with me: the preferred response to a show of hostility was often not to immediately retaliate, but to instead lure your opponent into initiating a subsequent action that rendered him even more vulnerable, thus enabling you to draw him off balance and attack him more effectively from there.

I found these sadistic teachers easy to so manipulate.

I would wait until the discussion reached a topic upon which I was particularly well versed. Then, as the teacher posed a series of especially difficult questions, I displayed blatant signs of daydreaming: I'd shift my body completely around in my seat to stare out a window, or gaze at a pretty girl across the room. This ploy never failed. The hands of eager students would shoot into the air, some barely able to control their zeal, their erect bodies stretching out of their seats while they emitted tiny groans of supplication, importuning the teacher to call upon them.

But the teacher would ignore them, and instead stare rapaciously at the side of my turned head for a moment before bellowing the name "Samuel Baron!" to catch me by surprise. The instructor would then strike a smug predatory pose, expecting me to be startled into unbearable fumbling and mortification.

I'd calmly stand and without hesitation recite a litany of impressive facts and observations on the matter at hand, which I had rehearsed throughout my pretense of distraction. Upon finishing, a quick glance enabled me to relish the look of stupefied humiliation on the teacher's face, after which I'd sit down, and serenely look away.

On a brisk New York evening during our recent fall stay, Sapphire and I made the long walk from my condo overlooking Central Park down to Jake's place in the West Village. As usual, the plan was to begin with what Jake had referred to for decades as a "lab," where we worked to perfect a specific cocktail. We then planned to couple our beverages with some very good East Indian food delivered from a favorite restaurant. Depending upon the lateness of the hour and how much I'd had to drink, Sapphire and I would probably wind up staying the night in his spare bedroom.

When Sapphire and I arrived, Jake had out on his kitchen counter the three reagents required to concoct the perfect sidecar: cognac, Cointreau, and fresh lemons. "This next batch needs a bit more of the Cointreau," he said as soon as he returned to the kitchen after letting us in.

Jake crouched and peered intently through the lower edge of his bifocals as he slowly poured the Cointreau, making certain the elixir's level in the pitcher conformed precisely to his desired specifications.

A half-empty glass sat beside him. That, coupled with his manner and posture, persuaded me that he had downed a couple prior to our arrival.

"Sidecars tonight, Dockles!" he announced. "Fine old cocktails, these sidecars. It's a shame how they've lost favor among the young. Even worse, some bars now mix them with bourbon rather than brandy unless you instruct them otherwise. It's a travesty, Doc!"

I found a stainless steel bowl in Jake's lower cabinet and filled it with water for Sapphire, then took a couple of dog treats from my pocket and placed them on the floor in front of her. Sapphire gobbled up the tidbits immediately. In the past I enjoyed feeding her such treats from my hand, but Sapphire's near vision had now become so blurred that she could no longer take a treat from my hand without inadvertently catching my fingers.

Jake handed me my sidecar in a chilled martini glass with a twist of knotted lemon rind artfully displayed. As always, Jake was meticulous about denuding the lemon rind of all residual white pith prior to garnishing the drink with it. He often said, "The pith is bitter, Doc."

Neither of us was much for sugared rims, but Jake did lightly rub the knotted lemon rinds along the rim of each martini glass prior to serving, perfuming the glass with a barely perceptible aroma of citrus oil. We toasted.

"It's delicious, Jake," I said. "Another gustatory masterpiece."

"Thank you, Doc," he said.

The conversation then turned to a documentary we had viewed together recently on public television, concerning experiments conducted with honeybees. The question we posed for conjecture was this: is a hive of bees a single organism or a group of individual bees?

The experiment featured in the documentary dealt with how bees choose a hive.

Each spring, if a honeybee colony has outgrown its current space, a swarm consisting of thousands of bees with one new queen breaks away to form a new colony, and searches for an alternative nesting location. Their search can take anywhere from a few hours to a few days, but the manner in which the search is conducted, and the way the decision is finalized, is quite astounding.

Bees seek natural or artificial environments for their new hive. These must meet certain prerequisites, the two most important being a large enough cavity to store sufficient honey for the winter, and a relatively small aperture for entry and egress so that the colony can defend itself from predators. Height above the ground is also a key consideration.

In order to create a controlled environment for this experiment, the scientists moved a hive of bees to an island on which no other bees existed, and which had no trees to provide natural hive cavities for the new swarm. Instead, the scientists constructed a number of wooden structures of different shapes and sizes, all of which could serve as serviceable hive environments, but only one of which was ideal with respect to the bees' preferences. The scientists wanted to see if the bees would choose the ideal home and, if so, how they would reach that decision as a group.

As the scientists expected, female scout bees were dispatched by the new swarm to investigate different parts of the island for suitable structures. Each time a scout found and inspected a new potential home, a scientist would capture the bee in a net, quickly mark her with a drop of paint to distinguish her, and then release her so that she could conduct her inquiry and return to the swarm to report on her findings.

When reporting back to the swarm, each scout performed a mid-air dance indicating the direction and distance of the recently examined hive site. These dances also expressed the degree of enthusiasm the scout felt for the site: the more frantic and passionate her dance, the more she was able to promote her choice and convince additional scout bees to fly out and inspect the site themselves. A sort of bee congress then convened, with groups representing one potential site or another trying to persuade others of the supremacy of their choice, first by the vigor and persistence of their dances, but eventually by headbutting opposition dancers as well. Fairly quickly, a decision was made. The scientists found that the process was quite effective—in repeated experiments, the optimal location was chosen in the vast majority of cases.

Even more interesting, though, was the striking similarity between this exercise and the decision-making process of human brains. In people, neurons play the same roles as those of individual bees. Information can be contributed by many different neurons, but the same sort of competition based upon quorums and enthusiasm ensues, leading to a decision by a majority of the competing brain cells.

Hence, our question: is a hive of bees more accurately characterized as a single organism or as a group of individuals?

Jake posited his argument with authority: "A hive is clearly a single organism, Doc. There's no question about it. It operates as a unified whole. It's obvious from observation."

"I'm not so sure of that, Jake," I replied. "Each bee is clearly a fully formed animal, capable of living on its own. Each bee has eyes, antennae, legs, and internal organs for digestion, elimination, and all other life-sustaining functions."

"Actually, Doc, bees are *not* truly capable of living on their own, given the strict and limited roles each are assigned throughout the hive. The behavior of the hive as a single entity clearly trumps the fact that individual bees appear to be discrete organisms. The fact that neurons in our brain are wired together, whereas individual bees in a hive are not physically attached to one another, does not significantly affect the way that these components interact to make necessary life decisions."

Jake seemed quite satisfied with this last salvo, and stood to pour himself another drink in celebration. To his chagrin, he found the pitcher empty and traipsed off into the kitchen to mix another batch.

"You know, Jake," I said from the sofa, "it's fairly evident that both behaviors are present: bees display unmistakable signs of individual behavior, whereas the hive's decisions are clearly made as if it were a single organism. It's akin to the polar opposites in our human psyches that cause us to view the world as an endless array of dualities: the continuums of positive and negative currents, gravity versus centrifugal force, archetypal warriors versus archetypal priests, good versus evil, power versus love, God versus devil. But are these dualities real? I don't think so. An overwhelming sense of unity can be obtained through classic mystical experiences as documented throughout history, be it the rapture of a Christian in prayer, the engrossed trance of an artist creating new work, or the state of samadhi experienced by a meditating Yogi."

Jake rolled his eyes and lowered his head as he mixed the reagents for the next pitcher of sidecars. "You're getting spiritual on me again, Doc," he exclaimed. "You're driving me to excessive drink!"

I sipped slowly on the remnants of liquid in my glass. "It saddens me now, Jake, to think back on how combative I was throughout nearly my entire life: in martial arts, in business, in relationships. I even taunted my teachers with cruel ploys in the guise of punishing the wicked."

"You mean staring out the window to entice them to call upon you? That was brilliant. Totally deserved on their part. Please, Doc, don't question yourself about things you did fifty years ago."

"All through my life," I said, "I asserted my strength and ego tirelessly. But what's fascinating is that the polar opposite of my belligerence asserted itself just as powerfully at times. The need, especially during sex, to be the vanquished, the submissive."

"Have another drink, Doc."

"The key is surrender. I know that now from my training in meditation. Surrender is the gateway to the spirit."

Jake took my glass, refilled it, and handed it back to me. "I know what you're saying about surrender, Doc. I used to be so full of myself. What a relief to get over that."

***

Leonard Levitzky chewed upon his necktie. It was the only distinguishing aspect of his character that leaped out at me when I initially observed him sitting near the back of the room in my eighth-grade geometry class. It would have been odd even if he persisted at it for just a moment. Yet Leonard Levitzky gnawed his tie incessantly. Every time I glanced in his direction, the bottom portion of his tie was looped up in his mouth.

All male students were required to wear neckties. The long-held New York City Public School dress code of neckties for boys and skirts for girls was still strictly enforced in the 1950s.

Perhaps because of his tie-chewing, and his shy and gentle manner, most fellow students dismissed Leonard Levitzky as odd and a bit slow. But we were in the same honors science and math classes, and although he never raised his hand, he always seemed to know the answer to any question posed to him. It occurred to me that Leonard Levitzky might just be as bored in school as I was. I decided to find out a bit more about him.

I asked some boys with whom I was friendly if they knew anything about Leonard. Their responses intrigued me. Many of them repeated the same rumor: it was believed that Leonard possessed the ability to read people's minds. I began to observe him unobtrusively.

He was somewhat taller than I, paunchy and soft around his hips and belly. Leonard's gait was a slow, stooped shuffle. His pants sagged and were baggy, and his shirts tails often protruded haphazardly from his waistband. He wore glasses. His thick, wavy hair was reddish brown and always unkempt.

Our junior high school had a large, paved schoolyard. During lunch hour, the yard was open for congregating and usually quite crowded unless it was raining or very cold and snowy. While the girls generally stood and chatted, many boys organized informal games—there were basketball hoops, areas where you could throw a ball and play catch, and a few one-wall handball courts.

One-wall handball never gained much popularity outside of New York City. The rest of the country played four-wall handball and soon moved to racquetball. But one-wall handball was a cheap outdoor game accessible to anyone who owned a small rubber ball. Courts sprang up initially at beach clubs but spread quickly to New York's public parks and schoolyards. It was a fast game and could be rough—New York City rules allowed you to physically block your opponent's access to the ball as long as you didn't move your feet after taking your last shot, so collisions and shoving were commonplace tactics. If you believed your opponent had moved his feet prior to blocking your access, you could call a "Hindu" and insist on playing the point over, though an argument over whether your call was legitimate almost always ensued, and occasionally led to blows.

It wasn't until years later when I played a polite game of four-wall racquetball with a client at his private club in Illinois that I learned that four-wall rules never allowed blocking regardless of whether your feet moved, and even the slightest obstruction was routinely called a "hinder," and the point was immediately replayed without discussion. Thinking about it in my hotel room before I went to bed that evening, I suddenly realized that our New York term *Hindu*, which I had screamed out so frequently as a boy, was just a decades-old New York mutilation of the word *hinder*. It reminded me of the first time I had ever seen the word *whore* written out. At first I didn't recognize it at all, assuming the word would be spelled something like *hooah*, the way it was pronounced on the street.

Perusing the schoolyard one day at lunchtime, I noticed Leonard Levitzky playing a heated game of one-wall handball, and acquitting himself surprisingly well. I played handball from time to time—this presented a convenient pretext for approaching him. After his game, I complimented his technique and invited him to join me some Saturday for a game of handball at the schoolyard where I had attended elementary school, which was closer to my home. He told me he was free this coming Saturday, and the meeting was set.

When Leonard Levitzky finally arrived on Saturday, I had been waiting on the stoop in front of my apartment house for over half an hour, wondering if he had forgotten about our rendezvous.

"Hi, Sammy," he said. "Sorry I'm so late. Walking over here from my neighborhood was crazy. It should have taken fifteen minutes and it took close to an hour. All this construction on the new highway. I couldn't cross over to get to East Tremont Avenue for blocks."

"The Cross Bronx Expressway," I said. "I know. It's insane. My mother sends me to this delicatessen, Izzy's, for stuff now and then. All the streets to get there now are blocked. I have to walk something like ten blocks out of the way there and back."

"I don't get why they're doing it right here," Leonard said. "There was an alternate plan to move it a couple of blocks south, along the north end of Crotona Park. They wouldn't have had to rip down all those apartments and evict everyone. Did you know they tore down over fifteen hundred apartments?"

"I heard that," I said.

"Did you ever meet that woman, Lillian Edelstein?" he asked.

"Yeah, she knocked on our door once. For like two years she was doing fundraisers and rallies and petitions to stop the evictions and move the highway. My father always said she didn't have a chance in hell of making it happen."

"Actually, she almost succeeded," said Leonard. "She got a lot of people on her side, including politicians. But then Robert Moses got the city to take title of all the apartment buildings along his preferred route, and everybody got evicted and then they tore all the houses down. I lost a lot of friends who had to move away. The highway just missed my house by a couple of blocks."

Recollections of my early years in the Bronx, and ruminations about how the borough had fared since, preoccupied me. So I suggested to Jake that he join Sapphire and me on a visit to some of my childhood haunts in the South Bronx.

Jake's initial reaction was less than enthusiastic.

"You want me to spend an afternoon driving around the South Bronx, Doc?" he exclaimed. "Why on earth would I want to do that? Have you been in the South Bronx lately? The place looks like some bombed-out village from World War II. It's mummified in neglect, Doc! And it's rife with armed hoodlums looking for old white men like us to rob and kill."

"Actually, Jake, I've done a bit of research on the internet," I said. "That image of the South Bronx is certainly still widely held, but the reality is quite different. Granted, there are still dreadful patches, but there's been a good deal of slow, steady development, much of it indigenous and very positive."

"It's a dangerous place, Doc!"

I laughed and reached up to rest my hand on Jake's tall, broad shoulder. "We'll have Sapphire with us," I said. "She's a vicious beast. And I'm a feared black belt in several styles of jiu-jitsu."

Jake chuckled. "Doc, I hate to break this to you, but you're a short, skinny old Jewish intellectual who, twenty years ago, was moderately adept at jiu-jitsu. You practice tai chi now, which, at best, might be effective at disarming a wheelchair-bound octogenarian with failing eyesight. And Sapphire, with all due respect, is a lovely old girl, but if she was ever vicious, it was sometime in the Paleolithic era."

Jake's diatribe caused me to laugh so hard that I had to bend over to catch my breath.

"All right, Jake," I acknowledged, "I actually gave this some serious thought and have a more nuanced plan. Do you remember Gus, the guy we've used as a driver now and then, here in the city? I talked to him yesterday. He'll take us around the Bronx and doesn't mind bringing

Sapphire in the car. Gus is an ex-cop, so he's not going to get lost or get stuck in the wrong place. And if you recall, he drives an old sedan, not a limousine, so we'll be inconspicuous. And he always boasted to us about how he replaced his car's windows with bulletproof glass."

"He *is* a well-prepared fellow."

"Yes, Jake, I'd say that an ex-cop who packs a gun with him at all times could be described as a well-prepared fellow. You'll feel safe. And better yet, Gus said he knows a great Italian place on Arthur Avenue with some outdoor tables—they're dog-friendly, so Sapphire can join the three of us for lunch. There will undoubtedly be some good Chianti."

"Good Chianti, eh? OK, Doc, you've worn me down. Count me in, albeit reluctantly. And if we die in a hail of gunfire, my death will be on you."

"I'll pay for lunch, and for Gus and his car," I offered, "in order to compensate you for the psychological pain you're obviously feeling as a result of obsessing over the possibility of a violent and untimely demise."

Especially pleased by the way that last phrase had rolled effortlessly off my tongue, I looked closely to Jake's face, as I had for many years, for some sign of approval. The fact that he had no rejoinder and displayed a slight grimace of ironic disgust bolstered me sufficiently.

The next day, Gus drove us for hours around East Tremont and the surrounding neighborhoods that were my boyhood Bronx haunts. Jake sat in the front next to Gus. I was in the back, Sapphire asleep beside me on the sedan's cushiony rear bench seat.

I reminisced aloud as Gus meandered. We passed by the storefront where Emmanuel had his first radio and television repair shop. I reminded Jake that so much of the work he and I had partnered on, years ago, stemmed from lessons I learned in that storefront.

Nearby, the small local library branch where I read books and fantasized about Esther the librarian was intact and evidently still in the business of lending books. My old five-story apartment house, less than a mile from the library, also stood upright. A secured steel door now faced the street, and the outside windowsills and frames looked to have been recently repainted. I wondered if the long horizontal antenna wire that Emmanuel and I strung up on the roof had survived the intervening decades.

Most amazing, though, were the recurring parcels of new, well-maintained, suburban-style homes fronted by modest but immaculately groomed lawns. They sat like oases interspersed among vast stretches of decay and dilapidation.

As we passed a strip of dark, forsaken, graffiti-shrouded hovels, Jake gestured animatedly and shouted, "You see, Doc, bombed out and dangerous!"

"Not so dangerous by day, Kenneman," Gus said pointedly, "especially with me around."

Jake's comment had evidently struck a nerve with Gus. I recalled a conversation with Gus some years back when he shared with me how tired he was of the reactions he garnered as a large, imposing, African American man. People balked at entering an elevator alone with him, and crossed deserted streets to avoid proximity with him, especially at night. I wondered if Gus had perceived Jake's remark as racially tinged. I looked for a way to shift the conversation's tone without being overly conspicuous.

"The patches of new housing are interesting," I said to Gus. "It's not like the gentrification I see in the trendy new neighborhoods in north Brooklyn or east Harlem. This seems more indigenous, like it's growing out of these old neighborhoods themselves."

"That's right, Baron," said Gus. "The South Bronx still gets a bad rap. Most everyone, like your friend Kenneman, is afraid to go near it. So it doesn't get the high-priced real estate gurus investing in it. These homes you see come mostly from community-development groups. I think it's good, though. The growth happens more gradually. Doesn't kick out so many of the old people. Might last longer, too."

As we drove, the footprint of the Cross Bronx Expressway remained an unrelenting and palpable presence. It gutted the neighborhood mercilessly, constantly thwarting our trajectory. Gus was familiar with the bypasses, but even he seemed to grow frustrated accessing them.

And the whole area appeared sequestered from the rest of the borough, rimmed by a network of soulless expressways, all designed to feed traffic between Manhattan and the suburbs, isolating the South Bronx like a spurned stepchild.

"There's some really nice stuff here," Gus announced as he drove us into Bronx Park and slowly skirted the Botanical Gardens. The flowered meadows I could see from the car appeared even more meticulously maintained than I recalled from my childhood. We passed by the entrance to the Bronx Zoo.

"Best zoo in the country," declared Gus.

"I'd have to agree," I said. "Have either of you been to the San Diego Zoo? It's lovely, and a close second. There's a beautiful zoo in Basel, Switzerland, too." I paused. "But truly, the Bronx Zoo may be the best zoo on the planet. Admittedly, I'm biased. I came here so often as a kid."

It might have been nice to visit the zoo for a couple of hours, but neither Gus nor Jake seemed interested, and in any event, it would have meant leaving Sapphire, who was still asleep, alone in the hot car.

"Let me show you a new park you probably never heard of," Gus said, heading southeast to Barretto Point, a delightful, small neighborhood park packed with mothers and young children. Although the park itself was charming, some of streets we passed in accessing it seemed desolate and menacing.

Jake started to get cranky. "How much longer are we going to drive around?" he demanded. "I'm hungry, and I want some of that good Chianti you promised."

"All right, Gus," I said, "what do you say we feed Jake?"

"Good idea, Baron. I'm actually with Kenneman on this one. I'm getting hungry myself."

Gus parked on Arthur Avenue. To those of us who grew up in the Bronx, Arthur Avenue was New York's true Little Italy, as opposed to the two-block tourist lure in lower Manhattan adjacent to Chinatown.

I awakened Sapphire and put her on leash as we exited the car and began walking. It was immediately clear that the stretch of Arthur Avenue devoted to old-style Italian shops and restaurants had diminished in length over the years, but the colors, the aromas, and the energy of the people on the street seemed unchanged. Although I spotted a couple of large restaurants that were obviously new and geared toward tourists, the remainder of the delicatessens, bakeries, flower stands, butcher shops, tobacconists, and smaller restaurants lining the avenue seemed absolutely authentic—many were indeed owned by grandchildren and great-grandchildren of the original immigrant proprietors.

It was a short distance to the restaurant, which as promised had a number of wrought iron tables outside on the street, where dogs were welcome. The maître d' was a burly, middle-aged Italian man whose tattooed arms and gruff Bronx accent could not mask an innate gentleness and affability. He clearly knew Gus well. They hugged and sent regards to each other's families.

We were seated at a table in the shade. Sapphire reclined at my feet. Our waiter immediately brought Sapphire a stainless steel bowl filled with cool water, which the dog lapped up eagerly. A few minutes later, when the waiter brought us menus, a basket of bread, and a large carafe of the house Chianti, he bent down and dropped Sapphire a slice of rolled-up prosciutto. Sapphire took the offering, and affectionately licked the waiter's shoes—perhaps to show her appreciation, perhaps because the remnant of some enticing tidbit lingered there.

One of the things I love about traditional Italian restaurants is how easily wonderful vegan food can be negotiated. After abluting with my alcohol-based hand sanitizer, I began my lunch with some fresh Italian bread dipped in fruity extra-virgin olive oil.

In the Arthur Avenue tradition, we ordered large family-style platters for sharing. I ate most of the big antipasto salad. We asked the waiter to please bring the salad's cheese and salami on a separate plate. Jake repositioned the cheese and meat dish between Gus and himself, and they quickly devoured its contents, with a couple of salami slices tossed down for Sapphy.

Gus and Jake shared a large plate of veal parmigiana. Each also took a bit off our third platter, linguini with marinara, leaving the rest of that selection for me. They sprinkled mounds of grated cheese on top of their servings.

I took from my pocket a small plastic vial filled with a powdered concoction I had created that morning and poured the mixture over my dish of pasta. The topping was delicious, despite the odd glance it engendered from Gus as I took my first bite.

"What the hell is that shit you just slopped all over your pasta, Baron?" Gus demanded.

"It's ground raw cashew nuts, nutritional yeast, and salt."

Gus grimaced.

I pointed to his plate. "That tasty grated Parmigiano cheese that you just sprinkled over *your* pasta, Gus, actually exhibits only three discernable flavor attributes: the fermented tinge of aged dairy curds, robust saltiness, and an unctuous fatty mouthfeel. The vegan combination I put together of ground fatty cashews, sea salt, and fermented nutritional yeast mimics the flavor and texture of those three elements uncannily."

Jake rolled his eyes and turned toward Gus, saying irritably, "Don't encourage him."

But the house Chianti was very smooth. Over the next half hour, it had a markedly ameliorating effect on Jake's demeanor. The three of us talked and shared stories and laughed. We ordered a second carafe of wine. Sapphire slept under my chair.

I was surprised how much of the wine Gus drank, considering that he was our driver and a retired police officer. Gus didn't talk much on the ride home, but he drove impeccably.

Leonard hit the ball hard and made clever use of dink shots, forcing me to run around his wide body to get to the ball. I tried shoving him out of the way a couple of times, but he'd squat, creating a low center of gravity, and he was impossible to budge. He initially took a commanding lead. It required all my concentration and every trick I knew to come back and edge him out by two points for the victory. I finally figured out that hitting hard didn't work against him, but if I hit high soft shots that forced him to run from side to side and low dinks to make him sprint in, I could tire him out and take advantage of his lack of speed and endurance.

"That was a great game, Sammy," he said, panting heavily as he administered a light congratulatory smack to my shoulder. "Let's play another."

"Absolutely," I said, "but let's take a break for a couple of minutes. I have something I want to ask you."

"OK," he said.

"People say you can read minds. Is that true?"

He lowered his head slightly and flashed a sheepish grin. "Well, yeah, sometimes, but it's no big deal."

"What do you mean it's no big deal? If you can really do it, it's amazing."

"It only works sometimes, and only if a person really tries to focus on it with me. And really, what does it accomplish? It doesn't help me in school. It doesn't help me make friends. It's just like doing a magic trick."

"But it's real, right? Not like a magic trick," I pressed him.

"Yeah, it's real," he said softly.

"Can we try it?" I asked.

"OK," he said, "just think of a picture of something. Anything, but think about it really hard and don't think about anything else."

I pondered for a moment. I wanted to come up with a mental image that had nothing to do with where we were or anything we had talked about or seen on the way over, to prevent Leonard from making an informed guess. After a couple of false starts I settled on a mental image of a dirty alleyway sandwiched between two buildings. On the alley's asphalt surface stood a half-opened garbage can with a cat sitting on its rim.

"All right," I said. "I have the picture in my head."

"OK, really focus," he said softly as he stared unimposingly into my eyes for about thirty seconds. Then he said, "I see like a narrow courtyard, with a garbage pail and a cat." He paused for a moment. "Did I get it?" he asked.

"My God!" I said. I was utterly flabbergasted. "You got it almost exactly. That's amazing, Leonard. What an incredible gift!"

"Actually," he said, "I've never done it with anyone where I saw it so clearly and so fast. *You* have a gift, Sammy. You're a *sender*."

"A what?" I asked.

"In telepathy there are senders and receivers. I can recommend a really good book about ESP experiments if you like reading—it'll explain it really well. I'm a receiver, but what I see depends on the sender as to how much I get and how clear it is. You're amazing, Sammy. Your picture was as sharp as a television transmission. I think you ought to read this book. The library has it. Do you like reading?"

"I do, Leonard. And I love the library." The image of the beautiful Black librarian popped into my head, followed immediately by a stinging twinge of panic. I frantically willed myself to think of something else: the pegboard layout of my latest electronics project was the first thing that came to mind. I needed to get the librarian out of my thoughts; my secret wasn't safe with Leonard standing a foot away from me.

"OK," Leonard said. "I'll write down the name of the book and the author and I'll give it to you in school on Monday. Sammy, after you read the book, I think you'll see that *your* gift is actually a lot more useful than mine."

"Really? I need to read that book."

"Ready for another game of handball?" he asked, suddenly animated and enthused.

"Let's do it," I said.

Leonard won the next game. My mind was no longer on handball.

9.
Project Venus

I READ THE FIRST CHAPTER of the book on ESP without moving from the spot where I found it on the library shelf. I skimmed a few additional sections before even glancing up.

Leonard Levitzky's description of the book was quite accurate. The author detailed the results of various experiments he had conducted, and recounted some of his personal experiences with telepathy and clairvoyance.

The subject matter captured my interest powerfully.

From what I gleaned at first glance, while all people have ESP experiences from time to time, some individuals are more innately gifted than others, and almost all such people tend to fall primarily into the category of a sender or a receiver. The book also pointed out that ESP is far more likely to manifest when individuals are dealing with critical matters that carry a sense of urgency and are emotionally charged. For that reason, controlled tests conducted in calm and repetitive scientific environments generally are incapable of detecting such phenomena.

I decided to borrow the book to explore it in greater detail. The alluring librarian had not been on duty when I arrived at the branch, but she was there at the counter as I checked the book out.

"I see you have yet another new interest, young man," she said as I stood across from her. "For the past few months you've been focusing solely on books about how to throw people to the ground. Now it seems you want to read their minds as well!"

I looked up her. She was smiling softly. I was usually quite nervous in her presence, but her gentle facial expression now put me at ease. "Do my interests seem strange to you?" I asked.

"No, not to me," she said. "But you *do* seem to be a boy hiding some secrets."

Her assertion startled me. "You can tell?" I asked.

"Don't worry," she whispered, leaning closer. "I'm sure nobody else can." She paused a moment, then added, "I have some secrets too."

Over the next few weeks, I obsessively pondered that encounter in my mind, trying to guess what her secrets might be.

———————

If I was indeed a sender (and, as characterized by Leonard Levitzky, a powerful one), could I hone my skills sufficiently to enable me to transmit to people who were not innately gifted receivers?

I would have discussed that possibility with Leonard, but he was gone.

Like so many other Jewish families in that corner of our East Tremont neighborhood, his had fled to the suburbs. They vanished just a few weeks after he and I played handball together. He didn't say goodbye.

The work on the Cross Bronx Expressway had not just displaced the families whose homes fell in its destructive wake. Its havoc proliferated. The property values of nearby homes and businesses plummeted, causing many of those structures to be abandoned as well.

African Americans and Puerto Ricans took advantage of the lowered rents and moved into the vacated apartments and storefronts. The whites living nearby bought into the stereotype of dark-skinned thieves and killers. The white exodus became a vicious, recursive loop, nourished by its own momentum and racism.

The neighborhood began to look very different.

Without Leonard to confer with, I modeled my ESP experiments on those in the book he had recommended. I tried sending messages to my brother, David, and my best friend Michael. I attempted to transmit some when they were expecting them and some when they weren't. None went through successfully.

In school, trying to send messages to unwitting students or teachers helped break up the tedium that I found progressively more unbearable. I tried for a month to impel some random student in a row near mine to ask permission to go the bathroom. It never worked.

Nowhere did I spend more time on doomed ESP experiments than in Hebrew school. Thankfully, I had not been sent there from the age of eight or nine, as was the case with many of the boys from more observant families. But I was nearing my thirteenth birthday, so some months of bar mitzvah preparation was deemed necessary.

I found Hebrew school far more odious than ordinary school. Classes were held evenings, Monday through Thursday, from 5 to 6 PM, with an additional hour on Sunday mornings. I was not at all enthused about this intrusion into my free time. My disenchantment was exacerbated by the fact that so many streets in the neighborhood were now blocked by preliminary sections of the Cross Bronx Expressway that the walk to and from the temple had become long and convoluted, and took me nearly half an hour in each direction.

The classes had the oppressive feel of a primitive indoctrination ritual. I spent most of each hour trying to send a subliminal message to my shriveled teacher, Mrs. Hirsch, to induce her to undue the top button on her blouse. She never complied.

The lecture on Rosicrucian meditation was my second at the lodge, and in many ways quite distinct from the first.

That initial talk, on Shaolin mysticism, had been presented by an outside expert with no connection to the Rosicrucian Order. The current lecture on Rosicrucian meditation was delivered by a longtime adherent. More direct references to Rosicrucian teachings were therefore present. But present too was a conscious and meticulous effort to divulge only a precisely calibrated inventory of information, to maintain the deeper secrets of Rosicrucian meditation for members of the sect.

The lecturer seemed willing to discuss the same general and stylized overview of Rosicrucian meditation I had discovered on the internet in the tract by Joseph J. Weed. Both stopped abruptly at any detailed description of technique. But the two sources were quite aligned regarding the phases for advanced meditators.

It was these advanced phases that intrigued me. I tried, in a nonthreatening manner, to explore them a bit more deeply in my post-lecture chat with Virginia Ferguson.

"It's good to see you again, Sammy," she said. "Did you enjoy the lecture?"

"I did."

"I'm interested to hear your impressions about the Rosicrucian approach to meditation," she said with great enthusiasm. "You seem to know quite a bit about different styles of meditation, so you have a lot to compare it to."

"It's the *advanced* phases of Rosicrucian meditation that I find fascinating," I said. "The *initial* exercises and approaches are similar in all versions of meditation: learning to relax, focusing on a single sound or object, then eventually suppressing thought altogether for some period of time. But what is the ultimate aim? When an advanced student masters those basic techniques, what stages of growth is he then looking to achieve?"

"Did the lecture satisfy your curiosity in that regard?" Virginia asked.

"Pretty much," I said, "and it aligned precisely with what I had been able to cull from the internet. And that's where Rosicrucian meditation differs quite distinctly from classic Yoga and Buddhist traditions."

"How so, Sammy?"

"In all traditions, you get your first palpable glimpse of samadhi during your initial breakthrough experience. And it's powerful. And you've worked so hard for it. It seems overwhelming and life changing. But that accomplishment is just a beginning. From there comes the real work. The immersion. Reflection upon the illumination itself."

"That's right," said Virginia.

"But in Yoga and Buddhism," I said, "from that point on, it's all geared toward severing ties with the material side. Because the material side is seen as illusion. The only true consciousness is supreme consciousness. The only true self is the universal self."

"And how far have you come personally, Sammy, in rejecting the material side?"

"Not nearly as far as I could, Virginia."

"What's stopping you?" she asked. "Is the time commitment and the level of focus too demanding?"

"No," I said. "It isn't. I believe I'm capable of it if I wanted. I've been retired for many years, so I have time to devote to it. But something inside me fears crossing over that way. Abandoning the corporeal world."

"What are you afraid of, Sammy?"

"Maybe fear isn't the right word. It's not as if I'm too cowardly to take the plunge. It's more akin to being prudent. Not going before it's time."

"Sammy, you mean you might be more willing to take the plunge if you were older, closer to death?"

"I might. Let me compare it to something, Virginia. You and I have discussed the fact that we've both adopted vegan diets. For a variety of reasons. Spirituality. Health. The environment."

"Yes," she said. "My doing so was Rosicrucian driven."

I said, "Let me share something with you that I don't think I ever told anyone else I know. Every once in a while, like maybe every couple of months or so, I eat a small piece of cheese. Real cheese, from a cow. It's totally contrary, philosophically, to what I believe. And I hate doing it. But I do it."

Virginia looked at me with a bit of surprise. "Really, Sammy?" she said. "You just get a craving?"

"*No!*" I exclaimed. "That's just it. There's no craving. I could easily go without eating the cheese. It's a conscious, measured, rational response to knowledge and analysis."

"What knowledge, Sammy?"

"All vegans are aware that you can't get vitamin B12 from a strictly vegan diet without supplements. So we all take supplements."

"And that takes care of it," she said.

"Are you sure, Virginia?" I asked. "If a diet, no matter how spiritually satisfying, has been scientifically shown to be deficient in one measurable nutrient, who knows what other trace elements might be missing? And if we don't know, then we can't put it in a supplement."

"But even if you believe that, Sammy, eating one small piece of cheese a few times a year can't possibly provide an adequate volume of missing nutrients to fill the gap."

"Maybe it can, Virginia. I came across an experiment many years ago. Scientists tried to duplicate seawater. They analyzed every component they could detect in ocean water, and synthesized what they thought was an exact replica. They filled an artificial pond with their synthetic seawater and put a bunch of ocean fish in there. All the fish died. The scientists could not figure out why. But the scientists then added just a very small amount of real seawater to their pond—I don't know, maybe a quart or a gallon. Not nearly enough to populate their pond with what was missing. But somehow it did. After that, the fish thrived. Some unknown set of trace elements in that *real* seawater must have been necessary, and they must have begun propagating in some way. And that eventually made the pond self-sufficient to sustain life."

"That's fascinating, Sammy. I see the vegan analogy, but how exactly do you see that relating to meditation?"

"Supreme consciousness, or cosmic consciousness, or God can be compared to veganism, in that it's depicted as totally pure. It's supposedly completely devoid of contamination from the illusory material world. But if that's true, what if it therefore lacks some necessary trace elements that we, as material beings, require—and if we immerse ourselves totally in it, we cease to thrive?"

"It's a fascinating theory, Sammy," Virginia said. "But why do you need to worry about it? Nobody, not the pope or the Dalai Lama or any monk or nun, is so sequestered and so immersed that they lose all touch with their material body and the material world. Just the act of eating, or drinking, or urinating, or defecating brings you back."

"That might be insufficient," I said. "I don't know. Maybe I'm just afraid, irrationally. Or maybe I just enjoy my material life, and want to keep it vibrant, coexisting with the mystical component."

"This aspect of doubt bothers you, doesn't it?" Virginia asked.

"Well, yes. But that's why Rosicrucian meditation seems different and somehow enticing. No matter how much work it takes to practice advanced stages of Yoga and Buddhist meditation, doing so is still essentially passive. You empty your vessel and let samadhi fill it. But the final stage of Rosicrucian meditation, if I'm understanding it correctly, is absolutely nonpassive. Once you've achieved the mystical state, and can dwell in it at will, it becomes your duty as a Rosicrucian to begin making meditation a *willful* exercise, and turn your mystical power back onto the corporeal world, to try to effect meaningful change. Does this agree with your understanding, Virginia?"

"Theoretically, absolutely."

"In this way," I said, "Rosicrucian meditation seems related to psychic phenomena. Rosicrucian meditation is, at its most advanced level, almost akin to the practices of clairvoyance, telepathy, or psychokinesis. And this would further suggest that the reason that ESP can't successfully be measured or investigated or harnessed is that such phenomena live, at least partly, in the spiritual side of reality, which is immune to measurement, rather than the cause-and-effect side."

"Wow, that's really interesting, Sammy," she said. "In fact, personal training in opening and growing one's ESP capability is an explicit aspect of Rosicrucian study."

"So, does this definition of the final stage of Rosicrucian meditation suggest that this is, philosophically, where the two realms intersect?" I asked.

"I think so, Sammy," she said. "But honestly, I'm so far from that stage, it's hard for me to understand it or to even imagine being able to do something like that."

"Maybe you're closer than you think," I said. "Is it possible that this same medical condition that affects your lungs and makes your death more imminent physically also opens you up more to psychic abilities?"

Virginia looked downward for a time, clearly weighing whether to say something that had manifested in her mind.

Part of me regretted what I had just said. Mentioning her death was undoubtedly inappropriate. Even so, I waited and watched her eyes, silently encouraging her, furtively hoping she would reveal to me some secret related to Rosicrucian meditation that had not been touched upon during the lecture.

Finally she looked up and said softly, "I was meditating and had a vision of two orbs of light entering my chest. I don't know what it meant, but it seemed very powerful. Something from that other strata."

To my great delight, one Sunday in March, my Hebrew-school instructor announced that our morning class was canceled, and we were instead herded down to the temple's auditorium to view a musical play celebrating the festival of Purim. As I entered the auditorium, I was handed a sheet of paper with a bit of information about the musical. The performance was entitled "The Song of Purim." The flyer contained a list of cast members, headed by a girl named Sondra Walkowitz, playing the role of Queen Esther.

The handout also contained a paragraph summarizing the history of the Festival of Purim, describing it as a joyful Jewish holiday commemorating the rescue of Jews living in the ancient Persian Empire from a decree of mass execution. The heroine of the story is Queen Esther, recently chosen as the new mate for the King of Persia. The breathtakingly beautiful Esther, a Jewish orphan raised by her cousin Mordechai, opts to keep her Judaism secret from the king. Sometime later, when the king's evil chief minister Haman decides that the entire Jewish minority dwelling in the Persian Empire should be massacred, Queen Esther, after much prayer and soul-searching, girds up her courage, reveals to the king that she is a Jewess, and begs him to spare her people. Because he loves her, the king grants her request, and the Jews are saved.

As I perused the lists of performers to see if I knew any of them (I did not), the lights in the auditorium dimmed, and the musical commenced on stage. The chorus sang a song depicting the day-to-day life of Jews in the Persian Empire. Suddenly, bit players ran on-stage, announcing impending doom, and the chorus's song grew frightened and desperate as the Jewish community contemplated its future.

The performance was thus far ordinary and somewhat tedious. A seemingly interminable ensemble dance number was dragging on. To occupy myself, I retrieved from my briefcase the copy of the Old Testament that we were required to bring with us to all Hebrew-school sessions. I located the Book of Esther and skimmed it. My young eyes had no trouble reading in the dim light.

My experience with Bible stories was that the rabbis often omitted interesting and provocative details in their summaries. In the biblical text, it seemed that the Persian king had a prior queen who had fallen out of favor because she refused his drunken command to display her beauty to a group of partiers. The king explicitly ordered her to appear wearing her crown, but it was not clear to me if she was to wear anything else or if the king wished to display her naked. I assumed she was to be naked. Why else would a queen refuse to appear before a group of well-wishers?

Esther became queen during a sort of beauty pageant subsequently ordered by the king, during which the populace presented to him their most nubile young women. The king had no idea that she was Jewish, and Esther did not see fit to mention it. That too seemed odd—surely a king with all sorts of advisors and staff would be able to vet his new queen sufficiently to determine that Esther was of Hebrew stock.

And the sparing of the Jews from slaughter was a far more barbarous affair than a mere decree canceling their execution. Despite being an all-powerful monarch, the king was implausibly constrained from rescinding his royal edict, and instead empowered Jews in the empire to conduct a preemptive genocide of their own against all armed Persians they perceived as a threat. The biblical text states that over 75,000 Persians were killed by Jews but is careful to also point out that following the mass killing, Jews took no plunder from their victims.

This seemed both ridiculous and quite troubling. Although most Jewish holidays understandably celebrate some historical victory in the tribes' efforts to avoid annihilation at the hands of various enemies, in the case of Purim, the king's solution resulted in absurd and unnecessary loss of life, and might therefore not be appropriate fodder for an annual celebration in Jewish synagogues.

I was pondering this when my reverie was shattered by a haunting, high-pitched voice. I looked up. Sondra Walkowitz had made her entrance as Queen Esther and was singing a disquieting ballad onstage. She wore royal robes, a sparkling crown, and ornate jewelry.

She was the most beautiful thing I had ever seen.

The paralyzing chill that engulfed me as I watched Sondra sing on stage was a sensation I had never before experienced. Her voice was angelic yet piercing and fierce. The spell she cast over me was immediate and all consuming. I watched her from the audience as if she and I were the only two people in the auditorium. The play wore on, but I didn't follow the events on stage. I watched only Sondra.

———

I was obsessed with Sondra Walkowitz for weeks after the performance. I needed to meet her. I had never felt any desire to talk to or socialize with a girl. But Sondra Walkowitz had become for me an elusive goddess. I now searched for a way to enter her realm.

I swore my friend Michael to secrecy, and explained my plight. I asked for his help in developing a plan.

"Why don't you just go up to her and introduce yourself?" Michael asked.

"That would never work," I said. "She's beautiful, and she's a singer and an actress in these plays at the temple, and probably other shows at school or somewhere. Can you imagine how popular she must be? I'd just be some ordinary boy trying to talk to her, along with dozens of others every day. She'd never pay attention. She might even laugh at me. No, Michael, I need a plan that will make me seem special. Worthy of her. Something she's never seen."

"So it's another project!" exclaimed Michael. He thought for a moment. "We'll call this one Project Venus. Venus was the Roman goddess of love."

Michael was a mythology buff, and felt compelled to name our more significant mutual endeavors after Greek or Roman deities. The exercise seemed gratuitous, but my agreeing to it increased Michael's enthusiasm level so significantly that it made sense to let him do it. He had dubbed our daily jiu-jitsu practice "Project Ares" after the Greek god of war. And when I rigged a sort of tripod and used a rubber band to keep the lens on Emmanuel's old camera open to shoot the moon and surrounding star trails at night, Michael named that experiment "Project Selene" in honor of the Greek goddess of the moon. Michael never challenged my leadership of all such enterprises. As long as he got to name them, he remained an extraordinarily loyal and energetic assistant.

My plan started with the assumption that students who participated in a temple performance would likely be loyal attendees at Saturday-morning worship. Attendance at Sabbath services on Friday evenings and Saturday mornings was strongly encouraged, but not obligatory, for Hebrew-school students. I had never attended.

But on the next Saturday morning, Michael and I loitered across the street from the temple in the late morning and waited for the congregation to exit. The children's service was held in a smaller prayer room and ended earlier than the main adult service, so I knew they'd appear first. Michael and I scanned the crowd of young worshipers as they filed out slowly down the temple's big concrete stairs. Sondra was there with her younger sister. Sondra wore a beautiful blue dress revealing the suggestion of nascent breasts and hips.

I identified Sondra to Michael, and we proceeded to surreptitiously follow her and her sister, to determine where she lived. I trailed a quarter block behind them, while Michael walked closer to them but on the opposite side of the street.

Both girls carried a chocolate bar, the gift handed out to each exiting worshiper by Rabbi Katznelson, our Hebrew-school principal who presided over the children's service. Sondra gave hers to her younger sister, who accepted it with glee. While Sondra's sister worked on the chocolate bars, Sondra reached into her purse and pulled out a small transistor radio, which she held to her ear as she walked.

We followed her to the apartment house where she lived, on the other side of the neighborhood. That explained why I had never run into her. That area sat in a different public school district, so Sondra and I attended different elementary and junior high schools.

The radio had given me an idea. But I needed to work on it a bit, and experiment, before presenting the plan to Michael.

***

Three weeks later, I was ready to lay out my blueprint for Project Venus.

"You know, Michael, I've built lots of radios," I explained, "but in the last couple of weeks I built my first transmitter. I had to get some parts, and a schematic out of a book from the library. But I've got it working now. It's not strong—it can only transmit maybe fifty or a hundred yards. So far, I've tuned it to transmit to unused portions of the radio dial, but if I'm right nearby, I think I can sort of bust in on someone listening to a commercial station."

Michael looked at me vacantly. "I don't get it," he said.

"Well, I want to do an experiment with you today. You go back to your apartment, and tune your radio to the big rock-and-roll station near the beginning of the dial. When you're ready, I'll use the transmitter from my kitchen, and we'll see if I can send you a message on the radio while you're listening to a song."

"What if you can, Sammy? How does that help?"

"Don't you remember? Sondra was listening to her transistor radio on her way home from temple. She also passed right by your cousin Saul's house. You and I got invited to Saul's house a couple of times last year. You remember—he showed us how to work his model trains. So, it shouldn't be too much trouble to get invited back there again. If we can set up my transmitter in his kitchen, I can broadcast a message to Sondra when she walks past the window on her way to temple. She won't know where it's coming from. It'll be something mysterious like 'Sammy will contact you, Sondra. Wait for Sammy.' It'll baffle her. Then on her way home, I'll see her on the street and say, 'I'm Sammy. Did you get my message?' She'll be blown away."

I waited for a reaction from Michael, who appeared to be pondering the scheme. Then his face lit up. "It's brilliant, Sammy. If it works, she'll think you're some kind of genius. But how will you know what station she's listening to? Even if one of us walked right up alongside her, there's no way to tell what station the radio's on."

"Sondra's a beautiful girl. She's an actress and a singer, so you know she must be super popular. Cool people like that all listen to the big rock-and-roll station at the beginning of the dial. That's the one that I'm going to try to break into during our experiment. I'm positive that's what she's listening to. What else could it be?"

"You're smart, Sammy. That makes sense. Let's do the experiment, and once we get the radio part working, I'll set up the visit with Saul. I'll brief him on Project Venus."

It took a bit of effort on Michael's part to convince his aunt that setting up an electronics experiment in her kitchen early on a Saturday morning was a prudent course of action. She had little understanding of science and feared that her son might be exposed to a threat of electrocution. She wanted to know every detail in advance, and balked when Michael mentioned that I planned to wrap a ground wire around a pipe under her kitchen sink. She insisted that mixing electricity with water in any way was extremely dangerous.

Saul arranged a phone call where she could talk directly to me. I at first tried explaining that my whole apparatus employed only a small twelve-volt battery, which could not possibly generate sufficient current to be dangerous. But she had no idea what I was talking about, and grew angry. It wasn't until I asked if she had ever been to my father's television repair shop in the neighborhood that she appeared to positively engage. She knew and trusted Emmanuel. So when I explained that Emmanuel oversaw all the electronics projects I built, and that he and I had used this particular transmitter together on a number of occasions, she finally acquiesced.

On the designated Saturday morning, Michael and I arrived early and set up the transmitter in Saul's kitchen. Saul was curious and watched intently. His mother seemed impressed with my device and my professionalism. She advised Saul to "pay attention and learn something about electricity." Then she went off to make the beds.

I peered out the open window, four stories up, and waited several minutes before I saw Sondra and her sister turn the corner and come walking toward us down the block. Sondra was dressed in her Saturday-morning best, and as I predicted, her small transistor radio was pressed tightly against her ear. I closed the window and stepped back, out of sight, then switched on the transmitter and pulled the microphone close to my mouth. Michael was now across the street—his job was to monitor Sondra's reaction. I could see him from where I stood, but I could not see Sondra and her sister, who were directly below. When it appeared to Michael that Sondra had heard the mysterious voice over the radio, he was to signal me by pulling a rubber ball from his pocket and bouncing it on the sidewalk.

I began talking. "Hello, Sondra. This is Sammy, with a special message, only for you. Watch for me later, Sondra. Watch for Sammy. You'll see me later." I repeated that monologue three times, waiting for Michael to bounce the ball. But Michael stood still, his eyes on Sondra as she walked down the block. I could tell by the direction of his gaze that Sondra had passed under the kitchen window and was heading away from us. Why hadn't she heard me?

I spoke into the microphone again. I repeated my spiel, louder and faster, with a growing sense of urgency. But Michael still did not move.

Sondra had by now surely passed out of transmitter range. A gnawing fear of failure clutched my solar plexus. But I tried one last time, now with frantic desperation. "Sondra! This is Sammy. This message is only for you. Watch for Sammy. I'll see you later, Sondra!"

As I finished, to my great surprise Michael smiled up at me through the window, pulled the rubber ball from his pocket, and began enthusiastically bouncing it on the ground.

———⌣———

I waited in front of Saul's apartment house for Sondra and her sister to return from temple. Michael and Saul were across the street, far down the block. I told them they could watch, but they needed to be inconspicuous and out of earshot.

The girls approached. Sondra looked at me warily.

"I'm Sammy," I said.

Sondra seemed startled. "Where were you when you were talking to me?" she asked quickly, a bit frightened and agitated. "I heard your voice, but I couldn't see you. Where were you?"

"You heard the voice from your radio," I said. "I was transmitting to it. I built an electronic transmitter, just to talk to *you*."

"No!" she exclaimed. "The voice was *not* in my radio. The voice was in my head. How did you do that?"

I was afraid now that I had miscalculated how she would react, that my scheme had actually turned her off to me. "I'm really sorry if I upset you, Sondra," I said. "Please don't be angry. I'm sure the voice just seemed like it was in your head. I was transmitting to the rock-and-roll station. That's where you heard it. But it didn't sound like part of the song, so you interpreted it as being in your head. I'm really sorry. I just wanted to meet you. I saw you in the Purim play as Queen Esther. You were amazing. I just had to meet you. I'm so sorry."

Sondra smiled warmly and stepped toward me. "OK, I'm not angry," she said. "Actually, what you did was kind of sweet. But I swear, the voice wasn't on the radio. It was in my head. I don't know how you did it. I wasn't even listening to the rock-and-roll station. My mother would kill me if she thought I listened to that stuff. I want to be an actress when I grow up, in musicals, like on Broadway. I was listening to that station that plays Broadway musical scores. Do you know it, Sammy?"

"Yes," I said softly. I was now utterly bewildered. The station she was listening to was on the opposite end of the dial. My transmitter could not possibly have accessed it. "So," I continued, "you said you heard me but not from the radio?"

"I didn't hear you as if you were standing there next to me. I heard you as if your voice was inside my head."

At that moment I knew what had happened. There was no other radio near her tuned to the rock-and-roll station. I was four flights up behind a closed window—she could not have heard me from there. There was only one possible explanation. The strong emotions in me, triggered by a sense of panic and desperation over the failure of my plan, had somehow enabled me to call to her telepathically. Leonard Levitzky was right. I was a sender.

For an instant I considered sharing this amazing occurrence with Sondra, telling her exactly what had happened. But I decided against that course of action. She'd probably find the assertion absurd and think I was lying. In the unlikely event that she believed me, the whole thing would frighten her—she'd think me some sort of mutant sorcerer to be shunned at all costs.

"Ah!" I said instead. "Your being on a different radio station than the one I was transmitting to must have activated my transmitter's secondary circuits. Those transmit a fluctuating signal that can be picked up by any station on the dial, but the sound doesn't come through so directly. It has the effect of . . . Have you ever heard a ventriloquist, how he makes his voice sound like it's coming out of the dummy rather than him? It's just like that, Sondra. It sounds like the voice is in your own head."

I couldn't believe I had just spewed out such utter nonsense.

Sondra bought every word. "Wow," she said, "that's amazing, Sammy. You're some kind of genius. I'm going to check with my mom and see if we can invite you over for lunch. I think she'll really like you."

"I'd enjoy that," I said.

10.
Bejeweled Scepter

JAKE WELCOMED SAPPHIRE and me into his apartment. "Our lab this evening, Dockles, will involve manhattans!" he announced animatedly as he hurried back into the kitchen to continue apportioning his reagents.

It was late afternoon on a balmy spring day in New York City. Sapphire and I had made the long walk to Jake's place in the West Village. Following the lab, Jake and I planned to have dinner at a local Middle Eastern restaurant.

I strolled into the kitchen to observe Jake's efforts, and to provide Sapphire with water and a couple of treats.

Jake moved back and forth between two bottles of vermouth, pouring small amounts of each into the pitcher to achieve an elusive balance. "You know, Jake," I said, "the first cocktail you ever introduced me to, all those years ago when I was still really a kid, was of course the martini. But I believe it was the manhattan that we tackled next. It's nice to get back to it. I don't believe we've had a manhattan lab in quite a few years."

"Fine old drink, Doc. A true classic. But you'd be amazed how it's morphed of late among the trendy."

"How would you possibly know anything about what's trendy, Jake?" I asked, laughing.

Jake grinned facetiously and nodded. "I do access the internet on occasion, Doc," he announced in his most resonant baritone.

"Let's see what I remember from your many lessons, Jake," I said. "You've always preferred the 'perfect manhattan' over the standard. The ordinary manhattan supplements the whiskey with sweet vermouth. But the 'perfect manhattan' combines equal amounts of sweet and dry vermouth. Which is what I assume you're doing now."

"Excellent, Dockles! You've learned well. Perhaps you can mix the next batch."

"I'd be happy to."

"There are other modifications though, Doc. As I said, the drink has morphed significantly. Come closer and I'll clue you in. Then we can taste and see if this modern rendering is superior to the vintage model."

I scanned the counter to see if I could detect anything that deviated from the recipe Jake had taught me years ago. The bottle of whiskey immediately caught my eye.

"That's *rye* whiskey, Jake!" I exclaimed. "Haven't you always made manhattans with bourbon?"

"Very good, Doc. You're on the ball. I have indeed always used a very good and high-proof bourbon. This is one of the trendy notions we'll be putting to the test."

"Rye?" I asked incredulously. "Jake, you've always insisted that rye was a liquor of a lesser god that deserved to be shunned."

"That was my belief, and a well-founded one for many years," he said. "It was swill. But just as New York's saddest neighborhoods are periodically subjected to gentrification, it appears that young trendsetters have now resurrected rye and turned it into not just something palatable but something hipsters find divine and upscale."

"Will it produce a manhattan that's distinctly different from the ones we've had with bourbon?" I asked.

"I've done a bit of research, Doc. The two whiskeys, especially the way they're made today, are not really as different as we've been led to believe. By law, bourbon must be derived at least 51 percent from corn.

Rye must be at least 51 percent rye. But the rest can be any grain, and often there is a good deal of corn in these trendy modern ryes. Chemically, corn tends to make a whiskey sweet and full, rye tends to make it dry and spicy. Really strong rye, like the swills I tasted years ago, made me pucker and wince. But I've examined the distillers' websites. Some of today's ryes contain almost as much corn as rye, so they're really quite balanced, and the slight additional dryness may be a welcome change. Some bourbons overemphasize their more saccharine characteristics, Doc."

"Your scientific research capabilities have always been stellar, Jake," I said.

Jake sprinkled a precisely measured portion of bitters into the pitcher and stirred the cocktail to chill it with the ice. We had experimented with shaken manhattans years ago. While we liked the cloudy, foamy feel of a shaken cocktail for martinis, we both agreed that manhattans felt more velvety on the tongue when stirred.

"For this first batch, Dockles, we'll stick to the traditional Angostura bitters we've been using for decades, so that we can make a fair comparison on the rye versus bourbon issue. But it appears that the kids now have also questioned the sanctity of Angostura bitters, so I've purchased some of the alternative trendy bitters—Peychaud's, Regan's Orange, and a few others. We'll incorporate those into subsequent rounds, Doc."

"I see you're sticking to lemon twists for garnish, Jake. No experimenting there?"

"Maraschino cherries are an abomination!" Jake shouted.

"But you'll eat almost anything," I cooed sarcastically.

"Not those things, Dockles!"

Prior to meeting Sondra, I had bitterly resented the hour I was compelled to spend each weekday evening at Hebrew school in preparation for my bar mitzvah. But I now eagerly arrived at the temple half an hour early for each session because that was when Sondra's class let out, and it gave us a few minutes to talk before she had to head home.

Shortly after our initial encounter, I had been invited to Sondra's house for lunch. Sondra's mother, Gertrude, a heavyset immigrant with a strong Eastern European accent, took an immediate liking to me. Sunday lunches at Sondra's house soon became a regular event.

Sondra was not at all the girl I initially imagined her to be. I still found her devastatingly beautiful, but she was apparently not very popular, and certainly not a part of the in-crowd at her school.

Her mother asserted great control over every aspect of Sondra's life. On those occasions that Sondra and I had brief phone conversations, I'd hear Gertrude whispering in the background, coaching her on what to say to me. This clearly suggested that her mother was also listening to my end of the conversations, so I was careful to always be on my best behavior.

Gertrude was a most imposing figure. When I visited each Sunday, we'd start in the kitchen, where Gertrude prepared a simple lunch, usually a tuna fish sandwich and a couple of cookies. Sondra and I would eat, but Gertrude led the conversation, and we both geared our responses toward her rather than each other. I was always polite and courteous, mostly out of fear; Gertrude controlled my access to Sondra. Interestingly, although I was generally quite reticent around her, Gertrude seemed most pleased when she drew me out about the electronics projects I built. She'd point out to Sondra that such skills could make for a very successful career.

I was careful never to mention my daily jiu-jitsu practice to either of them. I suspected that their knowing about it might be detrimental to how I was perceived.

After lunch, Sondra and I were permitted to spend time together in Sondra's small room, playing board games. The door to the room was always kept open. During the first few Sundays, Gertrude poked her head in almost constantly. But after a couple of months she mostly left us alone for the hour or two Sondra and I spent together, checking on us only occasionally.

Our game of choice was generally Scrabble. It became immediately evident, however, that my vocabulary, my ability to focus, and my sense of strategy were far superior to those of Sondra. Moreover, Sondra clearly preferred interacting directly with me to playing a board game. It became Sondra's standard procedure to show me her tiles when it was her turn, and ask for my help in forming her word. I had never imagined playing a game in that manner. Games always seemed primarily about competition. But given Sondra's approach, it seemed wrong for me not to respond in kind. So when it was my turn to play, I too turned my tiles so that Sondra could see them. She offered only small bits of input, so in essence I played both sides of the game while Sondra engaged me in conversations about friends, school, hobbies, and movies.

At the conclusion of one particularly memorable game, during which I had come up with a remarkable number of little-known words, Sondra said, "I don't know how on earth you remember all these words, Sammy. How do you do it?"

"I guess it's just because I spend so much time reading. I even like reading the dictionary sometimes, just skipping around, letting one word lead to another."

"I could never do it," she said. "It would be impossible."

"It wouldn't be impossible, Sondra. If you really wanted to spend lots of hours memorizing words, I bet you could. Now, you most likely wouldn't care about it enough to actually spend all that time, so I admit, it would be highly improbable. But not impossible."

"Impra-what? What did you say?"

"Improbable. It means something is very unlikely but not actually impossible. Like, if you tried to fly from here to Brooklyn by flapping your arms. *That* would be impossible. But learning words? Not impossible. But improbable."

"Improbable." She smiled. "I like that word, Sammy. I'm going to start using it!"

One Sunday afternoon, Gertrude surprised us by giving both Sondra and me a small halved pickle alongside our tuna fish sandwiches. When we finished lunch, Sondra and I found ourselves alone again in her room.

When Sondra opened her closet to retrieve the Scrabble set, I noticed that sitting on the closet's top shelf was the crown she had worn when she performed the role of Queen Esther. I asked her if I could take it down and look at it.

"Sure, Sammy. Can you reach it?"

"If I jump, I can. Don't worry, I'll be very careful." I retrieved and examined the crown, and asked Sondra to put it on. "Do you have the rest of the costume?" I asked.

"The robe is hanging up at the end here, and the scepter is buried in the back somewhere," she said, rummaging in the closet's rear corner. "Here it is!" She let me touch the scepter. It was light plastic but decorated cleverly to appear as bejeweled bronze.

"Why don't you put on the costume?" I said. "Instead of Scrabble, we can play a game where you're the beautiful queen and I'm your servant and you can have me do anything you want."

Sondra laughed. "Anything I want? OK, that sounds great to me!"

Sondra was wearing a very pretty red-and-black dress. With my help, she now draped over it her sparkling, flowing Queen Esther robe and sat regally on a hardback wooden chair, pretending it was her throne. Lifting her scepter, she pointed in my direction.

"Servant!" she commanded. "I want my royal golden slippers!"

I found the slippers at the bottom of her closet. They appeared to be part of the costume, but she might have worn them at other times too.

"Remove my black shoes, and put me in my golden slippers!" Sondra ordered gently, placing her scepter lightly atop my head, and pressing it down, causing me to kneel before her. I delicately removed the black shoes she wore. I slid the golden slippers onto her feet, softly cradling her soles in my palm as I did so.

"Very good, my servant," she said. "Now, find the soft shoe brush hanging on a nail on the back of the closet door, and bring it here, and clean the dust from my royal slippers."

"Yes, Your Highness," I said. I found the brush, then knelt again at Sondra's feet, and began gently brushing her slippers. Sondra rested her scepter atop my head as I worked silently for several minutes. A tingling sensation swelled within me and permeated my loins.

Our reverie was disrupted suddenly by Gertrude's laughter, which caused us both to jerk our heads and gaze at the doorway where she now stood. I was certain Gertrude would be angry and disapprove of our game.

I was wrong.

"You two are so adorable," she chuckled. "Just adorable!" she repeated in her heavy Eastern European accent as she walked back into the kitchen.

Jake finished stirring the manhattans and filled two chilled martini glasses. He garnished with lemon twists and we toasted.

"Very interesting," I said after savoring a mouthful of the rye manhattan. "Delicious, but definitely drier than the bourbon version."

"Agreed, Dockles. I'll reserve final judgment until we've had a few more rounds." He swished a mouthful about with his tongue, to better draw out its subtleties. "You know, it might be just a tad too dry. I recall reading that the 'perfect manhattan' is losing favor of late. Trendy bar-hoppers are returning to the standard version. Perhaps this is why. If you fashion a manhattan out of rye, which is innately less sweet than bourbon, then it stands to reason that a traditional rendering, which utilizes only *sweet* vermouth, might produce a more balanced end product. Let's try that for the next round, Doc."

Jake and I strolled into the living room and sat with our drinks. Sapphire followed and curled up at my feet in front of the couch.

"So, what's been on your mind lately, Dockles?" Jake inquired. "You have the look of a man who's mulling something over."

"Yes, Jake. On the walk over here, I was definitely pondering something. Here's my question: why are bondage and pain tied so inextricably to our Judeo-Christian notion of religious passion?"

"I'm honored that you'd ask a confirmed atheist such as I to weigh in on this ticklish conundrum, Dockles. But you do make a good point. Tortured martyrs abound in the overpopulated sectors of the fictitious heavens depicted by Christians."

"Not just Christians. The Old Testament is redolent with such imagery as well. In the Torah, the Jewish people are held in bondage in Egypt, where Moses witnesses slaves being severely whipped and beaten. In the Book of Judges, Samson ultimately submits to the allure of Delilah and is captured, enslaved, bound, blinded, and tortured. In the Book of Genesis, Isaac is bound and prepared for sacrifice by Abraham at the behest of God, in a tale so archetypal that Hebrew scholars refer to it in their native tongue simply as 'The Binding.'"

"Intriguing, Doc. As you know, much to my dismay, I was raised as a Protestant. We listened to endless readings from the four gospels. Did you know that the facts in each one are different? So, as if the whole story wasn't too ridiculous to believe in the first place, they went ahead and published four versions with conflicting facts!" Jake's voice had become agitated. He ratcheted it back now. "But I will grant them one thing: each version is consistent in that Jesus is held captive, beaten, tortured, pierced by nails, and suspended on a cross. Sounds like the agenda for a heavy Saturday night SM party here in the Village."

"Did you know, Jake, that Orthodox Jewish men, each non-Sabbath morning, bind their arm and head tightly in leather straps called tefillin?"

"And Christian penitents engage in self-flagellation with a cat-o'-nine-tails and other such implements," Jake said.

We had finished our drinks.

"Come in and mix another round for us, Doc. I'll supervise. We'll try another brand of bitters and use solely sweet vermouth."

I arose and stepped carefully over Sapphire. She was asleep.

We went into the kitchen, and I combined the reagents as Jake directed. It came out very good, smoother and sweeter than our initial attempt. When we returned to the living room, Sapphire had not stirred.

"You know," I said as I sat back down, "it's not difficult to cite these kinds of examples of sadomasochism in religion. They're obvious and have undoubtedly been referenced by others. My enduring and as yet unanswered question, however, has been *why*. What is it about the psychological and physical extremes of pain, bondage, enslavement, and suffering that continue to be linked to experiences of spiritual illumination for humans?"

"There has to be some sort of brain-chemistry explanation, Doc. It's too persistent to be attributed solely to random irrationality. Do *you* have a theory?"

I took a few more sips. "Perhaps I am not the optimal person to attempt to probe this enigma, Jake. As you're well aware, my psychosexual wiring has always been partial to play invoking power and submission. For me it's innate."

Jake thought for a moment. "You may recall, Dockles, that for years I translated operas into English as a hobby."

"Yes," I said. "I remember your telling me that the standard translations you came across were abysmal and artless, so you decided to create new ones yourself."

"I can't tell you how many arias I've translated where during the very act of being tortured, a Christian martyr sings ecstatically. It's the holy rapture of suffering for Christ. It's almost as if the brain's been altered psychedelically. Perhaps pain, accompanied by intensive faith, combine to produce some powerful combination of endorphins. Do you think that could be, Doc?"

"Endorphins are indeed opioids," I observed.

"Endogenous opioid neuropeptides," Jake declared pompously and with a big grin. He took a long gulp of his manhattan.

"Whatever happened to your opera translations?" I asked. "You don't mention them much anymore."

"I stopped work on them years ago, Doc. I wasn't getting much done. I liked to drink while I created them. It impeded progress significantly."

———

I began participating in our synagogue's Saturday-morning religious services. The ritual's overwrought solemnity seemed ludicrous, but Sondra and her sister were invariably in attendance. So, on Saturday mornings, David and I, wearing suits and ties, would walk to Sondra's apartment house, wait for Sondra and her sister outside, and escort them to the synagogue.

Girls and boys were sequestered during the actual prayer service, with the girls seated in a side section in the rear of the room. But the four of us reunited when the service concluded, and Rabbi Katznelson handed us each a chocolate bar as we exited the chamber together.

My brother and Sondra's younger sister, Anita, had little to say to each other, and both seemed annoyed that they had lost the undivided attention of their older siblings. Sondra and I walked side by side and talked. David and Anita trudged alongside each of us silently, a half step behind.

We were a block from Sondra's apartment on our way home from temple on a cool autumn day when Anita uncharacteristically broke her silence and grabbed the sleeve of Sondra's coat. "It's that creepy guy from the high school again!" she screamed, pointing at a heavyset boy about a block away, walking toward us.

"Let's cross the street," said Sondra. "I don't want to deal with him."

The four of us crossed the street. "Who is that guy?" I asked.

"He's a jerk," Sondra said. "He goes to the high school near here and he has this thing for me. I keep asking him to leave me alone, but every time I think he's gone, he shows up again and follows me around. He's horrible."

As I suspected, crossing the street was a useless ploy. The boy crossed as well and now was heading right for us, less than fifty feet away. I observed him carefully—he was beefy and about a head taller than I.

He now stood directly in front of us, blocking our way. "Whoa!" he said mockingly to Sondra, "you got a new little Jew boyfriend? You wouldn't go out with me, but you like a little punk like this?"

"Leave us alone, please," Sondra begged.

He moved closer. I pulled Sondra back and stepped in front of her. "You heard her. She's not interested," I said. "Let's not make this a big deal, okay?"

He pushed me, and I stumbled back a couple of steps. "You don't want a big deal?" he mimicked. "That's too bad. I like big deals with punks like you."

He pushed me again.

When he pushed me a third time, I had by then formulated my course of action. Michael, David, and I had practiced this precise series of jiu-jitsu moves hundreds of times, a fully choreographed response to an opponent's aggressive shove. It consisted of separate maneuvers I had found in three different books, which seemed to fit perfectly when I spliced them together into a lightning-fast sequence.

The moment the boy's palms touched my chest, I clapped over them with my own, locking his hands tightly against my torso as I jerked my upper body forward and down, doubling his hands back over his wrists and forcing him to his knees. I thrust my right leg upward and smashed the bottom of his chin with the top of my knee, forcing his head back. When I practiced with Michael and David, I always held back and made just the barest suggestion of this blow—but now I smashed him as hard as I could. He emitted a groan; I saw a light trickle of blood from the corner of his mouth. He'd probably cut his tongue.

While he was momentarily dazed, I slid quickly down to the ground while retaining the grip on his nearest hand. I used my falling momentum to increase pressure on his wrist and destabilize him. This enabled me to easily yank him onto his belly. I transitioned instantly into a jiu-jitsu arm lock, holding his right hand tightly in both my own, and wrapping my legs around his upper arm in a sort of figure-four configuration. His outstretched arm was now securely immobilized. His prone position rendered him otherwise helpless. In his current circumstance, the slightest downward jerk of my legs coupled with upward pressure of my hands would easily have snapped his arm in two.

I applied a bit of pressure to assure his focus. He screamed in pain.

"You're going to listen to me now," I said, "so pay close attention. We have a number of things to go through, but first, you are going to apologize to Sondra, and promise never to come anywhere near her again."

I tugged his arm just enough to encourage his response.

"OK," he said, "I promise."

"You promise what? Say it."

"I promise not to go near Sondra."

"And now apologize to her for everything you did," I said, "and be polite. Address her as ma'am."

"I'm sorry," he said.

I pulled his arm sharply. He screamed again. "I'm sorry, *ma'am*," I reminded him. "Say it like that."

"I'm sorry, ma'am," he whispered sheepishly.

"Good. The next thing that you'll promise me is that you're going to stop bullying anybody, anywhere, ever. And you better mean it, because if you go back on your word, I'll find you. And next time I'll break *both* your arms."

He needed motivation for this one. I supplied it with another sharp jerk of his arm.

"I promise not to bully," he whined, clearly humiliated and in pain.

"Call me *sir*," I said. "Say I promise not to bully, *sir*."

Another tug assured his reluctant compliance. "I promise not to bully, sir," he moaned, almost in tears.

"I am going to let you go now," I said. "And when I do, you are going to get up and run away from here as fast as you can. If you decide not to do that, and try to come at me again, it'll be the biggest mistake you ever made in your sorry life. Do you understand me?"

"Yes," he groaned, and began to cry.

"Yes *sir*," I reminded him, wrenching his arm sharply.

"Yes sir," he croaked softly between sobs. His acquiescence now seemed complete. I released him and then immediately hopped back up to a standing position, knees flexed and hands ready in case he tried to reengage.

The boy arose slowly, momentarily rubbed his sore arm, and then ran off, never looking back.

Sondra and Anita seemed dazed. After a brief pause to compose ourselves, the four of us resumed walking toward Sondra's house. Sondra slipped her hand inside my upper arm. It was the first time she had ever touched me in that way.

"I didn't know you could fight like that," she said.

"We know jiu-jitsu!" David blurted out. I turned and looked at him menacingly. He lowered his head.

"David just means I know how to fight," I said, "even against big guys like him. I don't really like to talk about it much."

"You're amazing, Sammy," Sondra exclaimed. "My mother is going to be so proud of you."

"Really? You plan to tell her about this?" I asked incredulously. "I would never consider mentioning this to my parents. They don't like me fighting, no matter what the circumstance."

Before Sondra could answer, Anita suddenly stopped and yelped. "Your pants are split, Sammy!" she laughed, pointing at my posterior.

I moved my hand to the back of my suit pants. Anita was correct. "It must have happened when I dropped to the ground," I lamented. "Now my mother is really going to be angry."

"Don't worry, Sammy," Sondra reassured me, edging closer to my arm as we walked. "My mom can sew it up. It'll look like new, and your mother won't even know. And *my* mom will think you're a hero."

We all walked up to Sondra's third-floor apartment, where Sondra related the incident to her mother with great fanfare. As promised, Gertrude found my behavior highly admirable. She told me to go into the bathroom, remove my pants, and hand them to her from behind the door. She restored the back seam with the speed and skill of an experienced seamstress. I got dressed and rejoined everyone in the kitchen where I thanked Gertrude for her help.

"You were very brave and protected Sondra from that big bully," Gertrude said in her thick accent. "I'm very proud of you, Sammy. I knew you were a very smart and polite boy, but I never thought you'd be brave like this."

As I tried to think of something to say other than "Thank you," their front door opened, and Sondra's father returned home from synagogue.

As had been the case whenever I saw him, he muttered a barely intelligible greeting, grabbed a copy of the Yiddish paper, and retired to a back room to read it. Sondra had told me he was a jeweler and made a lot of money but didn't talk much. He was a slight man with thick glasses and a studious demeanor.

Gertrude gave both David and me a couple of cookies to eat on our way home, and again told me how brave I was as I exited the apartment.

Just before the door closed, I heard Sondra say, "You know, Mama, Sammy beating up that big boy, it was just so improbable!"

———⌣———

Following two weeks of persistent San Francisco rainstorms, I was overjoyed to awaken to a sunny morning. San Francisco was in its third year of drought conditions, so the storms were certainly needed—their appearance had in fact become a cause of celebration in the local media. Nonetheless, the two weeks of rain prevented Sapphire and me from enjoying our morning hikes. The trails upon which we habitually walked had grown slick and muddy.

We'd been taking shorter morning strolls on wet neighborhood streets, often in the pouring rain. It was difficult to practice walking meditation in such circumstances. I was successful at doing so on a couple of mornings, but the showers, the wind, and the need to frequently cross streets teeming with frenetic morning drivers made the exercise mostly futile. When I first discovered San Francisco, in the 1960s, one of the things that most impressed me was how courteous drivers were to pedestrians. While a few of us still valiantly tried to maintain that tradition, it had mostly vanished as the city's pace quickened.

But on this sunny morning, as Sapphire and I headed in the direction of Golden Gate Park, I anticipated making the long trek up to the summit of Strawberry Hill, and looked forward to achieving the mystical mind state its environs regularly engendered in me.

Sadly, when we reached the park's entrance a couple of blocks later, it was apparent that the ground was still too muddy for our customary hike, especially for Sapphire, who found wet ground increasingly difficult to navigate in her old age. This was partly due to her diminished leg strength, but more so, I think, because her eyes could no longer discern the small lumps and fissures that arose all along the trail, causing her to constantly stick and stumble. She was also no fan of the bath she'd need upon her return, to rid her paws of caked-on turf.

Disappointed, I decided that we'd walk a few blocks north to the Presidio, a former Army base now converted into a public recreation area, with many paved walking trails. I didn't visit this park often, but I had been there a couple of years prior and recalled that some major renovations were just then getting underway. I assumed those were now complete.

As our walk veered off familiar streets, Sapphire's sluggish pace slowed even more noticeably.

When we finally reached the Presidio, I identified a quiet road that I remembered hiking some years ago. It was wide and fully paved, curtained with foliage along both sides. I took Sapphire off leash, and we set off. I had not enjoyed a good meditation session for weeks. I wanted this opportunity to be fruitful.

During the half hour it took us to reach this path, I had a good deal of time to entertain unbridled thoughts. For that reason, and because I was somewhat unfamiliar with the trail, I was wary of trying to auto-schedule my shift into universal consciousness as I did on familiar routes.

So I began my exercise of mindfulness directly, gently recognizing stray thoughts and allowing them to dissipate, emptying my mind, slowly enabling it to open itself to universal consciousness. After several minutes I achieved the state of spiritual illumination I sought, experiencing its hallmark sensibilities of peace, joy, timelessness, and a sort of nonrational cognizance that thwarted all perception of duality and rendered the entire cosmos a unified whole.

Suddenly, though, as we traversed a bend in the path, I heard a loud bellow and saw, about a hundred yards in front of me, a burly, disheveled man with a long beard, cursing and gesticulating violently. I probably would have heard him sooner, but like Sapphire, my hearing had deteriorated somewhat with passing years.

The man appeared to be schizophrenic. He was large and seemed angry. He screamed incessantly, and threw sharp punches in the air in my direction. "Come here, asshole, I'm going to knock you down!" he yelled, underscoring his threat with a couple of surprisingly well-executed shadow punches. I knew from articles I had read that most schizophrenics were not actually violent except perhaps to themselves, but there were exceptions. I slowed my pace considerably. I was still about eighty yards away from him.

"Come on!" he shrieked. "I want to knock you down." He threw some additional savage punches and kicks into the air.

There was a time when I would have walked directly toward him. For so much of my life, that would have seemed the proper course. Though scrupulously careful not to be the one to start the fight, I would have been poised to react instantly to any attack he might initiate, cataloging the various responses from my repertoire of jiu-jitsu tricks.

I confess that at times, by employing the most subtle glances and shifts in body language, I'd provoke an assault. I would never admit to such connivance, not even to myself. My ploys were nearly imperceptible, and profoundly easy to rationalize away. When attacks did materialize, the violent perpetrator was invariably hurled brutally to the ground. I'd retain an unyielding grip on a hand or wrist, ready to wreak further damage upon my victim if he resisted. In every case, I silently assured myself that by disabling this attacker now, I was protecting the safety of others who might come this way later.

It has taken me many years to learn that while there are times when this sort of direct resistance is appropriate, such instances are rare, far rarer than I ever wished to acknowledge.

So I did not walk now toward the man who threatened us. Instead, I studied for a moment a narrow stone path directly ahead of me that meandered from the trail, steeply climbing the hill blanketing the road to the left. We were now about fifty yards from the madman. I reattached Sapphire's leash and veered slowly onto the sheer path. It was damp and slick. I kept Sapphire on a short tether to help steady her as we climbed the hill to the top. My recollection was that one of the renovations begun a couple of years prior was a tall wooden staircase connecting the small paths atop this hill back to the main road. I hoped to encounter that staircase up ahead. The maniac continued to scream and verbally harass us as we climbed.

At the apex of the hill, we followed the narrow path for several hundred yards. The new staircase was indeed finished. We used it to rejoin the main road. The lunatic spotted us in the distance. He screamed and thrashed violently where he stood as we disappeared around another turn.

I again detached Sapphire's leash and let her walk free. As she and I continued our hike, I silently pondered the billions of infinitesimal neurons and synapses in the brain that control our behavior, and the hormones and other chemical substances that maintain the proper environment for such neurotransmission. I marveled at how these components exist in such an extraordinarily delicate and precarious balance. We are, all of us, just a tiny variance away from madness or mental dysfunction.

Once, when I was in my forties, I contracted a very bad flu that had me bedridden for well over a week. At some point I exhausted my supply of soup and teabags and did not wish to ask anyone for help. I was unsteady on my feet as I dressed—the virus had clearly affected my balance. I drove slowly and carefully to the large grocery store a half mile away, and cautiously approached a space in the store's parking lot that abutted a long brick wall. As I proceeded forward into the parking space, I was shocked and jarred when I drove directly into the brick wall, smashing and cracking my bumper. I could have sworn I had several yards yet to go. The flu had completely altered my depth perception. I was reminded of the fragile intricacy of our neural wiring—how susceptible we all are to its arbitrary malfunction.

The encounter with the schizophrenic, and my subsequent conjecture on cerebral frailty, had an intriguing effect upon me. For whatever reason, it increased my receptivity to the mystical sensibility from which the disturbance had wrenched me. My mind now merged effortlessly back with the consciousness emitted by the surrounding foliage, and I sank into a spiritual mindset as Sapphire and I slowly paced the trail together.

11.
Émigrés

FREEDOMLAND, A MONUMENTALLY unsuccessful theme park in the northeast corner of the Bronx, was constructed on a patch of swampland and configured in the shape of the contiguous forty-eight states. The amusement park survived only five seasons and never showed a profit.

Freedomland was the ill-conceived brainchild of Cornelius Vanderbilt Wood, who had been Walt Disney's right-hand man in the early design work for Disneyland. But the two men had a bitter falling-out—not only was Wood fired by Disney, but all evidence of Wood's contributions to the formation of Disneyland was eradicated from Disney's corporate records. Wood's resentment over this Orwellian obliteration of his accomplishments may well have fueled his fervor to build an East Coast park bigger and better than anything that existed.

Freedomland was billed as "The World's Largest Entertainment Center," which might have signaled that it was conceptually overambitious from the start. Or perhaps its failure to thrive was due to its singular theme: all its amusements were focused on America's history and culture. Or maybe Freedomland was brought to its knees by the lowly mosquito.

The park was built on a marsh, and drainage to an adjacent creek was never properly filled. The blood of Freedomland's human patrons provided a culinary feast for hordes of mosquitoes every hot, humid summer day.

Following the park's demise, the land became the home of Co-op City, the world's largest cooperative housing development. Had Co-op City been a municipality unto itself, it would have been the tenth largest city in New York State.

<hr>

I should have known something was amiss when my parents sent David and me to a sleepaway camp in Upstate New York for a six-week session in mid-July. My father had never seen the point in spending money on such things. Even this camp, which was low cost with few amenities, was at variance with his belief that kids should play on city streets during the summer as he had done his entire childhood.

But when I returned home after the six weeks of camp, my East Tremont neighborhood in the South Bronx seemed profoundly different. So much so that it convinced me that my perception prior to departing must have been deeply flawed. Such changes could not possibly have transpired in a mere six weeks.

The cacophony of heavy machinery being used to construct the Cross Bronx Expressway roared ceaselessly during daylight hours. The fine dust from drilled and smashed concrete was present in every breath I took outdoors. Moving vans were everywhere—the people I knew were fleeing. Many families had evidently waited until the summer to leave so as not to disrupt their children's school terms. New faces walked the streets. They looked different from those I grew up with. The new people had dark skin. They carried themselves differently. Many spoke Spanish.

The day after I returned home, I went up the flight of stairs in our apartment house and knocked on Michael's door, anxious to resume our jiu-jitsu practice. The woman who answered the door was Puerto Rican. She had a bandana tied around her head. Two of her dark-skinned children ran to join her, gaping at me through the doorway.

"I'm looking for Michael," I said. "He's my best friend."

"We live here now," she replied in a heavy accent. "We moved in two weeks ago."

"Do you know where Michael moved to?"

"We never met the family that lived in this apartment before us. I'm busy unpacking. I gotta go." The door closed.

I ran downstairs and found my mother ironing. She looked even more gaunt than usual, draped in a baggy, flowered housedress.

"Michael's family moved!" I exclaimed frantically. "Did they tell you? Did he leave a new address where I can write to him?"

"There have been so many families moving, I stopped paying attention to who they were," she said.

"So you don't know where they went?"

"If Michael wants to contact you, Sammy, he has your address."

The new school term started just after Labor Day. I was in my final year of junior high school. Many of the students I had known were now gone. Puerto Rican and African American pupils were prevalent in the hallways, and a few were in my classes.

The first big junior high school event each year was the science fair. I had an exciting idea about an electronics project I could build. It began with a trip to the library where I perused numerous books on electronics until I found one with a schematic for a transistor-driven oscillator. As I envisioned it, that would be the basis for what would eventually become a light-sensitive metronome.

The African American librarian was on duty. She looked especially regal and beautiful, wearing a snug maroon sweater and straight black skirt that hugged her hips.

Every time I saw her now, I fantasized about her obsessively for days. Her outfits changed in each fantasy—her straight skirts might be black, blue, or violet; her tops alternated between skin-tight knits and sheer, fitted blouses. Sometimes I caught a glimpse of her changing clothes while

I was tied up; she'd strip down to her bra and girdle before slipping into the outfit she'd wear to tend to her errands while she left me alone and helpless.

I handed her the book on electronics I wished to borrow.

"Back to electronics again, young man?" she asked.

"Yes ma'am," I said.

"Your name is Samuel," she observed softly, glancing at my library card. "May I call you Samuel, young man?"

"Sure," I said. "Actually, you can call me Sammy."

She smiled broadly. "It's nice to meet you, Sammy. I'm Esther." She extended her hand across the counter. I hesitantly raised mine and moved it into hers. I felt chills when our skin touched, and an erection instantly bulged against the fly of my trousers. I glanced down quickly, then back up, into her eyes. They gazed directly into mine.

"I'm glad to see that your family hasn't moved away, Sammy," she said. "So many people have."

Our right hands were still interlocked. Now she added her left and held my hand in both of hers. I inched half a step forward and pressed my body against the counter wall, hoping to force my erection down and disguise it from anyone who might come by.

"Yes ma'am," I said. "I like it here. I hope we don't have to move. But everything's changing so fast."

"Call me Esther," she said. "Yes, things are changing. But maybe the new people and the old people can all live together happily, and have even more fun. Do you think that's possible, Sammy?"

"I hope so . . ." I paused nervously, and finally completed the sentence with "Esther." I was hypnotized by her gaze. Just saying her name in front of her made my penis even more erect. I pressed harder against the wall of the counter to try to dampen my excitement, but it was too late. I ejaculated in my pants. I felt my face flush deeply. I stood motionless, gaping at her.

She chuckled, looked down for a moment, then reestablished eye contact with me. She released my hand. "You're an adorable young man, Sammy," she said. "I'll see you next time. You may go now."

I picked up my book and library card and walked out, turning away quickly to shield from her any wet spot that might have appeared near my crotch.

As I walked home, I was distraught and agitated. I desperately hoped that Esther had not realized that I orgasmed. But her reaction suggested that she had, and I was mortified by that possibility. As I neared my house, however, my thoughts wandered more to Esther herself. I really had never considered the fact that she was Black—I had never wondered how it felt for her to be constantly surrounded by so many white people. Now there were finally African Americans and dark-skinned Puerto Ricans in the neighborhood. I became quite curious to know if that made her feel more at ease.

I pondered whether that would be an appropriate thing to ask her when we next met, or if she might find it in some way offensive.

A few days after the science fair ended, the exhibition room was emptied of its projects. I carried my electronic light-sensitive metronome home from school, balancing it carefully atop the binder and textbooks I held in front of me like a tray. It had won third prize.

When I arrived back at our apartment, I was very surprised to see Emmanuel home from work. He must have closed his shop early. Large cardboard boxes were strewn all over the house, and a pile of papers sat on the kitchen table. When I stepped into the kitchen, I saw a man I didn't recognize sitting at the far end of the table, showing my mother and father where to sign various documents.

"What's going on?" I asked.

Emmanuel turned his head to face me. "We're moving, Sammy," he said. "We're signing the papers to buy an apartment in Co-op City."

"Co-op City?"

"We made all the arrangements when you and David were at summer camp," he said. "The site visits, everything. These signatures finalize the deal."

It immediately became clear that David and I had been sent to summer camp to enable my parents to consummate this arrangement without our knowledge or input.

"But I'm in the middle of the school year. Can't we wait until the school year ends?" I pleaded.

My mother now shifted her body in my direction, clearly agitated. "For God's sake, Sammy," she said, "the school year just started. You'll do fine changing schools. It's David you should be worried about. He's already terribly behind in his coursework. How on earth is he going to cope with this?"

———————————

We moved into our apartment in Co-op City on the Monday prior to Thanksgiving. I registered the next day to begin the completion of my final year of junior high school.

Co-op City's initial impression upon me never faded. It was an oppressive, dehumanizing maze. Thirty-five high-rise buildings, each twenty-four to thirty-three stories in height, formed the massive labyrinth. Our two-bedroom apartment sat somewhere on the sixteenth floor of building number twenty-eight. Over fifteen thousand residents eventually occupied this sprawling city within a city.

Among the gargantuan apartment houses were scattered a few clusters of three-story townhouses, which seemed far preferable to the high-rises. I wished we lived in one of those, but Emmanuel told me that we couldn't afford them. The people in the townhouses appeared a bit more civilized and cultured, but were reluctant to mix much with us, the plebian high-rise dwellers.

As if in lockstep with the complex's overwhelming architecture, the boys in my age range all congregated in huge groups of twenty to forty. Each group was headed by a tough, athletic kid high up in the male pecking order. When I observed these mobs of boys, who congregated in the open spaces between the buildings, their expressions always came across as vacuous, their movements lethargic. Perhaps, for them, being part of the multitude was so reassuring that further stimulation became unnecessary. Their torpor was interrupted by sporadic minor scuffles that broke out among group members, or on rare occasions by more energetic fracases with some rival throng perceived to be violating their turf.

I could not imagine a more distasteful way to spend time. Living in a place that packed families into stacked, cramped boxes was sufficiently depressing. Being a listless member of a nondescript crowd would certainly have made it worse. I avoided all such assemblies.

I came across a few other loners in the development now and then, but I was never able to cement a friendship. Sadly, all of them seemed in some way flawed or maladjusted, and had little of interest to contribute to a conversation.

As bad as the move to Co-op City was for me, it was even worse for David. It rendered him so morose and bewildered that he was impossible to be around.

I was alone much of the time.

The northern border of the Bronx separates New York City from the rest of New York State. Just above the demarcation line, along the Hudson River on Bronx's western edge, sits the city of Yonkers, fourth largest in New York State. For decades a bustling manufacturing center, Yonkers in the 1950s was beginning its slow transition to a working-class residential community.

Our family would occasionally drive up to Yonkers to do our shopping. Whenever we did, I waited with secret anticipation for our car to pass a small jiu-jitsu academy on the southern end of the town's main shopping thoroughfare, Central Avenue. Fascinated, I'd peer through the car window as we drove by the tiny dojo, trying to glimpse the goings-on behind the storefront's big street-facing window. I sometimes saw boys my age wearing stiff white fighting coats cinched with belts of different colors, practicing with each other alongside an instructor.

At home I'd sit silently with my eyes closed, piecing together the snippets of images I managed to collect. I'd embellish them with my own musings, and conjure up entire classes in which I participated.

After several months of vacillating, I finally did ask Emmanuel if I could enroll in a jiu-jitsu class at the academy. Even though I was quite certain he'd say no, I nonetheless tried to build the most persuasive case I could. I had determined that if I took a New York City bus west and switched to the Yonkers bus that traveled up Central Avenue, I could get to the school in under an hour. I even offered to secure an early-morning paper route to pay for the training.

As I expected, Emmanuel dismissed the idea as ludicrous. He further characterized all such martial arts academies as anti-Semitic.

To my credit, I had waited for an opportune time to pose the question. My father and I had just finished discussing an interesting article on new applications of classic mechanical principles. He was in a cheerful mood. While I doubted that his lightheartedness would dispose him favorably toward my request, I did hope that it would at least dissuade him from losing his temper. In that small way I proved correct—he became a bit annoyed but did not succumb to a full-blown lycanthropic-type metamorphosis.

I waited a week to talk to my new science teacher, Mrs. Goldman, after class. She was generally sullen and seemed uninterested in her subject matter. I had waited this long in the hopes of observing some change in her demeanor that might make her more receptive to what I intended to ask her. But I saw no such change and felt that if I waited any longer, the credibility of my request might suffer.

The bell signaled the period's end. As the class began filing out and the pupils streamed into the hallways, I approached Mrs. Goldman and asked if I might have a moment of her time.

"What now?" she sighed wearily. She looked much older close up than she did from my seat in the back of the classroom.

"I have a note from my science teacher, Mr. Gershoff, from my old school," I said. "He told me to show it to my new science teacher when I moved." I handed her the handwritten note, in Mr. Gershoff's unmistakable block print that he used whenever he wrote on the blackboard. The note stated that I had won third prize in the school science fair, and was entitled to ten extra points on my final class grade that would display on my report card in June.

Mrs. Goldman glanced at the note. "What exactly do you expect me to do with this?" she asked.

"Well," I said softly, "I hoped you'd take it into account for my final grade."

"This has no standing here," she said impatiently. "I don't even know if this is a real note from a real teacher."

"You can call Mr. Gershoff and verify it. He said it would be okay if you did."

"I'm not calling *anybody* or verifying *anything*," she said pointedly. "Do you know how many new students I deal with every week? Every one of them thinks they're entitled to some special consideration. *I'm* your teacher now, and you'll earn your grade just like everybody else. If you were clever enough, Mr. Baron, to win a science fair prize in your old school, you should have no problem earning a good grade in *my* class."

She handed the note back to me and turned away dismissively. I left the classroom without another word.

My younger brother had been barely holding on in his grade level in our old neighborhood—now he seemed completely lost. His behavior grew increasingly dysfunctional as he failed repeatedly in his attempts to cope with his new school and surroundings. David spent almost all his time outside of school with my mother in unsuccessful efforts to keep up with his lessons.

Correspondingly, my interactions with my mother now dwindled to almost nothing. I encountered her only when she assigned chores to me or served our meals. But even at mealtime there was little communication between us. My father had a longer commute from work, so David and I ate an earlier supper by ourselves, and my mother waited for Emmanuel to return from work to dine together with him. All of us took breakfast and lunch on the fly. We had no family meals.

On the rare occasions that I had any sort of substantive encounter with Rachel, she reprimanded me for my selfishness in not making David a more integral part of my life. When we first moved to Co-op City, I tried to organize jiu-jitsu practices with David on the weekends, but he was inevitably tired and unfocused. David eventually forgot everything he had ever known about jiu-jitsu and lost all interest in practicing. At that point, he and I had little upon which to connect.

But for me, having no one with whom to practice jiu-jitsu fueled a persistent sense of indignation. The existence of that storefront jiu-jitsu academy just a few miles away in Yonkers exacerbated my misery. But sharing my frustration with Emmanuel would only have provoked his violent temper, and any mention of it to Rachel would have subjected me to an interminable lecture on my selfishness and my lack of empathy for David.

So I practiced alone. It was a poor substitute for sparring with a partner, and made me appreciate how productive those daily sessions with Michael had been. But the solitary practice at least kept me in touch with the discipline.

I found a small playground, one of several scattered throughout the Co-op City development. All of them had swings, monkey bars, and seesaws. This one was a bit more remote, surrounded on two sides by thick bushes and trees separating its border from a cluster of three-story townhouses. I had discovered a small clearing of grass amid the foliage. That was where I practiced. In the early evening, the playground and the area immediately around it were deserted, so my privacy was assured.

I especially enjoyed practicing there in the winter when there was snow on the ground. It would be dark by five, so foot traffic nearby was nonexistent. The cushion of snow made it oddly comfortable to practice falling. Light from nearby lampposts filtered through the trees, providing just enough illumination to see. I'd practice all the standard jiu-jitsu falls, rolling and springing to my feet in one uninterrupted motion. I'd also imagine an opponent and practice throwing him to the ground. My favorite trick in the snow was to grab my shadow opponent's lapels, thrust a foot into his abdomen, and roll onto my back, hurling him into the air above me.

One cold evening in March, I had just concluded my lonely practice in the clearing. There had been no snow for a while, so my practice had been conducted on the frozen soil and what was left of the brown, dead grass. I snuck out from the foliage, but I didn't feel like returning home just yet, so I made my way to the playground and found the one-wall handball court in its far corner. I took from the pocket of my winter jacket a rubber ball. In my wool hat and gloves, I began tossing the ball against the wall and catching it.

A figure appeared seemingly out of nowhere. Probably because I was in a self-pitying and deeply introspective stupor, I was completely oblivious to any sounds that the boy may have made while running toward me. All I knew was that he suddenly and without warning streaked in front of me, snatched my ball out of the air, and ran off at full speed, laughing heartily.

Instinctively, I set off after him.

I recognized him. He was a year or two older than I, and a good deal taller. He was built like a runner. He was on the track team at the local high school.

I had seen him often—he was one of the multitude of boys in the large group that hung out between my building and the high-rise it faced. He was loud and outgoing, frequently engaging in playful scuffles. I had heard people call him Malcolm. I did not know his last name.

Malcolm was much faster than I, but he didn't try to run away from me. He preferred to taunt me. He ran back and forth in the deserted playground as I futilely chased him. Malcolm lifted the ball above his head occasionally to show off his trophy. He'd periodically shift direction, dashing back toward me and then dodging me at the last moment to evade my lunge.

But one of those times he miscalculated by an inch, and I was able to grab the sleeve of his coat as he passed. That caused him to lose his balance and spin back around toward me, in perfect position for me to exploit his momentary loss of equilibrium. Without hesitation, I thrust my hip against his side, straightened my knees and threw him over my shoulder to the ground. He landed hard on the playground's frozen asphalt.

Malcolm was stunned. He tossed the rubber ball aside, probably hoping it would occupy my attention as he rose and ran off. But he was very wrong. I pretended to give him space to regain his feet, but instead I hovered behind him, focused intently upon his movements. Just as he attempted to balance in an upright position, I took advantage of his temporary instability, seizing his left arm and twisting it up into a hammerlock as I closed behind him. I slid my left forearm under his and cradled his captured arm in the crook of my elbow as my fingers reached up to grip his shoulder. He was now rendered helpless with his left triceps severely stressed. I clamped my right forearm securely under his chin, in a choke hold whose pressure I could precisely moderate.

I had come upon this combination hammerlock and choke hold in a book on self-defense from the library near my new school. Whereas the library in East Tremont had stocked books on classical Kano jiu-jitsu, the library serving Co-op City opted for more generic self-defense texts, combining moves from boxing, judo, wrestling, karate, and other disciplines into stratagems that could work in street fights. I had heretofore applied this combination only against my imaginary shadow sparring partner. But it seemed tailor made for Malcolm.

Because Malcolm was taller than I, the hold not only immobilized him but also forced him to bend his knees and lean precariously to remain upright as I held him from behind. I forced him to walk with me in that position to where the rubber ball had rolled.

"All right, Malcolm," I said, "we're going to bend down together and you're going to pick up the ball with your right hand and place it back in my jacket pocket."

"You're choking me!" he screamed. "Let me go."

"Actually, I'm *not* choking you," I replied calmly. "*This* is choking." With that I increased the pressure on his neck, preventing him from breathing until he coughed and sputtered. I loosened my grip.

"OK," I said. "Now you know the difference between choking and *almost* choking."

"You're crazy!" he yelled. Malcolm staggered as I forced him ahead of me. We reached the rubber ball. "Do as I said," I commanded. I lowered him down. He picked up the ball with his fingertips and gently placed it into my pocket.

"All right, I did it," he said. "Now let me go! Please!"

"Not quite yet. I think we're going to walk all the way home like this," I replied.

Slowly, we trudged in unison along the darkened, deserted path back toward the high-rises. He stumbled uneasily before me as we trekked.

After a couple of minutes, during which Malcolm continued to plead pathetically, I noticed some people congregating up ahead. Rather than risk any sort of intervention, I decided to release him.

"I'm going to let you go now, Malcolm. You be a good boy and behave yourself or next time I *will* choke you till you can't breathe at all." I momentarily tightened my choke grip and enjoyed hearing him gasp for air. "Like that," I said. Then I began to loosen my grip on his arm and neck.

Just before I let him go, I said, "As soon as you're free, run away and don't make any more trouble, or you'll be very sorry."

The instant he was free, he commenced running. "You're a crazy bastard!" he yelled back at me as he dashed toward his apartment as fast as he could.

Although New York City buses and subways would have made it easy for me to reach my old East Tremont neighborhood from our new home in Co-op City, Emmanuel forbade me from doing so. He insisted stridently that the routes had become too dangerous now that Blacks and Puerto Ricans constituted a significant portion of the ridership. I imagined

Emmanuel to be wrong about this—he never rode the buses or trains. He took his car everywhere, so he had no personal experience to draw on. And although I heard other people in Co-op City echo those same sentiments, news reports about assaults on public transportation were extremely rare. Any I heard about almost always happened very late at night.

But arguing with Emmanuel about the topic was futile.

My father was, however, very receptive to any interest I expressed in his television repair shop and my working there alongside him. With no friends and little to do outside of school in Co-op City, I began accompanying Emmanuel to work every Saturday. Doing so had the consonant benefit of stationing me in my old neighborhood.

His store was just a few blocks from Sondra's house. I hadn't seen Sondra in a couple of months, staying in touch via occasional phone calls. But now, Sondra's mother had agreed to change our weekly lunch day from Sunday, when my father's shop was closed, to Saturday. My father opened his shop between 10:15 and 10:30 AM, too late for me to attend Sabbath services, but Emmanuel had no problem with me taking a couple of hours for lunch if I worked hard the rest of the day. I spent those lunch breaks unfailingly at Sondra's house. Though my weekly time with Sondra was not nearly as copious as it had been, I was nonetheless grateful to renew my relationship with her in this way. Her house was situated in a corner of the neighborhood a good ways from the Cross Bronx Expressway, so the diaspora had not yet impacted them as greatly. I feared, though, that it was only a matter of time until it did.

As I spent more time at Emmanuel's shop, I learned a great deal about his business. He gradually allowed me to take on increasingly challenging tasks. In the beginning he'd have me do simple jobs, such as finishing up basic repairs after he and I had diagnosed the problem together. I became a whiz at testing vacuum tubes and locating suitable replacements for those that had burned out. Over time I systematically mastered intricate wiring and part-replacement projects. Eventually I could diagnose and repair, without Emmanuel's assistance, almost every nonfunctioning television set presented to us.

My father was initially hesitant to permit me to interact with customers, preferring that I shadow him and remain silent. But on a couple of occasions, after I had been there several months, when the store got busy and Emmanuel was helping customers, I proved adept at assisting other overflow patrons. Upon seeing this, and with adequate cautionary reminders about consulting him before quoting prices on complex repairs and such, Emmanuel grew comfortable with my working directly with the public. He eventually consented to my unsupervised manning of the cash register.

I never did master Yiddish sufficiently to converse fluently with his older, non-English-speaking clients. But there were increasingly fewer of them in the neighborhood now—and most who remained were religiously observant and therefore did not come into the shop on Saturdays, rendering the issue relatively moot. Emmanuel, however, continued to harp on this shortcoming, reminding me periodically that this would make it impossible for me to run the store successfully without his continued presence.

Malcolm, the young man I had roughed up just a few days prior, was a regular constituent of a large group of boys in my general age range that materialized regularly after school and on weekends between my high-rise building and the one directly across from it. On any given day, the throng numbered between twenty and thirty.

Ever since that encounter with Malcolm, I had been concerned about its possible violent ramifications. It seemed plausible that Malcolm might choose to keep the incident secret from his cohorts. Having been manhandled by a younger, smaller boy would be embarrassing to disclose.

But if he did reveal what had happened, some subset of the group—or the whole lot of them—might come after me. I thought long and hard about what action I should take if that occurred.

Even if I were able to throw the first one or two attackers to the ground, the others would soon be upon me. I imagined not even the most skilled jiu-jitsu master could single-handedly ward off twenty or thirty assailants. At that point, any resistance I offered might just further infuriate the horde, and thereby intensify my injuries. Perhaps accepting my fate and just trying to block blows directly to my face would be the least damaging option in the long run.

I was pondering that precise theoretical dilemma when it suddenly became real and immediate. I had stopped off at the library on the way home from school, and by the time I approached the entrance to my building, about two dozen boys loitered there and seemed to be eyeing me. I pretended to ignore them and act nonchalant. But the tenor of the group was such that I knew I was about to be confronted.

"Baron!" one of the boys yelled. "Wait up, I wanna talk to you." I turned. The boy speaking was the group's informal leader, Paul O'Rourke. Paul was short, just an inch or two taller than I. But I had observed that he exercised a commanding presence among the other boys. He had a solid and powerful physique; I had overheard that he was a member of his high school's wrestling team, presumably in one of the lighter weight divisions.

Paul walked toward me, displaying a particularly formidable posture. Malcolm and two other boys joined him, but he stopped and motioned for them to stay back. They complied immediately. Paul confronted me one-on-one.

"Hello, Sam," he said. "I'm Paul O'Rourke."

"I know who you are," I said.

He extended his hand to shake mine. I suspected it was a ruse—once he had my hand in his, he'd try to take me down with some wrestling hold. I glanced over his shoulder. Malcolm and his two cohorts watched intently from about twenty feet back, and behind them the rest of the swarm were equally focused on my interaction with Paul. I had little choice but to take his hand, but I did so warily.

To my surprise, Paul shook my hand firmly and then let it go.

"How're you doing, Baron?" he asked.

"I'm OK," I said softly.

"I hear you got into it with Malcolm the other day."

"Malcolm started it," I said immediately. "I'd never provoke a fight with him or anyone else. I have no interest in that. But if someone comes at me, I defend myself."

"Malcolm admits he stole your ball. But he says that then you put his arm in some kind of vicious hammerlock. He can still hardly move that arm. And you choked him. Choking can be really dangerous, Sam."

Paul now stepped toward me, and I braced for a shove or a punch, but instead he placed his left hand lightly on my shoulder and leaned in closer. "Frankly, Sam," he whispered, "you probably saved me from roughing Malcolm up a little myself. He gets out of control, and I have to settle him down every now and then."

I said nothing, but detected the slightest hint of a smile on Paul's lips as he continued whispering. "And I do respect a little guy who can handle himself. I know what it's like when everyone's bigger than you."

"Really?" I muttered, not knowing what else to say.

"But, Sam," he said leaning in even closer, "while I agree that he needed to be taught a lesson, your choking him like that, that was over the top, don't you think?"

My innate reaction was to resist his accusation and defend my position. But to my own astonishment, I responded quite differently. My rejoinder was not motivated by fear. It was rather that Paul's manner was so irresistibly disarming. He beguiled me into trusting him.

"Okay, yeah," I chuckled sheepishly. "It was way over the top, Paul. I've been having all sorts of frustrations since we moved here, and I guess I took it out on Malcolm. You're right; he deserved to be put in his place, but not like that. I was wrong. I'm sorry."

"Maybe you can tell Malcolm you're sorry," he said.

I began to move in Malcolm's direction to comply with Paul's request, but Paul momentarily tightened his grip on my shoulder. "Not now," he said, "maybe some other time when you two are alone so it doesn't look like it came from me. When you say you're sorry, he'll apologize to you too, for stealing your ball and taunting you—I made sure of that."

"Thank you, Paul," I said, extending my right hand to again shake his.

He reciprocated, and we held that pose, with our right hands interlocked, his left hand resting on my shoulder, as he changed the subject.

"You know, you can come hang out with us if you like. We don't bite."

"I appreciate that, Paul. But I'm more of a loner. No offense to your group. I'm just not into crowds."

"I can appreciate that, Sammy. So why don't you just come over and say hi to *me* now and then. You seem like a good fella. Us little guys need to stick together for moral support. And that judo or whatever it is you do, maybe you can show me a few tricks. They might come in handy on the wrestling team."

"I'd be happy to practice some jiu-jitsu with you in private, Paul." That seemed like the prudent thing for me to say, though I was quite certain nothing would ever come of it.

Paul chuckled, patted my shoulder, and walked back to his followers. I turned and went upstairs to my apartment.

I was at our kitchen table fiddling with electronic components I had salvaged from radios surrendered at my father's shop. My idea was to design an electric eye that would beep whenever anyone walked into or out of the bedroom I shared with David.

Emmanuel's keys jangled outside the front door. He was returning home from work. As soon as he entered, it was clear that he was in an extremely agitated state. He stormed into the kitchen and confronted me with a raised voice.

"You're not to see that girl anymore!" he exclaimed. "What's her name? Sandra? Sondra? Whatever her name is, you two are *done*. Do you understand me? *Done!*"

I was too shocked to respond. My mother strode through the foyer from the back of the house to see exactly what was going on. She stopped and stood silently just outside the kitchen. I heard David's footsteps behind her, but he remained safely out of sight.

Emmanuel turned to Rachel to continue his rant. "That girl's mother,

Gertrude, was in my shop today! Fat, first-generation Eastern European yenta. Obnoxious woman!"

My father turned back toward me. "What kind of sick games does that woman coerce you into playing with her daughter? Her daughter dresses like a queen and you kneel before her and clean her shoes? That's depraved! The woman is out of her mind!"

He faced my mother again. "Rachel, do you know what that sick woman said about that game? That it was *adorable*! Adorable? It's perverted! Do you know what that woman is trying to do? She's trying to kidnap and train some young boy to be her daughter's doting, obedient husband. Have you seen that woman's husband? He's a subservient schlemiel! A nebbish! Now she's trying to indoctrinate some boy to be the same way for her daughter. Well, not *my* son!"

I must have made some involuntary facial expression because Emmanuel turned even redder and he slapped my face as he shouted, "Do you understand? Do you understand, Sammy! No contact with that girl or her mother and their sick, depraved, old-world mentality. I told her that neither of them are to go anywhere near you. *Farshtey?*"

"I get it," I said softly. I gathered up my electronic components and slowly left the kitchen. My mother stared at me sternly. As I passed David on my way through the foyer to our bedroom, he flashed a stupid grin. It took all my self-control not to hit him.

In April, my junior high school closed for spring break.

I now had a whole week ahead of me. I had agreed to work with Emmanuel in his shop on Monday, Wednesday, and Friday, but reserved Tuesday and Thursday for play and relaxation. My mother spent every day of the vacation working with David on his studies—he had continued to fall further behind in all his classes. On Thursday morning I told my mother I was going out to play.

I hadn't seen or spoken to Sondra for three months, in compliance with Emmanuel's angry decree. But now, in direct defiance of that admonition,

I caught a city bus to the nearest subway station and took the train to my old neighborhood of East Tremont. I walked several blocks out of my way to stay as far from Emmanuel's shop as I could while approaching the apartment house where Sondra and Gertrude lived.

About half a block from their building, I stopped on the opposite side of the street and stared up at Sondra's bedroom window. I saw no movement inside. I paced back and forth there for two hours, hoping to catch Sondra on the street. Finally, I saw her leave the house. I followed her for a block, then ran to catch up with her.

Sondra was startled when I touched her lightly on the shoulder from behind. "Oh my God, Sammy!" she exclaimed. "What are you doing here?"

"I've missed you so much, Sondra. I had to see you."

"I can't talk to you, Sammy. My mother would kill me."

"What did your mother tell you?" I asked.

"That your father was awful to her when she went into his shop. He screamed at her and warned us to stay away from you. I need to go now, Sammy. She told me I can't talk to you."

"Wait. Please," I said. "We don't always have to do what our parents tell us. We can see each other secretly, Sondra. Don't let them do this to us."

"I have to listen to my mother," she said sadly.

"Why?" I asked. "Trust me, I'll keep us safe."

"I can't," she said. A few tears rolled down her face as she looked at me. "I'm not as smart as you, Sammy. And not nearly as brave. I'm too scared. I have to listen to my mother. You've got to leave. I can't see you anymore."

She started to walk away.

"I love you," I called out to her. "I need to see you."

She looked back at me for a moment, crying harder. "Don't say that, Sammy. Please, don't ever say that again."

My entire body felt deadened. I couldn't move. I focused despondently upon her fading silhouette, and could barely make it out as she turned the corner three blocks down. Then she was gone.

As I slowly regained my senses, I felt the unexpected urge to talk to Esther. I realized I hadn't seen the librarian since we moved to Co-op City.

I walked quickly to the East Tremont library, scrupulously avoiding any route that would take me near Emmanuel's shop, utilizing a newly built overpass to cross the ditch that would someday become the Cross Bronx Expressway.

Esther was not on duty when I entered. I killed time by perusing the bookshelves in the science section and cursorily reviewing schematics from a few books on electronics projects. But I returned to the front desk every fifteen minute to see if she had arrived. After an hour and a half, I decided I needed to inquire. The librarian on duty was a blond-haired man in his twenties, wearing a tweed jacket and bright-blue bow tie. I approached him hesitantly.

"What can I do for you, son?" he asked.

"Is Esther coming in today?"

"I'm sorry, son," he said. "Esther hasn't worked here in several months." The librarian spoke in a gentle voice with an interrogative inflection I had only heard females employ. "Is there something I can help you with?"

"Was Esther transferred to another library?" I asked. "Do you know where she's working now?"

"I was told she found a new job," he said. "In another state. I don't remember where exactly."

"So you have no way of reaching her?"

"No, son, I'm sorry. Are you sure there's nothing I can help with?"

I stared at the man blankly. I became viscerally aware that I was plummeting into a withdrawn and nonresponsive state.

"I gotta go," I managed to whisper hoarsely as I ran out of the library, directly to the subway station. I caught the next train north. As it sped along the tracks, my body rocked numbly with the car's undulations. Something Sondra said kept coming back to me during the ride, further dejecting me each time I replayed it in my mind: *I'm not as smart as you, Sammy.*

Why did she say that? I had always gone out of my way to share my knowledge and intelligence with her as if it was *our* gift that we could exploit *together*. I never once held it up to demean her, or to extol my own virtues. Why did she see it now as something that separated us? I had always treated Sondra with respect and deference.

It was true; I realized from the outset that she was not as smart as I. Yet it distressed me now to imagine Sondra characterizing herself as somehow inferior, and to realize it was I who caused her to feel that way.

By the time I returned to Co-op City, I had missed lunch and knew that my mother might be worried as to my whereabouts. But it was also possible that Rachel was so engrossed in David's schoolwork that she wouldn't even realize I'd been gone. In any event, I was in no mood to return to the apartment.

I ran at full speed, oblivious to anything going on around me, until I reached my secret clearing behind the playground. Shielded by the trees and bushes, I began hurling myself to the ground from every conceivable angle, covering the full array of standard jiu-jitsu falls. With each plunge, my body rolled momentarily through the grass, then sprang up instantly into a ready fighting stance. Following each iteration, I immediately threw myself down again, with even greater ferocity and speed.

After about twenty such exertions I was shocked to realize that someone was in the clearing with me, watching me as I practiced.

It was Paul O'Rourke.

"Hello, Sammy," he said. "It looks like you could use a sparring partner."

12.
Amplification

IT WAS EARLY MORNING, just past sunrise. The area around the secret clearing was silent and deserted.

Paul O'Rourke hurled me to the ground three times in rapid succession.

I was in no mood to subject myself to further punishment, so I backed off. Paul would have none of it, though. "Come at me, Baron!" he shouted. "Get into it! Come at me like a man!"

I charged at him, but this time stopped just before he could reach me. He was not expecting that, and had already pivoted and leaned slightly toward the spot where he anticipated me to be. That almost imperceptible loss of balance on his part created a sufficient vulnerability to enable me to step forward and throw Paul over my hip, onto the grass beneath us. I retained his hand in a wristlock, which I prosecuted just sufficiently to prevent him from rising.

"Good move, Baron!" Paul laughed. "Very good!" He then tapped the ground three times with his free hand, and I let him up.

Jake arrived in San Francisco yesterday to spend a couple of weeks with Sapphire and me, as he often does in late December. Ostensibly, he visits to escape the cold weather in New York.

I met Jake at the airport, waiting for him at the baggage claim carousel as always. I watched him come off the escalator and head in my direction. He did not look well. His tall, broad shoulders hung listlessly. His back was slightly stooped. His usual confident stride seemed more of a tentative shuffle. As he got closer, I saw that his face looked a bit gaunt. The skin around his neck and cheeks sagged, and appeared pallid and somewhat desiccated.

I waved and caught his attention. When we met he put down his carry-on bag, and we engaged in our customary hug. It seemed that he held me more tightly, and prolonged the embrace a shade longer than usual.

"Are you okay, Jake?" I asked.

"Fine, Doc. Just a bit jet-lagged."

"I could have sent that private jet I use," I said. "You never let me do that for you."

"I don't need a private jet, Doc. What I need is transporter technology so I can beam here instantaneously. But short of that, a commercial jet is fine. I treated myself to first class. They mixed me some nice gin martinis, Dockles."

"Gin, eh? OK, we'll stick to that theme tonight."

Paul O'Rourke was a surprisingly impressive fellow, though it took me a while to fully appreciate his skill set.

I realized, after prolonged consideration, that my father had trained me to assess people based solely on their intellect. I had initially appraised Paul in that manner, and he was not exceptional. Although he earned decent grades in school, he was not in any honor classes, and he took the minimum academic load required for graduation, eschewing any advanced science or math electives.

Yet Paul thrived in circles I knew little about and would have had no idea whatsoever how to infiltrate. He had excelled on the wrestling team for the past two seasons and was now about to enter his senior year as team captain. Paul was also very active in student government, and told me he planned to run for senior-class president this semester. In addition, Paul was on the committee that organized school dances and proms, events so foreign to me that they could well have been artifacts from another solar system. He dated many attractive girls.

So, Paul O'Rourke had adopted a completely different strategy toward life and achievement than I. When I once mentioned his accomplishments to Emmanuel, my father immediately dismissed Paul as a frivolous academic ne'er-do-well, squandering his time on worthless, short-term amusements. Emmanuel assured me that Paul was doomed to a life that would be unsuccessful personally and professionally, and that I'd be better off staying away from him.

Emmanuel's assessment felt completely wrong. I suspected that if I possessed a tad more of Paul's tendencies and a tad fewer of my own, I might be far more effective in school and elsewhere. But I saw no point in pressing the point with Emmanuel. Doing so would only result in his scrutinizing my actions for evidence of my attempting to imitate Paul in some manner. Jiu-jitsu had taught me the foolishness of alerting an adversary to my future intentions.

My enthusiasm regarding jiu-jitsu had been recently rekindled due to Paul O'Rourke's sincere interest in learning about it and practicing with me. But because of Paul's participation in so many extracurricular activities at school, and his perch as de facto leader of one of Co-op City's street hordes, he had convinced me to arise an hour early on Mondays and Wednesdays and practice with him in the secret clearing around dawn, before returning home to shower and dress for school. I hated getting up any earlier than I needed to, but Paul claimed this was the only time he had available, and I was desperate for a sparring partner. Paul insisted that brisk activity in the morning enabled you to more aggressively embrace your entire day. I was not quite willing to grant him that, but I acknowledged that I did feel much more energized on the mornings that we practiced.

Perhaps because of his natural athleticism and his years of experience on the wrestling mat, Paul took to jiu-jitsu quickly. He was very disciplined about technique, and he proved a terrific practice partner as long as we adhered to our assigned roles wherein one of us launched a specific attack and the other parried it with a preset throw or takedown. But Paul also insisted that we spar a bit near the end of every session, in freeform fashion. When we first started doing so, it was a humbling and frustrating experience for me.

The street toughs over whom I had triumphed in the past had been overconfident, and completely unprepared for my counterattacks. Unlike Paul, they were entirely ignorant regarding the principles of *ju yoku go o seisu*.

But Paul grasped both the theory and the execution of jiu-jitsu almost instinctively. He was physically very strong. In addition, he had the savvy of a trained grappler. Back when I had sparred a bit with Michael and David, I was the unquestioned master. With Paul, however, I initially felt out of my league. He threw me to the ground seemingly at will. But whenever I appeared discouraged, Paul taunted me to come at him harder.

Over time I got much better at sparring with Paul, and we were now almost even, though he still got the better of me a bit more often than not. The disparity between us was accentuated when we found ourselves in a position where neither had the advantage of surprise or momentum or superior balance. In those situations, his brute power inevitably prevailed.

Paul frequently advised me to work out with weights to improve my strength. But that seemed like a huge investment of time, and I remained convinced that I could eventually master enough tricks to triumph over Paul solely through guile.

———————⌣———————

It was uncharacteristically chilly in San Francisco. I started a log in the fireplace; Sapphire plunked herself down directly in front of the grate and stayed there the entire evening.

Jake had unpacked in my guest room. He now emerged and found me mixing a pitcher of drinks in the kitchen. Given Jake's debilitated appearance, and the fact that he had ingested several martinis on the plane, I thought it important to keep him on the gin theme and not subject his stomach to a mix of liquors. I also wanted to create a cocktail for the evening that was not quite so strong.

Blood oranges, one of my favorite fruits, are available in Northern California from December through May. I had purchased a bunch of the first specimens I spotted that season at a farmers market earlier that day. I also had ginger beer on hand. I filled a pitcher with ice and mixed in gin, ginger beer, and a healthy serving of freshly squeezed blood orange juice. I added the juice of a lime and a bit of ginger liqueur. I tasted it and added just a bit more ginger beer. It was surprisingly good.

Jake strolled over. "Exactly what sort of concoction are you throwing together there, Doc?" he asked petulantly. "That does not even *remotely* resemble any cocktail *I've* ever taught you."

"I'm not really sure what to call it, Jake. But I had a bunch of blood oranges fresh from the market that looked really good. I know you got started with gin on the plane and so I wanted to keep that theme consistent. Ginger beer seemed to round it all out."

"Doc!" Jake bellowed. "What you're doing is pathetically obvious. You've been pampering me since I got here—insisting on carrying my luggage, hanging up my coat, and subjecting me to all manner of other unnecessary niceties. You're convinced that I'm in some sort of infirm state. And now you're mixing some pansy-ass cocktail to protect me from an alcoholic stupor."

"No, no, Jake. I just thought we'd be drinking for hours tonight, so it would be nice to sip on something that would creep up on us a little slower. And I'm a real fan of blood oranges."

"You've always been an especially inept liar, Dockles. On you, however, it's an endearing trait. Pour me one of those pitiful concoctions."

"I'm quite certain you'll drink me under the table tonight, Jake."

He laughed and grabbed his tumbler as soon as I filled it.

My younger brother failed nearly every class the year we moved to Co-op City. That June, my mother was informed that David would be required to repeat seventh grade.

When Emmanuel first learned of this, he was incensed and flew into a lycanthropic rage as he confronted David in our living room: "You're a pampered crybaby!" he screamed. "Just suck it up and do your work!"

Then he turned to Rachel and continued his tirade. "And you! You coddle him! You're just as much to blame as he is!"

My mother remained silent but was clearly infuriated. She grabbed David's hand, dragged him into the bedroom with her, and slammed the door.

The crisis over David's failure to cope with school lasted months. Over time, it rendered my parents emotionally distant from each other and from me. Rachel and Emmanuel snapped at each other daily over inconsequential things: Emmanuel's dissatisfaction with how skinny and stick-like my mother had grown; Rachel's exasperation over Emmanuel's falling behind on household chores.

Clearly, though, these were superficial attacks, proxies for their deeper, underlying differences. The core principles over which they so heatedly disagreed remained shielded from David and me. No matter how palpable the anger and resentment they felt toward each other became, the two of them collaborated impeccably in hiding the intrinsic details from us. It was exactly what they had done when they shielded their planned move to Co-op City from David and me by sending us to summer camp. They were never going to change this approach.

So I resolved to infiltrate their nexus of secrecy by other means.

Unquestionably, their bedroom at night was their inner sanctum. Emmanuel left early every morning. Rachel cooked him breakfast and saw to it that David and I were ready for school. Both Emmanuel and Rachel always seemed harried and drowsy in the mornings. I doubted that they broached any vital issues then. By the time Emmanuel got home from work, it was evening, and he and Rachel were always in the kitchen or living room. Their conversations there could be monitored—they contained no salient information.

The only time and place left was their bedroom, before they went to sleep. Their door was always closed. I could hear hushed tones, but nothing decipherable.

Nothing decipherable *to the human ear.* I was certain, however, that those muted sound waves could be amplified electronically.

Ever since my construction of the light-sensitive metronome, I had become increasingly fascinated with the science of amplification.

At the heart of that metronome project was an oscillator, which created a tone on its own. Generating such a tone was far less difficult to accomplish than it first appeared. Inherent in any electrical current is some degree of "noise." Carbon arc lamps, the earliest form of electrical street lighting, popular in the late 1800s, were hot, glaring devices that produced light when electrical current jumped between two carbon rods. The strong current produced a loud, annoying hiss. By contrast, the six-volt battery that powered my oscillator produced barely discernable "noise," but that "noise" could be looped and amplified to the point where it was easily heard and modulated through a small loudspeaker.

Most of my electronics projects prior to that had been radio projects employing sensitive headphones to transmit sounds to my ears. The oscillator for the light-sensitive metronome was my first truly focused foray into amplification. In the past, I had dismissed electronic amplification as mechanical and simplistic, and had taken little interest in it. But this project convinced me that amplifying a signal of any sort required ingenuity.

While my oscillator's sound originated from very faint electronic "noise," it was a fact that all radio signals contained a good deal of "noise," and simply making any signal louder only succeeded in producing jarring and unlistenable racket because the noise was amplified along with the meaningful sounds. Amplification, it turned out, was an art, wherein you electronically filtered out the parts of the signal that were unwanted, and amplified only the desired portions. Accomplishing this was far trickier and much more intriguing than I had ever suspected.

As I constructed my oscillator, I spent a good deal of time observing exactly how the unwelcome noise was eliminated and the desired frequencies enhanced. My familiarity with the capabilities of resistors and capacitors, the tools that did most of the filtering, increased markedly.

That interest in amplification intensified when we first moved to Co-op City. I had envisioned installing a powerful rooftop antenna with vast range for my radio experiments. But rooftop access was strictly forbidden to anyone other than the building maintenance staff. Master television antennas were pre-installed on the roof, and jacks were provided in each apartment's living room and bedrooms.

But those didn't function well for radio signals. I had instead rigged a relatively short horizontal radio antenna between the two windows of the room I shared with David. The antenna was situated against the building's brick wall, which limited its effectiveness to some degree. Although our location sixteen stories up ensured a minimally usable signal, this overall configuration required that any radio I built be meticulously calibrated for maximum amplification.

David and I each had a small desk in our room. The two desks sat adjacent to each other, beneath the windows, against the wall. On my desk, amid the books and papers, sat the electronics project that Emmanuel and I had tinkered with inexhaustibly for months—my radio/amplifier breadboard.

We called it a breadboard because only the core radio components were soldered in place. Alligator clips secured the rest of the electronic parts such that the elements could be rewired and recombined in endless permutations. Through trial and error, and detailed chronicling of hits and misses, we were constantly refining and strengthening the amplification capabilities of the set.

With no sink in the room, I had rigged an acceptable ground wire by unscrewing the protective plate on the baseboard radiator, wrapping a wire securely around the iron pipe inside it, then replacing the cover. That rendered the radio unit self-contained and fully functional.

So Emmanuel, Rachel, or David would not think it in any way out of the ordinary to see me in the late-evening hours, before going to bed, sitting at my desk with headphones in place, tweaking the amplification components and noting the effects. It never occurred to anyone that I might be doing something quite different. With an instantaneous swap of the wires on a single alligator clip, I could disable the radio signal that had been feeding the maze of amplification components, and instead stream in the output from a microphone.

In old detective movies, I had seen people use a drinking glass to eavesdrop on a conversation through a plaster wall. I conjectured that a properly calibrated microphone pressed against the wall might do an even better job. I had several small, sensitive microphones lying around from prior projects—and the edge of my desk abutted the wall of my parents' bedroom.

I experimented with all the microphones I had; one was unquestionably the best for the job. Whenever I decided to eavesdrop, I'd surreptitiously wedge it against the wall with the help of my fat history textbook. By positioning the book with its spine abutting the wall, the ruse was impossible to detect by anyone in the room. The microphone's cord hung behind the desk until it reappeared at the breadboard and melded inconspicuously with the labyrinth of wires, components, and clips.

Over the next few months, I overheard a number of eye-opening conversations.

The first few nights of eavesdropping demonstrated that I could hear my parents' bedroom conversations distinctly. But what they said provided little new information for me. About a week later, the first truly revelatory exchange channeled through my headphones.

In prior conversations, my father had taken the predictable approach of insisting that David step up to his responsibilities, and that Rachel stop coddling him. Rachel, also unsurprisingly, had expressed concern about the situation, but remained insistent on the need to gently nurse David through the ordeal.

Throughout these discussions, however, I sensed an unspoken factor lingering just beneath the surface. Now that specter revealed itself unmistakably.

Following a good bit of back-and-forth on the most effective way to help David be successful, an exasperated Emmanuel finally blurted out, "You can't have it both ways, Rachel. Either he's mentally damaged from the problem during birth and you're refusing to admit it, or he's not, in which case I'm right and he needs to suck it up and do his work."

"I will not accept that he's damaged," said Rachel. Her voice quivered as if she was starting to cry.

"Why not?" asked Emmanuel in a slightly raised voice. "Rachel, if he's damaged and we're aware of it, then we can deal with it. Denial isn't helping any of us. It's certainly not helping David."

"And then it will be *my* fault," sobbed Rachel, "because *my* blood pressure dropped. You'll blame *me*. Everyone will." Rachel's crying intensified. I was afraid it would drown out Emmanuel's response, but it didn't.

"That's nothing you had control over, honey," said Emmanuel. "Even if that's the cause, darling, it's not your fault."

As I listened now, I was flabbergasted by the tone my father employed. It was gentle and reassuring. I had never in my life witnessed him speaking in that manner. Then I heard what I thought was a kiss.

Rachel cried uninhibitedly. Emmanuel comforted her. "Now, now," he said softly, "let's not allow this to destroy us."

Rachel whispered through her tears, "If we acknowledge that something's wrong with him, Manny, and we go for help, you know what will happen. The relatives, the neighbors, they'll all find out. They'll think we're cursed, just like the Silvios down the hall with their mongoloid daughter. Do you want that, Manny?"

"Rachel, honey, I don't give a damn what ignorant people say or think. They can all go to hell."

Nothing further was said. I heard rustling, and the beginning of heavy breathing. I disconnected my apparatus quickly. That was not something to which I wanted to be privy.

———————◡———————

After consulting with Jake, we placed an order for food from my favorite San Francisco neighborhood Chinese restaurant. Some months after my establishing myself as a loyal patron, the restaurant's owner had discerned my dietary restrictions and invented for me a fully vegan version of his wonderful hot and sour soup. It was truly comforting on a cold evening. Jake and I ordered the soup, lots of vegetables for sharing, some fried rice for Jake and some steamed brown rice for me, an order of tofu and black mushroom that I knew Jake wouldn't touch, and a container of kung pao beef to satiate Jake's carnivorous compulsion.

We'd have leftovers for days.

During dinner and throughout the evening Jake and I nursed seemingly endless rounds of what we were now calling "gocks" (ginger-orange concoctions). Jake drank at least three or four glasses to each one of mine.

I pointed that discrepancy out to him.

"You know, Doc," he intoned in his booming baritone, "because I'm a much bigger man than you are, and because my body weight is significantly greater, our relative blood alcohol levels have undoubtedly remained equivalent, despite the disparity in our intake."

Given the number of glasses he had consumed, I was quite skeptical of that claim, but did not consider it worth pursuing. "I must confess, your eloquence and articulation have remained unscathed," I said.

"Thank you, Doc." He paused, then blurted out, "Do you think I am without nuance?"

This utterly surprised me. "What do you mean?"

"In conversation, Dockles. Do you think I am without nuance in our discussions?"

"What brought *this* up, Jake?"

"I was thinking back upon many of our recent exchanges. I find myself adhering tediously to a doctrinaire line of the rational and empirical. For instance, do you recall our discussion about bees?"

"Yes, Jake. Whether a hive was a single organism?"

"Precisely. To what extent did you think I believed in everything I said that night?"

I laughed. "That's a fascinating question, Jake. I don't know, but if I had to guess, I'd say a moderate extent."

"And you'd be right. I'm not incapable of perceiving nuance, Doc."

"Then why do you take such a hard, ultra-rationalist line whenever we talk?"

"It's *your* fault, Doc! I'm forced to do it to enhance the quality of our debate. You've become so embroiled in representing both the rational and the metaphysical in every debate, you don't leave any room for me other than on the extreme edge. If I just agree or posit slight differences, the whole debate becomes enervated."

"Why must it be a debate, Jake? Can't we just share ideas because they're interesting to probe?"

"I wouldn't find that as entertaining, Doc. Neither would you."

I smiled. "It's funny. Emmanuel always used to say that to me too. I'm really not sure it's true, though."

"It remains true for me, and I think for you as well, whether you'll admit it or not. When we were young our discussions were more spirited. You left space for other ideas. You weren't obsessed with always merging the metaphysical and the rational into one overarching gestalt."

"I'm sorry if I do that, Jake. It's just where my mind goes these days. I think our discussions are very spirited."

"No, I'm taking a new tack. Starting tonight. I am going to find ways to fight you that are more nuanced. That should keep me a bit more energized here in my enfeebled old age."

I chuckled. Jake grabbed the pitcher and topped off both our glasses.

"All right, Jake," I said. "Then attack me with nuance. What is our topic of debate for the night?"

"One of your pet peeves, Doc. The growing hatred between religion and science. You posit that religion and science are two aspects of the same truth! Rather than simplistically adopting the ultra-rationalist line, I am going to mercilessly dissect your personal rituals in this arena and point out their inconsistencies."

I laughed heartily. "All right, Jakles, have at it. But you better let me gulp this down and pour a refill. I'm going to need fortification to fend you off."

"Yes, we'll both need refills. Drink up!"

We quaffed the remainder of our "gocks." I emptied what was left of the pitcher into our two glasses and went back into the kitchen to mix a new batch. Jake followed, and launched his first salvo:

"You posit that the culprit is the Old Testament. Or at least people's literal belief in it, do you not, Doc?"

"You mean the rift in people's minds between science and spirituality? Yes. I'd say a literal reading of the Old Testament is at the core of the problem."

"But you *love* the Old Testament, Doc. Like so many others you adopt mindless rituals from it and attribute some sort of magic to them. The problem is much deeper than the Old Testament. The Bible triggers innate behaviors and thought patterns that humans can only overcome through rational thought and education. And rational thought leads inevitably to atheism."

"What do you mean when you say I love the Old Testament and practice rituals from it? That's absurd, Jake. I practice yoga and tai chi. I'm a vegan, and if that makes me kosher, it does so only by coincidence. These things are nowhere close to the Old Testament. I admit that the Old Testament has some beautiful myth and allegory in it. It's poetry, Jake. We can learn from poetry as much as from science."

Jake had downed half his round as I spoke. "Drink up, Doc. Each round gets better."

I took a sip. "We do seem to be perfecting the gock."

"Doc, you need to come to grips with how Jewish you remain. It goes far beyond allegory and poetry. You embrace mindless ritual, and it's that kind of behavior, when taken to extremes, that fuels the rift between science and religion."

"Jake, the simple one-syllable word *Jew* carries two distinctly different meanings. Many people will identify themselves as, say, Irish-Catholic, or German-Lutheran. They use two words because one implies ethnicity whereas the other implies a religious belief. The word *Jew* has come to connote both, and that's too much baggage for one word. I have never denied that I remain ethnically and culturally very much an Ashkenazi Jew from the Bronx whose DNA can be traced back to people in the Middle East. That will never change. But that's not where I find my spirituality or my philosophical perspective."

"Dockles, that well-honed rhetoric is undoubtedly dazzling to people who don't know you well. But I've known you nearly all your life. You haven't overcome the primitive need for ritual. Like all non-atheists, you cling to its crutch."

"What rituals are you citing, exactly?"

"You light candles on Chanukah, Doc."

I laughed. Chanukah had ended just two days prior.

I finished mixing the reagents and carried the pitcher back into the living room. We resumed our seats. Jake quaffed what was left in his glass. I refilled it.

"Chanukah candles, Jake? Really?" I asked. "It's a *winter-light* thing. Winter-light rituals have been part of us since primitive man. Every culture has a winter festival with lights. It stems from the primitive fear that the cold darkness of winter will lead to starvation and freezing and death, coupled with the never-ending uncertainty as to whether spring will indeed ever come again.

"And that's why every culture also has a spring festival to celebrate rebirth or resurrection, and the people's relief that the fear of winter is gone—for that year, anyway. Winter festivals are harmless fun, Jake. And they satisfy an archetypal need that's wired into us, that no amount of rational thought can overcome. So, we all need winter festivals. I tried Christmas trees back when I spent time with Stephanie, but they never really resonated with me because I'm culturally an Ashkenazi Jew! So I've gone back to Chanukah candles. It's just something humans need."

"*I* don't need them," Jake said. "I survive perfectly well without such rituals. Because I'm *rational!* In fact, I find all the hoopla about Christmas annoying."

"I find it annoying too, Jake, but that's the commercialism of it, not the innate festival aspect. And even if we find it annoying, the whole Christmas thing *does* get to us. You claim that you visit me every December to escape the cold weather back East. But we both know that it's hard, emotionally, to be alone during the holidays. Neither of us have anyone else to spend them with."

"That's a bunch of mawkish nonsense. Let's get back to the matter at hand. You mentioned the spring festival of rebirth. I assume that for Jews it's Passover. You bake matzo on Passover, Doc. I've seen you do it. You've offered me pieces of it."

"Jake, I bake whole wheat flatbread all year round. And it's much more akin to Indian chapatti than it is to matzo. So when it happens to be Passover and I bake my flatbread, I just consider it part of the cultural ritual. But I don't do Seders or such. Again, it's harmless, and it in no way shapes my philosophical belief."

"Okay. Here's where I get you, Doc. You atone on the holy days! You can't get out of that one." Jake took a hearty swig of his drink, as if to celebrate the muscularity of his verbal assault.

"I do respect the Jewish concept of Rosh Hashanah and Yom Kippur. In my own way. And it's funny because for a long time I was angry and sarcastic about the way Jews celebrated the New Year. Everyone else on the planet dances and parties and drinks and sets off fireworks for their New Year's celebrations. But not the Jews. We dwell on our sins and atone. It seemed so depressing and guilt-ridden. Actually, it was a conversation with Paul O'Rourke that got me thinking otherwise. I'm sure you remember Paul."

"I wish I never knew the scoundrel, but yes, Doc, you know that I remember him well." Jake's tone grew more somber, and he leaned toward me. "But those inventions—for signal amplification—they were *ours*, Doc. We called him a partner, but O'Rourke was just our itinerant peddler."

"Well, when Paul O'Rourke and I were kids, we used to talk about the Catholic ritual of confession. He was Irish-Catholic, and his parents forced him to endure it every week. He said that he and his friends had always referred to it as 'the weekly car wash.' He once said to me, 'You know, Baron, even though Jews bitch about fasting and atoning, just be grateful you only do it once a year!'"

"So now you're attributing your source of wisdom to a loathsome miscreant like O'Rourke?"

"No, but he did get me thinking. There's a real value in examining yourself periodically. Not for *sin*, of course. I reject the whole concept of sin. But for years, every Rosh Hashanah, I've examined myself by category: how am I doing ethically, morally, financially, athletically, socially, spiritually, compassionately, creatively? Where can I do better? And I think about it for the ten days until Yom Kippur. I figure out where I can improve, and I try to work on those things. Not about sin. Just about personal improvement. Where's the harm in that, Jake?"

"You don't need religious holidays to do that, Doc. You can do that anytime. You can do it on your birthday!"

"But I don't do it any other time. And I'm too busy getting drunk with you on my birthday." I laughed and poured myself another round. "But back to the Old Testament," I said. "That's where the trouble between science and spirituality starts. It's the insistence on taking it literally. The Bible is allegory, fable. Great literature. Beautiful poetry. But it's not science, Jake. Why can't people just see that and appreciate both the poetic and scientific aspects of cosmic truth?"

"Because you're wrong, Doc. It has nothing to do with the Old Testament, per se. The Old Testament is the convenient crutch people fall back on in the Western world. But these mindless rituals exist in every culture, whether they read our Bible or not."

"I guess so," I said. "It just always seemed to me that for so many people, the Old Testament is the logical place to pin the fear of new ideas—ideas about the formation of the universe and especially how life evolved on our planet."

"Look at you, Doc. Who's being the ultra-rationalist *now*? You're trying to find a rational answer to irrational fear. You can't find a rational answer! The whole syndrome is *irrational!* These people hate science and scientists because of irrational fear. It's the newness of it. The discovery. The challenge to what we know. The grasping of new explanations. It terrifies them. That's the meaning of the word *conservative*. *Conserve* means to protect or perpetuate. Evangelical conservatives want to perpetuate their current beliefs, regardless of any evidence presented to the contrary. That is very comforting to people, Doc, but it is the antithesis of science, which is to constantly question and learn."

"You're right, Jake."

Jake laughed uncontrollably and chugged his drink. "Doc, why are you always so wound up in the rational? Why do I have to pull you out of the rational? You're supposed to be the spiritual guru here."

"Well, there is a profound difference between the *ir*rational and the *non*rational, but that's an entirely different conversation, for another time. For now, let me just say, I love you, Jake. Rational or not."

"I love you too, Doc. Drink up."

13.
Lungs and Ghouls

JAKE STAYED IN SAN FRANCISCO through the holidays and left a few days after New Year's. Perhaps I had overreacted to his haggard appearance when he first flew in. He was quite chipper throughout his visit.

Still, he never opted to join Sapphire and me on our morning hikes. "I don't walk much these days, Doc," he stated matter-of-factly when I asked.

Instead, he slept in each morning and then helped himself to breakfast.

I never stocked white bread or eggs in the house, except when Jake visited. When Sapphire and I returned home after our hikes, we often found him still munching on fried eggs and toast, reading the paper, and washing it all down with a tall bloody mary. During a visit from Jake some years back, I had mentioned to him that if he planned to make a bloody mary for breakfast, he should be aware that the Worcestershire sauce I kept in the refrigerator was a vegan variety, made without the customary anchovies. "I can live without anchovies, Doc," he said.

The evening before Jake left, we had another manhattan lab. During our last such foray in New York City, we became convinced that good rye was superior to bourbon for this classic cocktail. For our lab tonight, Jake and I had purchased three very high-end rye whiskeys. We were now going to determine which one made the definitive manhattan.

"I'll leave the mixing of the reagents to you tonight, Dockles," Jake said. "You are quite familiar with the pertinent ratios."

I was surprised but gratified that Jake would trust me completely with such responsibility.

As the night progressed our conversation returned to the theme that we had examined on so many such evenings: the conflict between religion and science. We were on our second round of manhattans. Both Jake and I thought this whiskey superior to the first. Surprisingly, it was brewed almost entirely from rye, with very little corn or other grain.

Jake was reclining on a soft armchair, sipping on his cocktail, resting his laptop computer on his knees. He brought up a series of articles dealing with the history of the schism between science and religion in the Christian church.

"It's hardly a new phenomenon, Doc," Jake observed dryly. "Did you know that the Catholic Church persistently denounced the depiction of a heliocentric design for our solar system as advocated by such great scientific minds as Copernicus and Galileo for *centuries*."

"Am I correct that 'heliocentric' means they postulated that the earth revolved around the sun rather than the other way around?" I asked.

"Precisely, Dockles." Jake scanned the article for further facts. "Copernicus first posited such a design in the mid-1500s, and Galileo provided scientific support for the theory in the mid-1600s. It was not, however, until 1835 that official Catholic opposition to their works was fully expunged from all Church documents, and not until 1992 that Pope John Paul II formally acquitted Galileo of crimes against Christianity. Is that not *outrageous*, Doc?"

"It really never changes, though, at least for some people," I said. "I would guess, Jake, that the cultural impact of reimagining the relative movements of the earth and sun in the 1600s was not all that different from the intellectual upheaval engendered in our own society by more recent scientific advances."

"Quite right, Dockles. The big bang theory offered an explanation for the development of the cosmos quite different from the creation story in

Genesis within the Old Testament. It was not received well by the Judeo-Christian community."

"But nothing has provoked more uproar and contention than Darwin's theory of evolution."

Jake sipped his cocktail. "You know, Doc," he said, "it bothers me greatly that we still refer to it as a *theory*."

"I could not agree more, Jake," I said. "Evolution can hardly be called a theory any longer."

"If I'm not mistaken"—Jake paused a moment to confirm his reference on his laptop—"yes, Darwin wrote *On the Origin of Species* in 1859. If you examine the fossil record unearthed since then, along with associated advances in DNA analysis, there are endless instances of proof."

Jake downed the rest of his cocktail and became even more impassioned.

"We hear it all the time, Doc! Uninformed people still scream, 'Where's the missing link? Where's the missing link?' It's their tedious mantra. In fact, so many transitional fossil specimens have been found along the evolutionary continuum that the only feasible response to such a query is, 'Which one would you care to see?'"

"I agree with everything you're saying. This schism between science and religion bothers me more than almost anything I witness day to day."

"Then why haven't you become an atheist?"

"Jake, I've experienced something more. I can't deny what I've experienced."

"What you've experienced, Dockles, is just an altered brain state."

"Only people who haven't experienced it say that," I said. "Nobody who has actually experienced mystical illumination would ever say that, Jake. It's not possible."

"Let's for a moment posit, just hypothetically, that what you experienced was authentic. Even if that were true, it still in no way suggests that the teachings of traditional religion and the Bible have any validity whatsoever."

"People grossly misunderstand my attitudes toward religion and holy scripture, Jake. You do too. When I say that I do *not* reject the Bible, I'm saying that the Bible contains some of the greatest and most profoundly moving stories ever conceived. Many of these stories form the basis of Western thought. The Bible is *not*, however, a work of science."

"It certainly is not, Doc. Throughout history, human culture has used science and mathematics to meticulously explicate facets of cosmic truth extant in the material universe. Actions controlled by the laws of cause and effect that can be produced, repeated, measured, and codified. The Bible does none of that."

"Granted, but the other aspect of cosmic truth—the vast, nonrational, spiritual aspect—does not lend itself to such methodical probing. Instead, we have, throughout the ages, employed allegory, fable, and myth to try to convey the elusive truths inherent in this side of cosmic reality. Storytelling has been our sacred vehicle. Given that science and storytelling serve these completely different purposes for the human psyche, it is entirely possible that the Bible was never intended to be a factual scientific treatise on the origins of life and the cosmos. It is, in fact, more likely that in the great tradition of storytelling, the tales in the Bible were intended as allegory from the outset."

"That's a stretch, Dockles. But your manhattans are so good I'll concede the point if you mix another pitcher."

———⌣———

I continued surreptitiously monitoring my parents' conversations each evening. What I heard convinced me that they had at last acquiesced to the reality that David was somehow impaired. Emmanuel had reassured Rachel that no one was to blame, which finally ensured her acceptance. The tension in my parents' relationship began to subside.

Most astounding to me was their conclusion that it made no sense to seek help. They agreed that the consequences would be as Rachel predicted. And to what end? They were convinced there were no cures or treatments for such things, just the stigma of a child being labeled as damaged.

I could have decided at that point to stop my nightly eavesdropping. I had acquired the clarification that I initially sought. But the excitement of secretly encroaching upon their private confidences had become too enticing. And my listening felt in some way fair, because the two of them persistently opted not to share information I had a right to know.

My mother continued to spend hours working with David on his schoolwork, but with palpably less tension. She made his studies a sort of game, and constantly reassured him that as long as he tried, she and his father would be happy with whatever grades he earned.

Emmanuel now seemed far less distant and preoccupied. He resumed spending time with me. Frequently, in the early evening, he'd pull a chair into the room I shared with David and sit next to me as he and I tinkered with my radio breadboard, swapping resistors and capacitors in an attempt to maximize signal clarity for a given radio station. Whenever we did this, part of me participated fully, but another part observed from afar, savoring the irony of my father working with me on the very device that I'd use to spy upon him just a couple of hours later.

———⌣———

It was a brisk, sunny morning in San Francisco.

Virginia Ferguson texted me. She hoped that Sapphire and I could join her after our hike. She proposed a short stroll in a portion of the park nearer her home. She wanted to share some news with me.

We met in the concourse between Golden Gate Park's art and science museums, at the fountain that houses a statue of a saber-toothed tiger wrestling a serpent. I knew it well.

I had concluded a lovely walking meditation session. The time with Jake had been cathartic, clearing me of pent-up cerebral baggage. Sapphire also seemed rejuvenated. Perhaps she was relieved to have the house back to just the two of us. She enjoyed sleeping on the carpet in the guest room, and she couldn't do that when Jake was there.

We saw Virginia standing near the fountain, her tank of oxygen on its hand truck beside her.

She offered a quick hug hello, and a few strokes for Sapphire's head and neck. She seemed very excited.

"I'm on a list for a double lung transplant, Sammy!" she exclaimed.

"Really!" I said. "I thought you told me that a transplant would be of no help to you."

"That's what all my doctors told me. But yesterday I met someone who told me something different."

"Where did you meet this person?" I asked.

"At the post office, of all places. I was standing on line to mail a package. At the post office, for God's sake!"

"And who was it you met?"

"It turns out he's a transplant surgeon at UCSF Medical Center. He was just standing in front of me in the line, and he noticed my oxygen, and he asked me what disease I was suffering from. I told him it was a rare condition, we got into the details, and then he asked if I'd been offered a lung transplant. I told him my doctors all said it wouldn't help. He said there's a brand-new protocol for my condition. Recent breakthroughs have made a double lung transplant doable for me. This could cure me, Sammy. It's like being reborn!"

I hugged her. "That's wonderful, Virginia. Just wonderful. When are you scheduled?"

"I'm on a list. Within a few months, most likely."

"You know that dream you had," I said, "about the orbs of light entering your chest? This must have been what it was about."

"Yes, Sammy. It must have been."

———

I was permitted to stay up late on Friday nights. At 11 PM on Fridays, a local television station played old horror movies, hosted by a bizarre fellow named Zacherley.

Zacherley's makeup sculpted his features into a gaunt, metallic scowl. He wore old aristocratic garb flawlessly congruent with his mellifluous baritone. Surprisingly witty and articulate, he billed himself as "The Cool

Ghoul" and inserted his character, via brief, absurd film clips, into the most intense moments of each monstrous melodrama.

Zacherley's mad utterances, rife with sarcasm and innuendo, fused magically with the late hour. The selection of films featuring mutants and misfits intensified my sense of isolation in a dark apartment where everyone else was asleep. The gestalt was the very real impression that I was engaging in a deeply subversive act. It was that sensibility that made the ritual unrelentingly seductive.

Emmanuel initially refused to permit me to watch these films, insisting that the noise from the television would prevent the rest of the family from sleeping, but I proposed a solution. I hacked into our television set and installed a switch on its rear that enabled me to reroute the program's audio away from the television's speaker and into a pair of headphones instead. Emmanuel was overjoyed with my ingenuity. His only caveat was that I create an extension cord to elongate the headphone cable so that I could sit on the sofa across the room—he was convinced that if I sat too close to the television screen, I would be exposed to radiation that could lead to impotency.

Emmanuel also cautioned me that he wanted to hear no complaints of drowsiness when I arose early the next morning to join him for Saturday work at his shop. I agreed without hesitation.

On one of those Friday nights, prior to the movie's start at 11 PM, I sat in my room with the lights dimmed, presumably tweaking the amplification components on my radio breadboard but actually eavesdropping on yet another of my parents' private conversations.

I was surprised when, after several minutes of uneventful banter, Emmanuel whispered, "Rachel, I want to discuss your relationship with Sammy."

This piqued my curiosity. It was the first time either one of them had even *mentioned* me in these late-night discussions. Their conversations had been focused on David and his learning issues. I postulated that because they had at last achieved a tenuous consensus on that matter, their attention was turning now to their neglected firstborn son. I was eager to hear their thoughts.

"You know, Rachel, you barely interact with Sammy at all," Emmanuel said. "I realize that David needs a lot of your attention. But Sammy needs a mother too. You practically ignore him."

Rachel's response jolted me. "Sammy doesn't matter, Manny!" she said defiantly. "You don't see it. You can't see him clearly. He doesn't need anything from either of us."

"What are you saying, Rachel?" asked Emmanuel, sounding as stunned as I was.

"Sammy's brilliant," Rachel said matter-of-factly. "But he's entirely self-contained, to a point that's scary. He's going to be extremely successful because of that. But, Manny, it's almost sociopathic the way he doesn't really care about anybody or anything but himself. He doesn't care about David. He doesn't care about me. And he doesn't really care about you either, but you can't see it because the two of you are always discussing all your science and electrical gadgets, and you see him as a little *you*, who's going to make all the great scientific discoveries you never did."

"That's not fair, Rachel. Yes, he's a smart, independent boy. But you're painting him like some sort of monster."

"Not quite a monster, Manny. Just a scary creature in his own cocoon. Completely self-serving. What's the point in caring about him? He doesn't need it, he doesn't give a damn, and he sure as hell doesn't give anything back."

I ripped my headphones off, threw them down on the desk, and shut off the breadboard. David had been asleep. I heard him stir momentarily; then he turned over and began snoring softly again. The ceiling light in our room was off. I had been working by the faint illumination of the small reading lamp on my desk. Now I switched that off too. I yanked the microphone from its hiding place and shoved it in a drawer.

I was enraged. I knew my mother and I were distant, but I never suspected that she thought of me that way. I remained silent, but I trembled with anger and devastation. Images welled up in my head. I imagined myself beating Rachel unconscious, then standing over her and cursing her with a slow painful death. I imagined her suffering, and I took pleasure in it.

I glanced at the luminescent dial of my alarm clock. It was now nearly 11 PM. Still livid and shaking, I trudged into the living room, too distraught to be fully aware of my actions. I switched the television to play through my headphones, and then turned up the volume up as high as it would go. The audio rattled thunderously into my ears, then reverberated as a distorted din inside my cranium. The Friday-night feature starred both Frankenstein's monster and the Wolf Man. I let it overrun my consciousness as I watched numbly from the sofa.

———————⌣———————

The harsh words I secretly overheard my mother share with Emmanuel that Friday night continued to haunt me.

When my mind was focused on something else, I could escape. But Rachel's words reverberated savagely in my brain in the interstices.

My mother considered me a monster, undeserving of attention or love.

When I was alone and idle, my vicious fantasies in which I attacked Rachel, tortured her, and saw her dead became habitual. Their violence and vitriol intensified with each internalized iteration.

I yearned to stop conjuring up these images. But I couldn't make them go away.

14.
Fixers

THERE WAS A DECONGESTANT tablet popular in the 1950s and 1960s. It had three layers formed into a round white-and-yellow sandwich. While it is still on the market today, its chemical components have morphed considerably over the decades, along with those specific side effects the medication once produced in certain users.

During the winter of my junior year in high school, I contracted a harsh respiratory virus. I missed a week and a half of classes. Even when my mother decided that I needed to return to school, I was still quite congested, and my energy level had not yet returned to normal. Rachel had me take two of those decongestant tablets prior to leaving for school each morning, and supplied me with a small container of the pills along with her instructions to take two additional tablets every four hours to help get me through the day. I was to keep to this schedule for the next couple of weeks.

What I had not mentioned to anyone was that being sick provided me with a much-needed respite. Many aspects of school had become oppressive.

Paul O'Rourke had graduated and found a job selling boys' wear in an upscale department store just north of us in the town of New Rochelle. Paul still made time for our twice-weekly early-morning jiu-jitsu practices, but he seemed less passionate about the whole endeavor. I no longer spotted him in the crowds of boys who hung out between our buildings, or anywhere else in Co-op City.

For me, the most jarring aspect of Paul's departure was the loss of his assistance in navigating the social morass of Christopher Columbus High School. The year before he graduated, Paul was elected president of the senior class, and he helped me become a member of the science fair committee and installed me as technical advisor to the theater club for lighting and sound. With Paul gone, I still clung to those posts, but was unable to summon initiative to pursue fresh alternatives, and sank further into my shell. I made no new friends.

Even more frustrating was my growing annoyance with the classes I was forced to sit through. While the honors trigonometry and physics classes I had in the late afternoon remained interesting and exciting for me, the tedious array of English, history, French, and art appreciation classes that comprised my morning had become unbearable.

To my great surprise, though, the decongestant tablets from my mother helped that situation markedly.

Rachel had no idea that aside from making it a bit easier for me to breathe while my nasal passages and lungs sluggishly evacuated their detritus following my severe virus, those white-and-yellow decongestant tablets threw me into a mental state wherein I became groggy but not especially tired. It was certainly nowhere near the high I'd experience later in life through alcohol, marijuana, and cocaine. But at that point in my existence, the sole experience of altered sensibility I had ever encountered was a momentary, self-administered electrical jolt from simultaneously touching my kitchen sink and refrigerator. The pleasant, gentle haze induced by these decongestant tablets was far more useful to me and much longer lasting.

My lungs and nasal passages eventually cleared, but the pills proved irresistible. I developed a personal regimen of taking three on my way to school each day, and another couple midway through my morning. Those abysmal early classes now floated by effortlessly. My solitary lunches shed their aura of self-conscious discomfort, and by the time I finished afternoon gym class, and dived into trigonometry and physics, my mind had returned to its normal alert state.

I knew, though, that if I continued to siphon decongestant tablets from the bottle in our bathroom medicine cabinet, I'd quickly be found out. So I bought a small container of my own from a drugstore on my way to school. But when I returned to the same store a few days later to purchase another, the look on the face of the pharmacist as he rung up my purchase suggested that continuing in that manner might also become problematic.

So, for the next week, I carefully surveyed the shops within a three-block radius of the bus stops and subway stations I utilized each school day. I discovered six drugstores and seven small groceries that carried the decongestant tablets.

Once, years earlier, I had spent a couple of hours perusing an intriguing library book on the use of ciphers to encode messages. My favorite was a simple ploy where the letters of the alphabet were printed out in the boxes of three tic-tac-toe boards. Each letter could then be represented by the lines and spaces of the box it inhabited, with one, two, or three dots to indicate from which of the three boards it had emanated. It occurred to me that if the symbols were laid out a bit haphazardly on the page, the result looked so much like mindless doodles that a casual observer might not even perceive the shapes to be an encrypted message.

I now used that cipher to list the thirteen shops I had found that carried the decongestant tablets. I buried the sheet of paper in the middle of the thick, unkempt loose-leaf binder that I carried to school each day. Next to each entry, I made a small mark each time I visited to buy a bottle of pills. By buying larger bottles and never revisiting a store until I had patronized every other one on the list, I was quite successful at keeping my addiction fully undetected.

It took a good while to become obvious, but my mother was evidently enduring some sort of ongoing health issue. She now frequently stayed in bed, taking naps. She appeared increasingly lethargic. From notations on our wall calendar and snippets of overheard phone conversations, I surmised that Rachel was seeing several doctors, and had been for some time. I asked both Rachel and Emmanuel about the situation. Both said it was nothing serious and that I shouldn't worry about it.

I did not believe that to be the case.

I had not eavesdropped on my parents' late-night conversations for several months. Their discussions had grown predictable and redundant, causing me to lose interest. But now I resumed my surreptitious monitoring, and it did not take me long to ascertain that their whispered nightly discussions now focused entirely on Rachel's physical state. They discussed nothing else.

Curiously, neither ever referred to the illness by name. Rachel termed it "my condition." Emmanuel used the phrase "your health issue." I pondered what medical term was so frightening or repugnant that people would recoil from using it. Only one such word came to mind—*cancer*.

My parents' whispered bedroom conversations frequently made mention of a doctor named Axtmayer. His advice and information seemed of most concern to them. It occurred to me that the name Axtmayer was sufficiently uncommon that it might lend itself to a bit of reconnaissance. One afternoon, instead of heading directly home after school, I caught the bus that went to the medical clinic building in the Bronx where our family received all its care. I consulted the physician directory posted in the lobby. Dr. Leo Axtmayer was indeed listed. He was an oncologist.

A couple of nights later, as I listened through my headphones, Emmanuel asked Rachel in an almost inaudible whisper whether she thought it would be a good idea to do some worst-case planning. Rachel began to sob uncontrollably. I turned off my device.

A terrifying thought leaped into my mind. Was it possible that I had caused this?

I was a psychic sender. I knew that to be true no matter how many of my ESP experiments had failed. I had transmitted thoughts to Leonard Levitzky, and to Sondra. In both those cases, my focus was amplified by newness, intensity of emotion, or a sense of extreme urgency—factors never present in my unsuccessful ESP experiments with David and Michael.

During the past few months, I had obsessed over the cruel comments that my mother made about me. In retaliation, I angrily and repeatedly conjured images of Rachel suffering and dying. Those visions were vivid, accompanied by overwhelmingly hateful emotion. That was precisely the sort of mind state that could initiate a telepathic transmission.

I sat silently at my desk in the darkened room. The thought of this possibility immobilized me with fear.

———————⌣———————

Rachel's napping during the day greatly curtailed the time she was able to spend with David on his schoolwork. His grades plummeted. David grew even more sullen and withdrawn. His despair now conveyed a sense of helplessness, as if he felt it was something from which he could never escape.

In an apartment down the hall was a couple named the Silvios. They had a daughter with Down syndrome, though nobody used that term then. Everyone referred to her as the "mongoloid." We never saw her attend school. It was impossible to determine how old the girl was; although she was small in stature, she did not carry herself like a child.

I often thought about David, and the mongoloid girl, and children I had seen in the special classrooms that every Bronx public school kept concealed in inconspicuous corners of their buildings. The children with the most extreme developmental issues seemed to have no idea they were flawed—they just existed in their own worlds. The less severely retarded, though, or the invisibly impaired people like David, *knew* they were different, unequal, inferior. That had to be so much worse.

Why couldn't somebody make David better? Why would God, if he was perfect and all-knowing as Emanuel insisted, make some people suffer that humiliation and sadness? It suggested that something more random was at work.

There was so much then that we didn't know. There was not yet any understanding of dyslexia, ADHD, or the many other learning disabilities for which we now devise coping strategies. Then, you were labeled "slow" or "retarded," hidden away, trained minimally, kept by parents as a perennial child.

The Silvios down the hall assigned their small Down syndrome daughter simple chores, perhaps to make her feel useful—nothing that required leaving the building. She carried the garbage to the incinerator shaft. She hauled dirty clothes down to the laundry room in the basement, loaded them into the washer, dumped in detergent, and seemed especially thrilled to pop a quarter into the slot and watch the cycle rev up with a rumble. I had once heard her parents call to the girl; her name was Geraldine.

There was a boy who lived on a lower floor of our building. He was younger than I, but big boned, heavy, and a couple of inches taller. I had noticed him making fun of Geraldine whenever he passed her in a hallway or encountered her in an elevator. It sickened me. He was careful never to do it when adults were around, but he had no compunction about doing it in front of me or other younger people.

Rachel had sent me down to the laundry room in the basement with two loads, one white and one colored, accompanied by her predictable long-winded reminders on exactly how to treat each batch. Geraldine was down there when I arrived, watching a dryer spin, laughing at the flying clothes she saw through the round window on the front of the machine. I loaded my clothes into two adjacent washers and got them going.

The boy who frequently mocked her then entered the laundry room. He had no batch of clothes to wash. It appeared he had joined us with the sole intent of mocking Geraldine. He positioned himself between her and the dryer she was observing. He hunkered down, squinted, grinned idiotically, and began spasmodically wobbling. With an exaggerated slur he said, "This is how a mongoloid looks!"

I came at him suddenly from the side and pushed him hard. He staggered backward and careened off another dryer. "You want to make fun of somebody?" I said. "Try making fun of me, you asshole."

I knew he would come right back at me and push me with both hands centered on my chest. I positioned myself precisely, and just as his hands extended toward me, I flexed my knees, grabbed his left sleeve, and pivoted sideways. I thrust my buttocks into his pelvis, instantaneously rose up, and threw him over my hip onto the stone floor of the laundry room. I executed the throw perfectly. He landed on his back with a loud thud, and groaned in pain. I grabbed his hand with both of mine and gave his wrist a sharp twist. He winced and cried out.

"Leave her alone from now on, asshole," I said. "If I catch you making fun of her again, it'll be far worse. Now, get out of here."

Watching me carefully, he slowly rose and backed out of the laundry room, then disappeared down the hall.

Geraldine looked at me and smiled. She stepped closer and touched me lightly on the arm. Did I recoil? I wasn't sure—I know I tried not to. If I did, it was involuntary.

I didn't know what to say. I wanted to tell Geraldine to let me know if anyone caused her a problem in the future. But I was unsure if she'd understand me, or perhaps misinterpret what I said. I looked at her and nodded uncomfortably, then left.

Later that night, I could not sleep. I kept reliving the incident with the boy and Geraldine. The fellow I hurled to the ground was fat and stupid. He was ridiculously easy to throw down. People undoubtedly made fun of *him* all the time too. In his ignorance, it probably made sense to him to pass along the mockery to which he was constantly subjected.

There were so many people born with so much working against them. It seemed horribly unfair. I wished I could change it. But I knew that my throwing a pathetic fool to the ground, or recoiling from the touch of a developmentally disabled girl, was not any type of solution. The more I pondered my actions, the more contemptible they seemed. I was mortified by my behavior.

I wondered if the elusive sensibility of peace and illumination promised by the Rosicrucians might have provided a perspective for all this. But I had been denied that secret, and I had failed to identify a proxy.

I remained too agitated to sleep. Finally, I got out of bed, and as quietly as I could, so as not to awaken David, I accessed the pencil case where I kept my secret supply of decongestant tablets. I swallowed four. Sleep followed soon thereafter.

———◡———

Rachel's condition worsened. She napped frequently during the day. She depended on me to shop for groceries and do the laundry. She tried to spend time with David but had little energy left for him.

Several times a day I'd observe her fill a glass with water, take it into her bedroom, and close the door. She'd emerge soon thereafter with the water level in the glass just a bit lower. I deduced that she was swallowing some sort of prescription medication and didn't want David or me to see.

The possibility that I had telepathically inflicted this awful disease upon her still tormented me. I wasn't sure whether such a thing was even plausible, but there was no way to know, and no one in whom I dared confide. I frequently tried to impel myself into a sender's trance and transmit healing thoughts to Rachel, to try to undo the harm I may have caused. But how would I know if this had any effect?

Most importantly, I vowed never to think hurtful thoughts about her again, no matter how annoyed I became with her nagging or her admonitions. If she did somehow manage to regain her health, then my negative psychic transmissions would have ultimately caused no lasting harm, and my burden of guilt would be lifted.

But on several occasions, when she reprimanded me for not doing more to help David, my instincts overwhelmed me. I found myself recalling the cruel remarks she had made about me, and I again involuntarily propelled angry thoughts of harm in her direction. I'd immediately force myself to stop and try instead to replace the vitriol with healing telepathic transmissions. Sometimes, though, I was unable to calm myself sufficiently to make that shift.

I wallowed in self-loathing for days each time this unspoken cycle occurred.

No matter the havoc I experienced internally, I somehow outwardly projected a perfectly placid demeanor. Like an animal who conceals an injury for fear of becoming prey, I intuitively sensed the need to camouflage any disquiet.

By late spring, as my junior year in high school neared its end, the weather grew warm in the Bronx. Paul O'Rourke and I took advantage of the beautiful mornings by lengthening our early jiu-jitsu practices by fifteen or twenty minutes. He had clearly regained his enthusiasm for the training—he sparred with increased focus and discipline. These morning sessions were the only occasions I saw Paul now, and I cherished the short conversations we managed to fit in before he had to rush off to work.

During one such discussion, I was surprised when Paul brought up the year-end dance for high school freshmen. He had grown so detached from Christopher Columbus High School, it was odd to hear him mention it now. He claimed that the teachers overseeing the dance were having difficulty identifying upperclassmen to act as student chaperones and had reached out to him for help. It didn't make sense to me.

"I don't get it, Paul," I said. "Why would they come to you with this problem? You've graduated."

"I keep in touch with people, Sammy. You never know when you might need a favor or some advice. You should get into the habit of doing that."

"I'd be uncomfortable keeping people around just in case I needed them for something someday. I wouldn't know what to say to them."

"Well, maybe you can work on it. Anyway, I hoped I could count on you to be a chaperone at the freshman year-end dance. All you have to do is stand around and keep an eye on things."

I laughed. "Are you serious, Paul? Me? At a dance? That's way out of my element."

"I could really use the favor, Sammy. I have no one else to ask."

"How can you have no one else to ask? You keep in touch with everybody. You just said so. Ask someone else."

"Sammy, have I steered you wrong yet? The science committee and the theater club both worked out really well for you, didn't they? Trust me on this."

"But it's a dance. I don't *know* how to dance.

"Chaperones aren't even *allowed* to dance, Sammy. You just have to stand around. Please, Sammy. Trust me on this."

I sighed.

"Great! You'll do it."

It was impossible for me to say no to Paul O'Rourke.

The following Friday night I found myself at the freshman dance, dressed in a suit and tie, self-consciously pacing the perimeter of the floor, periodically checking the punch table and the bandstand as instructed. My presence accomplished absolutely nothing tangible that I could detect.

About halfway through the seemingly interminable evening, a girl in a blue dress approached me. She was also a chaperone—I recognized her from a math class I had taken a couple of semesters ago.

"Hi," she said. "You're Sammy, right?"

"Yes," I said. "We were in a math class together last year."

"I remember," she said. "I'm Joan."

"Hi, Joan," I replied perfunctorily.

"Paul O'Rourke suggested that I introduce myself to you," she said. "He thought we might have a good deal in common."

Now Paul's ploy made perfect sense. He was setting me up with a girl in an environment where I'd have nowhere to escape.

"So, Paul recruited you to chaperone this dance too?" I asked.

"Guilty as charged." She smiled.

I laughed. "Wow! He is such a character. I can't believe he did this. This is kind of embarrassing. What did he tell you about me?"

"He said you're really smart. Totally into math and science. And a solid good guy."

"He really said that?" I chuckled. "He never says anything nice like that to me in person!"

"He's that way. He dated my cousin for a while and I got to know him.

Oh, he also said that you're a jiu-jitsu champion and you could protect me if we were attacked in a dark alley."

"Oh God."

"Well, I'm not planning on being in any dark alleys, so you're off the hook. Anyway, I'm very much into math and science, like you."

"Really?" I asked.

"I know. People think it's odd for a girl. Sometimes it makes it difficult dating-wise, you know?"

"You mean boys aren't looking for a girl who's smart?"

"You could put it that way." She smiled again. "Paul thought you might feel differently about it."

Joan and I talked for the rest of the evening as we made our rounds together. At the end of the dance she gave me her phone number and said she'd like it very much if I called her. She already had her name and number written on a small piece of paper in her purse, so I assumed she had planned this ahead of time.

———⌣———

I recalled how Sondra bowled me over the first moment I saw her. Joan hadn't at all, but after spending time talking to her as we performed our chaperone duties, I began to like her. She was intelligent and interesting. And she seemed to grow prettier as we chatted. I was excited about the prospect of calling her.

I put off doing so for two reasons. The first was an ill-conceived notion of decorum on my part. I somehow believed that it was polite to wait a while before calling a girl back, so as not to appear overanxious, desperate, or creepy. I think it was Emmanuel who stocked my brain with such conceptions.

The other cause for delay was more compelling—my need for privacy. I did not want Emmanuel, Rachel, or David present when I made this call. If they were, all sorts of questions, probes, and taunts would undoubtedly follow: warnings from Emmanuel on the dangers of limiting myself to a relationship with just one girl; interrogations from Rachel on the girl's looks, family, religion, and future plans; and finally singsong teasing from David, who would skip through the house imbecilically intoning, "Sammy loves a girl. Sammy loves a girl."

The problem was that there was only one phone in the house. Emmanuel insisted that extensions were a waste of money, and that they encouraged bad behavior in teenagers.

The phone was mounted on a wall in the kitchen. By the time I returned home from school in the afternoon, Rachel was up from her naps and preparing dinner, with David keeping her company. After David and I ate, Rachel started setting up for her later meal with Emmanuel. And when my parents were finished with dinner, Emmanuel often sat at the kitchen table, reading newspapers and magazines until his bedtime. That was after 10 PM, too late to initiate a call to Joan.

I considered asking for a few minutes alone to make the call, but I was quite sure that Emmanuel would refuse and I'd be subjected to a rant I had heard several times before: "Why do you need privacy? What are you going to say that's such a secret that I can't hear it? Make the call. I'm not going to bother you. I'm just going to sit here and read. If what you're going to say is such a secret that I shouldn't hear it, then you probably shouldn't be saying it."

So I waited. I knew that if I remained vigilant, a five or ten-minute window would open up in the kitchen one of these evenings, and I'd seize it.

———⌣———

I had continued electronic monitoring of my parents' late-night bedroom discussions. I kept my eavesdropping sessions brief, but it was the only means I had to track the progress of Rachel's health.

A conversation I overheard a week after the dance offered a disquieting and completely unexpected turn of events. I wound up listening for nearly half an hour that evening—there were a great many details to absorb.

We were moving again, to a new neighborhood.

Riverdale, an upper-class enclave along the Hudson River in the extreme northwest corner of the Bronx, was not a place that I imagined our family could afford. Even today, Riverdale remains an almost separate entity from the Bronx and the rest of New York City, a bastion of wealth and exclusivity, primarily white, with a substantial Jewish population.

But we were indeed moving to Riverdale, although we weren't buying a home there. We'd be moving into the lower flat of the large two-family house owned by Rachel's sister, Eve, and her husband, Irving. They had three children, two of them older than I. My uncle Irving owned a grocery and appetizer store that catered to the many wealthy Jewish families in their Riverdale neighborhood. Irving and Eve did well. Their home was a spacious three-story structure with a brick and stone façade, a perfectly manicured front lawn, and a large backyard with trees and flowers.

The tenants who'd been renting the smaller lower flat were apparently moving out, and we'd be moving in.

Rachel's voice grew fainter. I adjusted my volume control to hear her more clearly through the wall. She made a point of reminding Emmanuel several times that they were giving us a big break on the rent. "Manny, you need to be nice to them and do a few favors for them here and there," she said. "Maybe you can get them a couple of radios or a TV."

"I can help them out with radios and a TV. But I don't need charity, Rachel."

"It's not charity, Manny. It's family. Just be nice. Remember, Eve's going to be doing all the cooking for everyone and she'll be helping with David. I can't do it anymore. We need the help. Especially David. Just be nice to them. You're such a sweet man when you're nice."

My father chuckled. "Well, I can't argue with that."

"Manny, I think we should tell the kids."

"It's still six weeks away. They don't need to know yet. They can finish the school year here, start the new school in September. It's not a big deal."

"They were so upset when we sprung it on them last time. I think they'd handle it better if they knew now."

"Okay, dear," said Emmanuel, "let's split the difference. We'll tell them at the end of the month so they'll have four weeks to process it. That's sufficient for them. Will that work, honey?"

"Thanks, Manny. That will be better."

When I felt I had siphoned out all the salient details from that night's conversation, I switched off the amplifier and removed my headphones. I sat motionless, trying to put this news into perspective. As hard as I tried to remain calm and see the positive aspects, I could not. Anger welled up in me. Soon I was quivering with rage.

Moving again! Just when I meet a girl, and maybe am starting to fit in a little bit. Sure, I hated Co-op City, but I'd been saying that since we moved here. Did anybody ever give a shit about that? No.

The only reason we were doing this now was because Rachel wanted it for herself and for David. *David again. Not for me. That's what she said. David needs the help.*

I found myself blaming Rachel for all of this, and again hurling furious and hurtful thoughts at her, wishing her ill. I tried as hard as I could to stop myself, but I was unable to.

After twenty minutes of struggling to calm down but succeeding only in growing angrier, I submitted to the sole remedy available, and silently swallowed four decongestant tablets from my secret stash. I went into the bathroom and washed my face over and over with hot soapy water until I felt more relaxed.

Then I went to bed.

⁓

My junior year of high school ended on June 30, the same day we moved to Riverdale. I never called Joan back. There seemed little point in doing so.

When I said goodbye to Paul O'Rourke, he appeared genuinely sad, and told me how much he'd miss our jiu-jitsu practices and our chats. I was surprised. Paul knew so many people. I didn't think our friendship meant that much to him.

Although Paul disagreed with my decision not to follow up with Joan, he didn't dwell on it as I thought he would. He seemed more intent on insisting that we not lose touch with each other.

"Listen, Sammy," he said. "I'm making decent money now. It turns out I'm a pretty good salesman and I'm racking up the commissions. I'm planning on getting my own apartment soon. We can get together there. Practice some jiu-jitsu and have time to talk."

I said that sounded like a fine idea. When I reached out to shake his hand, he pushed my arm aside and grabbed me in an enthusiastic bear hug. Its snugness affirmed his years of wrestling experience as well as his affection for me.

The move to Riverdale was remarkably seamless. While the psychological and emotional circumstances leading up to it had been harrowing for me, I had to now acknowledge that I greatly preferred living in Riverdale to living in Co-op City.

My uncle Irving always referred to his dwelling as a "two-family house," but that suggested two flats of relatively equal size, which wasn't at all the case. Our apartment was more an in-law unit, far smaller than the expansive living quarters of the host family. Still, it had two bedrooms, two bathrooms, a kitchen, and a living room, and wasn't significantly smaller than our previous apartment. Better yet, we had access to the roof, and Emmanuel and I wasted no time in installing a long horizontal radio antenna with a lead wire down to the bedroom I shared with David. I could at last resume serious work on radio projects.

While up on the roof with me, Emmanuel observed that the television antenna someone had installed for the family was cheap and poorly mounted. When we brought it up to Irving, he acknowledged that their television reception had never been as good as he had hoped, despite his purchasing one of the best sets available. He shook his head, chuckled facetiously, and lamented in his thick Hungarian accent, "So, the weasels hoodwinked me with a shoddy antenna that they charged me good money for! I'm a grocer, what do I know? I should have asked you for your expertise, Emmanuel. Any chance you can make it better for me?"

I liked Uncle Irving. He was a big, bearish man, always cheerful and energetic. He was our only immigrant relative, a Hungarian Jew. I loved listening to the stories he would tell after dinner as he puffed on a fat cigar and sipped on a glass of schnapps. His tales invariably highlighted his roundabout and arduous journey to America. Initially, the United States refused to grant him entry. So he somehow got into Canada, and spent a year and half wending his way back down to New York State, doing odd jobs.

Emmanuel found him far less charming than I, and confided in me secretly that he believed Irving to be a boorish drunk who entered the country illegally. I didn't argue with Emmanuel about it, but I disagreed strongly. I found Irving outgoing rather than boorish, and aside from wine on Jewish holidays, I never saw him drink anything other than his habitual shot of after-dinner schnapps, which always seemed to put him in a good humor. And if Irving did enter the country illegally and still became as successful as he had, then that seemed impressive.

Despite my father's less-than-reverential feelings toward Irving, Emmanuel immediately offered to replace the house's shoddy television antenna with a top-of-the-line model, free of charge. Emmanuel and I spent a couple of very enjoyable hours the following Sunday installing the unwieldy contraption.

First, we went up to the roof together, tore down the old antenna, and mounted the newer, bigger model. Then I climbed down into the family's living room while Emmanuel remained up on the roof. I opened a window near the television so the two of us could shout to each other, and we fine-tuned the setup, with me iteratively channeling through the three networks and the four local stations that were then available in New York City, while Emmanuel repositioned the antenna until we found the optimal orientation for the home's location. It was a give-and-take, and required many realignments, because the signals emanated from different source locations, and an antenna orientation that was perfect for one station might be quite poor for another.

An added benefit was that by using a splitter and a preamp to boost the signal, we could run an additional feed down to our in-law apartment and gain the advantage of the terrific signal for *our* family's television as well.

I did not reconfigure an eavesdropping capability in Riverdale for my parents' bedroom. I felt no pressing need to do so, and the apartment's configuration dissuaded me as well—the bedrooms were not adjacent. Two small bathrooms sat between them; one bathroom had a doorway into the master bedroom that my parents used, and the other opened out into the foyer.

I fantasized occasionally about planting a bugging device with a transmitter inside the wall of my parents' bedroom, just over their bed's headstand, and building a single-frequency radio receiver to pick up the bug's signal a couple of rooms away. I had no doubt that I could effectively rig the electronic components. I had less experience patching and painting walls, though, which would have been necessary to install the device. Still, I imagined that with enough time, and the proper plaster and paint, I could probably do it. But I never seriously considered going through with it.

While Riverdale was certainly a much more pleasant neighborhood for me than the overcrowded and dehumanizing maze of Co-op City, I had changed schools too many times in the past few years. Any meager reservoir of energy that I might once have possessed for social mingling had been fully sapped. The idea of starting over again, in a new school, where I knew no one, was devastating. I decided not to even try.

By the end of junior year, I had amassed lots of academic credits, including several science and math classes. I had nearly enough to graduate, and the few additional credits I required could be garnered with just a few classes in one semester. So, when I registered with the new high school, I arranged to graduate in January rather than June, and to take the minimum load necessary to do so. I explained to the assistant principal that my goal was to get to college as quickly as possible, and he had no problem with my stated plan.

I attended classes from 9 to 11:30 each morning, and made no attempt to fit in or socialize with anyone. By noon each day I was back on the subway, taking the line into old East Tremont to work at Emmanuel's TV repair shop. I'd arrive before 1 PM, pick up a couple of sandwiches in the delicatessen next door, and Emmanuel and I would have lunch together. Emmanuel was happy to have me there every day—one of us could repair sets while the other waited on customers. Also, with televisions getting bigger and heavier, I had for months lobbied Emmanuel to offer house calls where we'd perform repair services at customers' homes. At first he rejected the notion as unworkable, but he gradually warmed to it. Now, with two of us available six days a week, we began offering the service. It generated a few calls a week, and I performed the remote repairs.

The shop became my sanctuary, where I could escape from school, my mother's illness, David's incapacities, and my own lack of friends. Back in Riverdale, my aunt Eve had taken over pretty much everything that Rachel used to do. Our family ate dinner upstairs with the relatives every night. Eve tutored David in his studies, and even dusted and vacuumed our apartment weekly.

East Tremont was changing at a rapid rate. There were few white people left. Last year, when I worked at the store only on Saturdays, I had on a few occasions seen Sondra through the store's front window as she walked by with a fellow who I assumed was her new boyfriend. But I hadn't seen her now for months. At one point, I was called to repair a television in the building where Sondra had lived. Everyone I encountered there was Black or Puerto Rican. I assumed Sondra's family had moved.

The streets grew more dangerous, especially at night. Elderly Jews too poor to move but still wealthier than the newer residents were frequent victims of late-night apartment break-ins that had come to be called "crib jobs." The term insinuated that the senior citizens being victimized were as frail and helpless as infants, and thus easy prey.

Moishe Horowitz, a short, fat man in his sixties, bald with a bushy, dark-grey mustache, owned the Jewish delicatessen next to Emmanuel's shop. I was in his store frequently, first for our lunch sandwiches each day, and later for snacks and sodas. He enjoyed talking to me. Whenever he caught me with no one else in the shop, he'd lean over the counter and bring up the "fixers" in hushed tones.

"Sammy, you need to get your father to listen to me. This neighborhood is *fakacta*. It's getting worse every day. You think either one of us could sell our store and get anything for it? The whole thing's *shtick drek*! There are men, they call them 'fixers,' who burn down buildings for insurance money. You heard about them? Maybe we could do that. Burn our stores down. If both shops burn down, the police won't know which one of us to blame. We'll collect insurance. Start somewhere fresh where the streets aren't filled with animals. I've mentioned it to Emmanuel a hundred times. He's too scared. He won't do it. He'd rather let us die here. Talk to him, Sammy. Make him see."

———◡———

Fixers did indeed exist. They were white-collar criminals, expert at insurance fraud, and could find no cozier terrain than the South Bronx of the 1960s and 1970s. Property had plummeted in value and could not be sold. For many desperate owners of homes and businesses, burning their buildings to the ground for insurance money appeared the only remaining alternative. Fixers worked with street gang members known as "finishers," who stripped the structures of wiring, plumbing, metal fixtures, and anything else of value before burning them down. By the 1970s, firefighters were battling over half a dozen fires per day, driving from one to the next without even a break to return to the firehouse. Cases of suspected fraud eventually grew so rampant that police could not handle the volume and stopped investigating the occurrences altogether.

Individuals working on their own also tried burning their homes to the ground for gain, and often succeeded. There were many recorded instances of Section 8 residents torching their hovels in order to immediately secure an apartment in Co-op City. Existing law actually encouraged such action, because by rendering themselves homeless, the perpetrators became eligible to legally avoid the two to three-year waiting list for a subsidized space in the now popular development.

But when I was in my senior year in high school, the south Bronx was still relatively early in its incendiary progression. Fires were not yet endemic, though incipient occurrences had certainly become evident.

Every time I talked to Moishe Horrowitz about the fixers, I'd relay his sentiments to Emmanuel. At first, I always reported the conversations passively, suggesting that the ideas were all Moishe's and I was merely the messenger. Emmanuel's response was always the same.

"Moishe's a *schmuck*. He's reckless and foolish. If you get caught doing that, you go to prison, Sammy. It's not worth the risk."

But as months passed and the situation worsened, I began playing devil's advocate, and probing the possibility more aggressively with Emmanuel. Finally, in late November, after months of polite discussion, I put it to my father more bluntly:

"We're making less money all the time," I said. "Most of the people here in the neighborhood now can't afford televisions, and if they can and their sets break, they try to fix them themselves. We're going broke. We need to move, and we can't sell the store. We have to consider burning it down. What alternative do we have?"

Emmanuel flew instantly into a lycanthropic rage. "You want to go to prison?" he screamed and slapped me on the face. "You're *meshuggah*! We're not criminals! We can't do that. Don't ever bring it up again!"

After that conversation, I began a new ritual. Each night, as I lay in bed before going to sleep, I'd try to contact Moishe telepathically. I'd spend ten or fifteen minutes picturing his face and focusing on it unwaveringly. I'd attempt to penetrate into Moishe's subconscious mind and convince him to set fire to both our shops, without Emmanuel's consent or participation.

But every morning, our shops were still standing.

On a Thursday evening in mid-December, Emmanuel and I closed up the shop early. It had been a very slow day, as was generally the case now. It was also the middle of the festival of Chanukah. Along with Moishe and the other Jewish shopkeepers on the block, we closed a bit early so that we could get home and light the candles with our families as soon after sundown as we could wangle.

This Chanukah, we were lighting the candles upstairs with Irving, Eve, and their family. Their observance of the ceremony was pleasantly different from the more somber and subdued version over which my father had always presided. Emmanuel's interpretation was a brief prayer chanted in Hebrew, followed by the candle lighting, and nothing more.

Irving's version had all sorts of frills and fun.

Most importantly, Irving always served wine. Granted, it was sweet Manischewitz, which I'd sneer at today, but it was wine! And I was turning eighteen on my next birthday, so Irving thought it perfectly fitting to include me, along with his two older children, when he poured out the glasses. Emmanuel clearly would have greatly preferred that I received unfermented grape juice along with David and my younger cousin, but Rachel had harassed my father extensively about avoiding any confrontation, so he said nothing. I loved drinking that wine.

Each of the eight nights of the festival, Irving dispensed little gifts to the children. (Emmanuel wasn't a believer in gifts, even on birthdays or anniversaries. He had always insisted that because he provided his family with nice things all year round, he shouldn't be obligated to abide by holiday traditions imposed upon him by others.)

Often, Irving's nightly gifts to us were Chanukah *gelt*, which in Yiddish means money but which were actually round, chocolate discs covered in gold foil, embossed on top and bottom with symbols of the holiday to resemble large coins.

After reciting the prayer and lighting the menorah, everyone was encouraged to pick a winning candle, the one that would burn longest. As we waited and watched the tapers burn down, Irving would bring out the dreidel, which we'd spin to gamble for more Chanukah gelt.

Irving loved explaining why the dreidel game—a gambling contest somewhat akin to throwing dice—was associated with a somber holiday like Chanukah, which commemorated a successful Jewish insurrection against Syrian-Greek oppressors. In his booming voice, holding his glass of wine in front of him, he'd narrate the tale in his heavy Hungarian accent:

"Before the uprising that was led by the Maccabees, all the Jews lived under harsh rules. The worst was that they were prohibited from studying Torah. But the Jews were clever. They set up secret Torah schools on the upper floor of buildings. They posted a scout at the window overlooking the street. Whenever the scout saw a soldier coming to check on activities in the house, he'd give the signal that meant that everyone in the room had to hide their Torah books and cover the tables with money and dreidels. When the soldier arrived upstairs he thought the Jews were gambling. Gambling was permitted, so the soldier left, and the Jews could go back to studying Torah again. Pretty smart, eh?"

Although Irving related the tale with great charm, even I had to acknowledge that he repeated it far too often. The recurrences bothered Emmanuel so much that he'd roll his eyes and grip the seat of his wooden chair as if he were trying to crush it with his fingertips. But Emmanuel held his tongue as he endured each retelling—and he smiled and nodded to Rachel each time he did.

Eve served greasy latkes, or potato pancakes, symbolizing the oil that burned miraculously for eight nights in the fabled menorah of the original Chanukah story. I soon learned that if I wandered off into the kitchen under the guise of procuring seconds on the latkes, I'd encounter either Irving or his oldest son sneaking additional gulps of wine, a tradition they were more than happy to share with me.

The effect of the wine was remarkable. It buoyed my whole being. But unlike my decongestant tablets, the wine caused me to feel happy and energetic rather than just groggy.

So, as Emmanuel and I closed the TV repair shop that Thursday night, I was in good spirits, very much looking forward to another night of wine and celebration with Irving, Eve, and their family.

I was putting away tools and electronic components in the back room as Emmanuel cleared the cash out of the register for our nightly bank deposit. At that moment I heard the shop's front door burst open, followed by loud footsteps. I peeked out of the back room and saw a young man with a knife running toward Emmanuel. The man was short and wiry, with dark skin. It was difficult to tell whether he was Black or Hispanic.

He held the knife up to Emmanuel's chest and demanded money. I saw Emmanuel shaking, his hands quivering so violently that when he tried to scoop up the bills he dropped most of them, scattering them under the counter. The robber grabbed the front of Emmanuel's shirt and yanked my father toward him. It appeared that he was going to stab him.

I leaped out of the back room and ran toward them.

"If you're going to stab somebody, try stabbing me, you asshole!" I screamed.

The man kept his grip on Emmanuel's shirt, but turned to look at me. He appeared surprised that someone else was in the store. My father howled at him pitifully, "Just t-t-take the money, please."

I drew closer to the robber. As I did, he let go of Emmanuel's shirt.

"This stupid asshole isn't getting anything!" I taunted. That succeeded in infuriating the intruder.

The moment he started coming toward me, I halted and assumed the ready position, exactly as I had so many times in my jiu-jitsu sessions with Paul—left foot ahead pointing forward, right foot behind splayed outward, knees slightly bent, hands ready, eyes focused.

Every book on jiu-jitsu and self-defense said the same thing: never physically engage an attacker armed with a knife unless absolutely necessary. Surrender money or other valuables, and attempt to talk the assailant into leaving peacefully with your goods. But do not try to disarm him unless your life is in danger.

Paul and I had simulated knife attacks hundreds of times in our practice. The inexpensive toy rubber knife that I purchased one day on my way home from school had been wielded from every possible angle— from above, below, the side, and, most difficult to parry, a straight jab. I had disarmed Paul flawlessly every time he came at me. Although he and I hadn't trained together since I moved, I had reinstated my solo sparring with imaginary shadow opponents, and felt entirely ready should an encounter ensue.

Emmanuel screamed, "Just take the money. Don't hurt him."

The robber held the knife low, in his right hand, as he came toward me. When he lunged, the knife flew with a slightly upward trajectory. I deflected the blow by smashing my left forearm against his right wrist. I simultaneously slammed the back of his elbow with my open right hand and, employing that as a fulcrum, used his forward motion to spin him around and trap his knife-wielding arm behind him in a hammer lock. To my surprise, as I did so, I felt his blade slice into my left forearm. I glanced down at it momentarily and saw my blood dripping to the floor. It immediately occurred to me that when I trained with Paul, the rubber knife in his hand might have grazed me a hundred times during this maneuver—I would never have known.

In this position, when sparring with Paul, I would have exerted sufficient pressure to cause him to drop the knife, and ended the trick there. This time, though, I pressed the robber's elbow inward and downward with my right hand as I used my left to smash his arm up and outward with all my might. I heard a bone snap and saw the man's shoulder violently dislocate. He screamed in pain as he dropped the knife.

I now twisted his broken arm back the other way, causing him to shriek hysterically and shift his weight to his right leg to help alleviate the pressure. I kicked that leg out from under him and threw him down on his back. I leaped upon his chest, pinned his upper arms with my knees, and applied a choke hold with my right forearm across his neck.

"Call the police," I yelled to Emmanuel, who was still shaking.

Emmanuel couldn't move. He was paralyzed with fear.

"Call the goddamn police," I screamed. "I can't hold him here all night. And I'm bleeding."

"Oh my God," cried Emmanuel. "I d-d-don't want any trouble."

"You already got goddamn trouble," I howled. "Call the fucking police before I bleed to death."

I was exaggerating. The wound to my left arm was superficial. With adrenaline coursing through my body, I barely felt it. But my statement did arouse Emmanuel's attention—he turned toward the wall behind the counter where the phone was mounted.

I endeavored to apply just enough pressure with my choke hold to incapacitate the robber without killing him. This required me to periodically increase and decrease the pressure to his throat, while I monitored his breathing and consciousness. I had never practiced this. But I'd read vivid descriptions of the technique.

Emmanuel was still shaking as he picked up the telephone and called the authorities.

Emmanuel did not open the store on the Friday and Saturday following the attempted robbery. I was kept home from school as well. Ostensibly, all this was to give me time to rest and allow my arm to heal.

My arm did require ten stitches, but the laceration was shallow. The wound had stopped bleeding on its own long before I reached the emergency room. The police, who arrived ten minutes after receiving Emmanuel's call, took a quick look at my arm and assured us that we could take half an hour to answer their questions prior to leaving for the hospital. They cuffed the robber's arms behind him, which caused him to writhe in pain, and threw him into the back of their patrol car while they spoke to us on the street outside the shop. They made notes in their little pads. The policemen briefly praised me for my heroics, but spent far more time lecturing me on the danger of confronting men with knives.

"You were lucky this time, kid," said the older officer. "Next time, just give him the money and let him run. You can get yourself killed doing this."

Emmanuel agreed wholeheartedly with the policemen. "What got into you, Sammy!" he said. "I can't believe you did such a crazy thing! There wasn't even that much money in the register."

When Emmanuel and I finally checked into the emergency room, it was crowded. The initial assessment of my injury was that it did not require immediate attention, so we sat in the waiting room over two hours while the physicians dealt with more urgent cases.

As the weekend wore on, I realized that Emmanuel was using my wound as a pretense to keep his store closed. He was terrified of reopening, fearful of retaliation from friends of the injured robber. All through Friday, Rachel and Emmanuel harangued me on the recklessness of my actions.

"Samuel!" cried my mother. "That had to be one of the stupidest things you've ever done! You could have gotten both you and your father killed! How could you be so stupid to try to fight a grown man with a knife in his hands?"

"He was going to stab Dad," I said. "I saw it."

"That's not what happened, Sammy," interjected Emmanuel. "Yes, the robber got a little hot when the money accidentally fell on the floor, but I was going to pick it up and give it to him and he would have left. Our lives are more important than a few bucks. "

"He wasn't waiting," I said. "He grabbed you."

"You taunted him!" Emmanuel yelled. "You goaded him into attacking you!"

"I was just trying to get him away from *you*," I said.

"That's a bunch of crap!" screamed Emmanuel. "And now all his friends will be angry. They'll come after us! God knows what they'll do."

That exchange, which encapsulated the entire content of the discussion, was repeated for hours, couched in slightly different phrasings. The entire time, David, who had been kept home from school as well, stood behind my parents at the edge of the room, grinning moronically.

A newspaper reporter with a camera showed up at our door on Friday afternoon, requesting photos "of the young hero" and a statement from the family. Emmanuel shooed him away and told him emphatically that we did not want any publicity.

"God, that's all we need!" Emmanuel exclaimed when the man left. "Sammy's picture plastered in a paper so that animal's friends can identify him and come after us!"

"God forbid," said Rachel.

At sundown we went upstairs to light the Chanukah candles. It was a welcome relief. Both Eve and her daughter Beth hugged me and told me they were so glad I was all right. Irving announced that I was a hero and could drink all the wine I wanted that night. I took him up on that offer.

After the hours of admonishment at the hands of my parents, the wine did wonders in settling me down.

On Saturday morning, a police detective rang our doorbell and announced that the robber had confessed fully, so there would be no need for us to testify at a trial.

"Thank God," said Rachel.

"Your son did quite a number on the suspect's arm," the detective said to Emmanuel with a wry smile. "That actually helped quite a bit in eliciting the confession." He winked and turned toward me. "Where did you learn to fight like that, kid?" he asked.

"I dabble in jiu-jitsu," I said.

"Looks like you do more than dabble, son. Just be careful. Knives are dangerous. Anyway, we got the guy on armed robbery and attempted murder, so he won't be around to bother you for a long time."

Emmanuel stepped toward the detective and asked softly, "Do you think the man's friends might come after us. You know, for revenge?"

"It's possible, but unlikely," the detective answered matter-of-factly. "In cases like this, associates of the perpetrator usually lay low and try to stay out of trouble for a while."

The detective's opinion did not appear to set Emmanuel's mind at ease.

A couple of hours later the doorbell rang again. I was surprised to see Paul O'Rourke step into our hallway. He introduced himself politely to my parents, who had never met him. When he saw me standing behind them in the living room, he dashed toward me and gave me a gentle hug, careful not to squeeze the wound on my arm.

"Wow, Sammy," he said. "Are you feeling OK? How's your arm?"

"How did you know about this?" I asked.

"There was a very small article in the paper, and then I asked around." Paul turned back toward Emmanuel. "And you, Mr. Baron, are you okay? That had to be a very traumatic thing to go through."

"I'm okay," said Emmanuel, a bit nonplussed by Paul's poise and the sincere concern he appeared to be expressing. This was clearly not the way he had pictured Paul O'Rourke.

"Tell me, Paul," Emmanuel said, "I know you practice this judo *chazari* with my son. What do think of someone who wrestles with a man who's holding a knife instead of just handing over the money?"

"Is that what happened, Sammy?" Paul asked me.

"I thought he was going to stab my father," I said.

"That's nonsense," Emmanuel shouted. "He was threatening me, but he just wanted the money. Stores have been robbed all over East Tremont. No one's ever been stabbed if they gave up the money."

"I gotta go with your dad on this one," said Paul apologetically. "Listen, Sammy, in the spur of the moment you gotta think fast, but you know what all the books say. You never take on a man with a knife unless he's coming at you."

"He *was* coming at me," I said.

"Only because you taunted him," yelled Emmanuel. "You wanted him to come at you!"

"That *does* sound like my Sammy." Paul smiled as he walked toward Emmanuel and rested his hand on my father's shoulder. "Look," he said softly, "you're both okay, the guy's arrested, it's gonna turn out fine. I don't think we need to say anything more. I'm sure Sammy's learned his lesson and he won't do anything crazy like this again."

The ease of Paul's manner diffused the tension that had manifested. Emmanuel shook Paul's hand and thanked him. My father then turned to me. "This friend of yours makes a lot of sense. You should listen to him!"

Paul had to get back to work, so he excused himself and left. I made a mental note to remind Paul, if we ever resumed our jiu-jitsu practice, that we needed to replace the rubber knife with something rigid, perhaps a stick of wood, so we'd know if it grazed us during the disarming of the opponent.

That evening was the last night of Chanukah. Eve and Irving had invited a couple of other families to join us for the final night of candles and partying. Eve served appetizers and cake along with piles of latkes. The festivities ran late, and secret wine refills flowed freely in the kitchen.

At about 10 PM the phone rang. It was our extension. Because Rachel spent so much time every day upstairs with Eve while the rest of us were at work or in school, Irving had ordered an extension line for our downstairs phone installed in their kitchen.

Emmanuel answered. His face froze as he listened to the voice at the other end. "Yes, Officer," he stammered, "we'll be there as soon as we can." He hung up the phone and yelled, "Turn on channel seven. Turn it on now. The police say my shop is on fire! It's on the news!"

My cousins raced to the television in the living room and switched it on. The set seemed to take a very long time to warm up. When the picture finally stabilized, there was a news story being narrated about a fire in the East Tremont neighborhood of the Bronx. The film showed our shop and the delicatessen next door, engulfed in flames.

"Oh my God!" cried Rachel. Eve grabbed my mother and held her tightly.

"Sammy!" my father shouted in my direction. "Come with me; we're driving down there. They said police and firemen are on-site."

When we arrived, the entire scene seemed surreal. Moishe's delicatessen and our shop were burning wildly—the two stores on either end of them were also ablaze, but with smaller flames. The firefighters were trying to contain the fire everywhere with their huge hoses, but it appeared that they were focused primarily on rescuing the two peripheral shops. The deli and our TV repair shop were evidently beyond saving.

The same two police officers who had taken our statement following the robbery came over to talk to us. They had little information to offer, other than to tell us that the fire had started about an hour earlier, and that the owner of the delicatessen was celebrating the last day of Chanukah with friends in Brooklyn and that they had contacted him, but it would take him a while to get there.

The policemen asked where we had been that evening. When we said we were at a party with a good number of people, they took down a few names of those we were with, closed their notepads, and wished us well.

During the ensuing weeks, inspectors from the police and fire departments collaborated on an arson investigation. No one was ever charged. Our insurance company conducted its own additional inquiry, which stretched on for a couple of months but was ultimately inconclusive. They eventually presented us with a sizable check.

A detective later confided in us that it was possible that associates of the felon might have set fire to our store as payback for the robber's injuries and his arrest, but they couldn't prove it.

I believed that it was also possible that Moishe Horrowitz had hired a fixer to set the blaze while Moishe was establishing an alibi in Brooklyn, perhaps in response to telepathic commands bombarding his subconscious mind.

But I'd never know.

15.
The Ramble

JAKE PASSED AWAY this week. Acute symptoms manifested only days prior to the end. I was in San Francisco when he contacted me from his hospital bed in New York.

On such short notice, I was unable to secure the private charter plane that usually shuttled Sapphire and me between San Francisco and New York. I instead booked a seat on a commercial jet. I had to leave Sapphire in San Francisco—commercial airlines handle animals as cargo, for me a wholly unacceptable practice. Virginia Ferguson had often insisted that she'd be happy to take care of Sapphire for a week or two if I ever needed to be out of town. I now took her up on that offer.

When I reached his hospital room, Jake looked frail and weak. His hair was unkempt, and he needed a shave. It was awkward seeing him like that, with me fully dressed and him disheveled in an ill-fitting cotton gown. His cell phone sat on the small nightstand beside his bed, amid a clutter of paper cups, wadded tissues, and a pile of books. Jake had lost weight since I saw him last, but I chose to observe his still broad shoulders. They dominated the narrow hospital cot on which he reclined. I had always envied his shoulders.

"Thanks for coming, Dockles," he said.

"How are you, Jake?"

"Well, as you can probably assess, I've been better."

"How bad is it?" I asked.

"My heart and lungs are shot, my liver's failing. Most everything else is failing too." He raised his left hand, wiggled his index finger playfully, and smirked. "The good news is that this finger remains miraculously robust. I've been working the television's remote control flawlessly, Doc." Jake was left handed.

"What's the prognosis, Jake?"

"A couple of weeks at best. More likely, just a few more days. Dockles. I'm dying."

My eyes welled up and tears rolled slowly from them. I attempted to retain my composure but failed. Soon I was crying uncontrollably.

"Stop it, Doc!" he said adamantly. "I won't have this. I didn't bring you here so we could wallow in sorrow and self-pity. I've had a good run. I just wanted to have a few more entertaining chats before I go."

"Okay, I'll try," I said.

He leaned forward. "So, Doc, challenge my beliefs!" he said. "You've always been superb at that. The way you do it, seemingly politely, with your probing questions. But now, come at me hard. Show no restraint. If I ever needed to cement my positions, I suppose it's time."

I had not completely stopped crying, but Jake's demand made me smile.

"So, are you holding strong and going out an atheist?" I inquired softly.

"Absolutely, Doc."

"Wouldn't it be comforting at least to afford the *possibility* of something more?"

"You mean my disembodied soul joyfully finding itself floating in some nebulous ethereal venue?"

I chuckled. "Or something like that," I said.

"Actually, I think my stance is more comforting."

"And exactly *how* is it so comforting, Jakles?"

"I go in expecting nothing. I'm at peace with that. I'll just be gone, and not realize it. Nothing could be more tranquil. And if it turns out there *is* more, I'll have no trouble acknowledging my error and enjoying the proceeds."

"That's very big of you, Jake."

"I doubt it will be the case, but if it is, I look forward to seeing you again, Dockles, and picking up where we left off. No rush, of course. A few years wouldn't be long to wait when weighed against eternity, wouldn't you agree?" He flashed that impish grin I'd come to know so well. It was unmarred by time or physiological decline.

I started tearing up again as I looked at him.

"Focus, Doc," he said. "I need a couple of favors."

"Sure, Jake. What can I do?"

"I've been remiss in making any sort of final arrangements, so I was hoping you could get me cremated. I hate to have you take care of something so mundane, but I have no one else to ask, and I don't want it botched." He laughed. "Not that I'd be around to notice. But you remember when we were in business together, how much I hated anything being botched. You never botched anything that I can recall, Doc. You have a botchless record."

"And where would you like the ashes to reside?" I asked.

"You know, I was thinking that maybe you could sneak them in a backpack onto one of those hiking trails you talk so much about, where you walk with Sapphire, and the spirit of the trees infuses your spirituality. It's undoubtedly illegal, but if you could strew them on a hillside there, I think they'd be happy, reuniting with the earth."

"That's beautiful," I said, crying again. "I'll do it for you."

"I may be an atheist but I am not without sentiment, Doc."

"Did I ever tell you about the conversation I had once with my father, Emmanuel, about cremation?" I asked.

"Yes, but tell me again, Doc. It was a good one."

"It was after he retired. I was running the business. I mentioned to him that I intended to be cremated. Emmanuel was infuriated. He insisted it was against Jewish law. I told him I didn't care about Jewish law, and being cremated just made more sense in a crowded world. He said it was an abomination. I asked him why. What difference could it possibly make once your body was dead?

"He thought for a moment and said, 'What if you exist in heaven, for eternity, in exactly the form you were last in on earth? I'll be walking around heaven looking wonderful, in a beautiful suit, with my hair perfectly combed and my face just washed. And every time I see you, you'll look like some monster from the old horror movies, all burnt ash and crumbling bones, limping slowly through heaven forever. All the pretty dead women in heaven will want to talk to me and they'll all run away from you. I'll laugh at you every time our paths cross!'"

"He was a character," Jake chortled.

We sat silently. Jake seemed to doze for a few moments, then opened his eyes and caught me crying again.

"Stop it, Doc," he said. "Listen, I have another favor to ask. I know this is a lot, but I'd like you to go through all my stuff, and sort out anything worth saving. You can have anything you want. It's all yours anyway—I left everything to you in my will. Well, I left a few thousand dollars to a small, horrifically underfunded group of research scientists I came to know. They're doing technology research. You'll come across that, Doc; you'll probably find their research interesting too. But all the rest is yours."

"OK, Jake," I said. "That's no problem. And thank you. I mean, for leaving me your stuff. That's very kind."

"I know you don't need it, Doc. But there's no one else. Oh, and that reminds me. Please, no announcement in the paper, no ceremony, no memorial. I don't want any of that. And it would be a waste of time. Nobody would show up anyway."

The nurse came in and said it was time for Jake to take some medication. She told me it would make him drowsy and suggested that I come back tomorrow.

"I need some sleep anyway, Doc; I'm pretty tired," Jake said. "Come back early in the morning. We'll have time to talk."

I left the hospital and took a taxi to Jake's apartment. Years ago he had given me a key to his place. I was tired, but I knew that once Jake was gone, I wouldn't want to prolong my time in New York beyond what was absolutely needed. So I wanted to start going through Jake's things as soon as I could.

The doorman, Ray, knew me well. He greeted me solemnly as I exited the cab. "Hello, Mr. Baron," he said. "How's Mr. Kenneman doing? Did you visit him?"

"He's very sick, Ray," I said. "I'm afraid he doesn't have much time left. I'm here to start going through his things."

"I'm so sorry," Ray said. "Let me know about the funeral. I'd like to come if I can get away."

I rested my hand on Ray's shoulder. "You're a good man," I said. "I don't think there'll be a funeral, but Jake will very much appreciate the sentiment. I'll pass it along."

Jake's apartment was messier than I had ever seen it. I did a quick perusal and projected that the job would take me several days. I'd spend as many hours as I could there this evening.

Before I started, I went to Jake's liquor cabinet and poured myself a stiff shot of the single barrel bourbon we both liked to sip. I took the glass with me to his study where I began going through papers, envelopes, and folders. I felt oddly alone without Sapphire, and I made a quick call to Virginia in San Francisco to make sure that everything was all right.

A couple of hours into the work, I came upon a stash of well over a hundred letter-size envelopes, held together in rubber-banded piles. They were decades old—the rubber bands crumbled the moment I handled them. The envelopes had come through the mail, and their canceled stamps were all from Costa Rica. I knew what that meant.

The dozen envelopes with the earliest postmarks had been opened; the rest were still sealed. I unfolded the letter from the first envelope. As I expected, it came from Paul O'Rourke. It contained a heartfelt apology, and an offer to make restitution.

Each of the subsequent envelopes contained a check from Paul, in amounts ranging from five hundred to over a thousand dollars. The postmarks indicated no regular periodicity. Some were a couple of weeks apart; others showed a gap of several months.

Jake had not cashed a single check.

When I saw Jake the next morning, I mentioned that Ray had inquired as to his well-being.

"Thank him for me, Doc."

Then I brought up the checks.

"Ah, so you found those, Doc," he said. "Good. I wanted you to see them. You can throw them away now."

"Why did you do that, Jake?" I asked. "Paul was trying to do the right thing. Trying to make it up to you. Why didn't you cash any of his checks?"

Jake began formulating a response but then paused, distracted by a small container I had just taken out of a paper bag. "What's in the thermos?" he asked.

I leaned closer. "It's a bit of that fine single barrel bourbon we like," I whispered. "I thought you might enjoy some. What harm can it do now?"

"You are a fine fellow, Dockles! Start pouring! Here, use one of these paper cups they gave me. If the nurse comes in, she'll think I'm drinking water."

Jake downed the first two shots ridiculously quickly. By the third, he started sipping more gingerly.

Jake handed me an empty paper cup, and I poured a small shot for myself. The bourbon tasted especially good.

"Those checks, Doc," he said. "They weren't mine to cash. They didn't belong to me. And they certainly didn't belong to that reprobate O'Rourke either. They belonged to Jill. And if I didn't cash them, they'd stay with her. And they needed to."

"Jill and Paul stole that money," I said.

"No, Doc, not really," he said sadly. "We all make mistakes, Dockles. But some are much bigger than others. You and I both made huge mistakes with very special women. I made my mistake with Jill. You made yours with Stephanie. Our lives would have been very different. So much richer. We were both fools, Doc."

"And you see the checks as related to that?" I asked.

"Of course, Doc. That was money I should have shared with Jill, not hoarded. I was a lousy son of a bitch, Doc. I screwed around on her, lied about my assets, treated her like chattel. What she and Paul did, I deserved. That money needed to stay with them."

I gazed at him.

"I know what you're thinking, Doc. You reimbursed me for all that. Out of your own pocket."

I nodded.

"Believe me," he said, "I'll more than make it up to you in my will. And you never missed it, did you? You're a goddamn multimillionaire, Doc. You fly on private jets and you own beautiful homes in San Francisco and New York. In the end, I believe I did the right thing." He gazed at me achingly. "Do you forgive me, Doc?"

I looked down and thought for a moment. "There's nothing to forgive, Jake." I stared at him with affection. "I agree with everything you said. You did absolutely the right thing. No wrong was perpetrated. No apology needed."

"Thank you, Doc. You've always been a gracious soul." He took a few more sips of his bourbon. "I was thinking about when we were young and you bought your first car," he said, smiling wryly. "Tell me what you remember of our antics driving down Broadway."

My eyes began to tear but I smiled.

"Oh, Jake!" I said. "We were drunk and stupid. God, those were fun days."

"Tell me, Doc. Tell me your recollections." Jake leaned back and grinned broadly as he listened to me narrate:

"We'd been drinking on the Upper East Side," I said. "We both had way too much. We always did then. We staggered back to our cars and started driving toward Greenwich Village. Your apartment was there. It was about eleven at night. We were following each other down Broadway.

Slowly. I was in the lead. I stopped at a red light, and you rear-ended me. Gently. Just hard enough so our rubber bumpers crashed and both our cars rocked and gyrated. Then you pulled in front of me. And when *you* stopped at the next light, I rear-ended you in return. The same way. The cars rocked and gyrated. Then I passed you and we did it again. And on and on. We alternated. We must have crashed each other two dozen times, Jake. It was as if we were screaming out to the cops, 'Hey, look at us, we're drunk and stupid and playing bumper cars on fucking Broadway!' God, we really did that. And we got away with it! Is that how you remember it, Jakles?"

The grin on Jake's face remained broad for a moment. It then slowly decompressed into a vacuous stare.

He was dead.

———————⌇———————

When I left Jake's hospital room, I gave the nurse on duty my cell phone number and informed her that I'd be responsible for having his body picked up and delivered to a crematorium as soon as I could arrange it.

Outside, it was a mild winter day. The sun was bright. I pulled a pair of woolen gloves from the pocket of my coat and slipped them on, along with my sunglasses. I began walking slowly, in no particular direction. I soon was sobbing heavily, my head bowed, tears streaming down my face.

I was aware that I had a lot to do. I needed to find a cremation service and arrange for them to pick up Jake's body at the hospital morgue. And there were still endless piles of papers and belongings in Jake's apartment to sort through.

But right now, I could do none of that.

I found myself instinctively walking toward Central Park, just a few blocks away.

As I trudged, crying, toward the park, I realized how much I missed Sapphire. During our regular spring and fall visits to New York City, Sapphire and I took our morning hikes in an area of Central Park called the Ramble. Unlike most of Central Park, which consisted of wide footpaths and relatively flat terrain, the Ramble was a labyrinth of narrow, twisting dirt trails winding through the hills north of the park's lake. It was the quietest and most remote area I'd been able to uncover in Central Park. Even in the early morning, when Central Park was teeming with walkers and runners, the Ramble remained relatively tranquil.

In contrast to the benign nonenforcement of leash laws in remote areas of San Francisco's Golden Gate Park, there was rigorous enforcement by Central Park's patrolling legions, comprised of a mix of park rangers and New York City police officers. However, Central Park leash regulations were not in effect between dawn and 9 AM. So, during our New York visits, I roused Sapphire at 6 AM, assuring that she was free to saunter unfettered on our morning hikes.

Even so, because Sapphire had lost much of her eyesight, I kept her on leash until we reached the quiet trail along the lake leading to the wooden footbridge that crossed into the Ramble. On the wide main park roads, with the sea of runners dashing around us, I was afraid that without her tether Sapphire might lose me in the crowd, or be knocked to the ground as she paused to sniff an alluring remnant.

In the Ramble, Sapphire and I usually encountered a few pairs of dogs and owners we knew, and also some avid bird-watchers who were older and retired. The Ramble at one time enjoyed a reputation as a hotbed for gay assignations, but I saw little evidence of that anymore, especially in the early morning, though I did spot the occasional used condom lying on the edge of the trail, which always engendered a perfunctory sniff from Sapphire before she ambled on.

I imagined Sapphire by my side now as I walked alone along Fifth Avenue until I came upon a park entrance. I meandered the paths that took me to the Ramble.

After slowly climbing the trails that wound upward from the lake, I found a tiny meadow surrounded by trees and shrubs. The grass was damp, but there was a low tree stump. I sat on that.

I wanted now to clear my mind and enter into deep meditation. Too many memories and too many tears had prevented me from calming myself and clearing my mind as I walked. Usually, during walking meditation, such clutter dissipated spontaneously at some point. Today, however, there was too much distraction. I needed to sit, and focus purposefully on emptying my mind.

I sat upright on the tree stump, my legs crossed beneath me in a relaxed half lotus. In the chill air, I rested the back of my gloved hands on my knees, thumbs and forefingers forming classic yogic finger halos.

I began by simply watching my breath. But today that was insufficient. Too many recollections of moments with Jake fired in my brain's synapses.

It was rare anymore that I employed a mantra for meditation, but I needed to today. Although I always had viewed "om" as the purest of mantras, I had come to accept its more accessible cousin "so hum" as the sound pattern that worked best for me when I required it.

"So hum" contains the same vowel sounds and final resonating purr as "om." Those tones are designed to reverberate within the human vessel, evoking the oscillations of prana, or life force, entering and exiting the body with each breath.

In addition, for me, "so hum" offered more consonants upon which to comfortably anchor those tones and, perhaps more importantly, two syllables, enabling "so" to occupy me on the inhalation, and "hum" during the prolonged exhalation, leaving my mind less opportunity to digress back into bustle.

Silently, I repeated "so hum" over and over. My breath gradually slowed, elongating the sounds. I began to relax. At first, images of Jake haphazardly inserted themselves and I'd let them drift away, but after about twenty minutes, my mind emptied. I achieved the state I sought. I rested there, allowing myself to experience universal consciousness, immersing myself in its powerful sensibility of symmetry, peace, timelessness, and nonrational unity.

Suddenly a new and unfamiliar sensation filled my being. I had never before, during meditation, felt anything remotely like this.

It was Jake.

However, it was clearly *not* an internally generated recollection of Jake interrupting my quieted mind. This was very different. It was external. Massive and powerful. Transmitting to me from the mystical aspect of reality. I knew it to be Jake, even though it took no visual form, and did not announce itself with a name. It was Jake's spirit, now free and unfettered. It expressed such joy, such boundless freedom, such appetite for discovery.

Its overwhelming presence lingered briefly—then it was gone. But a remnant of its joyful abundance now filled my meditative state. A few tiny tears leaked from my closed eyes and trickled down to my chin.

Jake's soul had begun its journey. But not before taking a moment to bid me farewell.

I sifted through Jake's papers, made arrangements to donate his furnishings, and finally dealt with the logistics of his cremation. The effort drained me. It took me two weeks to finish the work.

But when I was done, the feeling of resolution was cathartic.

I had arranged for my usual charter jet to fly me home and boarded that flight exhausted. But I was exhilarated at the thought of returning to San Francisco.

Virginia Ferguson and her husband, Doug, picked me up at the San Francisco airport in their large SUV. Sapphire was sprawled out on the back seat and could barely contain herself when she saw me approach from the window. For a few moments she seemed to possess the energy of a puppy, frenetically climbing on my chest and licking my face. I was just as happy to see her. Virginia and Doug had apparently done a terrific job taking care of my girl.

The next morning was foggy and cool. I was very anxious to get back to our customary routine. I felt no jet lag whatsoever as I tugged on my sweats for a long early-morning hike with Sapphire on familiar trails in Golden Gate Park.

As we entered the park, I anticipated a rewarding session of walking meditation. I began to intensely process the thoughts occupying my mind, to work through them actively so as to more promptly dismiss them when I was ready to access the meditative state, later in the hike.

I pondered the extraordinary experience of being visited by Jake's soul. This and other recent occurrences suggested that I was becoming psychically more of a receiver now, not just a sender. *What exactly does it mean*, I wondered, *to be tuned in passively to transmissions from the mystical side?* It certainly made me more cognizant that we, along with all living creatures, were part of a web of supreme consciousness that infused all of our processes, every aspect of our lives. The fact that messages from that stratum could be conveyed to us, if we were in a receptive state, did not seem surprising.

I recalled that while walking on these same trails in the past, I had frequently thought about nature, and the evolution of plants and animals on our planet. I wondered now whether it was possible that the overarching mystical energy to which I was becoming increasingly sensitized had in any way guided those mutations that had been part of the natural selection process of evolution. Would my opening myself to such a possibility label me an adherent of intelligent design, a doctrine I had always found ludicrous? I wasn't certain. But if one can immerse oneself in the nonrational experience of universal consciousness, how is one then able to draw a rational distinction between "consciousness" versus "intelligence" or "intent"?

I felt no need to answer that question but was drawn to focus instead on my own spiritual practices and rituals. I felt that I was at a crossroads. What I had been doing had served me well, but I needed now to go deeper, devote myself more fully to the quest.

I resolved to immerse myself more zealously in the meditative state, to rely not solely on walking meditation but to return to a daily practice of silent, seated, traditional meditation as well. I had rejected that, years ago, as boring and nonproductive for me, but perhaps I had evolved spiritually now to a point where I was ready to embrace it.

I resolved also to stop drinking alcohol. Yoga and other Eastern traditions taught that alcohol deadened the mind and rendered it less disposed to the meditative state. Rosicrucians believed so as well. The only times I ever drank heavily anymore had been with Jake, and he was gone now. When I was by myself I rarely had more than a glass of wine or two with dinner. It would be easy to give that up, and might clear my psyche and make me more receptive to a regular discipline of seated meditation.

I also vowed to forego my periodic precaution of eating a chunk of cheese to supply trace elements, and to instead embrace my vegan diet fully and unconditionally. The spiritual benefits of doing so, I was certain, more than outweighed any fears I might harbor.

This new direction excited me and buoyed my spirit. I consciously allowed all these thoughts to slip away now. My mind emptied, and I transitioned quickly and effortlessly into a mystical mindset. I ambled peacefully along the trail, feeling a deep connection to the foliage around me and, on a more abstract level, to all living things. Time seemed inconsequential—the moment I was experiencing felt infinite.

I took Sapphire off leash when we reached the path on the inner island of Stow Lake. As we made the steep climb now to the top of Strawberry Hill, I glanced back periodically to make certain that Sapphire was walking behind me and had not slipped back too far or become distracted. My doing so did not in any way interfere with my mystical sensibility.

During one such check, I noticed that Sapphire had fallen back quite a ways, and was stationary, exploring some scents on the side of the trail. I stopped and watched her. She seemed aware that I was doing so, and turned to look in my direction. Sapphire then began slowly walking toward me, narrowing the gap between us. As she did, a man moved quickly behind her, and soon passed her, climbing the trail in my direction. For a moment I could have sworn he was Paul O'Rourke—he looked just like him. But I realized that it was the way Paul had looked the last time I saw him, more than thirty years ago, so the man was far too young to be Paul. As the stranger came nearer and walked beyond me on his way to the summit, I was surprised to see that he looked nothing like Paul.

Sapphire and I had a lovely stroll down from the top. She seemed especially energized and walked faster than normal. She favored her right side, which was racked with arthritis, but she was nonetheless moving with an athleticism more reminiscent of her younger days. At one point she jogged so far ahead that she stopped and turned back with that look I used to see so often but rarely did now, an expression in her eyes and the cock of her head that appeared to call me to hasten my stride and keep up with her pace.

Once we exited the park, home was just a few blocks away. Sapphire was back on leash. As we approached the house, I noticed an older gentleman sitting quietly on the sidewalk, leaning against our front gate. When the man saw us approaching, he stood and faced us. I paused to examine him more closely. Sapphire looked back and forth, from my gaze to his silhouette—the heavy fog and dim shadow from the house somewhat obscured his features. I stepped closer. Then I recognized him.

Sapphire brushed her snout against my thigh to ask if there was danger. I tapped her head and whispered softly, "It's all right, Sapphy. He's an old friend. His name is Paul O'Rourke." I knew Sapphire couldn't make out what I said; she had lost far too much hearing to detect such a faint whisper. She understood perfectly, though.

I gave Sapphire's leash a gentle tug and approached Paul slowly. When I was just a few feet away he grinned and said, "You're not going to beat the shit out of me again, are you?"

I began laughing. "I was going to hug you," I said.

He opened his arms and walked toward me. We embraced warmly and did not let go for quite some time. Sapphire sniffed Paul's lower legs thoroughly and seemed to find him acceptable. She retreated and lowered to her belly to watch us.

I took a couple of steps back and stood facing Paul. I chuckled. "That would have been quite a sight, eh, two old geezers like us throwing each other to the ground!" I said. "It's good to see you after all this time, Paul."

"It's good to see you too, Sammy. I'm relieved that you're willing to talk again. I was afraid you might just send me away."

"No. It's wonderful that you're here, Paul. Come in, have some tea."

We entered the house, and I began to say something to Paul when

Sapphire commenced a series of high-pitched yelps, loud and regular. It was her way of saying she wanted her breakfast before I became preoccupied with Paul.

I laughed. I didn't want to take the time to prepare her usual concoction, so I laid out a small pile of very delectable dog treats on the kitchen floor. They were among her favorites but required a good deal of gnawing and chewing to ingest. Sapphire seemed pleased and dug in.

"Please, sit down," I said to Paul as I returned to the living room, motioning toward the sofa. "I recall you liked your tea with honey," I said. "Right now I have only green chai tea, with soy milk and agave syrup, but I think you'll find it tasty. It's all brewed and mixed—I just have to heat a couple of cups in the microwave. Give me a moment and I'll be with you."

As I waited for the microwave oven to complete its cycle, I realized that my mistaking the fellow on the trail for Paul had been a premonition. In my meditative state, I had sensed Paul's proximity—further evidence that I was becoming more of a receiver psychically.

I brought out the tea and set Paul's on a coaster on the low table in front of him.

"This is such a surprise, Paul," I said. "What brings you to San Francisco?"

"I'm just up here for one night," he said. "Got in yesterday, flying back to Costa Rica later today. But I needed to see you, Sammy."

"I'm glad you came," I said.

"The tea is good," said Paul after a couple of sips.

"How is the bed-and-breakfast doing?" I asked.

"Very well, thanks. We actually have three now, with people running them for us—we just oversee, and schmooze with our guests."

"That's good to hear, Paul."

"Listen, Sammy," said Paul with a solemnity that instantly cracked the pretense of polite small talk. "I heard about Kenneman's death. That's what prompted me to come. Maybe close the circle."

I was surprised. "There was no announcement in the papers," I said. "You live in Costa Rica. How did you hear about his death?"

"I still have some connections up here," Paul said, smiling momentarily. Then his expression turned serious again. "Did he ever forgive me, Sammy?" Paul asked. "I really need to know that."

I took another sip of tea and put down my cup. "He did better than forgive you, Paul," I replied. "Jake said there was nothing to forgive. The money belonged to Jill—he was at fault for hiding it from her. In the end, he thought you did the right thing."

Paul looked down and closed his eyes. "Kenneman was a good man," he whispered. "We had our differences, but I knew you loved him, so there had to be something decent about him. I'm very relieved to hear what he said."

Sapphire walked into the living room where Paul and I were seated, carrying the last remnant of one of the treats in her jaw. She plopped down on the throw rug and began gnawing at the snack.

"And the money you put in to reimburse Kenneman?" Paul asked.

"So you know about that too," I said. "All repaid through Jake's will."

"That's good," said Paul.

The two of us were silent for a time.

Paul finished his tea. "Look," he said, "I'm sorry, Sammy, I have to catch a plane. I'm already late. I didn't realize how long I'd have to wait for you. I miscalculated. I better be going."

We stood and hugged. Sapphire looked up but didn't rise.

"Let's stay in touch, Paul," I said.

"I was hoping you'd say that, Sammy. I'd love to. For as long as we have left, you have my promise that I'll keep in touch. Maybe you can come down to Costa Rica sometime. Stay with us, on the house."

"Thank you, Paul. I'll give that some thought. Please say hi to Jill for me when you get back. Do you need a ride to the airport?"

"No, I have a car." He paused and looked at me. "I guess I should have stayed a few days," he said. "We would have had more time. But I really didn't know how this would go."

"I understand, Paul."

We hugged again. I saw him out.

I abluted thoroughly after Paul left. I had hugged him fully and unreservedly, even once touching my temple to his cheek.

I relaxed for a few moments and revisited what had just occurred before making myself breakfast. I fixed a thick peanut butter sandwich on whole grain bread, with slices of cucumber, tomato, and red onion. I topped the mélange with just a dash of salt and pepper.

When I finished eating, I heated up another cup of tea and swallowed one of my supplement capsules designed for vegans. I carried what was left of the tea into the back room with me and turned on the computer for my morning checks of email and news.

Sapphire sprawled out in the doorway of the room and went to sleep.

There was an urgent email message from Virginia Ferguson's husband, Doug. The hospital had found a donor, a young man who died suddenly in a motorcycle accident. Virginia and Doug had rushed to the hospital just a few hours ago. Virginia's double lung transplant was already underway.

16.
Chinese Checkers

SAPPHIRE AND I ENJOYED a lovely morning hike around the perimeter of Lake Lagunitas. The water and the lush foliage are part of the Mount Tamalpais watershed of Marin County, twenty miles north of San Francisco.

It was a cool weekday morning. The trails were mostly unoccupied, making them especially conducive to a tranquil session of walking meditation for me, and leisurely off-leash exploration for Sapphire.

An occasional lizard scampered across exposed rock and disappeared almost instantaneously into the heavy brush. Whenever one caught my eye, I'd immediately glance at Sapphire to see if she noticed it. But with her hearing almost completely gone and her eyesight increasingly compromised, she did not seem to spot even one of the darting creatures.

During the drive home, Sapphire lounged and dozed on the back seat. But as we approached our neighborhood in San Francisco, she perked up and launched into a familiar pattern of rhythmic high-pitched squeals emanating from the back of her throat. Sapphire now lunged forward, enthusiastically placing her front paws on the center console, her head right next to mine. The series of whimpers meant unmistakably that she was waiting for breakfast. She kept the barrage up nonstop as we entered the house, and did not desist even as she stood in the kitchen watching me ladle food into her distinctive red-and-white bowl.

Sapphire employed that same vocalization at other times as well, always indicating impatience or anticipation of some imminent event. On hikes, if I ran into someone I knew and stopped to chat, Sapphire allowed me three or four minutes to do so, but then predictably broke into that series of pulsating whines while staring at me, as if to say, "You've talked enough; it's time to resume our walk."

I had always wondered if this vocalization was unique to Sapphire. Then some years ago, while hiking on the cliffs at Lands End in San Francisco, we encountered a fellow hiker and his purebred Australian cattle dog. I am always intrigued when I meet cattle dogs, because Sapphire's personality and behavior patterns appear to be fully cattle dog, even though her morphology is about equally divided between cattle dog and Welsh corgi.

The owner of the purebred dog and I had been comparing notes for several minutes when both dogs simultaneously broke into that same whine, in almost identical pitch, signaling their owners that it was time to part ways.

This morning, as always, Sapphire's whimpers ceased the moment I laid her bowl of food on the floor and she commenced her manic guzzling. As she ate, I washed my hands thoroughly, and prepared my own breakfast, which started with a whole wheat bagel that I halved and toasted. I placed each piece cut-side up on a large plate, and slathered on hummus. I topped the open-face sandwiches with thin slices of dill pickles. I also brewed a big cup of green chai tea, to which I added soymilk, and a touch of agave syrup to sweeten.

I was anxious to get back to a science documentary I had recorded and watched a few days earlier. It dealt with primitive man's evolution and culture. I moved to the den and switched the television on as I munched upon my sandwich. There was a segment I wanted to see again.

I fast-forwarded through the first twenty minutes, which dealt with well-known tenets of Darwin's theory of evolution. Although there was no new information in this portion of the film for me, it did remind me how basic principles in this area of study are so frequently misconstrued, even by those who accept as legitimate science Darwin's original hypothesis and the tremendous body of related subsequent research.

For example, people still believe that the theory of evolution posits that we evolved directly from apes. It does not.

Humans and apes did, however, share a common evolutionary ancestor, a now extinct species that lived about thirteen million years ago. Ongoing mutations of that species' DNA eventually resulted in genetic lines that produced orangutans, gorillas, chimpanzees, bonobos, and humans.

Further down the evolutionary line, after the apes had split off, there was another significant common ancestor species, a tribe of hominids from which all humans would ultimately descend. That species lived around six million years ago. Only one of its progeny, however, was successful in avoiding extinction: *Homo sapiens*, the name we have given to ourselves, from the Latin *homo* meaning "man" and *sapiens* meaning "wise" or "rational."

But another branch stemming from that same common ancestor culminated in one of the most misunderstood of our extinct cousins: *Homo neanderthalensis*, a group more commonly known as the Neanderthals. It was the portion of the documentary concerning Neanderthal life and culture that I wanted to view again.

In books and films, Neanderthals were for years portrayed as savage brutes, with sloping foreheads, huge brow ridges, and small brains. But the facial differences between our species and theirs were far subtler, and Neanderthal brains were as large or larger than ours. Their brains did, however, differentiate to focus more on pragmatic survival skills and less on cognitive thought and reasoning.

Whereas we share 98.7 percent of our DNA with chimpanzees, recent studies suggest that we share as much as 99.84 percent with the extinct tribe of Neanderthal humans.

They were a fascinating and endearing bunch.

Evidence shows incontrovertibly that Neanderthals manufactured and utilized an array of surprisingly sophisticated tools, employed fire for cooking, lived in shelters, and made the clothing they wore. They skillfully used weapons to hunt large animals, and also gathered plant foods to supplement their diets. They even played music; a recently discovered flute constructed from the hollow femur bone of a juvenile bear attests to this remarkable fact.

But most startling was the compassion Neanderthals displayed toward members of their tribe. Neanderthals buried their dead. There was no practical need for that behavior because scavenging carnivores would have quickly devoured corpses left out in the elements. Excavations have discovered Neanderthal graves marked with symbolic offerings such as flowers. No other animal or early human species engaged in that sort of ritualistic behavior.

A number of Neanderthal skeletons have been unearthed revealing individuals who were crippled, deformed, blind, paralyzed, or missing limbs. Older tribe members who had lost all their teeth have been found as well. These afflicted humans could not possibly have survived on their own, yet their bones clearly establish that they endured for years with these disabilities. The only explanation is that Neanderthals cared for their sick and incapacitated tribe members, where necessary carrying them about or chewing food for them.

As I watched this segment for the second time, I was once again moved by the kindness demonstrated by these primitive people, and was painfully reminded how, for so much of my own life, I was utterly incapable of displaying even a fraction of that sort of humanity to the people around me. My mother was harsh when she called me insular and uncaring. But she was accurate.

As a boy I obsessed over the shortcomings I perceived in people like my brother, or the girl with Down syndrome, but my only intervention was to fight off those who mocked them, making a show of my own power. I never once made an effort to get to know the afflicted themselves, to interact intimately with them as people. They were the "other"—I had a fear of contagion.

Later, in business, although I was always beloved by my employees, whom I treated well, I made a science of exploiting the weaknesses and vulnerabilities I perceived in my peers and competitors, and gloated when I was successful in doing so. It has taken me so long to get beyond that.

I have come quite a ways, but am still not nearly where I'd wish to be. Late at night, when I cannot fall asleep, I still sometimes fantasize about those old conquests, and viscerally experience the adrenaline rush of my triumphs.

The primitive Neanderthals undoubtedly experienced joy in their own triumphs, yet still found time to nurture and support the frailest among them. Is it fair that they went extinct, ultimately unable to compete with a more cunning and cognitively gifted human tribe?

It is not.

But that is also not what happened. Their story had a far more ambiguous conclusion.

The Neanderthals somehow discovered the same stratagem employed by two of the spiritual disciplines that resonate so powerfully with me today: Jiu-jitsu teaches that you never attempt to overpower your assailant. Instead, you yield and become one with his force and momentum. Similarly, meditation teaches that you cannot fight your way to illumination. Only when you surrender, and empty yourself, does universal consciousness finally fill your vessel.

The kind and gentle Neanderthals thrived in Europe and Western Asia for several hundred thousand years. They abruptly and mysteriously went extinct about thirty thousand years ago, but not before they coexisted for a period of time with our ancient ancestors, early *Homo sapiens*, who had left Africa and begun colonizing Europe and Asia about sixty thousand years ago.

The Neanderthals could not overpower or outthink the *Homo sapiens* who invaded their territories. And in some instances, we *Homo sapiens* probably just slaughtered the Neanderthals we found in our midst.

But during those thirty thousand years of coexistence prior to the

Neanderthals' demise, there were occasional primitive souls who were drawn more to love than to conquest. These remarkable individuals interbred across the two competing species. They produced children who continued to breed and contribute to the gene pool. So, in the end, the Neanderthals did not perish. They yielded, and became a small part of us.

Scientists now postulate that most modern humans of European or Asian descent possess genomes that are between 1 and 4 percent Neanderthal in origin. Their traits are in us.

I often wonder to what extent kindness and generosity are inherent in those specific genes. As I continue to work on my spiritual self, I hope to someday fully tap into the unrealized well of compassion within me. When I do, I will not know from which ancient forebear it emanates. It will not matter then. I will be one with all of them.

———

The months following the fire that destroyed Emmanuel's shop were trying. I had graduated high school but deferred any thought of college so that I could work with Emmanuel to open a new store.

Ostensibly, he and I went out each morning to inspect vacant storefronts that might serve well for his new shop. If we found one that looked promising, we'd park nearby and count the people who passed in either direction for half an hour, to gauge how much business might be generated through foot traffic. If the initial count reached a certain threshold, we'd repeat the counting exercise at specific times during the morning and afternoon to compare with other sites.

But Emmanuel seemed listless and preoccupied. He found something wrong with every location. I suspected that he did not really want to open a new business.

More likely, his mind was on Rachel, whose physiological and emotional decline had hastened. It was now impossible to hide, and Emmanuel finally gathered David and me together to inform us of what had already become painfully obvious. In hushed tones and guarded language, Emmanuel explained to us that Rachel was very sick.

David asked if she was going to die. Emmanuel said he didn't know but he hoped not. He was not at all convincing in that assertion. I inquired as to what she was suffering from. While Emmanuel was willing to acknowledge that it was cancer, he refused to be any more specific. He only said that both David and I needed to be on especially good behavior, and support her in any way we could.

Emmanuel now tried to spend as much time as possible with Rachel. After squandering a few hours each morning cursorily considering and rejecting potential sites for the new shop, he'd rush back home to be with her. He'd find her either in bed in our flat, or upstairs with Eve, reclining on the living room couch.

Rachel was frequently listless and disoriented. I assumed she had been prescribed more powerful pain medication, perhaps morphine. She had by now lost a frightening amount of weight, and sometimes seemed barely recognizable.

Emmanuel remained insistent on not revealing details about the type of cancer from which she was suffering, and Rachel rarely acknowledged any pain she might be feeling. But on a few occasions, when she was sitting alone with Eve and unaware that I could see them, Rachel would let out a soft moan and grasp her abdominal area.

David spent time with her when he could after school, if she was awake. They would sit together, whispering and cuddling. These seemed like the only times that both David and Rachel were truly happy.

I attempted on a few occasions to approach my mother and have a brief conversation. But there was no longer any connection between us—the encounters were unbearably awkward and I finally ceased trying.

It was impossible to know whether I had caused Rachel's illness. My attempts to telepathically transmit healing energy had clearly failed, and it was by now obvious to me that my transmissions had been designed to assuage my own guilt, rather than to help someone I loved.

Emmanuel sustained the pretense of searching for a new workplace for months, exploiting Irving and Eve's largesse. I overheard snippets of whispered conversations between Rachel and her sister that convinced me that our family was no longer paying rent, nor even contributing to the food budget for the house. Rachel's illness coupled with the tragedy of Emmanuel losing his business had rendered our dependent status legitimate in the eyes of my aunt and uncle.

But none of this seemed right to me.

I wanted to be a more integral part of Emmanuel's new business, and I had postponed entering college to help get the enterprise going, giving me a sense of urgency to move the process forward. I envisioned that once the store was open and we had an initial period to settle in, I could work there by day and get my degree via evening classes at the City College of New York. CCNY's campus was in the upper part of Manhattan, not far from the Bronx by subway, and it offered free tuition to city residents who qualified academically. My understanding was that it had an excellent engineering department.

Emmanuel's procrastination about the shop got me pondering, though. What if there was more to his hesitation than just Rachel's illness and the need to get past the trauma of the fire? What if he sensed intuitively that there wasn't an especially lucrative future in a small television and radio repair shop? He would feel frightened and stymied. Radio and television repair was all he knew how to do.

The more I thought about it, the more I became convinced that not only was this precisely what Emmanuel was thinking, but he was undoubtedly correct. Moving the same small repair operation to a storefront in a nicer neighborhood like Riverdale would make the job a bit more pleasant and marginally more profitable, but in the end it would only provide enough to minimally sustain the family.

We could do more.

I secretly envisioned a much larger store, one that stocked an array of high-quality but reasonably priced televisions, radios, phonographs, tape recorders, and any other electronic equipment that customers might want. Emmanuel and I certainly understood the workings of these sorts of products. We could offer a full-service package; we'd deliver and install the items, repair them if they broke, even put up and align rooftop antennas for optimal television reception.

For a couple of weeks, I examined this idea from every angle, searching for shortcomings and potential obstacles. It seemed absolutely accomplishable. There was some risk involved, of course, but that was true of any new endeavor. Stores like this were going to exist. Why couldn't we own one of them?

Finally, I brought the idea up to Emmanuel. I anticipated that he'd react one of two ways—either become angry and reject it out of hand, or see it as a possibility and ask for some time to ruminate on it.

The reaction I received, however, was utterly bewildering.

Emmanuel just stared at me blankly. I had pitched the idea with great enthusiasm, including vivid descriptions of what the store might look like and how we'd lay it out. I was met with dead eyes and an expressionless face. After a long and uncomfortable period of silence, Emmanuel bowed his head and chuckled softly.

"Sammy," he said. "Oh, Sammy." Emmanuel addressed me now with more warmth and affection than I had ever experienced with him. "I'm sorry, Sammy. What a dream. What a lovely dream, for you and me. The two of us, working together in a place like that. You know, I'm very proud of you. But your idea, Sammy, it's impossible. You don't understand that because you're young and eager. I used to be like that. But this dream, lovely as it is, it can't be done."

"Why not?" I asked.

"Do you know how much it would cost to open a store like that, Sammy? You have to stock it. You have to buy all those televisions, and radios, and what were those other gadgets you talked about? Phonographs? Tape recorders? You need a variety of each type of thing, and you need to stock at least one or two of every item. We don't have that kind of money, Sammy. I wish we did."

"What about the insurance payment?"

"It was a nice payment. It's enough to open the kind of repair shop we had, replace the tools and spare parts that we lost. But not much more. I'm sorry, Sammy. I feel like I'm a disappointment to you. Holding you back."

"No," I said. "Please don't think that."

"You're a good boy, Sammy. Don't worry. We'll look harder. We'll find a new location for the repair shop soon."

Paul O'Rourke was happy to see me but did seem surprised.

He looked very sharp in a crisp blue blazer and a patterned tie. I was wearing a sweatshirt and dungarees, and felt a bit out of place.

Paul was waiting on a customer, fitting a fidgety young boy into a new black suit, marking the cuffs and the inseam with white tailor's chalk. I heard Paul chatting with the boy's mother as he worked. From their conversation I surmised that the woman had a daughter who was getting married. The young lad seemed horrendously uncomfortable with being forced to wear a suit. Paul and the boy's mother were good-naturedly reassuring him how handsome he'd look at the big celebration.

Paul had noticed me when I entered the boys'-wear department. He nodded almost imperceptibly and glanced over to a corner where I waited quietly until he had completed the sale. It was just prior to noon. There were no other customers around. I hoped he'd get a lunch break soon.

"Sammy!" he said. "What a surprise! It's great to see you." He shook my hand and slapped my right shoulder warmly. "What's up?"

"I have some stuff I'd like to talk about," I said. "Do you have a lunch break soon?"

"I'm here alone today, so I'm not taking lunch. I have a sandwich—I can sneak bites off it behind the counter. But it's dead here today. I have time to talk. What's on your mind?"

"It's about business," I said. "I think you know more than I do about this kind of thing. How people go about it."

"Sure thing, Sammy. What's the situation?"

"You know that my father and I need to open a new store. Because of the fire. We'll move it to a different neighborhood, of course. But here's the thing. Emmanuel is dead set on opening the same little kind of repair shop. I think we can do more. You know, open a bigger store that sells televisions, radios, all kinds of electronic equipment. It would be full service, with delivery, installation, repairs, the works. What do you think of that idea?"

"It's a great plan," Paul said. "If you had the right location and approach, you could make it work big-time."

"I think so too," I said. "But Emmanuel says we don't have the money to stock it with inventory. Don't other people have this same kind of problem? What do they do?"

"They get loans." He shrugged, as if it was so obvious that it hardly required stating. "That's what banks are for. Who can open a big store with just cash on hand? Not anyone I know. Almost everyone who opens a business gets a loan."

"So you think *we* could get one?"

"You could try. You'll never know if you can or can't unless you give it a shot. The worst they can do is say no, and then you're no worse off than you are now."

"Would you be willing to lay this out for my father?" I asked.

"Me?"

"Yes. If he hears it from me, he's not going to even take it seriously. But he seemed impressed with you that time he met you."

"Sure. Okay. If you think it'll help."

———

I had told Emmanuel only that Paul was coming over and wanted to talk with us both. When my father pushed for details, I said it was about business. I wouldn't go any further.

Paul arrived directly from work, still dressed in a suit and tie, which I thought lent him an air of additional authority. Together, we laid out the idea of trying to secure a loan for a bigger business. It took us several minutes. Paul seemed especially persuasive.

When we were done, Emmanuel smiled, turned to me, and spoke very softly. "This is what you brought him here to tell me?"

"Yes," I said. "What do you think?"

"Well, Sammy, I appreciate how much concern you have about this and about taking care of our family. And, Paul, you seem like a hardworking young man with a good head on your shoulders, and you came all the way here to talk to us, and I appreciate that too. But this loan idea. It's too risky. What if the business fails? Then I have to pay back all that money with no income. And what if the business gets off to a slow start? All my profits will go to paying back the loan, and I won't make anything. I've never borrowed money from anyone for anything in my life. I don't think it's a wise thing to do."

Paul nodded sympathetically. "I see your points, Mr. Baron. This is new to you. But I can tell you that lots of people do this successfully. There's always going to be some degree of risk in anything you take on. But at least this way you give yourself the opportunity to do something much bigger."

Emmanuel's face softened into a set of furrows that were sad and knowing. He spoke quietly, staring downward:

"There's something you boys don't understand. It's about failure. If I try this, it could fail. I've experienced that. I never want to experience that again. There is nothing in this world worse than the feeling of having failed at something that you really wanted. It's too painful. It's better to stick with what's safe. You protect yourself. Believe me, boys, you have to avoid failure at all costs. It can kill you."

"But if you don't at least try, how can you succeed?" asked Paul.

"If I don't try, I can't fail," my father answered.

I said, "I read an article once. It was about the most successful men in the country. The one thing they all had in common was that they had all failed several times, some almost catastrophically, before they found what worked."

"Those are different kind of people," Emmanuel said. "They're not like us, Sammy. They're the big *machers* who can talk their way into anything.

We can't do that. People like you and me get crushed if we try to play in that league. Listen to me, boys. Leave this alone. Protect yourselves. Don't fail like I did."

"What did you fail at?" I asked. "You never talked about it."

"No, I can't talk about it. What's the point? It's done. I am who I am." Emmanuel rose. "You boys take care," he said.

———————⌇———————

Rachel had been hospitalized for several weeks. Prior to that, she had grown very frail, and began experiencing occasional episodes of disorientation. She was admitted to the same hospital in the Bronx where she had given birth to David and me.

She initially shared a room with an obese woman who had horrible sores and splotches of dark pigmentation over most of her skin. That woman died a couple of weeks after my mother was admitted. Rachel mentioned to Emmanuel that the two of them had never spoken.

Eve and Emmanuel visited Rachel every day. David spent time with her after school and on weekends when he was able to find someone to drive him there and back. My encounters with Rachel were far less frequent, always polite, but very perfunctory and brief.

One evening, Emmanuel, Eve, David, and I arrived at the hospital together. The four of us had a short visit with Rachel, and then Emmanuel asked David and me to wait outside, while he, Eve, and my mother discussed private matters.

In the waiting room, David pulled from his pocket the miniature boxed Chinese checker set Emmanuel had bought him. David never seemed to tire of playing. Rachel, and more recently Eve, often indulged him in games during breaks from his homework assignments.

Chinese checkers, the creation of an American game company and not even remotely Chinese in origin, was a popular children's game then, far simpler than checkers or chess, requiring minimal strategy.

As had been the case dozens of times when David and I were banished together to the waiting room, he begged me to play Chinese checkers with him. I found the game so simplistic that it became tedious almost immediately. And David's inept grasp of even the most basic tactics assured that he never once came close to beating me. Yet he was always eager to play, and attacked every game with the same optimistic energy.

I won the first two games easily. During the third game, one of my mother's doctors entered her room and closed the curtain around Rachel's bed. That encouraged me, because generally when a doctor made his rounds, visitors were asked to leave. I thought we might get to go home a bit earlier.

But Emmanuel and Eve remained there with the doctor, so David and I played on. By the time we began the fifth game, I was so bored that I decided to see if, in addition to playing with David, I could solve a system of algebraic equations with three variables completely in my head. I had brought my old high school algebra textbook with me to pass the time— equations were enjoyable puzzles. I had pencil and paper too, but I kept those in my pocket, and picked a system of equations to begin attacking cerebrally while I played the game with David.

The algebra challenge proved fascinating, and took intense concentration to solve. David had to good-naturedly shout "Come on already!" several times because I had become so preoccupied that I forgot to make my move on the board. By the time I finished solving the system of equations and checked the state of the game in earnest, I realized that David was on the verge of beating me. In only a few moves he would be victorious.

But after studying the board intently, I came upon an ingenious line of play, one that might stymie David long enough to allow me to catch up, and possibly win. It depended on David not consistently finding his strongest move. I considered that possibility quite likely.

I hesitated, though. *Perhaps I should just let David win.* He had never beaten me at Chinese checkers, and in fact had never defeated me at anything else that I could recall either. I looked into his eyes, and he seemed so excited at the prospect of finally doing so.

I decided to cede him the victory.

But just as I was about to, at the last moment before I made the move that would assure my demise, I stopped. I told myself that David wouldn't want to win that way. He'd want to truly earn it. If I lost intentionally, he'd be insulted.

So I executed the strategy I had devised. As expected, David faltered, and I won as always.

The moment the game ended, David's expression withered and his whole body appeared to go limp. I was surprised—he sometimes seemed more disappointed to lose than at other times, but this reaction was extreme.

I had misconstrued the entire situation. I completely failed to grasp that on this occasion, the possibility of his winning was so imminent that he fully expected it to happen. When it didn't, the blow was especially devastating. He was on the verge of tears. I now wished that I had gone ahead and allowed him to win, but there was no way for me to retrieve the moment.

As I sat silently with David, miserably wishing that I had made the outcome different, the doctor exited Rachel's suite. He walked somberly through the waiting room and into the hallway. His head was down. He seemed especially pensive.

Emmanuel and Eve trudged behind him. Eve was crying. Emmanuel's face was ashen.

I immediately intuited what had happened.

The doctor had just ended my mother's life.

In those days, such transactions between physicians and families took place regularly. There were no grand debates about euthanasia in the press, no overarching scrutiny in the medical community. The deed was done quietly, by a doctor who had come to know the patient and the patient's family. The physician increased the dosage of pain medicine in the intravenous flow—the end followed quickly. Other hospital staff undoubtedly knew it had been done, but respected the decision.

Emmanuel now came toward us and knelt in front of David and me. He put a hand on each of our shoulders.

His voice broke and was barely audible. He said, "I'm so sorry, boys. Your mother just passed away."

David began to sob uncontrollably. Emmanuel strained to remain stoic, but tears tracked slowly down his cheeks. Eve stood off to the side, still crying as well.

I watched the tableau in a numb and detached state.

After observing for a time, I began to once again ponder whether I had caused my mother's illness—and if I had, what cosmic retribution might now await me. I momentarily wondered whether the doctor's intervention might mitigate my culpability; any chance for my telepathic efforts to reverse the effects of the disease had been short-circuited by his action. But I soon concluded that my attempts at therapeutic psychic outreach had long ago proved themselves futile. The doctor's intrusion had no meaningful impact on that extant metaphysical truth.

***

It was a warm summer evening. Eve cooked dinner for the family, as she had every night since my mother's death. It had become our ritual to light a *yahrzeit* candle and set it at Rachel's place at the dinner table before we began eating. Eve said it represented Rachel's spirit, so Rachel could still be among us.

David, Emmanuel, and Eve, and to some extent Irving and my cousins, all seemed to exhibit a deep sadness each time that candle was lit. For some reason I did not. All I felt was gnawing trepidation over the possibility of cosmic sanction for my role in my mother's death, although the immediacy of that fear had faded as the days since the funeral wore on.

Inwardly, I was a bit confused, and perhaps ashamed, regarding my lack of emotion. But rationally, I wondered if such ongoing remorse wasn't an indication of weakness, a detriment to moving forward with life. We were, after all, still alive, even if Rachel was not.

We had a quiet meal.

A few minutes after dinner I found Uncle Irving sitting alone on his favorite rocking chair on the front porch, reading the Yiddish paper. He was smoking a fat cigar and savoring his glass of schnapps. I asked if he had a moment to talk.

"Sure, Sammy," he said cheerfully in his thick Hungarian accent. "Go inside and pour yourself a few sips of schnapps. Then come back out and join me. We'll talk like men."

I complied. When I sat next to him, he clinked glasses, and I began sipping on the schnapps. I was surprised at how strong it tasted while being cloyingly fruity at the same time. I could see how that enforced a leisurely drinking pace. Downing it could be painful.

Irving said, "What's on your mind, Samuel?"

"I wanted to talk to you about my family's new shop," I said. "I realize that Emmanuel hasn't done much to move that along."

"Don't worry about that," he said reassuringly. "You and your dad should take as long as you need. Look, the two of you have had a lot on your shoulders. With the funeral, sitting shiva, trying to keep your brother, David, from losing his mind—it's been hard. Maybe it's not time yet to find a new business."

"That's very kind of you, Uncle Irving," I said, "but actually I wanted to discuss something more specific. An idea I have. You're a successful businessman and I thought you could help with this."

Irving seemed pleased with my characterization of him. "What's your idea, Sammy?"

"We're never going to get rich with a little neighborhood repair shop like the one we had," I said. "And in a few years, a shop like that might be completely out of date. We can do a lot better, Uncle Irving. I have an idea for a much bigger store, one that sells televisions, and radios, and other electronic appliances. Fair prices, and full top-to-bottom service. We'll deliver the stuff, install it, repair it, and whatever else people need, like running cable, putting up antennas, the works. We'll have a big selection for different price ranges."

My uncle was nodding positively. I continued: "There are going to be big stores like this competing for customers in the future. You know it and I know it. Why shouldn't we own one of them?"

Irving smiled and held out his glass to toast again. "You think like a real businessman, Samuel Baron. I like your idea. How can your uncle Irving help?"

"I laid the idea out for Emmanuel, and he's afraid. He's afraid of taking out a bank loan. And frankly, just afraid of failing. But we could make it work. I know it. I'm in this thing full bore. I'll do whatever it takes to make it successful. If we offer good products and high-quality service at honest prices, people will see that and come back for more."

"I agree with you, Sammy. What's Manny so scared about?"

"I think it's the possibility of not being able to pay back the bank in time and losing everything."

"That *is* a concern, Sammy."

"That's why I was wondering, Uncle Irving, would *you* be willing to loan us the money? My father might be willing to take on the challenge if the loan came from a relative."

Irving took a couple of long puffs on his cigar as he cogitated. He sipped his glass of schnapps and swished the sweet liquid around his tongue before replying.

"I want you to listen to what I'm going to say to you, Sammy. This is important, and if you want to be successful as a businessman, it's something you must never forget. What did I say to you when you came out here tonight? Do you remember? I said we'll talk like men. Do you remember that?"

"I remember."

"When you're dealing with people, even people you don't like"—he took another sip—"*especially* people you don't like, the most important thing is letting them keep their self-respect. Whatever you offer them, they have to be able to keep their dignity. *Farshtey?*"

"Okay," I said.

"And I like your father. So it's not only important from a business outlook that I don't disrespect him, but personal even more. Right?"

"Right."

"So, I'm not going to offer Manny a loan. He'd see it as charity. He probably wouldn't take it, but even if he did, he'd feel lousy. Like a failure. But that doesn't mean that I don't like your idea. I like it a lot."

"So, what then?" I asked.

"How about I be a partner? A silent partner of course," he laughed. "I don't know from electronics. I'm a grocer."

I chuckled and sipped on the schnapps. "Wow," I said, "a partner? That's an interesting idea. How would that work exactly?"

"I put up some money, your father puts up some money. We all go in together. The three of us. I don't work at the store, but my money helps pay for the inventory, the rent, fixtures, whatever. So I take a portion of the profits, whatever they are. A percentage."

"Forever?"

"Ha ha!" he exclaimed. "You *are* a shrewd businessman, Mr. Baron! No, not forever. Unless I'm dealing with a *putz* who wants to keep paying me forever." He laughed heartily. "No, say for two or three years. Enough to make back my initial investment and show a nice profit for myself. Of course, if the store needs some emergency cash along the way, I help with that too. Until you buy me out. Then you own the whole thing."

"And what percent profit would you propose to take, and how much more than your initial investment would the buyout price be?" I inquired.

Irving smiled broadly. "Such questions! These are numbers, Sammy. We can settle on numbers that everyone agrees to once we have the approach set." My uncle took a big swig of schnapps and laughed loudly after he swallowed. "And I'll get a hell of lot better deal with your father than I would with you. You're a shark, young Samuel Baron!"

I laughed and took another couple of sips.

"Thank you, Uncle Irving. It'll be great having you as a partner," I said. "But how do we break this to Emmanuel? He'll be angry if he thinks I came to you behind his back and got this thing rolling. He wouldn't go for it then."

"Good boy, Sammy. You see, you already learned what I tried to teach you before. You're worried about Emmanuel keeping his self-respect. And you're right. He wouldn't like it and he wouldn't go for it. So, I'll go to him myself. Without you. I'll just say I overheard you talking about this idea to someone. And it made sense, and I wanted in. Don't worry. I'll make him believe the whole thing was his decision."

I knew that Uncle Irving could accomplish that. "Fair enough," I said. I held out my glass. "*L'chaim!*"

"*L'chaim!*" he toasted. "To our success!"

Jake's ashes were delivered to me several weeks after his death.

When the UPS driver rang my doorbell, Sapphire could not hear it. But the moment she saw me spring up and walk toward the door, she knew it was a delivery. For so many years, she had signaled me, through excited barking and jumping, when a delivery was imminent. She used to do it before the doorbell rang—she'd hear the familiar sound of the truck's engine, the squeal of its handbrake, its sliding door slamming shut.

Now her barks were signaled by my own body language. Her attempts at jumping barely lifted her off the ground. But her enthusiasm was as sincere as it had always been. Did she realize that alerting me after I had already heard the bell was less useful to me? If she did, it didn't matter to her. Warning me of a delivery was her *job*. She did it to the best of her ability.

The corrugated shipping carton from the crematorium had been bruised somewhat in transit. I looked momentarily into the eyes of the deliveryman as he handed it to me. He had no idea it contained the remains of my closest friend. I smiled and wished him a good day.

I picked a special morning hike to spread Jake's ashes. I had, for several weeks, struggled to select a suitable resting place. I considered Mount Tamalpais in Marin County, Mount Diablo across the bay, and other iconic Bay Area sites. But none of these were trails that Sapphire and I frequented. In the end, Strawberry Hill in Golden Gate Park, where Sapphire and I hiked nearly every morning, and where I habitually practiced walking meditation, seemed the most fitting. We'd be in the presence of Jake's remains each time we visited, which was what I think he had in mind.

We went very early, just after sunrise. When we reached a lovely spot overlooking a heavily wooded hillside, I made certain we were alone, then removed the jar holding Jake's ashes from my backpack, unscrewed the lid, and watched as the ashes floated down the steep slope.

As Sapphire and I resumed our walk, I thought about the frailty of our corporeal existence. How we go through the cycle of gestation, birth, life, and death. We all feel immortal and invincible at first. But in the end, the allotment seems painfully brief.

Sapphire was off leash. I turned and watched her labor up the hill behind me. She walked so slowly now. Her time was nearly done. My lifespan was far longer than hers, but still short and fragile when compared to the rocks and trees that surrounded us on the trail.

I tried to imagine Sapphire when she was not yet born, when she was just a fetus, a potential life. Everything then lay ahead for her.

I too had been a fetus.

I recalled, from photographs I had seen, that human fetuses displayed physical traits inherited from all classes of vertebrates—common ancestors going back millions of years. An old, now discredited scientific theory speculated that the human embryo and fetus "recapitulated" all the various stages of human evolution in the womb. It is fascinating to see how the unborn human does appear to resemble fish or tadpoles early on, then becomes more reptilian, and finally mammalian. Regardless of whether an actual recapitulation has occurred, the physical resemblance indicates undeniable commonalities.

But just as every human embryo possesses inherited *physical* traits, there undoubtedly are *cerebral* legacies passed down as well.

We know that for many animals, instincts are hardwired, translating into behaviors that are critical for their survival. What instincts—or as Jung might have put it, "archetypes"—are hardwired into our human psyches?

Some of these inherited cerebral proclivities seemed in stark conflict with one another. I recalled an article I had come across on birds. It was accompanied by a photograph, which remained vividly etched in my mind. A dying chick, ignored by its parents, lay suffering on the ground, while its sibling, standing just to its side, was being fed from its mother's mouth. That photograph made me cry, yet pulled me back and made me stare at it over and over. These birds habitually lay two eggs. When times are good, the parents nourish and raise both chicks. But when food is scarce, they feed only the more robust offspring—and intentionally allow the runt to starve. Although it appears harsh, in evolutionary terms it makes perfect sense. The birds maximize the possibility of propagating the species by assuring that at least one chick survives to adulthood. In nearly all animal species, those physically unable to compete are eliminated.

But this tendency is clearly contradicted in the behavior of early hominids, Neanderthals in particular. Aiding their disabled was a priority; something in Neanderthal consciousness made them do it, even though it contributed nothing to the propagation of their species.

Today, our *Homo sapiens* DNA seems to contain bits and pieces of both attitudes. My father inherited, or at least chose to exhibit, more of the tendencies of the birds. When I was young he focused on me, neglecting my brother, whose prospects he perceived as limited. My mother, though, rest her soul, was the Neanderthal, so busy helping the disabled member of the tribe that she soon had no time for the others.

I had never, until that moment, cried over my mother's death. Now I cried, thinking about Rachel. I recalled how nurturing she was toward David and Emmanuel, both of whom needed that so much. It made clearer who my mother actually had been.

That morning, after distributing Jake's ashes, I finally forgave her. And perhaps myself as well.

When I finished crying, I pondered again the contradictions inherent in the hardwired human psyche. I was reminded that all of corporeal existence is riddled with these seeming contradictions, a reality defined by persistent duality in everything we perceive.

I knew from personal experience, however, that all such duality would be resolved in the unified, nonrational state of illumination brought on by meditation. That knowledge now spurred me to return to that sensibility, and extinguished in me any need for further rational thought that morning.

It took me only moments to slip into the meditative state.

17.
Antennas

MY FATHER EXHIBITED a barely discernable swagger as he announced to me that he had convinced Uncle Irving to become his partner in our new business venture.

Emmanuel explained that this would enable us to open a bigger store, somewhere in Yonkers, just north of Riverdale. It was important, he told me, that we immediately intensify our search for a new store location.

When I asked him why he had chosen Yonkers, he acknowledged that it was Irving's suggestion. Riverdale, according to Uncle Irving, had very expensive property costs, and the businesses in Riverdale tended to be small personal shops, like Irving's grocery and delicatessen. But big stores in Yonkers regularly attracted Riverdale shoppers, as well as patrons from all over the Bronx and Westchester.

So, with a renewed sense of enthusiasm, my father and I began monitoring potential store locations in Yonkers, sitting together in Emmanuel's car for hours, counting the number of people walking by whatever storefront we had under surveillance that day. He'd count the people passing directly in front of the store—I was assigned to count the people on the opposite side of the street.

In the evening, we'd pick up Uncle Irving after he closed his grocery for the day, and the three of us would drive back out to a promising location, to review our counts and get Irving's input. Irving knew the neighborhoods of Yonkers quite well. He and Emmanuel would sit up front, and although I at first resented always being relegated to the back seat, I soon found that it gave me an opportunity to monitor their conversations almost like watching a movie. I inferred a great deal from their facial expressions and body language.

Regardless of the property we were examining, or details concerning the level of foot traffic or the nature of surrounding businesses, Emmanuel invariably raised the same concern to Irving. "You need to tell me who lives around here," Emmanuel would demand. "I don't want my store in a place surrounded by *Schvartzes* and Puerto Ricans. Those animals destroyed my first store and the whole neighborhood in East Tremont. One of them almost killed Sammy. If there's any of that *drek* around here, we need to look someplace else."

Irving's reassuring responses followed a familiar pattern as well. "You're right, Manny," he'd say. "The *Schvartzes* and Puerto Ricans are animals. Thank God we got none of them in Riverdale. But Yonkers is pretty clean too. Very few of 'em here. And if they're up here, they behave themselves. Not enough of 'em to make a stink."

Whenever I heard them lapse into this tiresome palaver, my mind always drifted to Esther, the beautiful African American librarian whose whereabouts had become unknown to me. It seemed so sad that this sort of thinking undoubtedly tarnished the persona of even an alluring and charismatic person such as she. I was certain that there had to be many other members of those communities who were fine citizens. I wondered why entrenched powers considered it politically advantageous to marginalize these decent people.

Nonetheless, I was curious to know if Uncle Irving was just placating my father, or if Yonkers' demographic makeup corroborated Irving's assertions. A trip to the library confirmed that Irving was accurate— according to the 1960 census, Yonkers' population was 95.8 percent white.

Many of the available storefronts in Yonkers seemed like good candidates for our new electronics business. One evening, as the three of us examined a particularly attractive location, Irving casually inquired of my father, "So, did you tell the kid about the buyout plan?"

"No," said Emmanuel. "We haven't gotten to that yet."

"Well, you should tell him, Manny. It's his future we're talking about."

"What's this about a buyout?" I asked from the back seat.

"I'll explain it to you when we get home," muttered Emmanuel, obviously annoyed at Irving for having brought the matter up.

Later that evening, after dinner, in our small ground-floor apartment of Irving's house, I again pressed Emmanuel for the details of the agreement that he and Uncle Irving had hammered out.

"All right, Sammy," he said. "I'll tell you about the agreement." He whispered in my ear, "Just go make sure David's not awake. I don't want him to hear this."

I tiptoed into the bedroom that David and I shared. David was sound asleep.

My father had taken a seat at the kitchen table. I joined him there. "David's asleep," I said.

"All right, here's the deal." Emmanuel leaned closer and spoke in hushed tones. "We buy Irving out three years after we open the store. During those first three years, while he's a part owner, he keeps twenty percent of the profits every month, not counting anything we reinvest in new stock or improvements. The buyout price is ten percent over his initial investment.

"Now listen carefully, Sammy; this part involves you. You're going to make a good salary in this new store. Not like in the little shop back in East Tremont where I threw you a few bucks when you helped me out. You're a grown man now, and Irving and me expect a lot out of you. So after three years, it's *you* who's going to buy out most of Irving's share. He put in more money than me, but not that much more. I'm just paying him back enough to make up the difference. So when we're done, you and I are equal partners who made equal investments in the store. *Farshtey?*"

"So basically, I'm buying his share and becoming the other partner. Is that what you're saying?" I asked.

"That's right," said Emmanuel. "It may take you a while to pay him off, but he's willing to work that out with you."

"And I'll be an equal partner?"

"After three years, and once you pay him off. Yes, you'll be a partner. I expect you to work your ass off, Sammy, and save your money so you can buy him out quick. This is a big store and a lot of work. I'm giving you a big opportunity here."

I was elated. "I'll give it everything I got," I said. "How exactly did you come up with this plan?"

"This is just the way things are done in business, Sammy. You got a lot to learn."

Despite that condescending assertion, I doubted this partnership idea was his.

A few nights later, I caught up with Uncle Irving on the porch after dinner. He was, as I expected, in his favorite rocking chair, with a cigar and a glass of schnapps. He invited me to sit and drink schnapps with him.

"I'm very excited about the plan to make me a partner in three years, Uncle Irving," I said. "Thank you."

"You're welcome," he said. "Now you gotta earn it."

"Was this your idea?" I asked.

"Of course," he said, smiling. He took a long puff on his fat cigar. "Emmanuel liked my plan because he gets to keep more money instead of paying it back to me."

"I can see that," I said.

"But in the long run, Sammy, I did this for you. Now Manny will never be able to hold it over your head that you're not a real partner. Because you paid in, equal. And when tough decisions need to get made, when new ideas need to come into the business, that's when you'll thank me. He won't be able to shoot you down. You'll be an equal partner. And he'll have to listen to your ideas because they make sense. Oh, you'll have to pound him over the head with them for a while. But, Sammy, it's *your* ideas that are going to make this store a big success." He poked his cigar toward me for emphasis as he spoke. "Your father, he's a nice man. But you, Sammy, you're special. You're going to make me proud."

———————◡———————

My brother floundered severely after Rachel's death. He became oblivious to events going on around him. His grades in school plummeted.

On a couple of occasions, David's teacher asked my father to come in after school to talk to her. When Emmanuel returned home after each of those conversations, he slapped David around, yelling that David needed to shape up. Those beatings surprised me—I thought Emmanuel had written David off with respect to academic achievement. But I noted that during both of my father's tirades, he screamed out the same thing: "You're humiliating me! You're making the school think that I can't take care of you with your mother gone!"

My aunt Eve took Emmanuel and me aside one night and suggested that David was trying, in the only way he knew, to insulate himself from the pain of losing his mother. He needed time to work through it. Emmanuel rejected her perspective.

"That doesn't fly in life!" he yelled. "You got to get up, dust yourself off, and get back in the game. You can't wallow in self-pity."

"He's doing the best he can," said Eve.

"He has to do better," shouted Emmanuel as he stormed out of the room.

I started to leave too, but Eve grasped me gently by the forearm.

"Stay a minute," she said. "We need to come to some agreements about David."

"What do you mean?" I asked.

"I've spoken to his teacher several times this past month," she said.

I was surprised. "Shouldn't the school be talking with my father?" I asked.

"They tried that for a while after your mom passed away. But, Sammy, you know that Emmanuel's not always a reasonable man. Before your mother died, she gave the school my phone number and suggested they call me if they weren't getting anywhere with your father."

"Really? I wasn't aware of that," I said.

"Neither is your father."

"He won't be happy about it."

"No, but he'll be *more* unhappy to see David keep failing. Your father's hitting him isn't doing any good. You understand that, don't you?

I chuckled dryly. "It's been obvious to me for a long time, Aunt Eve," I said, "that Emmanuel doesn't hit his kids because he thinks it'll do any good. He hits us because he's angry and he can't control himself." I thought for a moment. "Actually, that's not true. He *chooses* not to control himself. He never hit my mother. And he's never hit Uncle Irving, or any of his customers, or David's teachers, and he's been angry at every one of those people too. He hits David because he can get away with it."

"What do you do when he hits *you?*" Eve asked.

"He stopped hitting me," I said. "Ever since I broke that robber's arm in the East Tremont shop, he hasn't done it. A couple of times he came at me like he was going to, but when he saw I was ready for him, he just backed off. I think he's afraid to hit me now."

"Well, I'm glad to hear that, for your sake," Eve said. "But now you need to get him to stop hitting David, and convince him that David needs to be on a different path."

"Me? Why do *I* need to convince him, and what path are you talking about?"

Eve stepped closer and put her hand on my shoulder as she explained: "Look," she said, "David's teacher and the school principal told me that by all rights they should leave David back and make him go through eighth grade again. But he got left back once already, and they really don't like to leave a kid back twice, because it destroys their spirit and it screws them up socially."

"That makes sense," I said. "Leaving him back again would be bad for everybody."

"Right, Sammy. So, here's what the school suggested: instead of David taking ninth grade as part of junior high school the way most kids do, we can move him into a high school and have him take all four years there, ninth through twelfth. But here's the thing—it has to be a *vocational* high school. He'll learn a craft. Plumbing, car mechanics, machine work, whatever it is. That's something he might be able to do, and even feel proud about it. He's never going to make it in an academic program."

I tried to picture what Eve described. It presented problems.

"Aunt Eve," I said, "I don't think that would work. Not in our family. My father would find it humiliating to have his son in a vocational school, and Emmanuel's not the kind of person who'd be able to hide that from David or anyone else. All David would feel is shame."

"David's too fragile," she said. "That could be disastrous. But what other option is there, Sammy?"

I pondered. "David's turning sixteen in a few months," I said, still working out the details in my head. "Why not just let him drop out? It's legal to drop out of school if you're over sixteen. He can come work in the store with Emmanuel and me. He'll feel like he's contributing. It'll be just like a vocational program, but with his family."

"What on earth will he be able to do in a *store*?" asked Eve. "You certainly can't have him selling to customers, and I'm sure Emmanuel wouldn't let him near a cash register."

"There's a lot to do in a big store," I said. "He can take inventory, dust the floor samples, sweep and mop, help with deliveries, take things out to people's cars. He'd actually be helpful."

"But he'd see *you* doing so much more. And then what happens when you become a partner and he's left behind?"

"We're *all* going to have to deal with that scenario no matter what we do. Believe me, I've thought about that. It's not pretty, but it's the way it is."

Eve sighed and shook her head. "All right then, I guess your idea is the best alternative we have," she said. "But now you have to convince Emmanuel to let it happen."

"How about Uncle Irving and I do it together?" I asked.

"I'm afraid not, Sammy. Irving and I talked about it, and neither one of us belong in a conversation with Emmanuel about his son. You're on your own for this one."

I took a deep breath. "All right," I said. "But I'm going to have to tell him that you talked to David's teacher and the principal behind his back. He's going to be majorly pissed off at you."

Eve smiled and moved her hand from my shoulder to my cheek. "Why, Sammy! I've never heard you use a vulgar expression like that in my presence. You must be feeling a bit closer to me than you used to."

She gave me a soft, quick kiss, then turned and walked into the kitchen.

At first, it was difficult for me to assess whether the storefront we leased in Yonkers was quite as large as I had imagined it to be. I was accustomed to seeing stores fully equipped with aisles, shelving, counters, signage, and stock. Here, though, I was faced with a vacant expanse, with bare plaster walls full of screw and nail holes, a few tattered electrical outlets, and an asphalt floor partially covered with scraps of soiled industrial carpet. In the far back corner sat a rusted toilet and sink with no enclosure around them.

We began paying rent on the storefront immediately. Our motivation was strong to get the shop ready for opening day as quickly as possible, with the lowest possible interim expenditure.

We'd opt for some professional help later on, to lay down linoleum and install the many shelving units and fixtures, but for now, Emmanuel and I tackled tasks like patching the plaster, painting, and pulling up old carpet.

After work each day, we met with Uncle Irving and discussed various layouts for the store. Of the three of us, I was the most adept at envisioning spatial variations, and it fell to me to create scale drawings of our various ideas for the shop's design. Emmanuel's prime concern was that the cash register and counter be situated right by the entrance so no one could abscond with merchandise without paying. I found Uncle Irving to be a far more thoughtful discussion partner in considering the configuration from the perspective of potential customers, and trying to lay out the televisions, radios, and other electronic appliances in a manner that might render them most appealing for purchase.

Of all the manual tasks that Emmanuel and I undertook, painting the expansive ceiling was the most difficult. One afternoon, after hours standing on tall ladders with our arms stretched upward while paint drops spattered our hair and faces, Emmanuel and I took a break. We sat on the floor and ate sandwiches that Eve had packed for us. I thought about how hard and tiring this work was. An additional hand would be most helpful. It occurred to me that this might be the right time to have that talk about David. My brother had just turned sixteen, so the option of his dropping out of school and joining us at the store was now viable.

We got up and disposed of the wax paper and crumpled napkins from the sandwiches. We were about to resume work when I asked Emmanuel if we could take a couple of minutes to discuss something.

"OK, but make it fast," he said. "We got to get this first coat on the ceiling by tonight so it'll be dry and ready for a second coat tomorrow."

"I want to talk about David," I said.

"Since when are you interested in David?" he asked.

"Aunt Eve's been talking to his teachers," I said.

This assertion flabbergasted him. Emmanuel's eyes widened and he stared at me motionlessly for a moment as his anger welled.

"What the hell do you mean she's been talking to his teachers?" he demanded. "Who the hell is *she*?"

"His teachers didn't think they were getting anywhere talking to you," I said. I saw no need to mention that my mother had planted that seed.

"And you knew about this!" he screamed. He was transforming now, entering a lycanthropic frenzy. His face was burning red. His features grew distorted. He hunkered his body down like an animal about to pounce.

He came at me as I expected. His open right hand hurled itself at my jaw. I blocked the blow with a standard jiu-jitsu parry and stepped back.

"Don't do that again," I said.

"Who the hell are you to tell me what to do!" he shrieked hysterically. He came at me once more, his hand lashing out at me so hard that he momentarily rose up on his toes. This time I pivoted as I parried the blow, and grabbed the assaulting arm at the wrist and elbow. I feigned pulling the limb upward, but as soon as I felt resistance, I used his own momentum to yank his arm across my body and maneuver it into standing waki gatame, a powerful jiu-jitsu armlock. His seized right arm was now stretched rigid, palm down, both my hands clamped on his wrist. My left side and upper arm formed a vise that squeezed his captured limb above the elbow.

Waki gatame is ingenious and powerful. The pressure forces the now vanquished aggressor to lean forward and crouch awkwardly. His imprisoned arm can generate no power from that position, and his body is so precariously balanced that he can barely stand, much less counterattack.

I had practiced the armlock many times with Paul and learned to precisely calibrate the intensity of the hold. By leaning forward and bending my knees even slightly, I could increase the pain by degrees; dropping quickly to my knees would have snapped the bone cleanly. In competitive judo, waki gatame is a submission hold.

Increased fury was Emmanuel's initial reaction to being held hostage in this humiliating manner. I was careful to gauge the pain I was causing him—just enough to keep him still and hopefully encourage him to calm down.

"Let go of me, you goddamn *schmuck*!" he screamed. "You attack your father? What the hell's the matter with you?" He quivered and squirmed spasmodically.

"You need to stop hitting me," I said calmly. "I'm eighteen. I'm a grown man. You gotta stop this."

"Goddamn you!" he sputtered, but I could tell from his body language that he was calming down, beginning to return to a normal state. I lessened the pressure on his arm slightly. I still held it fast, but allowed him to stand a bit more upright.

Emmanuel's resistance now lessened markedly. His entire body relaxed.

I watched his apelike scowl slowly morph, first into a grimace of discomfort, then finally into a sheepish grin. I loosened the grip a touch more.

"All right," he said softly. "You made your point. You can let me go now."

"So you won't hit me anymore?" I asked.

"What good would it do?" he muttered.

I let him go. He stood upright and massaged his right arm from the elbow down to the wrist. "You cut off my blood flow!" he said. "Maybe I should learn some of that judo stuff myself."

"There's a dangerous thought," I said. "Listen, we need to talk about David."

"You never gave a crap about David," he said. "Why the sudden interest?"

"According to Aunt Eve, his teachers say he needs to either be left back again or sent to vocational school."

"Vocational school?" Emmanuel exclaimed. "No son of mine is gonna be a grease monkey! Who the hell do they think they are?"

"All right. Don't get worked up again. I know a lot more jiu-jitsu tricks."

"*Gay cocken!*" he said, but with the hint of a smile.

"There's no way out of this if we keep him in school," I said. "He's sixteen. Let him drop out and come work with us, here in the new store. It's the only sensible answer. And he might like it. He'll feel included. And God knows we can use some help here," I said, pointing to the half-painted ceiling.

"You want him to quit school because you're too lazy to paint?"

"No. I want him to quit school because his choices are to get left back a second time and feel like a complete loser, or to get sent to vocational school and feel like a complete loser, or to come work with *us* and feel like he's part of a family."

"Why are those the only three choices?" demanded Emmanuel. "David could shape up, get his grades up."

"That's not going to happen," I said.

"Why not? How the hell do you know what's going to happen?"

"It's not going to happen because David suffered brain damage due to loss of oxygen during birth."

My father's jaw dropped in disbelief. He took a step back. "How do you know about that?" he asked incredulously.

"You don't keep secrets as well as you think you do," I said. "Let David work here in the store. It's the only reasonable choice."

Emmanuel looked down for a few moments to cogitate and compose himself. He raised his head, arched his back, and thrust his chest outward. "This is *my* decision, not yours," he said sharply. "I need to think about it."

But I could tell that my father had already inwardly acquiesced to my proposal.

Emmanuel looked up at me now with an expression I had never seen before. As if we were equals. I gazed back at him. He seemed a bit smaller than I normally perceived him.

He pointed to the ladder. "Get back up there and start painting," he said playfully, "or I'll kick your judo-boy ass. I'm still your father." He smiled broadly. "And I'm still your boss until you buy out your partner share. And that's three years away, you goddamn *mashugana*."

———

Garish neon signs were in vogue in the early 1960s. Large retail establishments featured them above their front entrances. Our new store's marquee flashed *BARON'S TELEVISION AND ELECTRONICS* in alternating phosphorescent green and red.

Within the display behind our front window, smaller painted signs were positioned strategically amid the featured stock items, declaring, *DISCOUNTS ON ALL ITEMS!* and *PERSONALIZED SERVICE AND HOME DELIVERY!*

Uncle Irving had talked up the new shop with his grocery store customers, his friends, and his fellow congregants at the Jewish Center. We also announced our grand opening through advertisements in several local papers.

Word had evidently circulated. We had far more customers that first week than we expected. And as the months progressed, we got even busier.

I did many things around the store, but my favorites were deliveries and home service. All the other tasks I did were in partnership with Emmanuel, but these responsibilities were solely mine. I had rushed to get my driver's license shortly before the store opened, when we realized that I was the only reasonable candidate for those duties and would need to use a vehicle. We utilized Irving's station wagon at first, but after a couple of months the store's profits enabled us to purchase a small van, the sides and back of which we had professionally lettered with our shop's logo.

Being totally in charge of that aspect of our business gave me tremendous pride. I was therefore scrupulous about doing the work in a manner that left my customers pleased.

The items I delivered were all housed in bulky, corrugated cardboard cartons. Despite my relatively short stature, I had always been strong and could handle most of them on my own. But for the deliveries of really big television sets and stereo systems, I took David with me to help, reminding him constantly to watch that we didn't graze walls, and that we always set the boxes down gently when customers were around.

In our fourth month it became painfully obvious that the store was so busy that we couldn't keep up without additional help. When I had to go out on deliveries or service calls, Emmanuel was left manning both the sales floor and the register. If David was there, he'd be stationed near the door to make certain no one left without paying, but David couldn't be trusted to work the register; he had to summon my father whenever anyone needed to check out.

I thought a good deal about how we might acquire more help for the store. We needed someone reliable—but more importantly, someone whom Emmanuel could accept and tolerate.

I recalled how impressed my father had been when he met Paul O'Rourke. And Paul was by now very experienced in retail sales. One morning, on the way into work, I suggested to my father that we hire Paul to work with us as a full-time salesperson.

Emmanuel's reaction was exactly as I anticipated.

"I don't trust anyone outside the family," he said. "And if I had to hire someone from the outside, I'd hire a Jew. Goyim will steal from us."

I was prepared with a response.

"There's no one in the family available," I said. "All of Irving's and Eve's kids are going to college or will be soon. And you *know* Paul. You met him. You were impressed with him."

"Yeah, I'll grant you he seemed like a nice fellow."

"And if you don't let Paul work the register, how can he steal from you? He'll be on the floor, doing sales," I said.

"What the hell does he know about televisions, or electronics?" demanded Emmanuel. "You told me yourself he didn't take any tough classes in high school. He's a charmer but he's a *schmo*."

"He's a *schmo* who knows how to sell. He's been doing retail sales successfully at a big department store for three years now, and he's gotten two raises and a promotion. He's good at it."

"But he doesn't know about electronics!" Emmanuel screamed, his face turning red.

"Don't get excited while you're driving," I said.

Emmanuel took a breath.

"Look," I continued, "if you think about it, what does Paul need to know? He's not repairing anything or installing anything. He needs to know that *this* set gets a slightly better picture than *that* set but costs twenty bucks more. And *this* phonograph has an automatic turntable and *that* one you have to set the arm down manually. You don't think he can learn that in one day?"

David piped up from the back seat. "Maybe I could do some selling?" he ventured.

Emmanuel looked back derisively, then focused back on the road. "You stay out of this," he yelled at David. "You already have responsibilities. Focus on those!"

"Paul knows how to sell," I said. "You don't want to hear this, but he probably knows how to sell a lot better than you or me."

"What the hell do you mean by *that*?"

"People *like* Paul. You said it yourself. He's charming. Not everybody decides whether or not to buy something because they did a ton of research or because they weigh the pros and cons scientifically. There are lots of people who buy things because they like the person selling it to them."

"Those people are idiots!" exclaimed Emmanuel.

"But aren't they idiots you want buying televisions from *you* rather than the next guy?" I asked.

Emmanuel sighed and was silent for a time. As we pulled into a parking space in front of the store, he turned to me and said, "OK, you can talk to Paul O'Rourke about it. But don't get your hopes up. He probably won't even want to leave the job he has." He paused as he started to get out of the car. "And before you talk to him we have to figure out what we're gonna pay him."

For Paul, taking the job with us meant a raise, and the opportunity to work in a smaller shop with people he knew. What seemed to motivate him more than anything, though, was that he'd have a much greater impact on the overall operation of the enterprise.

Paul's sales technique was an exquisitely nuanced dance. And an extraordinarily effective one. Paul approached each new customer with great enthusiasm, but cloaked his energy in a calm, nonthreatening demeanor. It reminded me distinctly of how he behaved in our jiu-jitsu sparring sessions. He'd appear placid and almost distracted, but he would pounce or parry instantaneously when the moment was right.

Paul worked instinctively. When I asked him to describe his approach to sales, he'd say to just watch him, that he couldn't explain it in words.

But after several days of observing him, Paul's pattern became clear. He'd first greet the customers warmly, ask a few questions, and listen very closely to determine their needs. His second step was informative. He'd show them the items available that might be of interest, provide salient data, and offer choices along the price continuum. It was his third step that surprised me. He'd leave his customers alone. He'd hover a distance away, keeping an eye on them, intuitively assessing when to reengage. But he allowed them time to think, talk among themselves if they were a couple or a family. He knew exactly when to reappear, answer further questions, suggest other options. At that point, if the customers needed more time, he'd retreat again. That process was iterative—he'd do it five or six times in certain situations, allowing the customers to feel unhurried and unpressured.

Often when he rejoined his shopper, the decision had been finalized. But sometimes, if he sensed that the customer was almost there and just needed a push, he'd close the deal deftly, often throwing in a small incentive, such as a few dollars off, or an inexpensive additional item free of charge. At first, he offered to pay for these inducements out of his own commission, but it was such an effective technique that Emmanuel and I began to employ it as well, and we built it into the sale price.

Paul's presence on the floor freed Emmanuel and me from frenetic multitasking, and stabilized the daily rhythms of our new store. Profits continued to rise.

As we neared the first anniversary of the opening of Baron's Television and Electronics, I felt ready to honor a pledge I had made to myself nearly two years earlier. I would return to school at night.

———————————⌣———————————

Today, New York City boasts the largest urban public university system in the nation. It is comprised of a network of twenty-four institutions, including eleven senior colleges and seven community colleges.

In the early 1960s, its oldest school, the City College of New York, was an academic gem, having graduated seven Nobel laureates throughout its history, in such disciplines as medicine, economics, chemistry, and physics. Other notable alumni of CCNY included Jonas Salk, Felix Frankfurter, Bernard Baruch, Paddy Chayefsky, Ira Gershwin, Edward G. Robinson, Henry Roth, and Leonard Susskind. Courses were rigorous, entrance requirements stringent. For residents of New York City, tuition was free. Students lived at home and commuted to and from school by bus and subway.

CCNY's thirty-five-acre campus sprawled over ten city blocks on a hill overlooking Harlem in Upper Manhattan. It was easily accessible from the Bronx, as well as from Yonkers, where our store was located.

I opted to start modestly, and to enroll in just two night classes so as not to disrupt my daily work responsibilities at the shop. I wanted to take introductory classes in physics and electronic engineering, but was immediately informed that both required me to have a solid grounding in calculus to tackle the more complicated equations that would arise late in the semesters of the science courses. After a brief conversation with one of CCNY's counselors, I switched my physics course for a class in introductory calculus, which I could take concurrently with a class in electronic engineering. I was duly warned that I would encounter a timing challenge when correlating my proficiency in calculus with the demands of the engineering syllabus. The counselor said it was doable though quite precarious for anyone who could not quickly and reliably grasp advanced mathematical principles upon initial presentation.

I felt up to that task.

My calculus and engineering classes that semester were held in Shepard Hall, the first building constructed on the flagship North Campus of CCNY when the university moved uptown in 1903. Built in Gothic Revival style, Shepard Hall was an immense stone castle comprised of Manhattan schist, a metamorphic rock native to New York City. The rock had been excavated on-site from pits dug for the buildings' foundations and for the underground tunnels that connected each of the campus's structures. Those tunnels were especially useful during New York's harsh, snowy winters.

When I first glimpsed Shepard Hall, I stood speechless and stared incredulously at its turrets, spires, and arched doorways. I was overwhelmed by its beauty and sheer size. I had never seen anything like it in New York.

The campus's renowned architect, George Browne Post, adorned Shepard Hall with thousands of terra cotta gargoyles, reminiscent of the grotesque figures bedecking the cathedral in various film versions of *The Hunchback of Notre-Dame*, which I had seen on Zacherley's late-night television horror fests.

My introductory class in calculus soon impressed upon me an aspect of the free public university that I hadn't considered: neither the school nor the professors benefitted from retaining students who fell even the slightest bit behind academically. Although the faculty could argue that rigorous standards were commensurate with high achievement, it was also true that smaller classes were easier to teach and meant fewer exams and papers for the professors to grade.

Introduction to Calculus was held four nights a week in a massive lecture hall, each row of seats one stair higher than the one before it, small wooden writing surfaces folding out from each right-hand armrest. As the professor, on his raised stage, gazed outward at the auditorium full of students on the first day of class, he announced confidently that by the end of the term, the few students remaining would be scattered among the first two rows of the lecture hall. This indeed came to pass. I was among the survivors.

My class in electronic engineering also conducted sessions in a huge lecture hall, but only three times a week. I was exhilarated to learn that our fourth class each week would be a small lab, run by a graduate assistant. We'd be broken up into groups of twenty or so, assigned to a graduate student, and we'd work together in teams, putting our theoretical knowledge to practical use in well-equipped lab spaces.

The graduate assistant assigned to my lab was a young man my father would immediately have labeled an archetypal WASP. Tall, with broad shoulders and narrow hips, he wore a tweed sports coat and walked with the grace of an athlete. His straight, soft, light-brown hair swept unpretentiously across his forehead, in stark contrast to the tight, wiry curls I had inherited from Emmanuel that clung so rigidly to my Semitic scalp.

Emmanuel had warned me that these sorts of WASPs didn't have to be intelligent or even good at what they did. They were given jobs and promotions because of how they looked and who they were. Emmanuel warned me that Jews had to work three times harder and be five times smarter to get ahead of them.

I was pondering the validity of those assumptions when the graduate instructor asked the class to quiet down and began to describe to us what the semester of lab work would entail.

I had never heard anyone speak the way he did.

He had a rich, stentorian baritone, but that was not what impressed me. It was the way he put words together. His vocabulary was vast, his diction perfect, and every sentence he uttered seemed to be recited from a book, perfectly composed and artfully constructed. Each phrase flowed effortlessly.

I was surprised, over the course of the semester, to learn how many of my fellow students were put off by how he spoke. They found him intimidating and condescending. I had exactly the opposite reaction. I was incredibly impressed, and began that day to try to mimic his style, to train myself to speak as much like him as I possibly could.

The instructor's name was Wayne Jakob Kenneman.

Every engineering student I encountered at CCNY was male. Almost all of them adhered to a self-imposed and extremely unflattering dress code. A long slide rule for complex calculations dangled from their belts, and a smaller, six-inch slide rule for less formal estimations was tucked in their shirt pockets. I noticed that Instructor Kenneman displayed no such instruments on his person—so I didn't either. We both owned slide rules, of course, but we kept them in our briefcases until we needed them.

I found myself trying to imitate Instructor Kenneman's speech patterns whenever I could. I was quite clumsy at it at first, slow and halting in my efforts. I practiced when I was alone in the shower, or when driving the store's van to make deliveries and service calls.

I realized I could use one of our store's tape recorders to monitor my progress. But when I did so I was horrified. I had no idea that my Bronx accent was so pronounced. For some reason I couldn't discern it when I spoke, but when played back on tape, it was jarring. I realized that even if I succeeded in imitating Instructor Kenneman's phrasing, my gruff diction would completely ruin the effect. So I started practicing articulation as well, consciously softening my vowels and learning to enunciate the letter *r* at the end of words. The tape recorder was invaluable, enabling me to focus on the areas that needed the most work. One morning, a few months into my efforts, Emmanuel and I were discussing inventory. He said, "That college stuff must be paying off. You're starting to sound like a goddamned professor."

CCNY's weekly electronic engineering labs became the highlight of my academic week. I looked forward to them and savored every moment. Other students on my team soon picked up on my facility for constructing electronic devices, and began asking for my help and advice on projects we were assigned. I was afraid that Instructor Kenneman might object to this as being contrary to the school's highly competitive environment, but he seemed to find it all quite endearing.

One evening, as I was working with a couple of other students to solder together the components for a transmitter, Instructor Kenneman posed a question to me. "Do you have much experience in electronic assembly, Mr. Baron?" he asked in his resonant baritone.

"It's been a hobby of mine for many years, Instructor Kenneman," I said.

"And how did you happen upon this admirable pursuit?" he inquired.

"My father owned a small television repair shop when I was growing up," I said. "He got me started by bringing home old parts and showing me how to build simple radios."

"That's very interesting, Mr. Baron," Kenneman announced spiritedly. "You appear to have an inherent gift for electronic assembly. Your intuitive tinkering unerringly leads you in productive directions, despite the fact that you have not yet been taught the theoretical underpinnings that would seem to be required for such accurate navigation."

He was embarrassing me now, in front of the rest of the class, but he persisted: "You have a more intrinsic feel for this than many I've met who hold doctorates in engineering. You're an innate 'doctor,' Mr. Baron!"

From that point forward, Instructor Kenneman referred to me as "the good doctor" when addressing me in front of the class.

When I first started the semester, I tried to find an undisturbed spot suitable for study in the small apartment that Emmanuel, David, and I still shared on the first floor of Uncle Irving's home. I was not able to.

There were large study rooms in Shepard Hall. By the time night sessions concluded, these rooms were quiet and empty. So I'd withdraw to one of them to do my reading and homework. It was a comfortable setting for me. There was a psychological factor at play as well. Within the grand, imposing walls of Shepard Hall, my mind focused firmly on schoolwork. Once I left campus, my thoughts inevitably wandered back to my responsibilities at Baron's Television and Electronics.

One evening, at the conclusion of my electronics lab, I was about to retire to the study hall down the corridor. I had packed my books into my briefcase and was on my way out when Kenneman asked if he might have a word with me privately.

"So, Dr. Baron, would you care to join me for a drink before beginning your commute home?" he asked.

His invitation caught me completely off guard.

"Oh, wow," I stammered hesitantly, "I'd love to, but I'm afraid if I don't put in some time studying this evening, I'll fall behind. I work long hours with my father in our shop. It might be hard to catch up."

I looked up at him, embarrassed and utterly convinced that the words I had just spewed out were ludicrous. He chuckled and placed his large hand reassuringly on my shoulder.

"A man of your intellectual gifts can well afford to skip one night of study, Dr. Baron, and substitute instead a bit of frivolity. It will recharge your cerebral coffers."

I was relieved to be offered a way out of the predicament. "Well, if that is your expert assessment, Instructor Kenneman," I said with a broad grin, "I would love to spend the time with you."

"Splendid. Let us be off then. I know a superb tavern just a few minutes away. But if we are to drink as friends, you must stop referring to me as Instructor Kenneman. We'll retain that appellation in class to avoid any suggestion of impropriety, but for our more jocular pursuits, you must refer to me more informally, Doc."

Doc—I liked the sound of it. However, I didn't know exactly what to make of his request to refer to *him* less formally.

"Would you like me to call you Wayne?" I ventured sheepishly.

"Oh God, no!" he roared. The sheer volume of his response made me fear I had committed a grand faux pas. "The name Wayne has never resonated with me, Doc. I hope you don't think I'm a 'Wayne.' Do you?" he asked.

"I guess not," I said.

"Certainly not!" He leaned down and whispered, "I do not have many close friends, but I ask the ones I have to call me Jake. My middle name is Jakob, after all. I would be honored to have you address me as Jake."

"All right . . . Jake." I smiled.

"Ah, good!" he said.

I assumed that we'd walk to a bar nearby, although knowing how dicey the neighborhood around campus turned at night made me wonder exactly how Jake intended to proceed. To my surprise, we strolled instead to a campus parking lot, where Jake led me to his car.

"Parking permits for graduate assistants who teach night classes are a most welcome perk, Doc!" he said as he opened the passenger door for me. We exited the campus and headed east, arriving within minutes at an upscale hotel with a plush lounge on the Upper East Side. "They know how to make real martinis here," he announced enthusiastically as he pulled up in front and handed his keys to a parking valet, along with a couple of dollars.

"I've never had a martini," I said as we entered the lounge, "but I'm anxious to try one."

"They are works of art!" exclaimed Jake. "I've been toiling to perfect the technique at home. It appears simple; it's mostly gin, chilled and poured, but it's deceptively nuanced. The amount of vermouth splashed in, the time it's permitted to sit on the ice, shaking versus stirring, the brand of gin . . . so many variables. There are actually philistines who believe a legitimate martini can be concocted with vodka, Doc! It's a travesty."

The bartender approached. "Two Beefeater martinis," declared Jake assertively, "up with olives." I was extremely impressed with how comfortable he was in this milieu.

"Driver's license," the bartender intoned, looking straight at me. I dug mine out. Eighteen was still the legal drinking age in New York then. "Thanks," he said, and handed the card back to me with a smile.

The drinks arrived, we toasted, and I took my first sip. "Wow, these are strong!" I said.

Jake laughed. "I'll invite you to my house some weekend night, Doc. You can assist me in my quest to formulate the perfect martini. It's a sort of laboratory experiment in itself—to create one of the finer things in life. I'll show you the proper reagents, and the technique as I have so far come to understand it. Who knows, perhaps your preternatural affinity for electronic assembly will translate to alcoholic amalgamation as well."

We drank and talked. Things were already growing hazy for me when I heard Jake order a third round for both of us. I tried my best to keep up with him, but while sipping on my third glass, I leaned toward him to emphasize a point and began to fall off my bar stool. Jake caught me and righted me on my seat. He laughed heartily, a resonant bass howl.

"A bit of practice will do wonders for your capacity, Doc. Fear not, I will guide you unerringly."

"I think I've had enough for tonight," I slurred.

"Indeed, Doc. No subway for you this evening. Jakles will chauffer you home."

The Empire State Building in Manhattan was for many years the tallest building in the world. When its construction was completed in 1931, the narrow column that stretched upward from its roof was designed to be a mooring mast for dirigibles. These lighter-than-air crafts were expected to become mainstream conveyances for air passengers in America, but airplanes soon proved the far more popular choice. The mooring mast atop the Empire State Building never hosted a single dirigible. Less than eight months after the building opened, the mast was replaced with a structure upon which huge broadcast antennas for radio and television stations could be erected.

For many years, the National Broadcasting Company had exclusive rights to the antenna location, which they used for their local television and radio stations. Even in 1941, ten years after the Empire State Building's construction, there were still only two commercial television stations operating in New York City, so contention for space atop the building was not an issue.

But by 1949 there were seven local television stations vying for consumers' attention. Each broadcasted from a different geographical site. This was an expensive solution for the broadcasters, but even more of a hassle for viewers, who had to reposition their sets every time they changed a channel.

In 1951, in an effort to alleviate these problems, five of New York City's television stations joined in a project to share the Empire State Building's rooftop as their broadcast site. This was a significant step forward. But this breakthrough embodied only half the equation. Each individual television set located in people's homes needed some sort of antenna to pick up these signals as well.

The earliest commercial television sets available in the American market looked like large radios with tiny viewing screens. Like radios, they had small internal antennas for receiving signals. This was not a particularly effective scheme.

In 1953, inventor Marvin Middlemark produced the first external home antenna: two telescoping poles mounted on a small swivel base that sat on top of the set. They came to be known as "rabbit ears." Resourceful viewers could fiddle with the two aerials endlessly to find the optimal configuration for each broadcast station, resulting in much-improved reception. The invention of rabbit ears boosted sales of televisions in America astronomically.

But for my customers who purchased television sets at Baron's Television and Electronics in the early 1960s, large rooftop antennas had become available as well. The reception they afforded was far superior to any indoor antenna. At my urging, our shop had established a profitable rooftop-antenna mounting and hookup service, which became part of my outcall and delivery purview.

The fact that five local stations all now transmitted from the Empire State Building assured our rooftop antenna customers good reception on those channels. However, there were still two stations broadcasting from other sites, and antennas aimed at the Empire State Building, no matter how carefully oriented, could not receive optimal signals for those. Expensive rotating rooftop antennas were fashionable in California and other warm-weather states, but not so much in New York and most of the Northeast, where winter snow and ice wreaked havoc with their exposed motorized components. New so-called omni-directional antennas did a bit better but still could not assure peak reception for all local channels.

I knew this was not ideal. There had to be better solutions.

I also knew that a great deal more content could potentially be made available to viewers. With powerful antennas, customers from Riverdale and Yonkers and other localities near the Hudson River could probably pick up some New Jersey stations. Customers from northern parts of Nassau and Suffolk Counties on Long Island could possibly catch transmissions from southern Connecticut cities like Stamford, Bridgeport, and New Haven.

Even more exciting was my discovery that the VHF frequencies that comprised the familiar channels from two to thirteen suddenly had new competition from higher UHF frequencies. The stations broadcasting on these new UHF frequencies were mostly small, independent operations, but had some interesting programming. Their signals were weaker, though, and far more dependent on antennas being precisely aligned directionally for decent reception.

All this seemed to me a fantastic business opportunity.

Till now, if a customer purchased our rooftop-antenna installation services, I'd drive out to the house with David. We'd go up to the roof together to mount the antenna. We'd start with the mast, a long aluminum pole, which we mounted on a wooden platform that we secured to the roof, with guy-wires to hold it erect. To that we'd affix the antenna itself, and attach a long, flat ribbon cable. We'd run that cable down the side of the house, threading it through a series of porcelain insulators called standoffs that looked like big eye bolts. We'd finally snake the wire into the house through the corner of a windowsill or a small drilled hole, and attach it to the back of the set.

I'd then return to the roof, leaving David inside the house to monitor reception on the television as he dialed through the stations. Based upon his assessment of picture quality on each channel, I'd make the necessary adjustments to the antenna's orientation up on the roof, trying to find the best positioning compromise. In private homes, we could communicate to each other by shouting through an open window. But I had discovered that one of our wholesalers of electronic appliances sold a new contraption called a "walkie-talkie." Perfected during World War II, these portable devices were now beginning to be used commercially. I ordered a couple to put out on our store shelves, and an extra pair for communicating with David when we put up antennas on the roofs of larger apartment houses. They were so effective that we now used them all the time, even for installations in small, single-family homes.

Even with the walkie-talkies, though, it was slow going. David's judgment was not reliable. I'd always go down inside the house to double-check his reports on picture quality. I inevitably found that some stations were not up to par and required more fine-tuning. I sometimes had to make as many as six trips up and down before we could call the job done to my satisfaction.

So, I was looking for a better partner than David.

And given the possibility of capturing transmissions from New Jersey and Connecticut as well as on new UHF frequencies, I was also looking for alternative technologies to offer customers that assured optimal reception for every station on the dial.

The profit potential for such an appliance seemed huge.

Jake invited me to his place for a martini lab on a Saturday night during New York's cold winter. Car exhaust had turned the light covering of snow on the ground to grey-black slush along the edges of the curbs and roadways. As soon as we closed up shop for the night, I drove the van we used for store deliveries down the Westside Highway to Greenwich Village where Jake rented his apartment. It was dark as I parked and walked to his building.

Our friendship was still new. I wanted to be sure not to arrive late. I had rehearsed some small talk so as not to appear awkward in his presence.

When I walked into his kitchen, he had all his accouterments laid out: a large bottle of Beefeater gin, a small bottle of dry vermouth, a jar of olives, a box of wooden toothpicks, a metallic canister for shaking, and a long-handled spoon and glass pitcher for stirring drinks. "I'm still working out whether shaking or stirring is more to my liking," he announced when he saw me glance at the two containers.

Jake had purchased a ten-pound bag of ice for the occasion. That seemed like a lot, until I realized that he filled his empty cocktail glasses with ice and a bit of water to have them well chilled for each batch, and used a large volume of ice to chill the gin inside the shaker or pitcher as he made the drink.

"So much of the art, Doc, is the interaction of the ice with the gin and vermouth," he said. "There is the chilling of the liquid, of course, and that needs to be thorough, but some of the ice will inevitably melt into the drink as well. More so with shaking than stirring. That bit of water will soften the final product, round out its harsh edges. It's quite critical, Doc."

"It doesn't appear you use much vermouth," I said.

"That's right. Just a wee drop. I read that when the drink was first concocted it was actually half vermouth and half gin. That would be grossly unpalatable by today's standards. And, Doc, the vermouth must be dry. There is a fine drink called a manhattan that we'll have to experiment with at a later date—it employs both sweet and dry vermouth. But I digress."

"And always gin," I said. "Never vodka. I remember you saying that."

"Vodka has its uses, Doc, but it's a travesty in a martini. And this misuse of vodka has given rise to the sad misconception on the part of the masses that a dry martini should have no vermouth in it at all. Vermouth adds such a distinction to a good martini. Of course, all these misguided fools who attempt to build martinis with vodka soon learn that vodka, which has no taste whatsoever, is completely overwhelmed by vermouth, so they advocate against vermouth and sully its distinguished reputation.

"If these philistines would just concoct martinis out of gin the way they are supposed to be made, they'd understand that gin's strong taste and essence of juniper blends exquisitely with fine dry vermouth. Are you absorbing all this, Doc?"

"I am for now, Jake. I suspect that once we start quaffing, my retention capabilities will diminish noticeably." That was a line I had rehearsed.

"Well put, Doc. But my pedagogical tendencies will have diminished by then as well," Jake replied.

We drank the first round, sitting on his living room sofa and making small talk about the strange mix of students in our electronics lab.

"You make the next round, Doc!" Jake suddenly exclaimed.

"Oh, I don't know if I'm quite ready for that!" I said.

"I'll watch your every move. I won't let you err."

"All right, Jake," I said, walking toward the kitchen. "But keep a close eye on me."

While we were back in the living room enjoying that second round, I brought up my ideas about antenna technology to Jake. I ventured first into whether he might be interested in assisting with rooftop installations.

"I know you teach labs in the evening, Jake. And I assume you take graduate classes during the day. But do you ever have days free?" I asked.

"Every Tuesday and Thursday, Doc. Saturdays and Sundays too, for that matter. Why do you ask?"

"I was wondering whether you might be interested in helping me out with rooftop antenna installations for our store. The activity can be somewhat interesting."

"Would this be a paying gig, Doc?"

"Oh, absolutely," I said.

"Then I'd certainly be available for you, Doc. We graduate assistants earn paltry stipends." He paused a moment. "I must say, though, the exercise of erecting antennas seems somewhat prosaic. Why seek out a man of my credentials?"

"Ah, Jake, we are exactly in sync on this!" I said. I sipped my martini and continued excitedly. "I think we can do a lot more. I'm envisioning new antenna technology. Perhaps multiple antennas on a single roof for different broadcast locations, and adaptors attached to the set's channel selector that will automatically route to the appropriate antenna for the station selected. Maybe signal amplification and filtering as well."

"Fascinating, Doc. With your preternatural tinkering ability, and my knowledge of electronic theory, we could undoubtedly construct the applications you envision. But do you have any customers who could afford to purchase such devices?"

"We actually have some very wealthy patrons from Riverdale and Long Island. I've run ideas by them. They're very interested. And this kind of thing grows upon itself. As we develop a reputation for high-end antenna technology, more such customers will seek us out."

"You know we'll need to patent anything we develop."

"I was hoping you knew something about that, Jake."

"I know a bit. And I can find out the rest from colleagues. A number of the professors at CCNY hold patents for electronic mechanisms."

"This is exciting, Jake. It will be an adventure."

"An adventure indeed, Doc!" He held his martini up to toast. We clinked glasses.

18.
Tai Chi

VIRGINIA FERGUSON WAS TOLD that she'd need to spend as long as three weeks in the ICU following her double lung transplant. But years of karate training had instilled in her a warrior's disposition—she was discharged in just eight days.

Sapphire and I, after our long morning hikes, became accustomed now to meeting Virginia and her tiny dog Kata once or twice a week for a brief stroll in the park. Virginia grew progressively stronger during the months following her surgery, but still wore a paper mask over her nose and mouth when we walked, to stave off infections.

Our human bodies innately attack invaders. Donated organs, though lifesaving, are seen by our immune system as foreign, so recipients of such must commit to a regimen of powerful drugs for the rest of their lives to suppress their immune systems and prevent rejection of their new organs. But those same drugs render the patients susceptible to all sorts of other itinerant microbes.

It was so good, though, to see Virginia rid of her oxygen hand truck.

"I'm really getting antsy, Sammy," she complained to me one morning. "I'm stronger now and I want to do something physical. I keep asking my doctors if I can return to karate, and they all tell me it would be too dangerous. I don't think I'm ever going to be able to do it."

"Have you considered tai chi?" I asked. "When an accumulation of recurring injuries meant that I could no longer train for jiu-jitsu, I found it a very welcome substitute. It was a little slow and frustrating at first, but the older I got and the more proficient I became at it, the more I realized how meditative it is, and how its forms truly are the foundation of a martial art."

"I *might* try tai chi," she said, "if I could do it with *you*. Where do you practice, Sammy? I see a group of people doing it every afternoon in the park between the two museums. I've never seen you with them. Where does *your* group practice?"

I smiled and spoke softly. "As I've mentioned to you, Virginia, I'm not much of a joiner. I practice tai chi alone. I learned the forms from a series of DVDs, and I practice at home. If it's a nice day, I'll do it out in my backyard—otherwise in my home office. That's where I do my yoga too."

"Alone? Well, that's no fun. Let's look into joining that group in the park. We can do it together."

"They're all old Asian people, Virginia. I don't know if we'd be welcome. I don't even know if any of them speak English."

"I'm sure some of them speak English, Sammy. I'll talk to them tomorrow afternoon."

I was not comfortable with this, but I said nothing.

＜━━━━━◡━━━━━＞

Baron's Television and Electronics was open Monday through Saturday. Both Emmanuel and I worked all six days and took only Sundays off.

Evening classes and study time at CCNY occupied my weeknights.

On most Saturday evenings, unless Jake had a date, he'd invite me to his apartment in the West Village for a cocktail lab. We had experimented with manhattans, gimlets, bloody marys, margaritas, whiskey sours, and mojitos. We had perfected all of those, but we inevitably returned to the martini. There was something about it that Jake considered noble and timeless—but alluringly elusive with respect to nailing down a consummate version. Most recently we were focusing on the olives. Olives with pits were superior in taste to those stuffed with pimento, but Jake found the presence of pits aesthetically unacceptable. We purchased a device that was mechanically similar to the tool that punches holes in paper, but which was designed specifically to pit olives. I came up with the idea of stuffing the pitted olives with something other than pimentos, and we were currently evaluating different types of cheeses.

With my schedule so full, Sundays seemed a perfect day for unwinding and recharging. But I grew restless and had an idea for Sunday mornings.

I wanted to take jiu-jitsu classes. That jiu-jitsu school in Yonkers still enticed me. It was just half a mile from our store, and I passed it frequently while out making deliveries or repair calls. I had stopped by the school's office one day and learned that they offered Sunday-morning classes for adults.

I no longer felt any obligation to seek Emmanuel's permission to study there, and didn't even mention the idea. I was an adult now and had a steady income of my own.

I asked Paul O'Rourke if he wanted to join me.

"No thanks, Sammy," he said. "You go ahead and do it yourself. It'll be good for you."

"I thought you'd want to join me," I said.

Paul smiled. "Maybe it's all those years I spent wrestling in junior high and high school. I've spent enough time on the mats."

"I'll miss you there."

"Jiu-jitsu is *your* thing, Sammy. Enjoy it. You'll be great at it."

I arrived forty-five minutes early for my first jiu-jitsu lesson, as the school had requested. I filled out the required paperwork and tendered my initial payment.

When the teacher handed me my white cotton *gi*, I felt as if I was touching something sacred. The stiff jacket, sleek pants, and wide white belt were folded into a neat square pile. I carried my *gi* down to the locker room and put it on, fastening it exactly as the instructor had demonstrated. After I knotted the belt, cinching the white coat around my waist, I ran over to the full-length mirror, mesmerized by my reflection. All those books on jiu-jitsu I had borrowed from the library contained photographs of combatants wearing exactly what I was now wearing.

In all the times I trained with Paul, I had never felt quite like this.

The improvised training sessions and many hours of sparring that Paul and I had shared in that secret grass refuge in Co-Op City—and more recently, on occasion, at Paul's apartment—had prepared me well. While there were a few holes in my knowledge, I patched those quickly and was soon promoted from the beginners' class to one for intermediate students.

The owner of the academy precisely fit my image of a martial arts master—he was a small Japanese man, solid as a granite slab, with a quiet air of mystery about him. He was referred to as "Sensei."

But the young instructor assigned to our beginner and intermediate classes, Mr. Hawkes, was more ordinary, much like the fellows I remembered on the football and baseball teams from high school. He was white, about six foot one or two, with the well-muscled physique of an athlete.

The large practice studio was unremarkable, with bare white walls and a dozen glaring fluorescent lights spaced evenly about its ceiling. The room's scent, however, was unmistakable. Hints of salty perspiration mingled with the alcohol-rubbed plastic surface of the mats. Those mats covered every inch of the floor; each time a body pummeled the mats' surface, a sweet, powdery dust puffed into the air and floated toward my face.

It was intoxicating.

I had about an hour before my calculus lecture started, so I picked up an egg salad sandwich at the CCNY cafeteria, planning to eat it in one of Shepard Hall's study rooms while I finished the assignment that was due for class.

On my way out of the cafeteria I passed a wire rack holding copies of the student-produced CCNY weekly newspaper. I picked up a paper to scan quickly before I started my calculus homework. I rarely found any articles in this paper worth reading, but there were sometimes announcements and notifications that were useful to me.

In the study hall, I flipped through the twelve-page newspaper in less than two minutes as I gulped down my sandwich. I found nothing of interest. I had turned over the paper's last page and was about to toss it away when a small advertisement on the back page caught my attention:

I pulled the paper closer and reread the ad several times, glancing about to make sure nobody was observing. I folded the newspaper neatly and tucked it in my briefcase. Over the next several weeks, I pulled the paper out when I was alone and studied that advertisement over and over. All sorts of thoughts raced through my brain.

I had never seen the ad before, and never saw it again, though I scanned every new edition of the CCNY paper for it. I wondered if the "Regal Mistress Angelica" had opted to only place the ad that one time, or perhaps it slipped past the faculty censors on that first occasion by some fluke but failed to ever do so again.

And who *was* this Mistress Angelica? What did she look like?

What sorts of people actually did this?

Should I call?

I had fantasized about precisely this sort of dominant/submissive sexual liaison all my life. Even as a young child, I perceived scenes in movies and television shows that involved any sort of bondage or subjugation as sensual, far more so than I did romantic episodes, no matter how steamy their portrayal. The endless daydreams I enjoyed while sitting in the East Tremont branch of the New York Public Library, gazing surreptitiously at the beautiful librarian Esther, all involved her binding and gagging me and suspending me from the ceiling in her secret office behind the checkout desk.

What damage could it possibly cause just to call this mysterious Mistress Angelica and inquire about her ad?

But every time I tried to picture the individuals who went to these secret places and did these things, I became more convinced that they all had to be dangerously depraved. Getting involved with them in any way could be horrifically risky. They might be homicidal killers. Ax murderers. Insane psychotic lunatics. Having any one of them recognize me, know my name, garner any information about me at all could lead to my death. Or they might blackmail me with threats to reveal my undisclosed predilections.

I could be ruined.

I eventually persuaded myself, with great certainty, that the people embroiled in New York City's bondage and sadomasochism community were vicious and insane. I was an odd exception, and I would be gobbled up like prey if I were foolish enough to explore their degenerate world.

I threw the paper in a public trashcan on a Manhattan street corner, and tried to never again think about that advertisement featuring Mistress Angelica.

But I thought about it constantly. And I thought about Esther. I wondered where she had moved and what she was doing.

With great enthusiasm I informed Paul O'Rourke that I was going to start regular strength training at the dojo. Mr. Hawkes told me it would help me immensely with sparring.

Paul was both amused and annoyed.

"How long have I been telling you that you needed to do weight training and improve your strength?" he yelled. "I've been telling you since we first started sparring when we were still in high school."

"Well, I guess you were right," I said.

"Damn straight I was right, but what bugs me is that when *I* told you to do it, all those times, you just ignored me. Now the jiu-jitsu teacher tells you to do it and you're all 'Oh, yes sir, I'll start doing it right away, sir!'" he taunted me in a mocking singsong.

"Well, as I said, Paul, you were right. By the way, are *you* still working out?" I asked him.

He sighed sheepishly. "No," he acknowledged, looking away. "I haven't worked out since I graduated from high school and left the wrestling team."

"Well, then let's work out together. We can do it before work, early in the morning. Three times a week. The dojo charges a nominal fee to use their weight room."

"Oh God," he muttered. "Getting up for work every day is bad enough. I'm not getting up hours earlier to lift weights." He thought for a moment. "I'd consider doing it in the evenings."

"I go to night school, Paul. You know that. I can't do it after work."

"Oh, all right," he whined. "We'll do it in the mornings. I guess it would be good for me to get back into shape. It just bugs me that *you're* the one talking me into it."

When we started weight training, I was determined to lift as much as Paul could. Despite his long layoff, he could still handle much heavier weights than I.

Mr. Hawkes was often in the dojo's weight room in the mornings too. Both he and Paul demonstrated exercises and helped me design a workout plan. They were scrupulous about pointing out when I violated proper form—and I did so often, particularly early on. In my zeal to catch up to Paul's capabilities, I took shortcuts: I jerked weights when I was supposed to move them slowly, with control; I used my legs to help with standing lifts instead of relying solely on my arms; and with straight-arm dumbbell lifts, I'd flex my elbows to enable me to utilize dumbbells heavier than I could control.

I grew fanatical about training. I had always considered myself strong—I carried televisions and other equipment without much effort— but now I realized how much stronger Mr. Hawkes, Paul, and many of the more advanced jiu-jitsu students were. I lengthened the duration of my sessions by arriving at the dojo even earlier in the mornings. After several months I asked my instructor if I could possibly get a key to the dojo's front door because I wanted to get started before the dojo opened. He said he'd need to get permission from the sensei.

Eventually the Japanese master acquiesced to my request and gave me a key to the front door. He handed it to me in person, and made it clear, in his soft, heavily accented monotone, that this privilege was contingent upon my always remembering to lock the door behind me before heading down to the weight room—failure to do so even one time would result in my losing this privilege. I found it fascinating that he was able to be so blunt and direct without ever seeming the least bit nasty.

The Japanese sensei was sometimes in the weight room when I practiced very early in the morning. He'd bow slightly to greet me. I'd return the gesture. We never spoke while we worked out. If he noticed me executing a set of lifts flawlessly, he'd sometimes give the barest nod of approval. But if he caught me cheating, bending my elbows or distorting my frame to handle heavier weights, he'd turn away in disgust. It was so humiliating that I soon learned to take lighter weights and maintain my form immaculately in his presence.

Eventually I stopped cheating when I was alone as well.

Paul O'Rourke's dedication to training ebbed over time. He would show up only once or twice a week, and his workouts became somewhat brief and perfunctory. On most exercises I had now caught up or surpassed his capabilities. He eventually stopped coming.

As I lifted heavier and heavier weights, I grew much stronger. Oddly, though, every time I examined my naked body in the mirror, it looked almost exactly as it had before I ever started training. I was a bit more solid and wiry, but I had added almost no bulk to my frame.

I was disappointed but assumed that if I kept lifting with my current zeal, the bulk would eventually materialize.

———⌣———

Virginia Ferguson related to me, with great enthusiasm, how she had been successful in befriending one of the younger women in the tai chi group that met each morning in Golden Gate Park. Many of the older people did not speak much English, but Virginia said that this woman was quite fluent, and was excited to invite non-Asian people into the group.

"And the others share her sentiment?" I asked.

"I guess so," said Virginia.

"How much does it cost?" I asked, somehow believing that if I probed enough aspects of the plan, I might find one to disqualify it from consideration.

"It doesn't cost anything," Virginia said. "It's an informal group. There's no teaching, per se, that goes on. There's one old man who's been practicing tai chi since he was a child—he leads and everyone else just watches him and does what he's doing. The woman told me that the old man only practices a few different forms, so pretty soon you learn them all and it's just a place to practice with other people and share the energy."

"I don't know," I said. "I've become so accustomed to practicing alone."

"I can't quite figure you out, Sammy," she said. "All those years you practiced jiu-jitsu, you attended classes and sparred with other people."

"I did," I said. "In different dojos throughout New York, and in various cities of the United States, and then here in California. I enjoyed the interaction with different opponents and seeing the variety of different approaches in the teaching. And it was sort of necessary to move around as I did, because Baron's Electronics opened stores in the different boroughs of New York, and out on Long Island, and then stores in Philadelphia and Chicago and Denver. And my broadcast-technology company had clients

I visited all over, eventually here in California. I found dojos in all those places. But you can't practice jiu-jitsu or karate alone. They're competitive sports. You need opponents. Tai chi is more of a spiritual discipline. If you're competing with anyone, it's yourself."

"But think of how the mystical energy will compound and reflect when you do it with a group of people," Virginia said. "And it won't take you long to feel comfortable in the group. You're actually a rather charming fellow when you're not being curmudgeonly and standoffish."

"You're lucky you're still too sick for martial arts," I laughed. "I'd toss you over my shoulder for trash talk like that."

"That's the spirit, Sammy," she said. "Let's go over tomorrow afternoon."

"Will we be the first white people to ever join their group?" I asked.

"Absolutely. What an honor!"

Weeknights, I commuted to CCNY after work using buses and subways, and didn't get home till late. Saturday nights I was often at Jake's apartment in the Village. So, dinners with Irving and Eve and their children had become a Sunday-night-only ritual for me.

Surprisingly, I looked forward to those dinners each weekend, probably because they were followed by my weekly after-dinner "schnapps time" with Uncle Irving. In the summer, and on pleasant spring and fall evenings, we'd sit out on the porch, and he'd lean back on his rocking chair and smoke a fat cigar while we drank and talked.

But tonight was a cold winter evening, so we took the schnapps bottle with us into the small chamber off the kitchen that Irving called "the cigar room." Eve always referred to it as the library, though there were very few books in it. There was a worn copy of the Old Testament, a seemingly unopened copy of Herman Wouk's *This Is My God*, and a few other old dog-eared tomes, all on Jewish themes.

It was the only room in the house where Irving was allowed to smoke his cigar.

I waited until we were halfway through our second round of schnapps to share with Uncle Irving my latest dilemma with respect to Emmanuel and the electronics store.

"Our antenna-installation business is taking off, Uncle Irving," I began. "It's like pure profit because the customers pay for the antennas and the other equipment separately from the service."

"That's very good."

"But we can make it better," I said. "I have this instructor at CCNY. He's not quite a professor yet, but he will be. I want to bring him on to help with some of the more challenging antenna installations. David just isn't cutting it, especially with the fine-tuning."

Irving looked concerned. "Why would a big *macher* like your teacher want to put up antennas?" he asked. "And you'd have to pay him too much, wouldn't you?"

"What I really want to do," I said, "is work with this instructor to patent some custom antenna setups with channel-specific amplification systems that rich people can buy. They'll get super reception, and be able to receive a lot more stations than they do now. You can't get that anywhere else."

"And you know how to invent these things?" he asked.

"Absolutely."

"Then make one of those things for me! Free of charge, of course," Irving laughed, poking his cigar toward me. "I'm a partner, after all."

I chuckled and took a big sip of schnapps. "We'll make a good one for you."

"And don't give me the first one you make, either," he said. "Make a few—sell 'em to people. When you sold half a dozen or so and worked the kinks out, *then* make me a really *good* one."

"You got it," I said, and smiled.

"So . . . keep talking," he said.

"I just don't know how to approach Emmanuel to get him to buy into all this," I said. "He won't want to take on another employee. He'll say David can help with the antenna installations like he always has. We're making do, and Emmanuel's already paying David—not much, but he's paying him—and he certainly won't want to pay someone else to do what David's already doing. And as for the new stuff, Emmanuel will say that inventions and patents are too big a risk, and we're a store, not an inventor's lab for pipe dreams."

"Emmanuel would have a point there, Sammy. Inventions can fail. You can lose money."

"This stuff will work, Uncle Irving. It's just a bunch of things that already work, combined in clever ways. I've talked to customers about it. They want to buy it."

Irving rocked back and took a couple of long, slow puffs on his cigar. He curled his tongue to blow the smoke out in rings that floated toward the ceiling. He poured back a big swig of schnapps.

"What if you and your professor form your own little company?" he asked.

That was a suggestion I had not expected. "That's a fascinating idea," I said, leaning forward. "How exactly would you see that working, Uncle Irving?"

He shrugged and pursed his lips. "You and your friend form a company. You make Baron's Television and Electronics your exclusive customer for your inventions. For *now*, anyway. If this stuff really takes off, people are gonna find a way to copy it, so eventually you'll want to sell it to other people too. But for now, you do your inventions, you sell them through Baron's Electronics. Your new company and our store split the profits. And if you want your friend to help you with the tough installations instead of David, he comes in as a contractor, and gets paid a portion of the profits that you make on that installation."

"So Emmanuel doesn't risk a thing," I said. "It's brilliant. He doesn't take on a new employee—he makes a profit off everything. Emmanuel can't lose. How can he refuse?"

"Right, and it's even better," Uncle Irving added. "To Emmanuel, your friend is an independent contractor. You know what that means, Sammy? It means because he's not an employee, labor laws don't apply.

No vacations, no social security, no insurance. Nothing. No headaches. And Emmanuel gets more help in the store because David's around more."

"Right," I said. "And if the new inventions work, he makes money off them, and if they bomb, he doesn't lose a thing. How do you come up with this stuff?"

Uncle Irving laughed and drank some more schnapps. "I like working with you, Sammy. We get good ideas when we talk."

We clinked glasses.

"Listen, Sammy" he said, "let me tell Manny about this. He'll resent it if he hears it from you. I'll tell him that I was asking you about college and you told me about this professor you had and some inventions the two of you were going to work on. I'll pitch it to him as an idea I got to make the store more money, with no risk, and no investment, and no extra work. Partner to partner. He'll buy it."

"Thank you, Uncle Irving. That sounds perfect."

"I've never seen Manny say no to more money!" Irving laughed. He pointed his cigar at me again. "And speaking of more money, you better buy out my partner's share soon, Sammy. The store's making so much goddamn money that I'll be the richest man in Riverdale if you don't! This should be *your* money, Sammy. You're working hard. No matter how much Manny's paying you, believe me, it's not as much as you'd be making as a partner."

"I know," I said. "I'm working on it. CCNY is free. I'm not paying any rent. I'm saving almost everything I make. I'll be able to buy you out in the next year, maybe even in the next six months."

"Good." Irving's expression changed and he looked at me seriously. "Sammy . . . listen to me for one more thing. Your brother, David. We both know he's not all there in the head. But he's a sweet boy. He means well. And he's . . . How would you say it? He's easy to hurt, Sammy. He's gonna see you put up your antennas with this new guy instead of him. He's gonna see you become a partner, and he's not. You gotta take care of him in some way. Don't become such a big *macher* that you leave David behind. You're his big brother. You gotta look out for him."

"I'm not sure I know how to do that," I said softly. "But you're right. I want to. Maybe you can help me with it, Uncle Irving."

"I can give you advice, Sammy. I'm always happy to do that. But *you* gotta make the effort. If you don't, you're gonna look back someday and be really sorry you didn't."

I nodded solemnly. I slowly finished the schnapps in my glass while I thought about what Uncle Irving had said.

<hr />

I acquitted myself especially well in the sparring session that followed our jiu-jitsu class at the Yonkers dojo. I'd been strength training regularly for nearly six months now, and hadn't missed a single Sunday-morning jiu-jitsu lesson since I enrolled. The combination of skill and strength that I'd acquired filled me with confidence, and translated into vastly improved sparring.

This morning I sparred first with a student on my level, then with a more advanced student, and finally for a few minutes with Instructor Hawkes himself. The instructor rarely sparred, but I think after he saw me annihilate both my opponents, he felt that I needed to be put in my place a bit, so as not to get too cocky. And he certainly did get the better of me—but to my great surprise, I managed to throw him a couple of times as well.

Paul O'Rourke had invited me to visit him at his apartment after class. I showered, dressed, and made my way over.

He greeted me, and I plopped down on his living room sofa as he walked into the kitchen. I expected him to come out with a couple of beers and was quite intrigued when he emerged instead with a contraption I had never seen.

"It's a water pipe," he said. "You want to smoke some pot?"

I didn't quite know what to say. I certainly had heard about marijuana. Some claimed it was harmless, invoking a high somewhat similar to alcohol but a bit gentler and more cerebral. However, the government and other authorities painted it as an extremely dangerous and potentially lethal narcotic.

"Do you think it's safe?" I asked Paul.

He smiled. "You're not buying that government bullshit about pot being some kind of killer weed that will destroy your brain, are you?"

"I don't know *what* to believe," I said.

"I've been doing it for a few months now, Sammy. Pretty much everyone I know smokes it now and then. Nobody's been hurt. The only thing I didn't like about it was how the joints I rolled were harsh and burned my throat. So I picked up this water pipe in a shop in Greenwich Village. This makes it much smoother."

"Do you mind if I take a look?" I asked.

The construction of the device was simple but rather ingenious. It was mostly glass. The water came about a third of the way up the container. The marijuana was burned in a small bowl on the top of the pipe; the smoke was conveyed through a brass tube directly into the water. That cooled the smoke, which then rose out of the water and could be inhaled through the mouthpiece. "Well designed," I said.

"So, you want to give it a try?" he asked.

"You go ahead," I said. "I'll watch how you do it and then I'll take a puff."

Back in the early 1960s, marijuana was not only illegal, it was also far less potent than today's designer buds so easily acquired in either New York or California at local medical marijuana dispensaries. Now one need only complain to a sympathetic doctor about stress or sleeplessness, and procurement of extraordinarily potent cannabis is assured.

But early in the 1960s the weed was harsh and it took a good deal of smoking to extract sufficient THC to get high. People would sit in circles and pass joints for hours.

After watching Paul take a few hits, I was ready to try. Paul had me hold the pipe to my mouth as he lit a match and held it over the bowl. The first puff I took was far too big and aggressive. It singed my throat and sent me into paroxysms of coughing and choking.

Paul laughed. "Easy, big guy!" he said. "Go slower."

I waited until my coughing subsided and went at it again. This time I pursed my lips loosely around the mouthpiece, so as to incorporate some additional air along with the smoke. I inhaled smoothly and gently. That worked much better.

"Hold the smoke in your lungs as long as you can," Paul advised.

After a few minutes and many inhalations, I felt as if I had mastered the mechanics of smoking. I ingested a good deal of smoke and held each lungful to my capacity.

But I felt nothing.

"I just don't feel anything," I said to Paul. "Maybe I'm just a person who can't get stoned."

"Getting stoned isn't like getting drunk," Paul said. "You gotta *learn* how to do it. It's strange. I was like that at first too."

We smoked a good deal more. I still felt not the least bit high.

"Try something," said Paul. "Stand up, close your eyes, and take a really deep breath. Just hold it. No smoke, just air. Keep your eyes closed and stand completely still. Just try to feel your body."

It seemed a bit silly, but I gave it a try. The sensation was quite ordinary at first, but after a short time I became aware that it had morphed into something completely unfamiliar. It was as if my body were an entity separate from myself, which I was now inhabiting and objectively exploring. The more I focused on it, the more intense the impression of disembodied investigation and discovery became.

I opened my eyes and looked at Paul. "Oh yes!" I smiled. "I think I'm stoned."

We lit up the pipe every few minutes for the next half hour. During that time, we had what seemed like the most fascinating and revealing conversation.

"Get me a piece of paper and a pen," I finally said to Paul. "I have to write this stuff down that we're saying. It's amazing."

Paul laughed but didn't budge. "Don't bother," he said. "We've all tried that. It's just a bunch of gibberish when you look at it the next day when you're straight."

Even so, we reached a point in the conversation when I said something

I considered far too profound to let go. I raced into Paul's kitchen and rummaged through several drawers until I found a pen and a scrap of paper and wrote the thought down.

A few days later I found the note in my pants pocket. It said, *Wouldn't any other air be as thin?* I laughed hysterically and threw it in the trash.

———◇———

After long days at work, followed by hours at CCNY and then a subway and bus trip home, I found that a couple shots of bourbon helped me get to sleep. Uncle Irving's house had a basement where he stored old boxes and furnishings. No one was ever down there at night. I kept my bottle of bourbon hidden there, with a shot glass. It was a quiet and private place for me before I went to bed—I had been using it as such for months.

It occurred to me one evening that a few hits of pot along with the bourbon might help me sleep even better. Paul had invited me to his apartment several more times following that initial foray into entry-level psychedelics, and I'd become quite enamored of the sensibility that marijuana engendered. I approached Paul one afternoon at work when I found him rummaging around our large equipment storeroom underneath the shop.

"Are you with a customer, Paul," I asked, "or do you have a minute?"

"No, I'm free right now," he said. "I'm just checking to see if there's anything we're overstocked on that I might need to push."

"Knowing you, Paul," I said with a smile, "you only sell customers what's best for them."

"Well, I do, but knowing what we have down here helps too."

"Hey, I've really enjoyed the times we smoked together," I whispered, glancing about to make certain no one else was around. "I was wondering if you'd be willing to introduce me to your dealer, so I could get some myself."

"That won't work, Sammy. He only sells to people he knows."

"Well, if you introduce us, then he'll know me."

Paul chuckled. "It doesn't work that way, man. For all he knows I'd be introducing him to an undercover cop. Getting arrested is serious stuff, Sammy. No one wants to be gang-raped in Attica. I'll just buy some extra and sell it to you myself."

"OK, thanks," I said. I smiled broadly and gave him a light tap on the shoulder. "So I guess now you'll get to make a profit off *me*."

"I hadn't thought of that," he laughed. "But since you mentioned it, maybe I ought to reconsider!"

It only took Paul a few days to procure half an ounce for me. In the meantime, I bought some rolling papers from a head shop a couple of blocks from where Jake lived in the Village. A few tokes of marijuana became a regular part of my nightly bourbon ritual in Irving's basement.

Late one evening, as I was sipping on my bourbon while holding a lit joint between my fingers, I heard footsteps in the basement and looked up. My younger brother was standing in front of me.

"What ya up to?" he asked, with a mischievous grin.

I wasn't sure what to say. "I'm just unwinding, David," I ventured. "Between the store and school, I work really hard. What I'm doing isn't right, but sometimes I just need to do it."

"Can I try some?" he asked.

"Some of what? The booze or the pot?"

"I'll try both," he said enthusiastically.

I thought for a moment. "Okay, listen, David," I said. "If you join me here, this has to be our secret. You can't tell anybody. We can both get in a lot of trouble for this. Do you understand that?"

"Yeah," he said. "It'll be our secret. I promise. It would be nice to have something we can do together again, Sammy. Like we used to practice jiu-jitsu and play Chinese checkers."

The moment he said "Chinese checkers," I thought of that night in the hospital waiting room. The night our mother died. The one chance I had to let David win something, to let him feel he was a contender in my world. I had blown that chance. I wondered if introducing him now to liquor and pot would atone for that. Perhaps this was how I could do what Uncle Irving had so strongly advised—something for David.

"Okay, little brother," I said. "This is now officially our secret place. Gather round. I'm going to initiate you into the ways of manhood."

David stepped toward me. He hadn't looked this happy in months.

———⌣———

Baron's Television and Electronics was becoming an extremely busy place. Paul regularly juggled two or three customers at a time. I was out for hours each day on deliveries and lucrative repair calls. Emmanuel raced back and forth from the cash register to the showroom floor constantly. David was restocking shelves, sweeping, taking inventory, and helping customers carry purchases out to their cars.

And after a couple of pep talks from Irving, my father had given me the go-ahead to work with Jake to offer advanced antenna systems to our customers. Jake and I were still in the design stage, but we'd be producing products for sale very soon. That would take me away from the store even more frequently.

All this made it clear that we needed to hire at least one more employee. I had mentioned this to Emmanuel several times, and reiterated it one morning as he, David, and I drove to work.

"I know we need someone," Emmanuel acknowledged. "Your uncle Irving's been saying it too. But who can we get? No one in the family is available."

"We have to hire from outside the family," I said. "We have no choice."

"Damn it," Emmanuel said. "I don't have a good feeling about this."

"Would you prefer that the store was doing shitty and you didn't need anybody?" I asked facetiously.

"Don't be a smart-ass," he muttered.

"Let me take the lead on this," I said. "I'll put an ad in the paper and start interviewing candidates. I'll narrow it down to one or two people, and then they can interview with you. You'll make the final decision."

"You bet your ass I'll make the final decision," yelled Emmanuel. "You're not a partner *yet*!"

Emmanuel realized immediately that he shouldn't have said that. He glanced back nervously at David in the rear seat. David looked confused as he leaned forward.

"Sammy's becoming a partner?" David asked.

"Don't worry about that," shouted Emmanuel, now clearly flustered. "Who the hell knows who'll become a partner? Anybody might become a partner. Just do your job and don't think about it."

Emmanuel fumbled frenetically with the car radio buttons until he found the morning news report. He turned the volume up very loud.

———◡———

The first few candidates I interviewed did not impress me.

I was scheduled next to interview a young woman named Stephanie Kelly, whose résumé stated that she lived in Queens and had recently graduated from the State University of New York at Buffalo. I calculated that she'd be close to me in age, most likely a couple of years older.

I was waiting for Miss Kelly at the store's entrance when she arrived. She was an inch or two taller than I, but I noticed she was wearing rather high heels. Her strawberry-blond hair was wavy and fell on her shoulders. She had bright-green eyes. Her white blouse and dark-blue skirt were very proper but clung snugly enough to her slender frame that I needed to very consciously refocus my attention to the task at hand.

I greeted her with a handshake. "Hello, Miss Kelly," I said. "I'm Samuel Baron."

"It's very nice to meet you, Mr. Baron."

David, standing a few steps away, grinned at me salaciously as I led Miss Kelly to the small, enclosed office in the back corner of the store. I closed the door and sat behind the desk. She took the seat across from me.

"Thank you for coming in today, Miss Kelly," I said. "Did you have any trouble finding the store?"

"No, not at all," she said. "My parents bought a television here a couple of weeks ago. I was with them, so I knew where the store was."

I smiled. "Well, I certainly hope the television worked out for them."

"Yes, everybody's very happy with it," she said.

"So, you were here with your parents in the store? I must have been out on service calls. I'm sure I would have remembered you."

Miss Kelly smiled coyly. "Do you have a good memory for all the faces you encounter, Mr. Baron," she asked, "or is it more selective?"

I chuckled. "It's selective, I think." I looked down at her résumé. "It says here that you graduated from the University at Buffalo last month. What did you major in?"

"Sociology."

"And did you find that interesting, Miss Kelly?"

She looked a bit surprised, and laughed nervously. "Honestly? No. I probably shouldn't say that on an interview, but really. It's not actually a science, it just sort of pretends to be."

"So your ultimate goal is not to be a sociologist?" I asked.

"God no!" she laughed. "My goal right now is to get a job and make a living and move out of my parents' home. My father thinks that's a decent idea. My mother just thinks I should find a rich guy to marry."

I nodded and smiled. "That perspective appears to be prevalent among mothers. Do you have any retail experience?" I asked.

"Summers. I sold clothes in department stores."

"Really?" I said. "Our head salesman, Paul, did that very same thing before he joined us. He sold clothing."

"So!" she said. "You've already established that the transition from selling clothing to selling electronics is doable." She grinned. "There's a proof of concept for you, Mr. Baron!"

"Indeed," I said. "A proof of concept. I like that term. So, tell me, Miss Kelly, how would you describe your approach to sales?"

"My approach? I just try to be nice, and help people find something they really want."

"That makes sense," I said. "Our head salesman, Paul O'Rourke, developed an approach to sales that we've all now adopted. It works quite well. Would you be willing to learn a new technique?"

"Sure," she replied, then paused for a moment as if carefully weighing her next sentence. "As long as the technique isn't hard-sell or coercive," she said hesitantly.

"No, it's quite the opposite," I said.

"That's fine then," she said. "I'm always open to new things. Come to think of it, when we bought the set here, the young man who sold it to us was very helpful. Was that Paul?"

"I'm quite sure it was," I said.

"Oh, his sales technique was superb," she said. "It really put my parents at ease. He even left us alone for a while. I could learn from him."

"Excellent." I perused the résumé again. "It says here that you can't type, Miss Kelly. You never learned?"

"Does the job require typing?" she asked.

"No. No typing at all."

"Well, that's good then," she said. "So I'm curious why you asked me if I can type."

I thought for a moment. "That's an excellent question, Miss Kelly. I guess I was just looking for someplace to move the conversation and that caught my eye."

"Can *you* type?" she asked, smiling provocatively.

I laughed. "No, I'm a hunt and peck kind of guy. I'm taking night classes at CCNY in engineering. It's all exams. No papers so far. So not much typing needed."

"Engineering!" she exclaimed. "So, you're one of those smart guys, eh? Where's your slide rule, Mr. Baron?"

"I make a point of never carrying it outside my briefcase."

"Thank God. That means you really *are* one of the smart guys."

I laughed again. "So, Miss Kelly, do you have any questions you'd like to ask *me*?"

"No. I just want to say I'd really like the job. You seem like a very nice man, Mr. Baron. I'd enjoy working for you. If you give me the chance, I promise I won't disappoint you. I'm a hard worker."

"I think you'd do very well here, Miss Kelly. I'm going to set up an appointment for you to talk to my father. Hopefully, he'll think so too."

I led Miss Kelly out of the office. In the front of the store, we encountered my father near the cash register. I introduced Miss Kelly to Emmanuel and mentioned that I would be arranging a follow-up interview for the two of them. Emmanuel nodded but said nothing.

For the next couple of hours, I could see that Emmanuel was seething, but I wasn't sure why. I asked both Paul and David if they'd had any sort of run-in with him. They said no.

Shortly after 6 PM, the last customer left, and Paul and David started locking up the shop. Emmanuel grabbed my sleeve. "Get the hell into the back office with me," he whispered angrily. Despite Emmanuel's attempt to keep his voice down, both Paul and David saw clearly what was happening.

We entered the office together and Emmanuel slammed the door shut. He was now in full lycanthropic fury.

"A follow-up interview with that bimbo?!" he screamed. "What the hell is the matter with you? I give you one goddamn partner-like thing to do, and you make your decision with your *petzl!* What kind of a schmuck are you?"

"Don't you want to at least see what she's like?" I asked.

"I saw what she's like. A tight skirt and no brains!"

"So you're not going to meet with her?"

"I *have* to meet with her now because you *told* her I would! You promised her a goddamn second interview without even checking with me. So now *I'm the one* who gets to do the dirty work and tell her no. Because *you* can't control your goddamn *schvantz!*"

He was still livid as I walked out of the room.

Stephanie Kelly returned later that week for her follow-up interview. This time her blouse was pink. Her skirt was black, and perhaps even a bit snugger than the one she had worn when I met with her.

Emmanuel told her to go into the back office and wait for him there. As she headed that way, Emmanuel took a few steps toward me, rolled his eyes, and whispered, "This won't take long."

But it took quite a while.

I kept looking at my watch. The two of them had been together in the office for well over an hour and a half when they finally emerged and headed toward the front of the store where I had just rung up a sale. Emmanuel had his arm around Miss Kelly's shoulders. They were both smiling broadly.

"We're going to hire Stephanie here," Emmanuel announced with just the hint of a flourish.

"Thank you, Manny," she said, beaming.

I looked at the two of them. "*Manny*, eh?" I smiled. "So I see we're all on a first-name basis now. How nice. And it's great that you'll be working here, Stephanie. Please call me Sammy."

"I'm so excited!" Stephanie exclaimed. "Thank you both so much."

Stephanie hugged Emmanuel, then hugged me. Paul and David quickly lined up behind me, and each scored a very enthusiastic and cheerful hug as well.

Stephanie danced out of the store, thoroughly exuberant.

I caught Emmanuel alone a few minutes later.

I said, "So I was right about Stephanie after all, wasn't I?"

Emmanuel looked at me sheepishly for a moment, then started chuckling. Soon he was laughing so hard that it took him a moment before he could speak.

"No! You weren't right. You had no goddamn idea how good she was!" he howled. "You got lucky! You used your *schvantz* instead of your brain, but you made a lucky guess. Even an idiot makes a lucky guess now and then."

Emmanuel slapped my shoulder affectionately and walked away, still laughing hysterically.

19.
Restraint

VIRGINIA FERGUSON AND I joined the afternoon tai chi group in Golden Gate Park and were soon regulars.

It took some of the older members a while to warm up to us, but after a couple of weeks we were always greeted warmly and given hugs goodbye at session's end. It turned out they all spoke a bit more English than they were willing to fess up to at first.

I very much enjoyed the goodbye hugs. The increased risk of contagion the contact posed, though, remained foremost in my mind until I got home and showered and shampooed thoroughly. After bathing I also then daubed my face with rubbing alcohol (an admittedly ritualistic precaution).

But before engaging in such ablution I'd invariably walk Virginia to her house, which was on the way back to mine. We always had interesting discussions.

Virginia was far more comfortable probing private matters than was I.

"You're such an interesting and successful man, Sammy," she ventured one afternoon. "How come you're not in a relationship?"

"I'm happy as I am," I said.

"Doug and I know some women you might like. There are a few in the Rosicrucian order. You'd have the spirituality thing in common."

"I've told you about my sexual wiring," I said. "It's tricky. I'm not sure I want to venture there with another person again. I'm actually surprisingly adept at amusing *myself.*"

"With your imagination, I'm not surprised," she said. "But you told me there was a special woman you shared SM with, before it went bad. What was her name?"

It took me a few moments to respond—it was not something I especially cared to discuss. "Her name was Stephanie," I said finally. "I loved her, and I should have stayed with her. I've told you this before, Virginia, but I'll acknowledge it again. Leaving her was a huge mistake on my part." My voice grew softer. "A sad, unsalvageable mistake."

Because Yonkers was located in Westchester County, just north of the New York City border, customers at Baron's Television and Electronics avoided paying New York City sales tax. Many shoppers mentioned to me that this was an added incentive in their patronizing our store.

Shortly after I made my final payment to Uncle Irving and became a full partner, I began taking Sunday-afternoon drives to Valley Stream, a village on the westernmost edge of Long Island. Like Yonkers, it lay just over the New York City border, in this case to the east. Shopping centers and large stores attracted patrons from the boroughs of Brooklyn and Queens. These people too were lured by the avoidance of city sales tax.

Our store in Yonkers had been up and running for two and a half years, and continued to increase its profits every month. We had a full staff of employees now. As successful as the store was, the day-to-day job of running it had become quite predictable and redundant.

It seemed time to open a second store. Valley Stream looked to be an ideal location. I did as much research and investigation as I could to justify the idea, then went to chat with old Uncle Irving.

Irving was now retired. He seemed very happy. My payout to him, along with the profits from our store that he earned along the way, had padded his nest egg to a very comfortable level. His children were old enough to run his grocery store, and he still took a small stipend from their profits each month as well. Irving's rocking-chair time, along with his daily allocation of schnapps and cigars, had increased markedly.

Although Irving no longer had an official role in Baron's Television and Electronics, I felt he was a vital ally in my convincing Emmanuel to open a second location. Irving and I had our discussion. As I anticipated, he was enthusiastic in his approval. We decided we'd present the idea to Emmanuel together, out on the porch, after our next Sunday family dinner.

Emmanuel's reaction was eminently predictable. "Why open another store?" he yelled at Irving and me. "*This* store is doing better than we ever could have hoped. Why risk another store that could fail? Who needs it? You're both *meshuggah*!"

Irving and I agreed that the best approach was not to try to convince him immediately, but for both of us to keep hammering the idea at him every few days until he succumbed from exhaustion.

It took about three months.

It was obvious from the outset that I'd run the Valley Stream store and my father would run the Yonkers store, but how to divvy up our two strongest and most experienced employees, Paul O'Rourke and Stephanie Kelly, was much more difficult to work through with Emmanuel.

My father did believe Paul to be the stronger and more reliable person. But that was probably because Paul was male, and Emmanuel just couldn't fathom a woman being more adept at managerial responsibilities than a man.

Despite that prejudice, Emmanuel always had a special relationship with Stephanie and didn't want to give her up either. He tried arguing that because this whole idea of second store was a crazy pipe dream of mine, I didn't deserve to take either employee.

At his core, though, Emmanuel knew his position was untenable. I understood that, and so I knew he'd eventually acquiesce. It took patience to wait out his spirited protestations, but we finally reached a compromise. Paul would stay with Emmanuel full time. Stephanie would work four days a week with me at the new Valley Stream store but remain one day a week in Yonkers with my father.

The agreement was adequate for my needs. Perhaps more importantly, it adhered to the principle Uncle Irving had so gently ingrained in me—it allowed Emmanuel to retain his self-respect.

When I explained the plan to Stephanie, I was apologetic. She and I had discussed the possibility of her transferring to the Valley Stream store several times prior, and Stephanie was very eager to make the move. We enjoyed working together. And her commute to Long Island was a much easier one than to Yonkers.

But when I told her that Emmanuel insisted on having her with him at least once a week, she chuckled. "That's nice," she said. "I do love him. He's kind of an old curmudgeon, but he's a sweet guy at heart."

"And you're the daughter he never had," I added.

"I guess I am," she said.

Baron's Television and Electronics in Valley Stream was a larger property than the Yonkers store. It held more stock, and soon exceeded the original location in monthly profits. It drew customers from Brooklyn, Queens, and from the Long Island suburbs as well.

The Valley Stream store had a small second story, perfect for a few offices. I eventually consolidated all ordering, accounting, and inventory paperwork in those offices.

One evening, shortly after we closed for the day, I headed up there to review the accounting ledger. I found Stephanie Kelly in an office, typing what turned out to be an angry letter to one of our suppliers who had reneged on a promise to us. She didn't notice me watching her for nearly a minute. She was focused on her task—her typing seemed ferocious and passionate.

Finally she sensed my presence and turned to look at me in the office doorway.

"It's the assholes at Smithers and Sons," she said heatedly. "The lovely folks who supply us with the portable tape recorders that are selling so well? Their slime-ass salesman promised me a deal, and now he says he can't do it. So I'm taking it up with the owner."

"I applaud your tenacity," I said.

"And I'll call him, too. I just want him to read the letter first and have it in his hand when I call."

"I have no doubt you'll prevail," I said. "You can be fearsome when your mind's made up."

"Do not mess with *this* lady!" she said with a smile.

I waited until she finished the letter and pulled it out of the typewriter.

Then I said, "It *is* strange, though, that you type with such exceptional speed and precision. Two years ago, when we hired you, your application stated that you couldn't type, and you confirmed that in your interview with me. Do you remember that, Steph?"

She marched over and stood directly in front of me. In her heels, she was just slightly taller than I. She cocked her head and put her hands on her hips provocatively.

"So what are you saying, Sammy. That I lied on my application?"

"Well, you did!" I laughed.

"Because if I had said I could type, then you and every other man alive would have seen me as a secretary and nothing more. You know that's true!"

"But you did lie," I said teasingly. "It seems that you ought to suffer some sort of penalty for that." I thought for a moment. "I'll tell you what . . . if you have dinner with me tonight, I'll forgive the incident and wipe your record clean."

She sighed loudly and rolled her eyes. "Oh God! Are you asking me out, Sammy?"

"I'm trying to," I said. "I don't appear to be doing very well."

"Not the most romantic come-on, Samuel. Lying on my application! That's really the best you could come up with?"

"I'm sorry," I said. "I guess this sort of banter isn't my forte, Steph. But if you want to go grab some pizza and beer when we're done here, I really would like spending the time with you, outside of work."

She reached out and gingerly straightened my tie and ran her hands down the lapels of my suit jacket. "You know, everyone says it's a mistake for a woman to date her boss. They say it doesn't usually turn out well."

"I don't think that will be a problem for *us*," I assured her.

"Actually, I don't either," she said.

I wondered whether the cocktail-related knowledge I had absorbed in my many labs with Jake could help me look a bit more sophisticated in Stephanie's eyes. Steph and I had done two weeknight pizza runs after work. They went well, so I asked her to join me for a Saturday-night visit to an upscale restaurant on the upper eastside of Manhattan.

The waiter asked if we wanted cocktails. Stephanie motioned to me to go ahead and order first while she perused the cocktail list.

"A Beefeater martini," I said, "very dry. Up. With olives. And please, let it sit on the ice for a minute or two before you pour it."

"Very good, sir," the waiter said.

"I'll have a Singapore sling," Stephanie said.

The waiter nodded and strode off.

"A Singapore sling?" I asked Stephanie. "I know a bit about cocktails. I've never heard of that one."

"We used to drink them in college," she said.

My martini arrived looking as I expected. Stephanie's Singapore sling was a reddish-pink concoction sitting in a tall, curvy glass resembling those that New York candy stores used for ice cream sodas. The drink was garnished with a long wooden skewer holding a slice of pineapple, a slice of orange, and a maraschino cherry.

Jake would have considered it a monstrosity.

"You're looking at my drink like you've never seen anything like it before," she said. "Would you like a taste?"

She passed the entity over to me. I took a small sip.

"Oh God!" I said. "That tastes like candy."

She smiled. "It goes down very easy."

About an hour later we were each working on our third round of drinks. I was also finishing a large bowl of fettuccine Alfredo, sopping up the remaining sauce with some crusty Italian bread. Stephanie was halfway through her plate of veal parmigiana.

She looked across the table at me.

"This is our third date, Sammy," she said. "You haven't made a pass at me yet. Time to get on the ball with that."

"Actually, I've been meaning to talk to you about it," I said. "I have some very specific tastes in that area, and I wasn't sure if you'd be amenable. I've been waiting for the right time to bring it up."

"Well, I'm pretty schnockered, so I guess now's as good a time as any."

"Well, Steph, I'm partial to ropes, handcuffs, blindfolds—"

"Let me stop you right there, cowboy," she interrupted. "That's a dead end for me. I can't stand being restrained. When I was a freshman in college I pledged for a sorority. Their ritual involved putting manacles on my wrists for the evening of pledging. The chain between them was long and hung down to my knees, so I could move my hands pretty well, but even so, I couldn't stand it. After just ten or fifteen minutes I was so uncomfortable I told them I changed my mind. I had them take the manacles off me, and I left. I never pledged another sorority again. I'm sorry, Sammy, I just won't be restrained. By you or anybody."

I gazed at her face, and was reminded how lovely she was. "I think you've misinterpreted my predilection," I said. "I have no interest in restraining you, Steph. I'd like *you* to restrain *me*."

Stephanie's eyes widened and she leaned toward me.

"Well! That's different. You want me to tie you up?"

"And have your way with me."

"Do anything I want?"

"Well, within reason. I do have to show up intact and relatively unscathed for work on Monday."

"Wow. I never would have thought. At the store you're always in such control of everything."

"Maybe that's why I want to cede control to someone else on occasion." Stephanie smiled and took a long sip of her Singapore sling.

"I think I can handle this, big boy. It actually might be really fun."

"I'll do what you want, and worship you," I said teasingly.

"You'll *worship* me, eh? So, Sammy," she said with a sly laugh, "I'll be your shiksa goddess—*literally!*"

I laughed. "How the hell do you even know what a shiksa goddess *is?*" I asked her.

"Sammy, you're not the first Jewish man I've ever dated."

———————⌣———————

Emmanuel, Paul, Stephanie, and I were together for an evening meeting in the Yonkers store when we received the phone call. My brother, David, had been found dead of a drug overdose.

Emmanuel pummeled the wall with the phone receiver and screamed, "No, no, no!" He dropped the receiver and ran directly at me. I was still seated at the meeting table. I turned slightly toward him. Emmanuel yelled, "Your mother said to watch over him, goddamnit!" He began to bang his fists hysterically on my chest.

Stephanie gently pulled him off me and held him.

"We all saw David losing his grip," she said. "It got worse when Sammy became a partner, but we all tried to help him. Manny, you kept telling him that if he worked hard and saved his money, he could become a partner someday too."

"Do you think he believed me?" Emmanuel asked, sobbing now.

"I'm sure he did," Stephanie said. She embraced him tightly.

Paul glanced at me with a worried grimace, and then quickly looked away.

At my urging, Paul had convinced his dealer that he could work directly with David and me. While Paul and I limited our purchases to marijuana and an occasional gram of cocaine, we both knew David had begun experimenting with harder drugs. We had tried multiple times to warn him against it.

But when David learned I'd become a partner, he felt betrayed and no longer trusted anything either Paul or I told him.

I breathed deeply and gazed about the room. The phone receiver still lay on the floor, emitting the periodic yelps of a disconnected circuit. Emmanuel cried in Stephanie's arms. Paul was motionless, head bowed.

I remained silent.

I thought about that game of Chinese checkers I could have let David win.

20.
Chicago

SHORTLY AFTER LANDING at O'Hare International Airport, I retrieved my large suitcase from the baggage claim carousel on the lower level of the terminal. As soon as I did, I spotted Stephanie entering the arrivals area. She craned her head in various directions, trying to locate me.

With my bag in one hand and briefcase in the other, I scooted in the opposite direction, making a grand circle back toward her. The intense congestion surrounding the luggage conveyors effectively shielded me from her view, and my short stature assured that she would not glimpse my head above the crowd. I emerged from the masses, and tread softly until I was just behind her, then silently inched even closer.

When she felt the material from my open suit coat barely brush the back of her skirt, she stepped to the side and turned her head to see who had encroached upon her space, but guessed immediately that it was I. It was my habitual greeting ploy. Though Stephanie had become far more vigilant over the years, I was still almost always successful in materializing directly behind her before she noticed.

The hug and kiss we exchanged, there in public, was quick and polite. But her smile and the intensity of her gaze made it obvious that she was very happy to be with me again.

"It's good to see you, Steph," I said. "Thanks for picking me up."

"You're welcome, Sammy. It's good to see you too."

We set off for the terminal's parking garage. As always, Stephanie had to race a bit to keep up with my bounding stride. She didn't seem to mind.

"How was the flight in from New York?" Stephanie asked.

"Do you really want to know?" I laughed. "All right then. LaGuardia was a mess. This place, O'Hare, I'll hate forever. And they put me on one of those older planes where first class is hardly worth paying for. But I have to say, the service was good. The flight attendant remembered me by name. I had a few shots of bourbon, and that took the edge off." I paused a moment. "I'm looking forward to my stay here, Steph."

"Me too, Sammy. I know how busy you are with all the stores, but I really wish you could spend more time here." She looked in my direction for a moment as we walked. "Is it my imagination, or do you have a few more grey hairs than when I saw you last?" she asked.

"I don't think it's your imagination."

"You look very distinguished, and very handsome," she assured me. "I talked to Manny today."

"You talk to my father more than I do," I said, "since he retired."

"We go back a long way, Manny and me."

"You're still the daughter he always wanted. That's been well established. How did he sound to you?"

"Manny's hanging in. He sounds more bitter, more depressed, but that's a progression that's been going on for quite some time, Sammy. For the past couple of months I've talked to him almost every day. He's been insisting that he would have been happier if he'd just kept the business as one little neighborhood TV repair shop."

"That's sad," I said.

"Does it ever make you doubt what you did, Sammy?"

"No, Steph, not for a moment. What would he have now? What would any of us have? It's really not about that anyway. You know that. It's about all the family stuff—the change, the loss. He just can't get past it. When my mother passed away it was bad enough. But once David died of the heroin overdose, Emmanuel lost his grip on everything, and he's never gotten it back. I wish there was more I could do for him, but you know, he's a stubborn geezer these days."

"I know you love him, Sammy. I told him that."

We entered the short-term parking area and I immediately scanned the aisles, determined to locate the SUV before Stephanie revealed where it was. She knew exactly what I was up to, and walked passively by my side, careful not to signal a direction.

"I see it!" I exclaimed.

I tossed my luggage into the vehicle's rear storage compartment, then entered on the driver's side. As I adjusted the mirrors and seat, Stephanie climbed into the passenger's side, peered around the parking lot to be sure no one was nearby, shut the car door, and opened the glove compartment. From a small satchel she retrieved a mirror, set it gently on the horizontal surface of the opened glove box door, and carefully laid out two generous lines of cocaine.

I watched with rapt attention as she tore open the foil wrapper of a sealed, alcohol-soaked, square cotton swab, wiped her fingers, then carefully scrubbed down a small, translucent plastic tube that had once served as the core of a coiled roll of dental floss. As she waved the cylinder in the air to dry it, I thoroughly abluted my hands with alcohol gel from a small container in the pocket of my suit coat. I took the plastic tube from Stephanie.

"Just the way you like it," she said.

"Thanks, Steph," I replied as I reached over for the mirror, checked the lot again for passersby, then lowered my head and inhaled the line, being as precise as possible to take exactly half the line into one nostril, then switch to the other nostril for the remaining half.

The rush was immediate—invigorating and cathartic.

I returned the paraphernalia to Stephanie, who took her line quickly through an old segment of unwashed drinking straw.

Our SUV exited the airport parking lot. It was a relatively mild winter evening in Chicago. Small amounts of snow and slush lingered on the streets. The sky was clear and crisp. I drove toward the condominium I kept in Evanston, just north of the city. It had been a couple of months since I'd seen it.

"How's the apartment?" I asked.

"I haven't been there since your last trip, but I had the housekeeper do a thorough, off-cycle cleaning just yesterday," said Stephanie. "It should be nice. It will be so good spending some time with you again, Sammy."

"Yes, it will," I said, reaching over and resting a hand lightly on Stephanie's thigh. "So, you have me booked into the appointment with the alderman tomorrow afternoon, right? What time again?"

"Two thirty, Sammy."

"What were you able to find out about this guy, Steph? He's newly elected—I know that. I looked at a couple of newspaper articles. A bit of a blowhard populist, don't you think?"

"I've asked around and read up on him quite a bit. He's a straight arrow." She paused and chuckled, "My God, Sammy, by Chicago standards he's a goddamn product of immaculate conception! You remember working with his predecessor? That guy was a big schmoozer and wheeler-dealer. This guy's going to be the exact opposite.

"I think your biggest problem's going to be that the alderman is brand new at this and may not know exactly how the game is played. And his whole election campaign was based on his being the squeaky clean, all-American boy, so he'll probably be hesitant to deal at all. Also, whatever you're planning to pitch to him, you'll need to do it fast. He likes his meetings quick and done." She paused. "We could really use the zoning approval, Sammy. Expanding the store just that much would double our profits."

"I'm optimistic," I said. "By the way, Steph, you've been doing a great job running the Chicago store. I don't say it often enough. No matter what happens with the alderman tomorrow, you're going to get a nice bonus and a substantial raise for next year."

"Thank you so much," she said. "That means a lot to me."

"And the way you take care of me when I'm here—I appreciate that very much too."

"Taking care of you is my favorite part, Sammy."

Rush hour traffic was abating. The roads started to move well.

"Do you want to pick up some takeout for later from that Hunan place we like?"

"I picked up two bags of your favorites from there on the way over. I guess you didn't see it in the trunk. We can heat it up when we're ready."

"Amazing!" I exclaimed, laughing. "You're always one step ahead of me, Steph."

"I try," she said.

We reached the condo, parked the SUV in the underground lot, and stepped into the small, slow-moving elevator. As it conveyed us, I put down my bags, took Stephanie in my arms, and we shared a passionate kiss.

I plopped my luggage down in the entranceway as we entered the apartment. "I'm going to take a shower," I said.

"Do you want another line first?"

"No, I'll wait till I get out of the shower. Can you make me a bourbon on ice, though?"

"Sure thing. I'm in the mood for a drink myself," she said.

———※———

I emerged from the bathroom naked. Stephanie stood in the hallway, holding a cocktail in each hand and clad in sheer black lingerie. I was struck by the contrast of her luminescent, shoulder-length, strawberry-blond hair as it played against the sleek black shoulder straps of her outfit.

She handed me my drink. We toasted, and headed to the bedroom.

We climbed under the sheets and sipped our drinks. On the nightstand on my side of the bed was a plastic dental floss core identical to the one in the car. It too had been freshly disinfected and now sat on a clean paper napkin. I instinctively checked the orientation of the napkin's crease to assure that the tube now rested on what had been the napkin's inner surface, prior to its being unfolded. I had pointed out to Stephanie long ago that the napkin's outer surface was clearly more likely to have become populated with unwanted microorganisms.

She was incredibly good about remembering such things.

Stephanie put her drink down. From a tiny envelope she dumped a small pile of cocaine onto a rectangular hand mirror. Using a single-edged razor blade, Stephanie meticulously chopped and herded the pile into two ribbons of very fine powder. She gingerly handed the mirror to me. I inhaled my line and then passed it back to Stephanie, who took hers.

Stephanie snuggled beside me.

"Being at the airport made me think of the time we flew out to Las Vegas for the weekend," she said. "You remember? We were doing coke on the plane in the first-class cabin's bathroom."

"I remember. You went in first and laid out two lines," I said. "I was waiting outside to go in as soon as you came out. But I turned away for an instant and some guy tried to sneak in ahead of me just as you exited."

"You almost knocked that guy on his ass pushing in ahead of him!"

"You had a mirror with two lines laid out on the sink in there. Can you imagine what would have happened if I had let the guy go in ahead of me?"

We laughed hard, hugged and kissed, drank some more bourbon, and snorted two more lines.

She said she loved me. I told her I loved her too.

Stephanie whispered, "Would you like to be tortured a little, Sammy?"

"Oh, Steph, that would be great, if you're up for it. Are you sure you have the energy?"

"I've been looking forward to it all day."

Stephanie eased out of bed. From the back wall of the bedroom closet she retrieved a cloth satchel that contained my prized collection of leather restraints and sex toys. She cuffed my hands behind my back and used a wide strap to bind my upper arms tightly against my body. Stephanie carefully piled high the four pillows on the bed and positioned me gently so that I leaned against them.

She had become incredibly adept at this.

"Is that comfy?" she asked.

"Feels good, Steph."

"That's the last thing you'll say to me for a while, sweetie." With that, Stephanie scoured a black ball gag with a freshly unsheathed alcohol swab. I took the ball receptively into my mouth and felt her buckle the strap behind my head.

Stephanie kissed me lovingly on the forehead, then went to work on my nipples, squeezing and kneading them between her fingers and thumbs. She started gently but increased the intensity over time, finally using her teeth as well as her fingers to tug and stretch my vulnerable flesh. My muffled moans grew louder as she progressed. The sounds I emitted were visceral, with a raw and primal edge.

Stephanie paused and admired the effects of her initial handiwork. I had developed an unwavering and insistent erection. My nipples were red and slightly enlarged.

"I'll leave you for a here while I fetch the ice," she whispered, "but you do need the snakebite kit first."

From the satchel, Stephanie removed a standard camper's snakebite kit, which consisted of two rubber suction cups shaped like oversized pink thimbles. She licked their top rims, then squeezed their bottoms and placed one over each of my nipples. The moistened rims adhered to my skin as Stephanie slowly released her grip on each, inducing them to begin their merciless and unrelenting suction. Their purpose here was not to draw out snake venom, but to suck upon and enlarge my already compromised chest nodules.

As Stephanie walked into the kitchen and filled a large bowl with ice from the refrigerator's front dispenser, I knew she was listening closely to be certain that my persistent moans were those of pleasure-pain, and not spasmodic gulps of choking or panic. She took pride now in how adept she had become in satisfying my idiosyncratic needs. She had, at first, employed the restraints and paraphernalia precisely as I instructed, but over time she developed variations and embellishments of her own.

These nuances and enhancements brought me profoundly greater pleasure because they suggested true power and control inherent in her female being, rather than merely imitative pretense.

When Stephanie returned to the bedroom, the suction cups were pulling hard against my flesh—their efficacy had increased steadily and inexorably.

My erect penis started to throb a bit. My eyes were closed. Somehow, the fact that my cries were suppressed intensified my immersion. Stephanie cupped her hands together, shoveled up six or seven cubes of ice, then swaddled her palms tightly and suddenly about my member.

My eyes shot open. My high-pitched scream from behind the gag assured Stephanie that she had successfully wrenched me from my reverie and reminded me that *she* would control my focus. The ice engendered almost instant detumescence, leaving my penis splayed soft and powerless against my thigh.

Stephanie compressed and gently removed the snakebite cups. She took a moment to examine my nipples, now fully engorged and pinkish red. Her teeth had nicked them up a bit—she was careful now to curl her lips over her teeth as a buffer as she once again began to gnaw and tug at the nipples. She also dug her long, freshly manicured fingernails up and down the flesh of my torso, leaving raw red furrows in their wake. As she did, she gently massaged my limp member with her coarse pubic hair, and felt it gradually regaining life.

She now turned her attention entirely to my penis, licking and stroking it until it again rose high and thick, and began throbbing. She mounted me from above and rode me gently and slowly, massaging her breasts as she did, while monitoring me closely for the slightest sign of impending ejaculation. I watched her with anticipatory dread, and emitted a wide-eyed, muffled scream from behind my gag as she lifted herself off me, scooped up a handful of ice, and applied it with seemingly unfeeling precision to my erect penis, rendering me once more immediately and sadly limp.

I arched my back, and writhed and moaned for half a minute, then gradually relaxed my body. Stephanie waited while I did, then laid out a small line of cocaine and held the mirror and plastic tube to my nose. "You'll need a bit of energy, sweetie," she said. "I'll let you rest a couple of minutes, but then who knows how many more iterations I'll subject you to?" She ran her fingers lightly along my scalp. "And I'm sure you're aware that you'll need to provide me with at least two orgasms of my own before I even think about letting you come."

———————◡———————

I awoke at 4 AM, my habitual rising time. I had not set an alarm.

The condo was pitch black and quiet. I didn't want to disturb Stephanie, so I did not turn on a light. I sat on the edge of the bed for a moment, then bounded up. I tried to be silent as I threw on my sweats, grabbed my garment bag and briefcase, and left the apartment.

My ability to program my subconscious mind to awaken me, without fail, at the precise hour of my choosing was an odd gift, but one I appreciated, especially when I slept with Stephanie.

I took the elevator down to the garage, started up the SUV, and drove out alone into Evanston's dark, cold morning. Stars were still visible in the sky. On my way out, I made certain that Stephanie's sleek little sports car was parked in one of the garage's visitor spaces—she'd need no assistance from me in getting to work.

I had become accustomed to driving different cars in different cities. I did a good deal of business travel. Baron's Television and Electronics now had stores in Yonkers, Valley Stream, Harlem, Newark, Philadelphia, Chicago, and Denver. With Emmanuel retired, I ran the entire enterprise.

The independent company I co-owned with Jake specialized in advanced antenna systems and had customers all over the United States. Because Jake was now a tenured professor, he rarely could get away to meet with clients, so that fell to me as well.

As a result of my extensive travel schedule, I maintained an ongoing membership with a national fitness center that had branches in every major city of the United States. All were open twenty-four hours a day, every day of the year. I was quite familiar with the route to the northern Chicago branch—I had been there many times when I stayed in the condo with Stephanie. I generally arrived at the gym between 4:30 and 5 AM.

I did not enjoy getting up that early, but it was necessary. Early morning was the only reasonable timeslot to insert a physical workout that I knew wouldn't get gobbled up by work obligations. I found it odd that people who knew my schedule always assumed I liked arising at 4 AM and that doing so came naturally to me. Those who met me again later in life were often surprised to learn that I no longer kept those hours.

My daily workout never varied. It lasted ninety minutes, divided into three phases: I began with thirty minutes of cardiovascular work on either a stationary bicycle or a treadmill. Then an hour and ten minutes circling through various weight machines with sub-phases focusing on the upper body, the torso, and the legs. Finally, I did twenty minutes of yoga stretches.

I attacked the cardiovascular and weight work aggressively, pushing hard, endeavoring to do a bit more each session.

In stark contrast, I was not in those days overly enamored of the final twenty minutes of yoga stretching and cooldown. I executed the postures dutifully, but invariably became impatient with them. I never shirked, though, because I had discovered that as important as endurance and strength were to my proficiency at jiu-jitsu sparring, the elasticity, grace, and calm focus derived from yoga were equal or greater contributors to mastery over various sparring opponents. I took full advantage of this realization, but persisted in finding the potency of the gentle stretches annoyingly counterintuitive.

When I finished that morning's workout, I showered in the locker room, then walked over to the sink area to shave. As always, before lathering my face, I observed myself for a few moments, naked in the large mirror. I saw a short, slender man, solid and wiry, but devoid of exceptional muscular development. The cautionary reminders from Emmanuel, so many years ago, had been correct—I had stopped growing by the age of twelve and shed the baby fat that made me look husky as a boy.

When I first started working out seriously with weights at that small jiu-jitsu academy in Yonkers, it frustrated me enormously that despite the dedication and ferocity with which I attacked the workouts, I could not add bulk to my frame. I eventually consulted several personal trainers who all told me the same thing: my anatomy was not conducive to building muscle mass.

But this no longer bothered me. I used it to my advantage. My lack of bulk belied a body that was exceeding strong and agile. New opponents in jiu-jitsu sparring matches always underestimated my power. Whenever they did so, they made it easy for me to pounce upon them mercilessly.

Certain individuals with whom I had sparred many times over the years persisted in miscalculating my strength. No matter how many times these opponents sparred with me, they remained curiously incapable of recalibrating their perception of the man they were fighting, and thus continued to be easy prey.

I had packed a freshly pressed pinstripe suit and solid blue tie in my garment bag, which I now paired with a white shirt for a traditional look that I thought would be optimal for my meeting with the alderman that afternoon. I left the gym and made a quick stop at my favorite Chicago sandwich shop for my usual egg salad sandwich on whole wheat toast, and a bottle of whatever fresh juice struck my fancy that morning—today it was a mélange of carrot, beet, and apple.

One of the reasons for my longtime loyalty to this particular sandwich shop was its owner's scrupulous sanitation standards and the employees' consistent adherence to those guidelines. Anyone handling food donned a fresh pair of clean plastic gloves, and disposed of those gloves to handle money. Although I had never witnessed a breach of that policy at this shop, I nonetheless scrutinized my sandwich's construction. When traveling to a new city, I had on several occasions entered a sandwich shop with which I was unfamiliar, ordered a sandwich, and observed closely as the employees worked. On those occasions that I found the sanitation practices subpar,

I reacted in a measured and consistent manner. I never argued with the employee. I politely paid for my sandwich, disposed of it in the store's trash receptacle on my way out, and tried a different shop. But I never failed to accurately note the name and location of the offending establishment, and to write a detailed letter of complaint to the owner or corporate office.

I returned to my SUV, cleaned my hands thoroughly with alcohol sanitizer, and gobbled down my sandwich and juice.

I spent the rest of the morning driving around the city, cruising by each of the large electronic discount stores, and stopping to visit several. I was always interested in what my competitors featured, how much they charged, and especially in how aggressively or passively their sales-floor employees behaved toward customers. It was my long-held belief that overly aggressive salespeople turned away far more customers than they enticed. The sales training that Paul O'Rourke and I had developed for my chain of stores stressed becoming knowledgeable, helpful, and attentive, but also acquiring an ingrained sense of when to afford customers time to themselves to ponder and weigh the choices presented. It was particularly important, during such interludes, to keep an eye on the customers, and return to them promptly when most advantageous—the ability to gauge the optimal moment to reappear was an art form in itself. In many ways, that skill separated my most successful salespeople from their less skillful peers.

Interestingly, although Paul and I had developed the sales-training curriculum, we both agreed that Stephanie did a vastly better job than either Paul or I in presenting the course to new trainees.

Shortly before noon, I arrived at the Chicago branch of Baron's Television and Electronics, located in the Logan Square neighborhood of Chicago, about seven miles northwest of downtown. Nearly five years ago I had bought the property and built the store for a fraction of what a comparable property in the downtown Loop would have cost.

I found a parking spot down the block and perused the storefront as I crossed the street to approach the entrance. The store looked good. The expansive front window was sparkling clean. The displays behind it were well laid out and enticing. The new sign Stephanie and I had recently ordered to replace the original was similar enough to the old to assure continuity, but sufficiently different to suggest an inventory that remained cutting edge. With respect to the new sign, I had viewed endless design documents and photos, and had Stephanie's assurance that the finished product looked wonderful—but this was the first time I had seen the sign in person.

It was clear upon entering the store that Stephanie had prepared the employees on the floor to expect my arrival at some point during the day. Every employee, even those whom I had never met, identified me immediately, and greeted me with excitement and overt deference. As always, I sought to put every employee I met at ease, shaking hands, using their first name that I read off their name tag, asking how things were going, making jokes and small talk. I'm not sure I realized it then, but although I ostensibly demonstrated to each employee that I did not consider myself in any way superior, I would have been quite shocked and somewhat annoyed had anyone in the mix dared to actually act toward me as an equal.

Each time I concluded shaking the hand of an employee, I smiled, wished the worker a good day, and then closed my right hand into a tight fist as I straightened my arm. The pressure on my fingers and palm was my reminder that my hand had been potentially contaminated by skin-borne viruses and bacteria, and needed to be scrubbed vigorously with a dollop of alcohol sanitizer from the small bottle in my coat pocket—but only when the opportunity arose for me to do so inconspicuously. Sometimes another employee would materialize before such a safe haven presented itself, and I would find myself shaking hands with two, three, or four employees prior to finally discovering an ablution oasis. My sense of carrying with me an unfinished task requiring immediate resolution increased with each handshake. If sufficiently bombarded by well-wishers, I would eventually recalibrate my course toward a corner or a small cul-de-sac behind some appliances, to decontaminate and start afresh.

I developed these habits at our first store in Yonkers. Soon after its opening, I started coming down with annoyingly frequent colds and flus.

A bit of research at the library made it clear that these bouts of illness were due to the constant physical contact I had with customers and with the surfaces they touched. I instituted two changes to my personal behavior which in short time became habitual: I cleaned my hands frequently, and I never touched my face. That second measure took real focus and persistence to instill. Reaching for my lips, chin, and other facial areas was an instinctive reaction to a host of different stimuli.

I had methodically explored the Chicago store's expansive showroom for four or five minutes when I noticed Stephanie in the distance. She was calling an employee's attention to a large-screen television floor model—its display had grown a bit blurred and distorted, undoubtedly after thousands of hours of nonstop display broadcasting. She directed the employee to replace it with a new one immediately.

As Stephanie turned to walk toward the stereo displays, she was startled to see me standing less than a foot behind her. "You never get tired of sneaking up on me, do you, Sammy?" she laughed. I extended my hand for a polite and professional handshake.

"The store looks wonderful, Steph," I said. "You must have passed around my photo. Even the new employees recognized me instantly."

"I used a very flattering picture," she said with a smirk.

"Well, thank goodness for that," I chuckled. "Can we go to your office and talk? I want to review the alderman spiel and see what you think."

* * *

At precisely 2:30 PM, an assistant to Alderman Jarielski came into the waiting room where I had been sitting. "Alderman Jarielski will see you now," she said.

"Thank you," I said, smiling politely. I arose, grabbed my briefcase, and followed the young woman into the alderman's office.

Alderman Jarielski stood behind his desk, reviewing my request for a zoning waiver. He appeared a bit bigger and more imposing than the photographs I had viewed. Jarielski's biographical information prominently mentioned that the alderman had played linebacker on his college football team. His physique and general appearance were consistent with that—tall and broad shouldered, with light-brown hair and chiseled facial features.

I approached the desk and held my hand out for nearly ten seconds before the alderman lifted his head from the zoning application and shook my hand quickly and perfunctorily. "Sit down, Mr. Baron," he said.

As I lowered myself into the chair, I imagined for a brief instant the large, athletic alderman stepping toward me and throwing a punch. I blocked the punch and took firm hold of the alderman's wrist and sleeve. Squatting slightly, I pivoted and thrust my back into Jarielski's exposed abdomen, then raised myself up and threw the alderman over my hip and onto the floor. As Jarielski lay on the ground, I maintained my grip on his wrist, twisted his arm violently, and yanked it downward while simultaneously raising my own knee with sufficient force to strike the arm and fracture Jarielski's elbow with an audible snap.

"It's good to meet you, Alderman," I said as my reverie concluded, and I reached into my briefcase to retrieve my packet of information. "I've heard only good things about you, sir," I added.

"I see here that you're seeking to expand your store into the adjoining lot, Mr. Baron. By my calculations, that would increase your store's size by about forty percent. It would also significantly exceed our zoning limitations. I'm sure you know that I campaigned on preventing this neighborhood from being infiltrated by huge warehouse-size stores. Why should I consider your request?"

"For the past five years, Mr. Alderman, we've been good and responsible members of your community. We employ more of your neighborhood's young people than any other business. And ours aren't minimum-wage jobs, sir—they are jobs with good remuneration and a caliber of healthcare and retirement benefits that no one else in this neighborhood can even remotely approach. Expanding will enable us to offer more of these jobs in an economy that needs it, and will allow us to continue to offer televisions, stereos, computers, and other electronic equipment to your constituents at fair prices without them having to travel elsewhere in the city. When people stay in the neighborhood, the other local businesses benefit too. You campaigned on keeping this district vibrant and competitive. Expanding our store will help you do that."

"Allowing a *new* business to open on the lot next to yours would help the community as well. You know, Mr. Baron, the bookstore that closed and left that lot vacant had been there for forty years. I knew those owners very well. They had a family with a couple of kids in college. But their store closed because people buy more televisions than books now. So you help and you hurt. It's the nature of business. There's nothing special about your store, Mr. Baron. I'm strongly inclined to have a new business open in the lot next to yours. You've told me nothing that would prompt me to grant an exception to the zoning ordinance that I helped create and emphatically support. That ordinance engenders competition and diversity; *that* is what makes a district vibrant and competitive."

I smiled and nodded. "I understand your position, sir. Perhaps there is something I can offer that might change your mind. My store has been very successful in your community, and so I'm fortunate to have sufficient resources to bring to bear here."

Alderman Jarielski leaned forward in his seat. His demeanor grew stern and direct as he stared into my eyes. "I don't know exactly what you are suggesting, Mr. Baron. I've heard rumors about the relationship you enjoyed with my predecessor. I caution you, Baron, don't even think about offering me some little side benefit. That may be the way your people operate, but I don't play there, and if I hear anything out of your mouth even remotely suggestive of a bribe or personal inducement, I will report you to the district attorney in a heartbeat. Don't go there."

Jarielski concluded his diatribe and leaned back in his seat. He was evidently accustomed to seeing such displays on his part visibly intimidate the person sitting across from him. But many of my jiu-jitsu sparring opponents had attempted similar ploys.

It plainly annoyed Jarielski now that I remained unfazed. I enjoyed observing his irritation.

"Mr. Alderman," I said, "I have no idea what you've heard about my relationship with your predecessor, nor would I venture to guess what preconceived notions you may hold about *my people*, whatever exactly you mean to imply by that characterization."

That irked him even more.

I continued: "Let me assure you that I have never, in my entire life, in substance or even in appearance, skirted the law in the fashion you're suggesting. I don't do it in part because I'm an honest and ethical person, but I don't do it in larger part because it's bad business. Those tactics may achieve some short-term objectives, but in the long run, you'll get caught. They always catch you. You're living in a fantasy if you think they won't. And when they do catch you, you lose it all. Mr. Alderman, I intend to keep everything I have when I'm done. So I don't play there either."

"All right, Mr. Baron. I'll take you at your word. But if that's the case, then what do you have to offer?"

"As I said, Mr. Alderman, I'm fortunate enough to have resources in an economy where resources for public works can be very difficult to procure. You have wonderful plans for this community, sir, but there's so much that you need. A library, perhaps, or an after-school center, a playground and park, indoor basketball courts and a local league. I've spent a good deal of time in this neighborhood. Any one of those things, strategically located, could help enormously with the vision you've posited. Baron's Television and Electronics is poised to make a sizeable donation to this community and work with you on making one or more of those things a reality."

"In return for a zoning waiver," said Jarielski.

I smiled. "A quid pro quo here does seem a bit tawdry. But a general understanding, Mr. Alderman, that our store's agreeing to make such a donation would in turn cause you to consider our request for a zoning exception with an open mind could, I think, enable us to work together to great mutual benefit."

The alderman was silent for a moment. He probed my countenance, as if searching for a clue as to whether the man in front of him could be a trusted partner. Jarielski had made many promises to get elected. The sorts of donations I now suggested could help him enormously in bringing some of those to fruition. I believed Jarielski was now pondering whether he could successfully package and advertise such an agreement as both positive for the community and completely legitimate.

"Have you entered into this sort of understanding with any of the communities in which your other stores are located, Mr. Baron?"

"With our stores in Philadelphia, Newark, and Harlem—yes sir, we have."

"How exactly were such agreements characterized for the media?"

"As positive, aboveboard, robust partnerships between business and government, in economic times when tax revenues could not possibly finance these sorts of endeavors for the public good. And, as has been the case here in Logan Square, the vast majority of the staff and shift supervisors in all those stores were from the neighborhood, so there was an increase in jobs as well."

"This won't come cheap, Mr. Baron."

"Mr. Alderman," I said reassuringly, "write a ballpark figure on a piece of paper and slide it over here."

Jarielski tore a small yellow square off a pad, pondered a moment, jotted down a number, and pushed the note across the desk.

I glanced down at the paper, then looked up and smiled at the alderman. "I believe we can do business in that ballpark, sir."

"Baron, do you intend to be in town for a while?" asked the alderman.

"I can certainly arrange that, sir."

"I need to sell this to a few higher-ups, but that shouldn't present a problem. Let me set up a three-hour meeting next week with you and me, our planners and architects. We'll be able to get specific about projects and start the paperwork going."

"In the meantime, sir," I asked, "will you be considering the merits of our store's expansion request?"

"As soon as the donation is finalized, you'll get your zoning waiver, Baron. You have my word on that. Ask anybody here—my word is good."

"I've done my homework in that regard, sir. I have no doubt about the veracity of your word."

We stood and shook hands across the desk, the stark difference in our heights triggering me to once again imagine hurling the alderman to the ground and fracturing his arm with a loud crack.

———————

I left the alderman's office and headed back to the store.

Peering through the window of Stephanie's office, I saw her reviewing inventory reports. After a cursory knock I let myself in without waiting for a response. Stephanie looked up as I shut the door.

"Sammy!" she exclaimed. "You're back. So, tell me, tell me! How did it go with Alderman Jarielski?"

"We'll be expanding the store, Steph."

Stephanie screeched in excitement, leaped up, and ran to me with her arms raised above her head. "You did it!" she screamed as she embraced me excitedly. "You have some secret power, Sammy. I honestly don't know how you do it."

"All aboveboard, Steph. We'll be partnering with the community to deploy some new public facilities. It'll help the neighborhood, help us, and help the other merchants. Just like we did at the other stores. All good."

"That's wonderful."

"Tomorrow, you and I should sit down with the accountants. I have a ballpark idea of what we'll be donating, so we should start figuring out the most advantageous way to work it out tax-wise along with the store expansion."

"I'll make it happen, Sammy."

"And tonight," I said, "how about making a reservation at that fancy Italian place in the Loop where we celebrated last time. Make it for 8:30, Steph. I want to try to catch the 6 PM sparring session at my favorite Chicago dojo, the one across town. Work off some aggression."

"Sounds great, Sammy. A reservation that late should be no problem. I have more than enough work to keep me busy till then."

"I'll see you there," I said.

———————

In stark contrast to my decision to choose a single national fitness chain with branches in the cities I worked in, I carefully and meticulously identified an individual jiu-jitsu dojo in each of my travel destinations. Treadmills, stationary bicycles, and weight machines were relatively interchangeable. But as a fifth-degree black belt, I required experienced jiu-jitsu instructors for meaningful tutelage, and a sufficient number of advanced students to provide challenging sparring sessions.

I had been a well-known presence in my Chicago dojo for years now, and had become close with the head instructor, for whom I had great respect. This dojo, like most of the dojos where I now practiced, specialized in Brazilian jiu-jitsu, which was quite different from the traditional Kano jiu-jitsu that I studied as a boy. Kano jiu-jitsu, later called judo, was developed by Jigoro Kano in the late 1800s. Based upon hundreds of years of Japanese grappling tradition, it consisted primarily of moves designed to throw one's opponent to the ground.

By contrast, Brazilian jiu-jitsu was a much more recent innovation, pioneered by Mitsuyo Maeda in the early to mid-1900s and popularized in the United States by the Gracie family in the 1990s. The key difference was that Brazilian jiu-jitsu additionally incorporated extensive techniques devoted to ground fighting, which had been almost entirely absent from Kano's compendium of tricks. I liked that aspect, and enjoyed the emphasis on intensive sparring.

There was, however, a refined and deferential tradition imbedded in the culture of Kano jiu-jitsu that had vanished in concession to the Brazilian style's ferocity. I missed that somewhat then. In retrospect, I should probably have missed it far more than I did.

I arrived in the locker room about an hour prior to the sparring session, to allow sufficient time to stretch and warm up. Shortly before six, as I donned my gi and tightened its black belt about my waist, I was happy to see among the half dozen men also changing into fighting garb my old rival Vince Tesalio. Vince was in his late twenties and a firefighter whose size and physique were quite similar to that of Alderman Jarielski. Like me, Vince was an advanced black belt. I walked over to him and we shook hands warmly.

"Vince, my friend, I was hoping to see you here this evening. Are you already hooked up, or might we spar a bit tonight?"

"You never get tired of kicking my ass, do you, Baron?" replied the firefighter with a broad smile, glaring down into my eyes. "Yeah, I'll hook up with you tonight. But be on your toes; I've been working out and sparring like a motherfucker. I might just take you tonight."

"I'm just a small, middle-aged man with grey hair," I said. "You shouldn't have any trouble handling *me*."

"Yeah, right . . ."

Just a few minutes later on the mat upstairs, in our stiff white gis and impeccably knotted cloth black belts, the two of us executed in rapid succession a fierce but unremittingly graceful ballet of moves and countermoves. Each brief episode commenced with both of us upright. Dancing, feinting, clawing, each jostled for a positional advantage. Suddenly, one of us would pounce, throwing the other to the mat while landing atop or alongside him on the ground. Then another quick struggle ensued, arms and legs entwining, bodies rolling and pivoting, until one man achieved a submission grip, causing the other to lightly tap the mat or his opponent three times with an open hand, signaling surrender. Upon the issuance of that signal, we disengaged, leaped up without the slightest pause, and regained our standing grappling positions to begin our next encounter. Each tiny contest lasted only a few seconds. Neither of us tallied our victories and losses.

Vince Tesalio's warning was well taken—he had worked himself into terrific condition and had obviously sparred frequently of late. He surprised me several times with unexpected tricks and attacks. But as we wound down after forty-five minutes of grueling exertion, it was clear that, in the end, the small wiry man with greying hair had gotten the better of his larger, stronger opponent.

Vince and I strolled together back to the locker room. Vince wrapped his long, thick arm around my shoulder as we walked, in a gesture of friendship and congratulation. "I'll get you one of these days, Baron," he said, breathing heavily.

"I know you will," I said. "You fought great tonight. And I'm not getting any younger."

"Don't bullshit me, Baron. You'll kick my ass for the next ten years."

We laughed as we reached our lockers and undressed to shower.

As I soaped up under the pounding stream of hot water, I thought of Stephanie, and looked forward to our celebratory dinner in a couple of hours.

Alderman Jarielski encountered no problem in securing approval for the supplemental-community-funding agreement with Baron's Television and Electronics, Inc. The alderman now formed a team of planners, architects, staffers, and attorneys to finalize the details.

I had my attorney, Sid Weinberg, fly in from Manhattan to participate in the discussions. I set Sid up in a hotel just half a block from the alderman's office. I also invited Stephanie to attend the meetings.

"I didn't expect to be included in these talks Sammy," Stephanie said as the two of us dressed for the kickoff meeting on Thursday morning. "I really appreciate your inviting me."

"The Chicago store is *your* store, Steph. When we build the add-on, it will be a bigger store, a different store. And the community involvement is under your jurisdiction too. You need to be in on both from the outset, and help shape them. I have no doubt at all that you're up to it."

Stephanie was wearing a white bra and a black half-slip. Her freshly pressed, cream-colored blouse was still unbuttoned as she strode over, embraced me tightly, and gave me an intimate kiss. "You mean so much to me, Sammy, in so many ways," she whispered.

When Stephanie and I arrived at the alderman's office, Jarielski's administrative assistant greeted us warmly and directed us to a large conference room down the hall. The alderman had not yet arrived, but most of the other main players were already present. Stephanie and I made our way around the room, shaking hands, identifying ourselves, and extending polite greetings. We then wandered over to the buffet of pastries, bagels, and fruit. Stephanie prepared herself a cup of coffee, and also spooned some blueberries and pineapple chunks into a small bowl, which she topped with a dollop of yogurt. She asked me if I wanted anything, but I grabbed a plastic bottle of spring water with my left hand and told her that was all I needed at the moment. My right hand was clenched, awaiting unobtrusive ablution when I sat down.

We found two seats together on the far end of the table. I put down my water and held my hands underneath the table as I scrubbed with alcohol gel. I stood again and draped my suit coat over my chair. I was about to sit once more when I spotted my attorney conclude a brief conversation with one of the alderman's architects.

"Excuse me a moment, Steph. I need a quick word with Sid." I trotted to the other side of the table where Sid had seated himself. I leaned down, and he whispered a brief status update in my ear. All was going well.

I headed back around the table, past the open door of the conference room, just as Alderman Jarielski arrived for the meeting. I stopped abruptly, and the two of us stood face-to-face. I instinctively offered my hand in greeting, but then noticed that the alderman's right arm was in a sling, encased from his wrist to well above his elbow in a bulky plaster cast.

The alderman smiled. "Hello, Baron," he said. "I'm off handshaking for a while. Damndest thing; I was playing Wiffle ball with my kids, jumped up to snag a line drive, and the bone just cracked, right at the elbow. Doctor said it was a freak accident. I played seven years of varsity football through high school and college, and never broke a bone. Strange, huh?"

"I'm sorry you were injured, Alderman. When exactly did it happen?"

"Saturday afternoon, around half past two. We barbequed in the backyard, had our lunch, and then we decided to play some ball. Next thing I knew I was in the emergency room." The alderman chuckled and leaned his head down toward mine. "Don't get complacent, Baron. The arm doesn't affect my negotiating skills."

I laughed. "My suspicion is that if anything, it will make you tougher."

The alderman turned to visit the buffet. I quickly gathered up

Stephanie and Sid, and took them over and introduced them to Jarielski as the alderman selected his morning pastry. Stephanie immediately took the alderman's plate and asked him how he liked his coffee.

"Cream and sugar," said Jarielski, with a nod and a smile. Stephanie mixed his coffee and took his breakfast back to the meeting table, setting it down neatly in front of him along with a couple of small paper napkins. The alderman thanked her graciously, and in a voice sufficiently loud for me to hear, asked her, "Did Baron hire you?"

"Yes sir," she replied.

"My opinion of him just shot up significantly," the alderman announced with a wry grin and a glance in my direction.

As I returned to my seat, I tried to focus on the interactions Stephanie and I had just shared with Jarielski. They appeared to represent a significant leap in our personal relationship and level of trust. But I could not maintain that thought. My mind kept wandering instead to the heavy cast on the alderman's right arm, and the fracture the alderman had described.

It was that precise injury that I had twice envisioned inflicting upon Jarielski during our initial meeting. More disturbing to me was that on Saturday afternoon, the time the alderman reported suffering the accident, I had been driving across Chicago for a private jiu-jitsu lesson with the dojo's sensei. As I drove, I imagined over and over again throwing the alderman to the ground, and smashing his twisted, hyperextended arm against my raised knee. Each time I played the scenario in my head, I could hear the bone crack. The final iteration of the encounter in my mind, which I conjured up at exactly 2:30 PM as I pulled into a parking space across the street from the dojo, had seemed eerily vivid, as if it were occurring in real time.

———◡———

Securing approval to expand our Chicago store was a significant achievement and merited celebration.

I arranged for a long-weekend getaway to Jackson Hole for Stephanie and myself, then suggested to Stephanie that we should invite Jake and his longtime on-again-off-again girlfriend Jill and make it a foursome. Stephanie agreed; she had always liked Jill.

Organizing the trip as a foursome was also tactical on my part. I knew how much Stephanie enjoyed skiing. But I had grown up in the Bronx, playing stickball, handball, and other street games. Skiing was not something I had ever been exposed to, and the possibly of breaking a leg and endangering my jiu-jitsu practice was not a risk I was willing to take. Jill would be a perfect companion for Stephanie on the slopes—both women were experienced skiers.

And Jake would be company for me. It had surprised me at first to learn that Jake had no interest in skiing. For some reason, I imagined that all tall, athletic-looking WASPS skied. It was probably Emmanuel who had planted that notion in my head as a boy. But Jake explained his perspective on skiing quite directly once during a lab. "Why would I want to be cold and wet, Doc, mindlessly sliding downhill on some lump of snow, when I could be in the lodge, sitting by a fire, sipping on a fine cocktail?"

Businesswise, Jake and I had also identified Jackson, Wyoming, as a town now attracting wealthy homeowners, and I had recently been in touch with a company that installed rooftop television antennas in the area. They were interested in the products Jake and I produced, so I arranged a meeting for Tuesday morning before we flew out.

It always gave Steph and me a mischievous thrill to pack our SM gear and wonder what a luggage inspector might think if he came across it. More ticklish was masking a small bit of cocaine for the weekend. We purchased a dozen empty gelatin capsules with a brownish hue, and meticulously filled each one with cocaine. We took a small jar of multivitamins whose contents looked similar, disposed of the vitamins, and packed the jar with our capsules for the trip.

On Sunday afternoon, a light snow fell in Jackson. The women were skiing. Jake and I were in the lodge, each nursing our third martini.

Jake probed a bit: "Do I detect the slightest hint of malaise in your usually playful and sexually charged relationship with Stephanie, Doc?"

I looked up, a bit surprised. "You know me so well, Jake. It's the tiniest thing. I had no idea it even showed."

"Not so much until the four of us got schnockered at dinner last night, Doc. Then I detected a whiff of it."

"It's odd," I said. "We've always been really good at separating our unorthodox sexual dynamic from the rest of our relationship. But lately it seems to be creeping into Steph's day-to-day demeanor. Just a bit. Nothing I can even point out to her that wouldn't seem silly. But I just don't want it to go further."

"It won't seem silly to me, Doc. Point out an incident."

"All right. Here's something that happened just before we left. You know, Jake, when I'm in Chicago, if it's just for a day or two, Stephanie and I stay in my condo. But with all the negotiations to expand the store, I'd been in the city for several weeks. So we started spending a lot more time at Stephanie's house. She has all her stuff there, she can cook meals, and she feels more comfortable."

"And you feel less in charge, Doc?"

"She does have a different sense about her, in her own place. And it makes me wonder what it would be like to actually live with her."

"What happened specifically?"

"I don't know if all women do this, Jake, but Steph has what she calls the 'coaster rule' in her house. If you put a drink down on a table, you have to use a coaster. Otherwise she gets really upset. The only exception is the one glass-topped end table in her living room. She says glass is okay, so you don't need a coaster there. So, I've gotten in the habit of always sitting in the leather recliner next to the glass table, and putting my drinks down there to avoid any shit she might raise."

"Did you somehow run afoul of the coaster rule, Doc?"

"Not exactly. I came back to her house after a long day at work and jiu-jitsu sparring. I said hi, and as is my wont, I immediately went into the kitchen, mixed a martini, and left it to chill while I got out of my suit and tie, and into sweats. But as I walked through the living room on my way to the bedroom to undress, I see Stephanie sitting on the couch, looking at me with this weird expression on her face. I say, 'What's up?' and she just smirks and says, 'You'll see.' I asked her again, and she says, 'You'll figure it out.' So I'm a little annoyed, but I figure I'll just go into the bedroom, change my clothes, and then she'll tell me."

"Did she tell you when you returned, Doc?"

"No, she just kept staring at me with this condescending grin. So I went back into kitchen, poured my martini into a cocktail glass, and joined her in the living room. I sit down in the recliner and I'm just about to put my drink down on the glass table. It's maybe an inch above the surface of the table when I realize it's not a glass table anymore. It's a wooden table. I need a coaster. So I don't put the glass down. I stand up and turn around, and I realize I'm not sitting in the recliner. It's a different chair. And I look around and every piece of furniture in the living room has been moved to a different place. The whole configuration is completely different."

"Sounds intriguing, Doc."

"I asked her why everything is changed. She says, 'So, you finally noticed. You really are the most unobservant creature I've ever met. I worked for hours today dragging everything around, and you didn't even notice it. How can you be in a room and not see it?' So, she's getting angry about it now."

"Women do that, Doc."

"I say, 'Don't get mad. Why did you do it?' But that's not what she wanted to hear. 'Do you like it?' she yells at me. 'Aren't you going to tell me if you like it?'"

Jake was laughing now. "I'm quite certain, Doc," he said, "that the rearrangement of the layout made absolutely no difference to your aesthetic appreciation of the room. Your sole interest was to reposition yourself next to the new location of the glass table, so as to continue to skirt coaster regulations."

"That's exactly right, Jake," I exclaimed, pointing my finger at him to reassert his conclusion. "So I said it looks okay, and she lays into me: 'Just okay? I worked for hours dragging heavy furniture around to make the room look nice for you, and all you can say is 'okay'?"

"You realize, Doc," Jake said, laughing, "she didn't do it for *you*. Women get these seasonal hormonal cycles and have to reconstruct their nests. Jill drives me crazy with this insanity when we're living together. That's why we mostly live apart."

"Well, I asked Stephanie why she didn't just wait for me to help her move the furniture around, but she obviously didn't want to hear that either. She just wanted me to tell her how lovely it looked."

"So I assume you told her."

"Yes, I told her. But the whole thing left a bad taste in my mouth. Especially the way she teased and played with me before I figured out what was going on. She's only supposed to act that way when we're in bed, playing. It's insulting otherwise. I'm her boss, for God's sakes. It could get very ambiguous."

Jake chuckled. "Women do these things, Doc. You need to get used to it if you plan to live with her." He sipped on his drink and pondered a moment. "But you know, perhaps you could use a tad more ambiguity in your love life. Not everything is a mathematical equation."

I was about to refute his assertion when I spotted Stephanie and Jill, back from the slopes, heading to our table to join us. "They're here, Jake," I whispered.

The women sat and ordered drinks. Our conversation reverted to polite banter.

On Tuesday morning the meeting with the antenna installers went well. Jake and I secured a new customer. When it was done, Jill and Jake flew home to New York. Stephanie got on a plane to Chicago.

I flew into Denver, Colorado, where I spent a few days monitoring activity at Baron's Television and Electronics' newest branch store. I had just opened it there one year prior.

The store looked beautiful and sales were outstanding.

21.
Randomness

OUR TAI CHI SESSION was peaceful yet invigorating.

Virginia Ferguson had recovered much of her former strength and had by now become quite adept at the slow, graceful tai chi movements we practiced twice a week with the group in Golden Gate Park.

Today, for the first time, Virginia did not wear a surgical mask when she practiced—her transplant surgeon had given her the okay to go without it. The Chinese people in the group congratulated her graciously when she arrived unencumbered. Even the group's informal leader, an old tai chi master who was generally quite dour and serious, walked toward Virginia, smiled, and raised both his hands. Virginia lifted her hands as well. They interlocked fingers in a gesture of friendship and bonding. I had seen the leader greet certain long-term members of the group in that manner when they had returned after a prolonged absence.

When the session ended, I walked Virginia home.

"Your recovery is progressing so well, Virginia," I said. "Your power and endurance have improved remarkably. And the way you've mastered the tai chi forms is quite impressive."

"Thank you, Sammy. I'm feeling so much better. I'm trying to directly influence my physiological healing processes through my meditation."

"Really. How exactly are you going about that?" I asked.

"You once mentioned how you found Rosicrucian meditation interesting because there was an active element in it. Where the practitioner tries to directly effect change. I don't feel I'm nearly at the point where I can effect change outwardly in the world, but I think I have a shot at doing it within myself."

"That's interesting," I said. "Even mainstream medicine now acknowledges that one's own mind can assist healing greatly, and induce health. So there's no reason you shouldn't be able to do it."

"For me, Sammy, it's more than that. With a compromised immune system, I need to somehow ward off invasions from diseases like cancer. There are certainly known risk factors I can avoid, but beyond that, the onset of diseases like cancer are considered by science to occur randomly. But what is randomness, really?"

"Quantum physics says randomness operates on the atomic level," I observed. "In a way, everything else works up from that."

"Exactly, Sammy. And you know how you once mentioned to me that you wondered whether the universal consciousness we experience when we meditate might in some way have affected the genetic mutations that resulted in the evolution of life on earth? Why can't it also affect what we call randomness on an atomic level in our own bodies?"

"That's a fascinating concept, Virginia. So, you are trying to positively coerce the randomness in your atomic substructure through meditation."

"That's right," she said.

"I actually find the tai chi movements themselves profoundly meditative," I said. "Do you?"

"Yes, in a way," said Virginia. "But not nearly as intense as I find seated, silent meditation."

"We talked once," I said, "about our shared experiences of learning meditation in conjunction with martial arts. We agreed that it focused us for sparring but didn't have a more spiritually encompassing effect. It appears you're finding a similar pattern with tai chi."

"Yes, I am. That reminds me, Sammy, you told me that after your friend Jake's death, you had returned to a serious practice of seated, silent meditation. Are you still doing it?"

"No, I stopped," I said.

She seemed surprised. "Why? Did you find it difficult? Or boring?"

"You know, Virginia, I was trying to immerse myself fully into a spiritual lifestyle. Or I thought I was. But it wasn't right. I had stopped drinking alcohol, but it didn't take me long to see that a little wine with dinner wasn't interfering at all with that aspect of my life. So I went back to drinking wine."

"OK, the wine part I get, Sammy. But what about the meditation?"

"I find now that I truly prefer the walking meditation, Virginia. It's *right* for me. Not so much because seated, silent meditation is boring—it's more that it's isolating. It's the same thing that I felt about it in the past, but I couldn't conceptualize it then. I didn't understand that it wasn't a failure on my part to be unwilling to do the seated meditation. It was actually an active decision on my part, both consciously and subconsciously, that I *preferred* walking meditation."

"But why?"

"When I do the seated meditation, the mystical sensibility possesses me completely. But then, when I finish meditating, I'm thrust back into the cold, corporeal world, and it's a shock. As a result, the spiritual sensibility quickly fades. But for me, walking meditation melds seamlessly into my corporeal existence. While I'm meditating, I move. I navigate. I meet people on the trail. I keep an eye on Sapphy. All of these are phenomena of the material world. And as a result, the mystical mindset merges into my material being. And it lingers. It becomes integrated fully into everything I do. It lasts the whole day. That's really what I've always sought, Virginia. To have the spiritual mindset with me at all times. Walking meditation does that for me."

"It's so real, hearing you talk about this, Sammy. You truly have been so focused and courageous about your own spiritual journey. You've found what works for *you*, and you aren't ashamed or afraid that it might clash with what other people say is right."

"Well, thank you, Virginia. It's taken me a very long time to get here."

I paused a moment. "But you'll be glad to know that I did retain one very special commitment from the vows I made after Jake's death."

"Really, what's that?" she asked.

"I'm now fully and completely vegan. That fear I had that drove me to eat that one little prophylactic chunk of cheese every month or two seems to be gone for good. Other than Sapphire's dog food, every morsel in my kitchen is totally plant-based. I'll have to have you over for dinner sometime. You can bring little Kata to play with Sapphy."

"Actually, Sammy, I'd like to take you up on that next week. Doug is going to be out of town a couple of days at an insurance convention in the Midwest. It would be nice to join you then."

"We're on," I said.

———————

Two and a half years after my agreement was concluded with Alderman Jarielski, the expansion of my Chicago store remained unfinished.

I knew I needed to be on-site. Even so, I put the situation off for months; I was busy with other things, and I feared how unpleasant confronting it would be.

But I finally flew into Chicago.

I endured a very long day of meetings with Stephanie and the lead contractors working on the addition. I screamed at people for hours. When it was finally over, Stephanie and I had a late dinner of Chinese takeout at my condo.

I was still livid.

We ate in silence.

When I finished my food, I started doing lines of coke and shots of my favorite brand of amaretto. After half an hour of watching me do so at a manic pace, Stephanie began pleading: "Sammy, please. Stop that. You'll never get to bed. You'll be up all night and you won't be able to go in to work tomorrow. Please, honey."

She tried to gently pull me up from the table. I pushed her arm away.

"What difference does it make if I go in tomorrow or not?" I shouted.

"Nothing's going to change. You've been managing this expansion for over two years. Over two fucking years! How can it not be done? Where the fuck have you been?"

"That's not fair, Sammy. I've kept you informed every step of the way. You know everything that happened. First, we were hit with awful weather. Between the rain and the snow, we couldn't get the shell finished, and without the shell, we couldn't build the inside and stock it. Then there were two labor strikes and we lost the construction guys and the electricians for a while. By the time we got them back, the permits had expired and we had to go through all that again. Sammy, we've been through this over and over."

"All of that happened months ago. Why the hell are we stalled *now*? You should have made it happen. That's your *job*. *I* sure as hell would have seen that it got done if I were here managing it. I just can't understand it. You fucking blew it, Steph."

I quickly snorted two more lines. I downed a shot of the liqueur and was pouring another when Stephanie responded.

"Then why the hell weren't you *here*?" Stephanie screamed. "You're *never* here anymore. And when you *are* here, you're so fucking coked up and drunk that I wind up covering for you all the time anyway."

"Do you think I'm like this all the time?" I demanded. "You think I could run a goddamn enterprise the size of Baron's Electronics if I was drunk all the time? I do coke and booze when I'm here because it's the only way to deal with your goddamn incompetence. If you weren't fucking me, you would have been fired a long time ago."

"And if I didn't love you, I would have *quit* a long time ago. And by the way, when was the last time you had an orgasm with me? Six months ago? A year ago? You can't even get a goddamn erection when you snort that shit. So I guess the coke is more fucking important to you than our relationship." Stephanie started crying now. Her voice grew louder and became shrill. "You and I were supposed to stop being a secret. You kept telling me we'd get married. It was all a bunch of bullshit, wasn't it, Sammy? You never intended to marry me at all."

"If you weren't such a goddamn incompetent bitch, maybe I would have."

"You're a fucking bastard, Samuel Baron. I'm going back to my house. You stay up and snort your fucking lines and drink your fucking shots until you throw up and collapse. It's what you always do. And I'm goddamn sick of it."

The next day, it was late afternoon by the time I showed up at the store. I'm sure I looked a bit bedraggled.

Stephanie had left her letter of resignation on my desk. She was gone. My initial reaction, which persisted for quite some time, was an ambivalent mix of gnawing loss and profound relief.

Two weeks after her resignation, I learned that Stephanie had secured a position as a senior-level executive at one of our largest competitors. Just a couple of weeks after that, I decided to give up cocaine. I found it surprisingly easy. I tossed what was left in the toilet and never did another line.

I ran the Chicago store myself for the next three months and then promoted a long-term employee into the position. We completed the expansion shortly after that.

Jake and I didn't often drink rum. But Jake had recently read up on daiquiris and decided they were fine old drinks with a fascinating history. He told me they originated in nineteenth-century Cuba, and their influence eventually embroiled such notables as Ernest Hemingway and JFK.

Daiquiris were therefore deemed lab worthy.

I invited Jake to hold the lab in the New York City apartment I had recently purchased on the upper floor of a beautiful old brick building on Central Park West. It had a lovely view of the park, and a doorman who had once fought in the Golden Gloves tournament.

We scheduled the lab for Wednesday night. That day, I worked at the Yonkers store and had a chance to catch up with Paul O'Rourke, who ran that store for me now. He was doing well.

On my way home, as Jake instructed, I picked up three brands of high-end rum and a dozen limes. While I waited for Jake to arrive, I boiled equal parts water and sugar to create a pot of simple syrup. Just those three items, Jake said—rum, lime juice, and syrup. Nothing more was needed other than chilled glasses and ice. We'd experiment with ratios and the different rum varieties.

During the first couple of rounds, Jake and I dissected the pros and cons of the cocktails, and Jake talked at length about his recent efforts as a professor.

It wasn't until the end of the second round that I broached the topic foremost on my mind.

"I've decided to sell Baron's Television and Electronics," I said. "I got a fantastic offer yesterday, Jake, for the whole thing, all seven stores plus the mail-order warehouse."

"And you're ready to let it go, Doc?"

"I'm more than ready."

"How much, Doc?"

"I don't want to say, exactly. But tens of millions, Jake."

"Quite impressive, Dockles. I think that deserves another round."

We mixed up a third round together, trying yet another rum and slightly increasing the amounts of lime juice and simple syrup. We tasted it while standing in the kitchen.

"I think this is the best round yet," I said.

"As always, we are obliged to acknowledge that the cerebrally numbing effects of the first two rounds may have rendered us less discerning."

We laughed.

"What did your father say about your decision to sell the business, Doc?" Jake asked.

"Well, he's retired now, and our agreement has been that he has no say in my decisions, but he gets a third of the profits as a silent partner. So I was going to offer him a third of the proceeds from the sale, but I decided to give him half. He was quite happy with that."

"That was rather generous, Doc."

"Not really, Jake. Almost all of it will come back to me when he passes away. So the percentage is in some ways moot. And I knew this would short-circuit any bitching or haggling on his part. I just wasn't in the mood to deal with more of Emmanuel's shit."

"Are you sure he'll leave most of his share to you? How do you know he won't spend it?"

"On what, Jake? He barely leaves that little apartment he's lived in for decades. You remember it—it's in my aunt and uncle's house in Riverdale. He sits there all day long in his underwear and listens to lunatic right-wing radio stations."

"Then it sounds as if your inheritance is secure, Dockles."

"I actually insisted on giving a payment to my uncle Irving too. He fronted us the money to open that first store in Yonkers. But he refused to take it. He insisted he had no claim to it. So we had this insane negotiation, out on his porch with both of us drinking peach schnapps. Here I was trying to give more money away, and he was fighting to have me keep it. He finally got sufficiently drunk that he agreed to accept a token amount."

"Very quaint, Doc. So what are you going to do now in your copious spare time?"

"Brace yourself, Jakles." I paused and stared directly at him. "I want to do a major expansion of our antenna company."

"What? I barely have any time to devote to it now, Dockles. With my load as a tenured professor, you'd be taking it all on yourself. And what is there to expand? We sell paraphernalia to every big electronics store in the country as it is. What more is there to do?"

"A new line of business, Jake. I want to focus on big hotels, hospitals, old-age homes. Anyplace where there is, or should be, a TV in every room but the signal just isn't good enough to support that. Our equipment has been for home use, but we can expand those capabilities easily. It's not like we have to invent anything brand new, just take what we have and fine-tune the amplification algorithms so we can assure a clean, robust signal for any channel in as many rooms in a building that have a need to watch it."

"You're a bold man, Doc! Ambitious, impetuous, and very bold. I admire that." Jake sipped on his drink. "But as I said, you'll have to do the bulk of this on your own. I'll be more than happy to fiddle around on the electronics with you, improve the amplification algorithms, and help secure the patents. But the day-to-day legwork and selling would be up to you, Doc."

"I want to bring in Paul O'Rourke as our salesman. You've met him. The man can sell anything. People just love him."

Jake put his drink down. He bowed his head—his brow tensed, and the slits of his eyes grew narrow. "I don't know about O'Rourke, Doc. I certainly trust your assessment of his skills. I've only met him a few times, but he and I, there's a strain there."

"I know that, Jake. I'll act as the go-between. Paul's good at what he does, and as you said, I'll be handling all the day-to-day work, so you'll barely have any contact with him."

"All right, I'll trust you on that. If anyone can make a business work, it's certainly you. And I'll enjoy working with you on the upgrades to our inventions. We haven't done that kind of work in quite a while."

"It will be like old times back in the CCNY lab," I said.

Jake walked into my kitchen and mixed a fourth round of daiquiris. He returned with the shaker and refilled our glasses.

"Ah, Dockles!" he said wistfully. "Our days in the CCNY lab. They were good times. You were such a brilliant student. I wish you had continued on. Did I ever tell you I was heartbroken when you dropped out after just three semesters?"

"I had stores to run, Jake."

"And empires to build."

We toasted and drank in silence for a few minutes.

"You know, Dockles," Jake said, "there's been a change in you since you broke up with Stephanie. It's very subtle. I doubt anyone else would notice. But there's an emptiness I can sense. I suspect it's quite pervasive inside you."

I looked at him for a moment. "You're right, Jake. I do miss her. I didn't so much, at first. But the reality of not having her in my life gets to me now, more and more every day. She really was a beautiful woman, inside and out."

"Why don't you call her, Doc?"

"Believe me, I have. Dozens of times. She won't answer, and she won't return messages."

"Write her a letter. You write well."

"I tried that too. Three times, Jake. Three letters, and I poured my heart out in every one."

"She won't budge, eh?"

"I said too many really horrible things, Jake. And I took her for granted for way too long. So maybe this is right. Maybe we're really just not meant to be together. You know, I didn't do cocaine heavily except when I was in Chicago with her, and I was able to stop it completely when we broke up."

Jake sipped on his drink and sighed. "Well, maybe the two of you will get back together at some point."

"I don't think so, Jake. I'm not like you that way. You're able to get back together with your former conquests. Look how many times you've broken up with Jill, and you two always get back together. It's uncanny."

Jake chugged down the remainder of his drink in one large gulp. "What do you mean by *former conquests*, Doc? Women can't be *unconquested*. Words have meaning." Jake smiled broadly now and he feigned indignation. "A conquest *remains* a conquest. In perpetuity." Jake raised his voice and pointed his empty cocktail glass in my direction. "Remember that. There are no *former* conquests! A woman can't be *unconquested*! They're *conquests*!" He laughed loudly. "Drink up, Dockles."

Paul was thrilled to come on board.

Paul's initial sales at Baron and Kenneman Antenna Technology were to small and medium-sized hotels and motels. We equipped those establishments impressively. That led to work at a couple of larger hotels.

Through persistence and networking, and by utilizing the glowing endorsements of our hotel and motel clients, Paul then landed a very big sale at a prestigious academic medical center in Northern California.

What intrigued Jake and me most about this deal was that the medical center was not interested solely in television entertainment for every bed and waiting room. They certainly wanted that. But Paul had explored a further capability with them. This involved the transmission of output such as charts and displays from certain bedside medical instruments onto a patient's television screen. Doctors could then reference these images during conversations with the patient, and thus help explicate diagnoses and justify prescribed actions.

Neither Jake nor I had authorized Paul to offer such capabilities. Neither of us had even conceptualized the possibility. According to Paul, the spontaneous idea occurred to him during a critical negotiation point in his sales discussion.

"They were about to drop the deal completely," Paul explained when he briefed me by phone after the pivotal meeting. "They couldn't justify the cost of the technological upgrade just to improve television reception."

"Didn't they think it would help them recruit patients who might otherwise go to different hospitals?" I asked him.

"That's what I thought at first too, Sammy. But because it's an *academic* medical center, their three hospitals treat what they call tertiary and quaternary conditions."

"As opposed to primary and secondary?" I asked.

"Exactly, Sammy. I should have guessed you'd know what those words meant. I sure as hell didn't. Anyway, it boils down to the fact that the patients in their beds would likely be there no matter what. Less expensive local hospitals are just not equipped to deal with them."

"Interesting," I said. "I had no idea it worked that way."

"Neither did I. But when the medical center decided the cost for the television upgrade wasn't worth the benefit for them, I was going to lose the sale unless I upped the ante. So I started asking them what else they'd like the televisions to be able to do. And we came up with the charts and displays from bedside instruments. That would up the value of the project big-time for them, because now it's benefitting *doctors*, not just patients. But they're convinced that it's technically impossible to do."

"Did it ever occur to you that they might be right, Paul?"

He chuckled. "I've never seen you back away from a challenge, Sammy. I thought you and your egghead friend Jake would love tackling this one. I bet you can do it."

"I suppose the commission you stand to earn was somewhat of a motivator in this harebrained scheme too," I ventured.

Paul laughed heartily. "Lots in it for all three of us if you guys can make it work," he said.

***

I did not initially intend to buy a house.

I at first just rented a furnished studio apartment near the project site. The medical center was located in a residential neighborhood in the western part of San Francisco.

Jake and I had agreed that I needed to be on-site full-time to run the installation. The complexity of the circuits Jake and I designed, and the custom equipment required to collect output from the hospitals' bedside devices, necessitated close oversight.

Outside of work, I proceeded as always when relocating temporarily in a new city: I identified the closest fitness center for my early-morning workouts. I found a dojo with a jiu-jitsu instructor I could respect and sufficient number of high-ranking black belts to assure challenging opponents for sparring. And I acquainted myself with a few restaurants with full bars where I could dine comfortably each evening.

But it was the alternative newspapers, offered free from glass-and-metal dispensers on every corner along major San Francisco streets, that instigated an entirely unexpected trajectory for me.

The papers featured frequent articles about the various BDSM organizations in the city. BDSM, I learned, was a fascinating three-tiered acronym: BD for bondage and discipline, DS for dominance and submission, and SM, of course, for sadomasochism. At that time, I didn't personally see much distinction among those three categories, but apparently the many active participants in these Bay Area organizations did.

A variety of groups held meetings and periodic play parties, each catering to a specific orientation: male dominant/female submissive, female dominant/male submissive, gay men, lesbians.

There was also one large umbrella organization, the Society of Janus. It held monthly meetings, and quarterly orientations for new members. The group portrayed itself as offering support, information, opportunities for fraternization, and entrée into the community.

I was intrigued.

I recalled how years ago I had tossed out a CCNY newspaper with an anomalous ad posted by "the Regal Mistress Angelica." Ever since, I had stubbornly clung to the irrational view that I was the only otherwise normal person with a penchant for BDSM—the others were all dangerous degenerates and potentially violent criminals. But reading about these organizations made the psychosexual inclination seem ordinary and acceptable.

Perhaps it was the Bay Area itself. There was a tolerance and laissez-faire attitude toward sexuality seemingly ingrained in the population. Same-sex couples held hands on the street. Cross-dressers cavorted in public. Nobody seemed overly concerned.

I wondered now if perhaps the BDSM community was actually populated by exceptional people—creative, successful, eloquent individuals whom I might find to be brethren.

The orientation for the Society of Janus was held in the basement of a home owned by a big, bearish gay man obsessed with leather and whips. He wore a snug, black leather vest, his thick, curly chest and underarm hair spewing out prominently from its gaps. Every inch of his basement's walls was covered with whips, straps, and paddles hanging from hooks.

The orientation meeting itself was perfunctory. I and the other five people present were welcomed into the club, and the rules and nature of monthly events were explained. The bearish man then went on at great length about how his favorite personal fantasy was to be forced to clean the home of a dominant man while leashed by his testicles and led about. He encouraged each of us to discuss our own fantasies. We were all forthcoming but far less verbose.

The first monthly meeting I attended was held in a fairly large hall with a stage in front. Lots of wooden chairs were set up in auditorium fashion, but ample space remained around the perimeter for schmoozing after the presentation.

What struck me immediately was the vast array of different costumes, some designed to clearly indicate the fetish of the individual. Many people were dressed in leather, and most everyone who wasn't wore clothing that was either black or red. Some people had handcuffs hanging from their belts; there were a few men dressed as women. One morbidly obese man, who looked to weigh close to four hundred pounds, wore just a diaper and sucked on a pacifier.

Vastly more men were in attendance than women. Every woman present appeared to be part of a couple, be it with a male or another female. Among the heterosexual couples, most of the women seemed to be bottoms meekly following their men around.

The few women who were tops all wore leather dresses or corsets, and seemed to know each other—they congregated off to one side. Many kept their male slaves collared and led them about on leashes. They were clearly an established and distinct subset of the larger group, ensconced and seemingly impermeable.

I began to suspect that integrating into this community might be more challenging than I anticipated.

The presentation that evening was by a long-term member of the group. He was an accountant by day, but his fetish of choice involved piercing and suspension. He recounted how his interests manifested from as early an age as he could remember. He described many of his experiences in great detail, and offered tips to people interested in piercing and suspension on how to assure that the play was safe. He saved his proudest achievements for the end of his talk: He had, on several occasions, served as a stunt double in Hollywood movies, when a character needed to be realistically tortured. He projected onto a screen several photos of his work in films, including his most notable turn, in *A Man Called Horse*. He claimed that it was he, not Richard Harris, whose chest was impaled with blades attached to the ropes suspending the main character in that iconic scene. He unbuttoned his shirt and displayed the scars from that ordeal.

I observed his physique carefully, and compared it some weeks later to a poster I uncovered from the movie's promotion. I believe he was telling the truth.

But I had not come for the presentation.

I was there for the schmoozing period that came after. Though it was not a comfortable milieu for me, I had a specific goal. I therefore approached it as I did the many business meetings I had attended through the years. I would do what was necessary to get what I wanted.

After talking to a few people to gather information, the challenge became quite clear. There were literally hundreds of submissive men for every dominant woman. And when it came to dominant females, it was difficult to ascertain if they were sincerely oriented, or if they were doing it for convenience or profit.

The odds were clearly not in my favor.

Several unhappy and lonely submissive men quietly pointed out to me a woman who led a group that was female-dominant, but which included both heterosexual and homosexual couples. The general impression was that this group was slightly less couples oriented and might be easier to infiltrate.

None of the men, however, had been remotely successful in doing so.

I walked over and stood near the woman, patiently awaiting a brief word. She was engaged in conversation with two other women. I could not help but overhear. She was explaining that her group's numbers had increased, but the group was hurting financially, and had difficulty renting adequate space for parties.

The woman finally turned to me and spoke with a degree of disdain.

"Why are you hovering around here? Who are you? Do you want to talk to me?"

"I would very much appreciate a moment of your time," I said.

"What is it?" she asked dismissively.

"It appears that you need space for your parties," I said. "I'm thinking of buying a home in San Francisco. I'd be happy to let your group use it, free of charge."

"You don't have the house now?"

"I'm consulting here," I said. "So I'm in a furnished apartment. But as I said, I'm considering a purchase."

"Do you have any idea how much a house costs in this city?" she demanded.

"Yes," I said. "That won't be a problem. Are you interested in my offer?"

"What are you asking for in return?"

"Just to attend the parties."

"You'd buy a house in the most expensive real estate location in the country just to attend our parties?" she asked.

"I have the means. Why not?"

"Who the hell are you?"

"My name is Samuel Baron. I owned the Baron's Television and Electronics chain. You may have heard of it. I sold it recently. I have a new business now, specializing in broadcast antenna technology."

The woman's demeanor changed. She had been facing away from me, talking with a turned head. Now she shifted her body and looked me straight on.

"This isn't a bunch of bullshit, I hope," she said.

"What point would there be in my doing that?" I asked.

"None. But people do." She stepped closer and softened her tone to a whisper. "Listen. If you can do what you say, I can work out your attendance at the parties. Men can only come if they are coupled with women, but there's not a strict limit on how many slaves a woman may bring. I have a boyfriend who's my slave." She pointed to the silent, emaciated fellow at the end of the leash she held. "But I can bring you as a second slave. That will get you in. I don't offer anything beyond that with respect to me. Are you clear on that?"

"Perfectly clear," I said.

She leaned over and said something to her slave, then unfastened the leash from his collar. He immediately ran off and fetched a pen and a small pad and handed them to her. "Here's my phone number," she said as she scribbled. "Call me when you can absolutely guarantee the house. My name is Mistress Delilah."

"It's nice to meet you, Mistress Delilah," I said. "Is there a neighborhood in San Francisco to which you're partial?"

The first play party in the new house materialized less than two months following my initial conversation with Mistress Delilah. Paying in cash enabled me to close on the house quickly. Offering a bit more than the asking price rendered the haggling period quite brief.

One of the submissive men in Mistress Delilah's group was a carpenter by trade. Under Delilah's oversight, and with my cooperation, he equipped the living room and three bedrooms with over a dozen relatively inconspicuous ceiling hooks to which chains and slings could be affixed to serve as punishment venues during parties. The living room of the house was large and boasted a couple of structural wood pillars. Many homebuyers might have considered them eyesores. For us, though, they were perfect bondage posts, ideal for slaves whose behavior was deemed imperfect.

We furnished the house with durable upholstered chairs, sofas, and floor coverings. I paid for them—Delilah insisted they be secondhand so as not to take undue advantage of my largesse.

My willingness to collaborate, coupled with my vast experience in expediting projects, impressed Delilah and several of her close female cohorts. They promised me that at the party, I'd have playtime with each of them. But they reminded me that in accordance with my submissive role, I was to wait until each woman summoned me at a time convenient for her.

I rendezvoused at the house with Mistress Delilah and her slave, John, and two other couples about an hour prior to the party's start. We laid out the food and wine, hung the chains and slings, and attached pairs of leather manacles to the ends of each chain.

As guests started arriving, the norms and customs of the female-dominant party culture immediately became evident. The women, in leather dresses or corsets, sat on the chairs and sofas. The slaves, be they male or female, were either completely naked or adorned with scanty leather harnesses. The slaves fetched food and drink, brought the refreshments back to their mistresses, and knelt on the floor beside them.

Delilah caught me standing motionless, taking in the proceedings. I may have seemed a bit overwhelmed. She whispered gently in my ear, "Take off your clothes, Sammy. You don't have a problem with that, do you?"

"Not at all," I said.

Delilah was the first to grant me playtime—in fact, she played with me before she did with her own slave. I wondered if that was because she really wanted to, or because she saw it as an obligation that she wanted to fulfill and get out the way. Regardless, I was excited. I had not played with a woman since Stephanie.

Delilah tightened a pair of leather manacles around my wrists and attached them above my head to a dangling chain using double-sided snap hooks that were ubiquitous around the room. She placed a leather blindfold over my eyes, held my head gently, and whispered in my ear: "If you need me to slow down, say 'yellow.' If you need me to stop, say 'red.' Those are your 'safe words,' Sammy. Anything else, no matter how loud you cry out, I'm going to take as expressing pleasure. Do you understand?"

I nodded, and almost immediately felt her start to rub my chest. Soon she was squeezing my nipples, gently at first, then much more aggressively.

She moved to my torso, which she stroked with her palms and fingers for a while, then brought her long nails to bear, with increasing ferocity.

While she held my abdomen with one hand, she began spanking

my buttocks with the other. She started fairly softly, but increased the intensity slightly with each blow. Soon she was wailing at my flesh with all her might.

I moaned ecstatically.

After a few minutes she switched from hand spanking to what felt like a leather paddle, and then finally to a flexible leather switch that hissed audibly with each strike. The switch hurt badly and felt as if it might break my skin as the blows grew progressively swifter. I was about to yell out "Yellow!" but she stopped just before I did, and began gently rubbing my very sore derriere. Her hand fondled the side of my head. I felt her breath on my ear.

"You did very well, Sammy," she whispered lovingly, before removing my blindfold and unhooking my bonds. "Get a glass of wine for yourself," she said. "Look around. Take it all in. You helped make this happen. Thank you again, Sammy."

Delilah walked back to her slave. I stood motionless for a few moments and let my eyes readjust to the light. As I did, I thought back upon my many play sessions with Stephanie. At first Stephanie had limited herself to exactly the things I requested, but even later, when she developed her own variations and inventions, she remained acutely aware of my limits, and was always careful to remain safely within them. Tonight, Delilah was bolder, and exceeded my own perceptions of my pain tolerance when she whipped me with the switch. Yet she knew exactly when to stop.

It had been a fascinating experience. I looked forward to more.

I headed toward the kitchen to pour myself a glass of wine as Delilah had suggested, and to wash the part of my face where the blindfold had been. But as I walked, a couple caught my eye. They were two lesbians seated in the far corner of the living room. They must have arrived while I was blindfolded. The dominant, a middle-aged African American woman, sat on a loveseat. Her young, blond female slave knelt on the floor beside her mistress. The two sipped wine and chatted.

I strolled toward them and stood politely a couple of feet away.

I waited patiently, but the women continued their conversation.

I assumed the submissive was taking her cues from her mistress. Her mistress would not stop and acknowledge my presence.

"Excuse me," I finally said. "I'm sorry to interrupt."

The Black woman turned her head toward me. "My God, you're an impertinent young man!" she said sternly. "You must be the fellow who bought this house."

"Yes, I am," I said.

"Yes *ma'am*!" she corrected me, raising her voice sharply. "Have you no manners?"

"I'm sorry, ma'am," I said. "I just wanted to ask you a question."

"Why are you *standing* in my presence?" she demanded. "If you must speak to me, do so on your knees, young man. Don't you know anything at all?"

I knelt before her.

"I apologize again, ma'am," I said.

"All right," she sighed. "What is it you want?"

"I think we've met before," I said.

The African American woman looked at me with an almost bewildered expression, then rolled her eyes, turned to her female submissive, and started laughing.

"Did you hear what the boy said, Sarah? He said he thinks we've met before!" She turned toward me again. "Is that really the best line you can come up with?" she scoffed. "They told me you were somewhat accomplished."

"No, really," I said. "Were you ever a librarian in the East Tremont neighborhood of the Bronx?"

Her lower jaw grew suddenly slack—her eyes widened. She was absolutely silent and motionless for a few moments. Then she smiled slightly.

"Oh my God!" she cried. "You're the adorable young man who read all those books on electronics, and jiu-jitsu, and ESP. It was . . . Sammy . . . was it not?"

"Yes," I said. "I'm Sammy. It's so very good to see you, Esther. I've thought of you often."

"*Mistress* Esther," she reminded me softly. "Keep with the protocol, Sammy."

I grinned. "It's good to see you, *Mistress* Esther."

"And it's so good to see you too," she said. "You look wonderful."

"So do you, ma'am," I said.

"Well, I don't—but it's nice of you to say. I've become a rather fat middle-aged woman. Not like the curvy Amazon you used to fantasize about in the library with my tight skirts and slinky tops."

"Was it that obvious that I was fantasizing about you?" I asked, smiling.

She turned to Sarah. "One day I took Sammy's hand and held it, across the counter where we checked out books. He got so excited that he orgasmed in his pants. Right there as I held his hand."

Sarah laughed sweetly and looked at me with a mischievous grin.

I said, "I've been wondering for thirty years, Mistress Esther, if you realized I ejaculated that day. I guess I finally have my answer."

"Are you suitably mortified, Sammy?" she asked, chuckling.

"Very pleasantly so, ma'am." I smiled. I began to rise. "I'm so glad we had this time to talk, Mistress," I said, "but I'll go now. I want to be respectful of your time and preferences, and I don't want to interfere in any way with your evening with Sarah."

"Because you think I'm a lesbian?" she asked.

"Well," I stammered, and gestured toward Sarah.

"I *am* a lesbian," she said, laughing. "At least most of the time. But that doesn't mean that Sarah and I can't enjoy the servitude of a fine boy slave on occasion, especially one who's obedient, polite, and very cute."

"He's blushing, ma'am," Sarah noted to Esther.

"He is indeed," Esther said. "Go get yourself a glass of wine, then come back here and kneel down and visit with us for a while," Esther instructed. "The rule here is that you are submissive to *all* women, so you must be submissive to Sarah as well as to me, in your words and in your actions. Do you understand, young man?"

"Thank you, ma'am," I said. "I'd love to spend some more time with both of you."

22.
Crutches

JUST BEFORE THEY LEFT the party, Esther and Sarah invited me to their home for dinner the following Saturday.

I arrived, as instructed, at 5 PM. Their lovely two-story house was in Los Altos, a suburban town on the peninsula, about forty-five miles south of San Francisco.

I rang the bell. After a minute or two Sarah came to the door and let me in.

"Hi, Sammy," she said. "It's nice to see you again. Mistress is still dressing. I was upstairs, attending to her. Come in."

Their home was furnished beautifully with plush rugs and antique pieces. Sarah shut the door behind me. "Here," she said, "have a few hits off this and wait for us here in the living room." She handed me a lit joint, which was smoked down about halfway. There were lipstick stains on its end.

Sarah started to climb back up the stairs, then stopped and turned toward me. "Oh, and Mistress wants to see you completely naked when she makes her entrance. Please don't disappoint her. You can put your clothes on the chair in the corner," she said, pointing to a recliner near the window.

Clearly, our evening would involve more than dinner.

I took a couple of quick puffs on the joint and set it down in an ashtray on the coffee table. I smelled some sort of cheesy casserole baking in the kitchen.

After stripping completely, I wasn't sure if it would be considered appropriate to sit on a piece of furniture in that state, or to sit at all. So I stood and waited. I couldn't really tell if the house was cold or warm. My body was suffused with the heat one produces in anticipation of sexual contact.

As I anticipated Esther's arrival, my attention strayed to the bookshelves covering every bit of unoccupied wall space in their living room. During our conversation at the party the night before, Esther had mentioned that her love of reading led her to a career as a librarian. The many books in her collection attested to that. I was especially impressed with Esther's taste in novels.

It took about ten minutes before Esther sashayed elegantly down the stairway, with Sarah close behind her. Esther wore a fitted, satiny brown blouse, and a snug purple pencil skirt. She rested one hand lightly on the stair rail and balanced gracefully on tall brown stiletto heels.

Alongside the two of them scampered a small, furry white dog.

"Do you recognize the outfit, Sammy?" Esther asked.

"I do, ma'am. You wore it often at the East Tremont library," I said. "It was one of my favorites, ma'am."

"No. It *was* your favorite," Esther corrected me. "I could tell by the way you watched me when I wore it."

"Yes ma'am," I said sheepishly. "It was my favorite."

"And did you picture me in it when you masturbated back then?" Esther asked.

"He's blushing again, Mistress," Sarah said to Esther. "He seems to do that a lot."

They both laughed.

"Sammy," Esther said, "I purchased these clothes yesterday in honor of your visit. I tried to match them as closely as possible to the outfit I wore years ago in the Bronx. The skirt and blouse are both a few sizes larger. But judging from your erection, I suspect you find this ensemble just as enticing."

"You look absolutely beautiful, Mistress," I said.

"I'd like to introduce you to our dog, Cookie," Esther said. "She's a miniature terrier schnauzer mix."

"Hello, Cookie," I said, bending over and hesitantly petting her as she pranced over. I was quite unfamiliar with dogs at that time.

"Sammy, there's a chair in the back room that I want you to drag out here. Sarah will direct you."

I followed Sarah to a room down the hall. For the first time, I took a moment to look at her closely. She was quite beautiful too, in a much quieter and more understated way than Esther. She wore a snug beige sweater and tight jeans. Her hair was straight and blond and fell not quite to her shoulders.

We entered a room that appeared to be used to pot plants. Sarah pointed to a heavy wooden chair with leather straps attached at various points to its frame.

"It's too heavy to lift," she said. "Just drag it out slowly and try not to scratch the floor."

"I'm a bit stronger than I look," I said. I lifted the chair and carried it into the living room. I placed it down in the middle of the room in the spot that Sarah indicated.

"Does our little slave boy work out?" Esther asked. "That's a heavy piece of furniture you maneuvered there, young man."

"I do work out regularly, ma'am. I'm a fifth-degree black belt in jiu-jitsu."

"My my, how impressive!" Esther said. She turned to Sarah. "And yet he's about to be rendered helpless by two delicately dressed ladies just the same!" She looked back to me. "There's some irony in that, Sammy dear, don't you think?"

"Yes ma'am."

"Sarah, strap Sammy into the chair. Make sure the bindings are especially secure, given his superhuman strength." Esther's tone was playful and reeked of sarcasm.

I sat down. Sarah tugged my arms back and cuffed my wrists behind the chair. There were two thick upper straps. She pulled the higher one tight and buckled it around my chest. She did the same with the other, across my waist. My shins and ankles were then strapped separately to each chair leg, leaving my thighs spread and rendering my erect penis exposed and readily accessible to either of the women.

Esther strolled over, her arms swinging in a sexually ostentatious manner. Her hips undulated exactly as I remembered from the library in the Bronx.

She tested the straps to be sure there was no slack, and softly stroked my erection with the tips of her long fingernails. I noticed they were polished dark purple.

"Scrub the ball gag with alcohol, Sarah," she said softly. "I think the boy may be a screamer."

Esther watched as Sarah inserted the gag into my mouth and buckled the straps behind my head. Then Esther turned and walked into the kitchen. As she strolled off, I watched her hips sway hypnotically in her tight purple skirt. It was so eerily reminiscent of my recurring teenage fantasy of being left for hours, suspended from the ceiling of her office in the library, that my erection grew even bigger and harder, if such was possible at that point.

But unlike my teenage fantasy, Esther did not stay away long. She returned almost immediately, carrying an ornate bronze candelabrum with four large, flower-shaped sockets.

"Sarah, dear, take this and load it with four of our prettiest candles— the tall, thick ones I like with the spiral etchings." Esther cocked her head and pondered a moment. "Ah, yes, blue, red, yellow, and black, I think. They'll go nicely with his skin color."

"Right away, ma'am," Sarah said as she scampered out of the room.

Esther lightly scratched my testicles with the sharp, painted nails of her right hand. "Candles, Sammy. You grew up in a Jewish home, back in the South Bronx, did you not? I'm sure there were lots of candles. On Chanukah and many other occasions. They were holy artifacts. So, you're familiar with such things. Now—understand—this is *my* realm. I am the high priestess here, Sammy. In my church, it is I who creates the rituals."

I was transfixed, captivated by her words and her gaze.

Sarah returned, bearing the candelabrum with the four tall, colored candles burning majestically.

"Thank you, dear," Esther said to Sarah. "Hold it where I can reach it easily. It's my paint palette now."

Esther reached for a candle but stopped. "Oh, Sarah, before I start, be a dear and fetch the drop cloth and lay it down under his feet and around the chair. We don't want wax stains on the rug. I'll take the candles while you're gone."

Sarah handed the candelabra to Esther, who held the flaming tapers motionless, inches from my face. Their effect was hypnotic.

Sarah was back quickly with a large canvas cloth. She dropped to her knees and positioned it beneath me, carefully tucking it under my feet, which were still strapped tightly to the chair legs.

Esther returned the candles to Sarah, smiled, and stroked my cheek. Then she carefully gripped the red candle at its base and plucked it from its holder. "Red is one of my favorite colors, Sammy," she cooed. "It will look lovely on you."

She held the candle high and tilted it down, so that a slender stream of hot wax dripped onto my left thigh. I tensed and groaned, but then relaxed. The wax was hot, but not unbearably so. She maneuvered the candle such that it created a red pattern on my skin, moving from one thigh around to the other, and then allowed a few drops to adorn my erect penis. The skin there was more sensitive. I lurched, and squealed behind my gag.

Esther returned the red candle to its holder and grabbed the blue one. "Sammy, as a man of science, you'll appreciate the physics at work here. I was holding that red candle rather high. So the air had quite a bit of time to cool the wax as it fell. The closer I draw the candle to your flesh, however, the hotter the wax will become."

I strained at my bonds, but they held fast. She started the blue candle at the same height as she'd held the red one, but as she decorated my thighs, she slowly lowered it. As she promised, the wax grew hotter. When she got to my penis, she dipped the candle so that it was just barely above my skin. The heat became excruciating.

My loud, frantic screams were muffled by the gag, and though the leather straps nearly immobilized me, my torso convulsed sufficiently to cause Esther to turn the candle upright, and afford me a respite.

She handed the blue candle to Sarah and lovingly stroked my head. "You're such a sweet boy, Sammy. You're enduring my torture very well. I'll give you a couple of moments to recuperate, but I do need to finish my canvas. I have two colors to go, do I not?"

I tried to beg her to stop, but all I emitted were unintelligible howls.

Esther painted me with the yellow and then the black candle much as she had with the blue, but now she altered their height unpredictably, eliciting frenzied, muffled shrieks from me when she lowered them. She'd grant me brief periods of relief, only to swoop down again just as I regained my equilibrium.

"Have I been making you scream too much, Sammy?" Esther asked as she finished with the black candle and handed it to Sarah. "Your voice sounds hoarse, dear, and you seem a bit exhausted. We'll relax awhile."

She caressed my penis softly and turned to Sarah. "You may put the candles away now, dear. Find Cookie and bring her here."

She turned back to me. "You know, Sammy, all this screaming, all this fear on your part. I believe I know the cause. You're afraid I'm going to damage your penis. Your cherished appendage. You fear that the hot wax may render it dysfunctional. All this worry over that one silly thing. As if it is your very being."

Sarah reappeared, holding the small dog.

"Ah, Cookie!" Esther exclaimed, extending her hands. "Here, give her to me." Esther clutched the dog against her stupendous breasts and hovered over me. She spoke calmly. "There is a solution for all this consternation over your penis, Sammy. I can have Cookie here bite it off. She'd be relatively quick. I've trained her."

I jerked spasmodically, yanking upon my bonds. They did not yield.

"I know what you're thinking Sammy. Is this woman in front of me a deranged lunatic? Have I fantasized all these years about this mysterious librarian, only to discover, too late, that she's a psychotic and sadistic murderer?"

She had discerned my thoughts unerringly. She thrust the dog toward my groin. I emitted a frightful howl and strained with all my might against the straps.

Esther laughed, and pulled Cookie back before she touched me. Esther gazed at me as would a mother at a newborn child. "I will never hurt you, Sammy," she whispered. Then she chuckled and peeked briefly at Sarah. "Well, let me rephrase that, dear," she said. "I will most definitely hurt you, and in most creative ways. But I will never damage you. I take care of my slaves. I love them."

She put Cookie down on the floor. "Sarah," she said, "bring in the vibrator. The boy has earned a treat." Esther squeezed the base of my penis with her sharp nails. "I suspect you didn't take me all that seriously about Cookie, after all," she said. "Your erection has remained rock hard."

Sarah returned and handed Esther the vibrator. Esther turned it on, calibrated its intensity, and began rubbing it along the underside of my member.

"Sammy," she said, smiling, "you have been a very good slave. You have my permission to orgasm now."

After a minute or two I was very close to a climax, but self-consciousness held me back.

"If it's any added motivation, dear, it will be the only opportunity I'll give you this evening for a climax," Esther said.

She continued to stimulate me. I moaned and writhed, but I couldn't come.

Esther turned to Sarah. "Help him, dear," she said.

Sarah grinned mischievously and took each of my nipples between a thumb and forefinger. She squeezed astonishing hard, without once altering the knowing smirk on her face.

I orgasmed explosively.

Esther pulled the vibrator away and shut it off. She handed it to Sarah, who left the room and returned quickly with a warm, wet cloth to clean any residue off my member. Soon I had detumesced completely, but my nether regions remained brightly decorated with swirled configurations of red, blue, yellow, and black paraffin.

Esther walked to the side of the chair and lovingly stroked my neck and upper chest. She smiled as she glanced at the pool of semen on the drop cloth. "Do you know how much I wanted to do things like this to you when you were a boy, Sammy, visiting the library in the Bronx and staring at me for hours? I knew we were kindred spirits. Ah, to initiate a boy. It would have been extraordinarily exciting for me. And it would have been so comforting for *you*, to know that there was someone with whom you could share your secret. But society is not understanding in such matters. I would have lost my job, been charged with a criminal act, forsaken my entire career. Isn't it amazing that we get to do this *now*? I am so glad that you found us, Sammy."

I looked at her longingly. I wanted to tell her I felt the same way, but I produced only incoherent mumbles.

Sarah said to Esther, "He's a good deal more articulate when he's not gagged, don't you think, ma'am?"

"Yes, dear, he is," Esther replied. "We'll have to release him from all this before dinner. But let's leave him awhile and mix a shaker of cocktails first. He's so pretty trussed up like that."

Because it was a Sunday morning, I encountered little traffic on my drive south from San Francisco.

During a recent conversation with Esther and Sarah, I casually mentioned my boyhood fascination with the Rosicrucians, and how my father had dashed that dream. Esther immediately suggested that the three of us visit the Rosicrucian museum in San Jose. It was apparently one of Esther and Sarah's favorite diversions. They especially loved the many mummies and their heavy stone sarcophagi.

Esther asked me to meet her at her office the following Sunday morning. She had a bit of work to finish up, after which we'd head to the museum. She was the director of libraries for the city of San Jose, reporting to the city manager in that capacity. It was an impressive position.

My drive took about an hour. Her office was on an upper floor of a tall, modern building, part of the imposing city-government complex in downtown San Jose. She greeted me, filed away the papers she had been working on, and walked with me to the elevator to head back down.

"I'm very excited about visiting the Rosicrucian museum, Mistress," I said. "This whole adventure with you, the past few months, is like closing a long loop with my childhood—my secrets about BDSM, my sexual obsession with you, my fascination with the Rosicrucians. I'm really enjoying my time with you, ma'am."

"As am I with you, Sammy," she said. "Sarah unfortunately won't be able to join us today. She's working on closing arguments for a case, and it's taking her longer than she anticipated."

"Oh, I'm sorry to hear that," I said. "Sarah's a lovely woman. I have to tell you, ma'am, I was very surprised when I first learned that Sarah was an attorney. She seems so quiet."

"Sarah enjoys being submissive and laconic in our domestic arrangement," Esther said. "But don't let that fool you, Sammy. I've seen her argue a case. She's relentless when she's questioning a witness. Believe me, you'd want her on your side if you needed an attorney. She works for one of the most prestigious law firms in the country. She's greatly respected there, especially for someone so relatively young."

The elevator arrived. We entered and headed down to street level. About halfway down, the elevator stopped to pick up another passenger—

an African American woman about my age. She and Esther immediately made eye contact, cackled affectionately, and hugged.

"Yo!" shouted Esther with great excitement. "I ain't seen you fo' ages, girl. Where you been at?"

"It so good to see you too, girl," the woman responded. "This city got me workin' my sorry butt off. I been thinkin' bout quittin'. Never do it though! I'm just like you, girl—gotta prove the man wrong."

We reached the street. The women hugged goodbye and parted ways.

I remained silent.

"You look a bit dumbfounded, Sammy," Esther said, smiling broadly. "Are you surprised I'm bilingual, dear? Or you might more appropriately say I'm *bi-dialectal*, equally fluent in Black and white street dialects. Many African American women *are*, you know. You probably just don't get much chance to see it. We live in two worlds much more than you realize."

"How exactly do you gauge when to turn it on, ma'am?"

"Oh, it's generally pretty obvious."

"Have you ever gotten it wrong?"

Esther laughed loudly and rested her hand on my shoulder. "Oh yes, dear, one time that I recall vividly. These two Black women I didn't know approached me in San Francisco. I could tell they were going to ask for directions. I broke into Black talk big-time. It turned out they were visiting from England. Both had impeccable Oxford accents. Oh God, Sammy, I was mortified."

"*You* mortified, ma'am? There's a twist."

It surprised me now that in all the time I had been in the Bay Area, it had never occurred to me to visit Rosicrucian Park in San Jose. As soon as we drew near, I was overwhelmed by its size and beauty. The Rosicrucians were clearly not a paltry or impoverished organization. Aside from the Egyptian museum we were visiting, Rosicrucian Park housed a planetarium, peace garden, temple, and library. The grounds were exquisitely landscaped, and the buildings were architected in grand Egyptian and Moorish style, replete with pillars, cupolas, and statues of ancient gods. The museum building itself was modeled after the Temple of Amon at Karnak, from the age of the pharaohs.

The exhibits were fascinating. We lingered longest around the mummies. For some reason, both Esther and I were most intrigued by the mummified cats.

When we were done, we exited to the street. "So, how did you like the museum, Sammy?" Esther asked.

"I enjoyed it very much, ma'am," I said. "It's a magnificent place. But everything in there is about Egypt. There's no substantive information at all about the Rosicrucian order itself."

"They seem to keep their secrets intact and their organizational boundaries very secure, Sammy. I believe they've always been that way."

"Have you ever considered joining, Mistress?"

Esther chuckled. "Sammy, if I wanted to belong to a cult, I'd form my own. I'd be the empress and everyone else would be slaves."

"I'd join that," I said, laughing.

"How about you buy me lunch instead, dear? It's a more manageable commitment."

I smiled. "Sure. Is there a place around here you like?"

"There's an Ethiopian place near here. I'm very fond of it."

I had never tasted Ethiopian food. The place was small and homey. From the descriptions on the menu and what I saw on the plates of other diners, all their food, whether meat or vegetable in nature, had the same consistency—a sort of viscous stew.

A heavyset African woman with a thick Ethiopian accent greeted Esther warmly. It was evident that Esther visited regularly.

We each ordered a combination plate. When the two plates arrived, I noticed that my various dollops of stew rested on a round piece of spongy flatbread. Additional disks of the bread came in a basket for us to share.

There were no utensils.

"Does your friend know how to eat Ethiopian food?" the waitress asked Esther.

"You'd better show him," she said.

The waitress stood beside me. "You eat with your hands," she said in her heavy accent. "The sour bread is called *injera*. It is your spoon. Like this." With that, the woman reached for my plate, tore a piece of bread off with her hands, and used it to snatch up a glob of stew. She picked up the soggy lump and thrust it toward my face. I was so stunned I instinctively parted my lips, and she stuffed the food into my mouth. "Good?" she asked.

I nodded hesitantly as I chewed. She strode off.

"You look white as a ghost, Sammy," Esther said. "Do you not like the food?"

I finished chewing and swallowed.

"I didn't expect her to handle my food and feed me that way," I said apologetically. "I have an issue with germs, Mistress. I'm sorry."

"Oh dear!" Esther said. "Well, do what you need to regain your composure."

I reached into my pocket and accessed my plastic bottle of hand sanitizer. Until then, I had been scrupulous about hiding this aspect of myself from Esther. But now I had little choice. I abluted my hands thoroughly, then took another squirt onto my palms and fastidiously massaged it into my lips, cheeks, chin, and the bottom of my nose.

We had each ordered a glass of *tej*, Ethiopian honey wine. I took a big swig and swished the liquid around my mouth for a few moments before swallowing. The alcohol content did not seem very high, but I hoped there was enough to have an antiseptic effect.

"Are we quite done now?" Esther inquired derisively.

"I'm sorry, Mistress. Just one of my idiosyncrasies."

"Perhaps it's a bit more of a psychosis, dear," Esther teased. "But you're a charming boy, just the same. Was doing that in front of me humiliating for you?"

"Yes, ma'am, very much."

"Well, at least *some* good came of it!" She chuckled. "Too bad Sarah's not here—she'd enjoy telling me that you're blushing."

I smiled.

"Let's have a proper toast," Esther said, "despite your having already chugged down a quarter of your wine as disinfectant. We'll probably have to order another round anyway."

We clinked glasses and sipped the wine. We each ate a few mouthfuls of the food. The flavors were delightful.

"Have you played with many women in the past, Sammy?" she asked.

"Other than with the women at our parties, and with you and Sarah, there's only one other woman I've ever played with. Her name was Stephanie. She and I were involved for almost ten years."

"You sound regretful, dear. Did it not end well?"

"I ruined it, ma'am. I blew it as badly as I've blown anything in my entire life."

"I'm sorry to hear that, dear. What was the nature of your relationship?"

I looked at her for a moment. "What do you mean?" I asked.

"Were you submissive to her?"

"Well, yes. We played a great deal."

"That wasn't my question, Sammy. Listen carefully, dear. Were you *submissive* to her? As Sarah is to me, for instance."

"Yes, Mistress. Just like Sarah is submissive to you, and *I'm* submissive to you. I'm not sure I understand what you mean."

"Clearly you don't, Sammy. Sarah is submissive to me in a completely different way than you are. Sarah is submissive to me in everything we do. It's a lifestyle. We don't just play. Mind you that when Sarah goes to work, she's a lioness and a fearsome attorney. But when she steps through our door, or when the two of us are out socially together, she is my slave. In every activity and every discussion we share."

"And she likes that?" I asked.

"She loves it. And I love it. But I doubt very much that you had that sort of relationship with Stephanie."

"No. I couldn't do that, ma'am. In fact, Stephanie *worked* for me. She ran my store in Chicago. She had run other stores for me prior to that. She started as a salesperson for my father and me. So we had a professional relationship too."

"A professional relationship where *you* were clearly dominant and in control."

"Well—I owned the company. So yes."

"And in your private life, when you weren't playing, what was the nature of your interactions?"

I deliberated over that question. I really had never considered that. I looked hard at Esther, across the table. "I see your point, ma'am. I suppose that other than when we played, Stephanie catered to *me*."

"Was she good at that?"

"She was wonderful. I don't think I ever truly conceptualized that aspect of who we were until this moment. I don't think I appreciated it adequately."

"Do you realize, Sammy, that you *did* have a dominant/submissive relationship with Stephanie. Only *you* were the dominant. She catered to all your needs."

"But I was submissive when we played."

"Not really. In a sense, you ordered her to play with you the way you liked. She was obeying your orders."

"She seemed to enjoy it," I said. "She invented her own twists."

"You're rationalizing, dear."

I drank the wine that was left in my glass and pondered what Esther had just said. Esther flagged the waitress and ordered another round of the *tej*.

"I guess you're right, ma'am," I finally said. "I thought I was being submissive. I certainly felt very submissive when Steph and I played. Was I just deluding myself? I feel submissive when I'm with *you*."

Esther smiled warmly and reached across the table. She took my hand in hers.

"You're such a sweet boy," she said. "You like to play. You like being submissive when you play. There's nothing wrong with that, dear. You just have to understand who you are, and what you want."

"I want to be submissive with you," I said.

"Yes, when you're *with* me. Understand, Sammy, that the time that you and I spend together is, in a sense, fantasy time. No matter what we're doing, whether it's eating or attending a museum, or just sitting and talking. You're in a submissive trance. It's all play, and it's all lovely, and I truly enjoy having you in my life. But could you do what Sarah does? Could you live with me, and let me make every decision? Where we invest our money? How we furnish the house? What clothing you should buy? Whether or not you should spend time with jiu-jitsu? Even if you knew that I'd make compassionate decisions, and discuss things with you as I felt appropriate, could you do that? I honestly don't think you could."

"No, I couldn't," I said softly. "I wouldn't want to, ma'am. I'm amazed that Sarah wants to do that."

"She's wanted a relationship exactly like this all her life. So have I."

"Maybe I don't belong in the BDSM community," I said.

Esther laughed, gently at first, but then so hard she needed to catch her breath. She took a few sips of wine to moisten her throat.

"Oh, my dear Sammy, if that were the criteria, the BDSM community would be emptied of almost everyone in it! The *real* outliers are people like Sarah and me. The lifestyle people. There are very few of us. If anyone doesn't properly belong in the community, it's probably us."

"But you two embrace it purely."

"Let's not get caught up in some artificial hierarchy that defines extreme behavior as pure, and everything else as somehow lacking. Wanting to compartmentalize your submissive play is absolutely fine, Sammy. That's not what ruined your relationship with Stephanie. It sounds to me that what ruined it was how you behaved the rest of the time."

I was silent for a while. I finished the food on my plate and most of my wine. I put the glass down gently and looked up.

"Thank you, Mistress Esther," I said. "I really never understood any of this. I can't necessarily fix anything I did in the past. But I'm so glad I found you."

The injury occurred during a sparring session in Sensei Yamaguchi's dojo in Daly City, just south of San Francisco. I was working with Stuart Kowalski, an advanced jiu-jitsu student with whom I often sparred. We'd sometimes share a beer after practice.

I was masterfully executing one of my favorite throws. I had a firm grip on the lapels of Kowalski's gi, and had used his own momentum to yank him forward diagonally so that all his weight was, for that brief instant, on his right foot. I pivoted outward quickly on my left leg while I raised my own right foot and delivered a sharp, short kick just above Kowalski's outer ankle. It swept his right leg upward and rendered him suddenly airborne, precariously angled, more horizontal than vertical. I assisted the rapidity of his descent by tugging upon his lapels and hurling his torso down toward the mat. He landed with a crisp, thudding smack.

Unfortunately, just prior to that smack, I heard a very different sound as well—a hollow, disembodied pop. It seemed as if it had emanated from my left kneecap, but I felt no pain. It was only when I subsequently tried to take a few steps that the pain became apparent and the knee buckled. I fell to the mat, rubbed the area for a few moments, and got up, fully expecting the knee to be fine. Such tweaks were not uncommon during practice and sparring, especially as I aged. But a searing twinge of pain reasserted itself, and the joint immediately buckled again, sending me ignominiously back to the floor.

With an exhalation of disgust, and the instantaneous envisioning of all the inconveniences and indignities that undoubtedly lay ahead, I told Kowalski that I thought I had torn something in my knee and asked if he could help me to the emergency room of the nearest hospital.

A moment later, Sensei Shigeo Yamaguchi was standing above me as well, inquiring as to my well-being. He offered to accompany us to the hospital.

"It wouldn't be fair to the students in your next class to deprive them of your austere and imposing presence, Sensei," I teased. "Who would be left to instill fear and obedience into their hearts?" I sat up on the floor. "Kowalski can take me to the emergency room. We'll be fine."

"Since your sense of humor is intact, I'm sure your knee will follow suit shortly, Mr. Baron." He smiled. "Please give me a call and let me know the prognosis."

"Will do, sir," I said as I slowly raised myself on one leg and put my arm around Kowalski's shoulder for support. Kowalski was about six feet tall and solidly built—he had no trouble keeping me stable.

We made a quick stop in the locker room to gather my things, and then trundled slowly out into the parking lot.

I said, "On second thought, buddy, just take me to my car. I'll get myself home, catch a quick bite, and go to bed. Maybe it's just a strain and I'll be able to walk in the morning."

"You sure, Baron?" he asked. "It seems like it might be a bad one."

"It's my *left* knee, Kowalski—I don't need it to drive. I'll get home fine. I want to give it a chance and see what it does."

"Okay, Baron, I hope you feel better in the morning. You'll be okay getting up to your place? Don't you have some stairs?"

"I'll be fine," I said, "but thanks for the help, Kowalski. I appreciate it." I slid into the driver's seat of my car.

"Nice throw before your knee popped," he added.

"Thanks." I laughed. "Might be the last throw I make for a while."

"Good luck with it, pal. Give me a call and let me know how it turns out."

Accessing the furnished apartment I rented in San Francisco did indeed involve climbing a double flight of stairs. After I pulled into my garage, I grabbed my briefcase and gym bag and hopped as far as the staircase. I stopped, gazing upward, and whispered, "Fuck," more with resignation than with anger.

I sat upon the bottom stair, and eased up one by one, which took me finally to my flat's front door, where I stood, produced my key, and hopped inside.

Going directly to the kitchen, I first thoroughly washed my hands, then smeared a series of wheat crackers with peanut butter and gobbled them down. Then I drank a glass of water. I hopped into the bathroom, washed my face, brushed and flossed my teeth, and made it into the bedroom where I threw my clothes on a chair and plopped into bed for the night. Just before fluffing the pillow and crawling under the sheets, I cleansed my hands again using the pump jar of hand sanitizer on the nightstand.

I slept well and without pain. The next morning when I woke up, it took me a moment to recall that I had suffered an injury, but as soon as I did, I was very curious whether any healing had occurred overnight. I swung my legs over the side of the bed and rose very gingerly. I was able to stand on two legs. I tried taking a few hesitant steps. There had been some improvement, but very little. I could put just enough weight on my left leg to limp slowly across the room. But the pain I endured doing so was quite severe. My optimistic hope was dashed. The injury clearly required medical attention.

I called into work and explained that I'd be out. I then called my general practitioner, whom I knew from my project at the medical center. He agreed to squeeze me in among his morning appointments, sparing me hours of tedium and frustration in a crowded emergency room. I was most grateful.

An hour later, in his office, the doctor felt around my knee a bit, sent me a few doors down for X-rays, and at last surmised that I had sustained a fairly serious cartilage tear. He then subjected me to a series of semi-informative, lighthearted bromides, which he had undoubtedly recited verbatim scores of times to other patients:

"The knee isn't a particularly well-constructed joint—no ball and socket, just two bones and a bunch of connective tissue. Can't complain to anyone except God about that. This is the kind of injury that's usually cumulative, years of twisting and turning in sports like basketball or tennis, or in your case throwing people around. Some people's connective tissue holds up better than others'; you can complain to your parents about inheriting weaker connective tissue if it makes you feel better . . ."

"Where do we go from here, Doctor?" I asked him.

"We can go in surgically and clean it up a bit, but honestly, rest and incapacitation will do just as well."

He asked me if I had ever learned to use crutches.

"No," I said.

"My nurse Sally can fit you with a pair and provide a tutorial. Given your general fitness level, Mr. Baron, you'll be an expert in twenty minutes, going up and down steps and anything else you need to do: lindy, foxtrot . . . "

I chuckled. "How long will I be on crutches, Doctor?" I asked.

"I'd guess six to eight weeks. Keep off the leg completely at first. Come back and see me in four weeks and we'll figure out if you can start putting a little weight on it. Then there'll be rehab."

I had seen people navigating on crutches throughout my life but had never stopped to ponder the specific obstacles those people encountered. My education began immediately upon returning to my flat.

I made it up the stairs quickly enough, though I modified the stair-climbing methodology taught to me earlier that day by Sally. Sally's method demanded that I plant a crutch on either side of me on the current stair, and then rely solely on the crutches for balance and support as I swung my one usable leg up to the next step. But balancing exclusively upon the crutches seemed a tad precarious, especially as I climbed higher. A tumble backward from that height would exacerbate my problems notably. So I put both crutches under my left arm for support and used the stairway's banister on my right side to provide a somewhat more stable fulcrum.

Having negotiated the stairs reasonably adeptly, I ventured into the kitchen and filled a tall glass with water, planning to carry it into the living room to drink it on the couch while I watched television. But it suddenly occurred to me that the logistics of even that simple maneuver were beyond my current capabilities. I needed both hands to work the crutches. I had no way to carry a full water glass out of the kitchen.

I sighed, and resigned myself to the reality that I would encounter many such logistical puzzles in the weeks to come.

＿＿＿＿＿＿＿＿＿＿＿＿

Esther left a message on my office phone at the medical center on Thursday morning, asking me if I wanted some company at home the following evening. I was finishing my first week of work since the knee injury, trying to run the big project while hobbling on crutches. I felt I was adjusting well, but when I heard her voice and pictured Esther spending time with me at my apartment on Friday, a fresh spark of energy and joy infused me. I called her back and confirmed the rendezvous.

When I opened the door to let her in, I was quite surprised to see her decked out in a nurse's uniform. At the medical center, nurses wore loose-fitting green scrubs and dashed about in tennis shoes. Esther would have none of that. She was dressed in a stiff, freshly pressed white dress of the sort nurses wore back in the 1950s. The dress was snug about her torso, clinging to her magnificent breasts. She had the top buttons open to reveal far more cleavage than would have been permitted by a hospital dress code. The bodice was snugly cinched with a wide, white cloth belt, and the skirt fanned out and hung just above her knees. She wore sheer white stockings and tall stiletto heels of white patent leather.

Esther was an inch or so taller than I in flat shoes. Now, in high heels, and with me stooped a bit upon my crutches, she towered formidably above me. To add to the effect, she had pinned to her hair one of those classic white nurse's caps that haven't been worn in hospitals for decades.

I tried to greet her and tell her she looked lovely, but she cut me off abruptly.

"What are you doing out of bed?" she demanded. "Take off your clothes and get back in bed right now. I will not tolerate a disobedient patient."

I undressed, got into bed, and slid under the covers. Esther, who had been watching me with her hands on her hips, now strolled over and grabbed my crutches, which I had leaned against the wall at the foot of my bed.

"Hmm . . ." she groused.

The window of my bedroom looked out into a small courtyard overflowing with tall, unattended grass. The four apartments in my building theoretically shared it, but no one ever went out there.

Esther slid the window open, and casually dropped my crutches out the window. I heard them land on the grass, two stories down, with an audible plop. I gasped in shock.

"What have you done?" I cried. "I can't walk without those."

"Yes, you are quite helpless now," she said calmly. "I'm going to go mix myself a drink. Would you like one?"

"Yes, a strong one, please, ma'am," I whispered.

"Now, that's a much better attitude, dear," she said as she tucked the covers about my body lovingly. "You are desperately in need of treatment, Sammy. If you accept my ministrations obediently, then I'll try to remember to fetch your crutches and bring them back up here before I leave."

Before I could respond she sashayed out of the room and was gone for several minutes. She returned with two well-chilled martinis.

"Think of it as a mild anesthetic," she said as she handed me my drink and clinked her glass against mine.

Esther made fine martinis. Even Jake would have rated them highly.

We had two each. While we drank them, Esther sat on the edge of my bed and talked to me seriously about the injury, how I was faring on my project at the medical center, and if I needed anything day to day. She stroked me lovingly as we spoke, her hand rubbing against my body through the thin blanket. When we finished, she took the glasses into the kitchen. I heard her rinse them out and put them into the dish rack.

When she returned, Esther was fully back in character as the all-powerful nurse.

"It is time for your treatment, dear. This is a serious injury you've suffered—therefore you must understand that treatment is to be extensive. You will be restrained to better accept the required physical therapy."

Esther had brought with her a cloth satchel full of what I guessed to be restraints, whips, and other toys. She reached into it now and retrieved two hunks of soft but very strong mountaineering cord, which she used to tie my wrists to the bedposts. She also pulled out a ball gag sealed in a plastic bag. When she opened the bag, the aroma of rubbing alcohol was palpable. As she gagged me, I appreciated how thoughtful she had been about respecting my aversion to microbes.

"I've devised a form of acupressure, dear. Although small-minded caregivers might presume, in your case, that treatment should be limited to the area around the knee, a more holistic perspective demands that nerve pathways all over your body need to be stimulated to encourage healing."

With that, Esther pulled from her satchel a bag of small plastic clothespins with spring-controlled pincers. Slowly and meticulously, she ran her left forefinger about my torso, claiming in her cooing narration that she was tracing scientifically proven energy routes. Each time she came to a spot of her choosing, she used her thumb and forefinger to wad a small clump of flesh, and then clamped a clothespin mercilessly upon the skin. Each time she did, I issued a muffled scream of pain. Soon I was bedecked with a dozen such remedies.

As I writhed and moaned, Esther revealed a small metal box.

I knew exactly what it was.

A few weeks prior, Esther, Sarah, and I had dined together. Esther was reminiscing about the times we interacted at the library in the Bronx, when I was a boy. I mentioned that around that same time I briefly became addicted to self-administered electric shocks, induced by simultaneously touching the sink and refrigerator in our small apartment.

To my great surprise, Sarah exclaimed, "Oh my God! I did much the same thing when I was a girl. I had forgotten completely about it. I wonder if I'd enjoy electric shocks now?" That prompted Esther to turn to me and say, "Sammy, dear, you're a clever boy and an inventor of electronic paraphernalia. I'm sure you could build me a small device that I could use to apply electric shocks to Sarah. I'd like to be able to vary the intensity, but it would all have to be at a safe level for any part of the body. Battery powered, I'd assume."

I built Esther such a machine, and presented it to her a week later, with the lone caveat to not shock the torso near the heart. I wasn't certain, but my research suggested that even a small electric pulse near the heart could disrupt the body's systemic rhythms.

Esther now cradled the metal box in her hands. "It's such a lovely little machine you built me, Sammy. Surely you didn't think I'd spare you from its ramifications." Esther then placed the device on the bed and untangled its two cables. Each wire had a small metal probe on its end. "You might think, dear, that the current would best be applied directly to the injury," Esther said. "But actually, the nerve pathways that most profoundly control pain responses in the lower body are located here." She began stroking my erect penis. "And here." She lowered her hand slightly and softly caressed my testicles.

I tried to scream and beg her not to proceed, but my unintelligible mumbles were to no avail. Esther spent the next few minutes applying periodic electric shocks to my nether regions.

Each one made me roar and flinch. Yet, every time, my erection grew even stronger. That made Esther laugh.

When she finished with the machine, she put it away and removed all the clothespins from my skin. She stroked my penis a couple of times, then produced a condom from her satchel and put me into it, rolling it down my shaft. She produced a vibrator and applied it to the underside of the organ near its base. I ejaculated almost immediately.

Esther had never displayed the remotest interest in having either oral sex or intercourse with me. I assumed that was because she preferred females for intimate contact. But she and Sarah both seemed to enjoy bringing me to orgasm nonetheless. It often made me think about the very different pattern I had become accustomed to over the many years that Stephanie and I played together. When Stephanie had me restrained on a bed, she invariably found time to sit on my face and force me to perform cunnilingus. And we always concluded with her mounting me for a furious bout of copulation.

I expected Esther to untie me after she induced orgasm, but she did not. Instead she found a washcloth in my hall closet, dampened it with warm water, and wiped my member clean. Then, as I watched, she foraged through her cloth satchel and retrieved four odd-looking plastic items.

"Do you know what these are, Sammy?" she asked.

I assumed the question was rhetorical as she still had me securely gagged.

"Do you remember our conversation at the Ethiopian restaurant, dear? You were confused about exactly how submissive you wanted to be. These contraptions are male chastity devices. I purchased four different sizes. I'm sure we'll find one to fit you perfectly."

I moaned from behind the ball gag. Esther ignored that and began fitting the devices onto my penis. Each chastity device had a curved, penis-shaped compartment that fit snugly over a limp member, with perforations at the tip to permit urination. Plastic straps from the base of the cylinder were pulled down around the scrotum and secured with a tiny padlock behind the testicles. Esther found one that fit perfectly. I had to admire the ingenious design. It was lightweight and simple, but it seemed diabolically effective.

"I confess that it's a tad draconian, Sammy," Esther said soothingly, as she softly rubbed my belly. "It does not allow even an erection. At work you'll need to avoid the urinals and pee in a stall—it would be quite embarrassing if anyone saw this on you, big boss that you are. But it will be a good test of how submissive you actually can be, dear. To what extent are you willing to depend upon Sarah and me for your orgasms, to lose control over them, to be forced to ask permission to receive one?"

I looked at her helplessly.

"If you reach a point where you can't handle it anymore, just let me know and we'll end the experiment."

With that, Esther left the apartment briefly and returned with my crutches, which she leaned back up against the wall where they had been. She untied me, and gave me a sweet kiss goodbye.

"Thank you so much for visiting, ma'am," I said. "I really do enjoy your company so much."

"I enjoy yours as well, Sammy. Let's see how long you last with the chastity device."

I lasted one week.

I was curious to know if Sensei Shigeo Yamaguchi had any suggestions regarding activities I could engage in during the time I was on crutches, and afterwards while rehabilitating the knee. I explained to him that I was still working out with weights, limiting my training to upper-body exercises I could perform while seated. I told the sensei I was anxious to return to jiu-jitsu practice but knew that might be months away.

"We've talked, Mr. Baron, many times, about your interest in becoming more adept at meditation. This might be a fine time to pursue that."

"That's an interesting idea, Sensei," I said. "All the meditation techniques that you've shown me, I continue to practice. They focus me and relax me. I think they help me at work, and I know they make me better at sparring. But that *breakthrough* that I've heard so much about, that experiencing of another realm—that continues to elude me, as you know. Other than just meditating more, which I've tried, what would you suggest?"

"I've been thinking about you in this regard, Mr. Baron. I think an immersion might do you good. There are a number of intensive Buddhist meditation retreats I can point you to, all within an hour or two of the Bay Area. The approaches vary slightly but not importantly. Most retreats are a week or ten days. But with your work and all, maybe a three-day retreat would be a good start for you. You could take a Friday off, no?"

"I could, I'm sure. What are these retreats like?"

"You meditate almost all day."

"All day?" I exclaimed with some alarm. "I'm not sure I can do that, Sensei."

"You have incredible focus, Mr. Baron. If you put your mind to something, you can do it. You are my most advanced black belt and the dojo's champion at sparring. You even get the best of *me* in sparring once in a while."

"Not very often." I chuckled.

"But on occasion. Why? Are you an incredibly gifted athlete? No. You keep yourself in marvelous shape and work hard, but no. It's your focus. Your mind. That sort of mind can master advanced meditation."

"Do you really think so? It's something I've always wanted."

"It's not easy, Mr. Baron. The commitment of meditating for hours at a time, to reach the breakthrough point, is something you need to decide you really want to do. I have information and brochures from some of the retreats if you wish to consider it."

"All right, Sensei. I'll look into it. Thank you."

The Buddhist temple held its meditation retreat in a remote wooded area two hours north of San Francisco.

I drove slowly into the small gravel lot. The ground was rutted and uneven, and the car lurched from side to side. A fine white dust formed a cloud around the vehicle.

I sat in the car a few moments—in part to let the air clear, but also to gird myself for the three days ahead. I thought back to the first descriptions of meditation I had come upon as a boy, combing the library for information on the arcane practice. I assumed that any discipline capable of opening one to spiritual illumination had to incorporate intricate contortions and machinations of the mind. When I first discovered that it consisted merely of emptying the mind and thinking of nothing, I was dumbfounded. How could something so simple produce such a profound result?

But I had learned, through practice, that stilling the mind was extraordinarily difficult. Now I was about to immerse myself in a retreat where I'd spend hours attempting the feat.

I had read the rules for the meditation retreat carefully, at least a dozen times. Absolute silence for the entire duration of the retreat was strictly enforced. No sex or fraternization with any other students was permitted—this explicitly included gestures, facial expressions, physical contact, or written notes. Males and females were kept segregated. Books, radios, musical instruments, and writing materials were all forbidden. Even masturbation was taboo.

All forms of prayer, worship, or religious ceremony were prohibited. Also prohibited was all exercise other than walking meditation during one assigned period each day.

No outside communication whatsoever was allowed. Eating after midday was forbidden as well. Food was simple vegetarian fare, eaten in silence. One break for tea in the afternoon was the only thing ingested past noon.

Most of the three days was spent in the Zendo, or meditation hall. We participants all sat around the perimeter, facing the wall, our backs to the center of the room. Many sat cross-legged on a cushion. The rest of us used chairs. I would have preferred to sit cross-legged on the floor, and would normally have been capable of doing so, but my knee could not possibly have withstood that stress. I was embarrassed about being one of the people in chairs. I wanted badly to explain to the others why I needed to avoid the floor, but the edict mandating silence prevented me from doing so.

The cabin assigned for sleeping was a small shack, with a wooden floor and five pairs of bunk beds along its walls. In the center of the room was a small wood stove, which the monks lit if they felt it was too cold to sleep without it. Initially I felt very uncomfortable with the lack of privacy. I was accustomed to private hotel suites when I traveled. But we spent so little waking time in the cabin that the concern turned out to be inconsequential.

Despite being arbitrarily assigned an upper bunk, I found I was able to ascend the small ladder without a problem. I was still limping slightly, but I don't think it was especially noticeable.

The schedule every day was the same. The wake-up gong rang at 4 AM. Most of the students found this ungodly—they appeared groggy and disoriented. But the hour was quite normal for me. The first meditation session in the Zendo was from 4:30 to 6:30 AM.

That was followed by an hour and a half for breakfast. We ate rice gruel and pickled vegetables. We took the meal in the same seats in the Zendo that we used for meditation, silent and facing the identical section of wall. The isolation was all the more eerie because people were all around, but we were forbidden from interacting.

After breakfast concluded, there were two more hours of meditation.

Lunch at 11 AM unfolded exactly like breakfast, and consisted of more pickled vegetables, rice, and simple vegetable soup. It was the last bit of food we'd be permitted for the day.

We were then granted an hour for rest or walking meditation. The group reconvened for meditation from 1 to 5 PM. A tea break from 5 to 6 PM offered tea that was green and bland, taken without sugar or dairy. Two more hours of meditation followed.

From 8 to 9:30 PM there was an hour and a half of discourse from a teacher, and a brief period to entertain questions. That question-and-answer session was the day's only exception to the imposition of silence. There really was not much to query about, but a few students asked a stream of questions that seemed entirely gratuitous. I was certain that they found the silence unbearable and just needed to hear their own voices.

We returned to the bunkhouse at 9:30 PM, and the lights went out almost immediately.

The hours of meditation were, of course, the most challenging aspect of the experience. The Buddhist monastery offering this retreat employed a style of meditation that began by watching the breath. Once the mind was more focused, we were advised to observe, without emotion or judgment, the thoughts that jumped into our minds, and let those thoughts slip away. Patience and persistence were stressed. We were warned that any anger or frustration we might experience in trying to empty our minds would be self-defeating. Eventually, if we stilled our minds sufficiently, the enlightenment of cosmic truth would fill our vessels.

Just sitting still for that long was at times agonizingly difficult. I wished that Esther were there and could tie me tightly to the chair, and gag and blindfold me. It would have made it far easier for me to remain motionless for so many hours. Fantasizing about that distracted me and at one point gave me an erection, a clear breach of protocol. Fortunately, I was facing the wall, which hid the bulge in my pants from the monk facilitating the session.

I had brief periods where my focus was good, but many where I lost it altogether and suddenly realized that I had spent minutes, or possibly even hours, thinking about work, jiu-jitsu, and incidents from my past. A couple of times, I awoke and realized I had been asleep, and had absolutely no idea for how long.

By the third day I did experience some extended intervals where my mind appeared completely empty. I felt no surge of mystical illumination, but I did experience a profound feeling of peace. If the breakthrough point I had heard so much about really did exist, I was close to it, but not yet there.

23.
Shortwave Radio

WHEN I RETURNED HOME from the retreat, I began practicing seated meditation for half an hour every day. There was still no breakthrough, but I became much more comfortable and adept at the practice.

In retrospect, though, the most intriguing thing about the entire retreat experience had been the food. At that point in my life, I had never equated the food I ate with spiritual progress or lack of it. The monks insisted that because flesh food of any sort involved imprisoning and slaughtering an animal, it had inherent in it violence, cruelty, and a lack of compassion. Ingesting such food, they insisted, transferred those sensibilities to the eater, and stunted his spiritual growth.

I was not prepared to adopt the sort of meager rations offered at the Zendo on a permanent basis. But the assertion that food and mystical illumination were intimately linked resonated strongly with me.

I gradually changed my diet. I first eliminated red meat. A few weeks later I stopped eating poultry as well, and relied on fish and seafood as my primary protein sources. Six months after that I gave up fish and seafood too, and adopted a fully lacto-ovo vegetarian eating plan.

When I spoke to Emmanuel on the phone and told him I had become a vegetarian, he screamed that I was an idiot and insisted that the diet would surely kill me. From that point forward, every weekly phone conversation with Emmanuel opened with him launching into the same tirade:

"Are you still a vegetarian? Are you still following that idiot diet?"

When I told him I was, he'd roar on:

"You're an idiot! Why do you listen to these lunatics? That idiot diet is going to kill you. You want to die? You're an idiot!"

———◇———

I was surprised to receive a phone call from my aunt Eve. Over the years, when I found myself in New York, I still occasionally joined Eve, Irving, and Emmanuel for a Sunday dinner. But I hadn't been in touch with either Irving or Eve since I arrived in San Francisco to manage the big medical center project. It had been eight months.

Eve sounded concerned.

"Sammy, I have some bad news. But not *so* bad."

"Is everyone all right?" I asked.

"No, Sammy. Your father, Emmanuel. He had a small heart attack."

"A heart attack?" I exclaimed.

"Sammy, it was a minor one. He's home now."

"Is he going to be okay?"

"He's going in for a procedure. They're inserting a stent into his artery. They think that's all he needs."

"When is that?"

"They're getting back to us with an appointment time. Probably in a week or two."

"How did it happen?"

"It wasn't that dramatic. He felt pain in his chest and down his arm. So we called the paramedics and they took him to the emergency room."

"And he's okay now?"

"He has angina, Sammy. Heart disease. They think he had it for a long time, but he never went to the doctor, so no one knew. But it's manageable."

"And how's Emmanuel holding up psychologically?" I asked.

Eve chuckled slightly. "As big a curmudgeon as ever."

"Well, then he can't be *that* sick," I said reassuringly.

"Sammy, listen. We know you're busy. But Irving and I, we're getting old ourselves. We really can't take care of your father anymore, now that he has a heart condition. We need you to come back and have him live with you in your apartment in Manhattan."

"He won't want to do that," I said.

"Irving and I talked to him. He knows he has to do it. He's still grousing about it. But he'll do it."

I hesitated before speaking again. I realized that this phone conversation was about to change my day-to-day life drastically for the foreseeable future.

"Okay," I said, "the project here is wrapping up. The final testing should be done in two or three weeks. We go live over a weekend right after. Can you wait till then? I'd be able to make a clean break and come home, and not have to split my attention between here and there."

"That will be fine, Sammy. Thank you. I'll talk to you again before then."

"Doesn't Emmanuel want to get on the phone to say hello?"

"I asked before I called. He said no."

I snickered. "You're right. He's his old self."

***

I helped Emmanuel into the passenger seat of the van I had rented.

At first I considered hiring movers, but he had only a few things, which I had loaded into the van earlier. There were a couple of suitcases and a half dozen cardboard boxes filled mostly with electronic paraphernalia.

I went back to the house to say goodbye to Uncle Irving and Aunt Eve, who were standing in their doorway. I thanked them again for all they had done. Eve had a few parting reminders about Emmanuel's care.

From Riverdale in the Bronx, I crossed the Harlem River into Manhattan and headed west. Manhattan is very narrow at its northern tip—it took only a couple of minutes to reach the Henry Hudson Parkway at the city's westernmost edge, which would take me south to my apartment on Central Park West.

"How are you feeling?" I asked Emmanuel.

"I'm all right," he said gruffly. He pointed his finger in my direction. "And listen. Just because we'll be living together doesn't mean you get to tell me what to do. I'm still your father. I don't have to listen to you. *You* have to listen to *me*."

"It's a pretty big apartment, with two floors," I said. "There'll be enough room for both of us to do whatever we want."

"Just don't get any ideas about being the big boss with me."

We drove for a while in silence.

I turned my head slightly so that I could see Emmanuel out of the corner of my eye as I drove. "Eve mentioned to me that because you've had angina for quite some time, your doctor recommended that you adopt a vegetarian diet."

"Yeah. So?"

"And he gave you articles to read about the health benefits of a vegetarian diet," I continued.

"What's your point?"

"Oh, I don't have much of a point," I said. "I was just wondering if you still thought I was an idiot for adopting a vegetarian diet."

Emmanuel became agitated and his face reddened. He pondered my question for ten to fifteen seconds. Then he shouted thunderously while shaking his finger in my face: "You're still an idiot! You made a lucky guess! Even an idiot makes a lucky guess now and then!"

I considered what my father had just posited. It took a moment or two before I started giggling. Soon I was laughing so hard that I had to slow down and focus hard on keeping my car in the lane. I could not control myself. I was roaring hysterically.

Emmanuel watched me, seemingly nonplussed, for about thirty seconds. Then he started laughing too. Soon his guffaws had him rocking violently forward and back. He banged his palm deliriously on the dashboard.

"A lucky guess!" Emmanuel shrieked breathlessly in a high-pitched voice between howls and cackles. "An idiot with a lucky guess! It's classic!"

We laughed together irrepressibly until we arrived at my building and the doorman came to the car to assist us.

Emmanuel and I had not laughed together like that since I was a young boy.

———⌣———

Shortwave radio utilizes electromagnetic waves of a specific frequency range. Broadcast signals in this span behave in a surprising manner. They exhibit a tendency known as "skip propagation." Rather than broadcast in a straight line until they dissipate, shortwave signals hit the ionosphere and bounce back to Earth. Water or ground can then reflect the waves again, sending them back into space, only to hit the ionosphere and again reflect back to the surface. This cycle can occur two or more times before the waves lose their strength.

As a result, shortwave radio broadcasts can effectively bend around the horizon and be picked up thousands of miles away. The reflection patterns are affected by sunlight, so certain stations tend to be received by day, whereas others become available at night. The different seasons also alter the ionospheric layer sufficiently to affect what stations can be accessed.

Constructing shortwave radios had become Emmanuel's favorite pastime.

As he unpacked, Emmanuel decided immediately that the large table in my dining room was the perfect spot for his electronic tinkering. He emptied the contents of his various boxes onto the table. Soon, there were numerous fully constructed radios and a plethora of loose components strewn from one end of the table to the other. The radios didn't look like radios you'd buy in a store. There were no cabinets, or station delineations, or knobs. Just mazes of components wired together on slabs of pegboard. The volume and selection of stations were tuned via potentiometers and variable capacitors soldered to the wired connections.

At first, I was glad to see that Emmanuel had a hobby. But it didn't take me long to understand the horrific lure that shortwave radio now held for him.

No matter what Emmanuel was doing, be it eating, tinkering with electronic components, or reading the newspaper, he had some shortwave talk-radio show blaring so loudly it could be heard rooms away.

The content was shocking.

It was relentlessly racist, homophobic, and jingoistic. The people spewing their hateful right-wing propaganda were incessantly angry, screaming their messages of hostility in loud, accusatory voices.

After a couple of hours of trying to ignore the barrage of noise, I finally confronted Emmanuel.

"What the hell are you listening to?" I asked.

"This is what I listen to. I live here now. I can listen to whatever the hell I please."

"I know you used to listen to conservative talk radio," I said. "That was always on the AM dial. This is shortwave, isn't it?"

"Damn right it's shortwave," Emmanuel said. "The laws governing AM radio are pansy-ass rules. They can't broadcast the truth. There are no rules on shortwave. This is the real stuff. You should listen to it. You'll learn something."

"You're a Jew!" I exclaimed. "Don't you think these people hate Jews just as much as they hate the Blacks and Hispanics they're constantly railing against?"

"Don't give me your liberal bullshit," Emmanuel yelled. "There are a couple of anti-Semites I've come across. I don't listen to them. These people I listen to speak the truth. Just look at how everything around you is falling apart. Look at how the neighborhood where you grew up in the Bronx turned into a pit of filthy uncivilized animals. You're just like all the other idiots, kidding themselves. Look around and stop denying the truth."

I realized that living with Emmanuel was going to be far more challenging than I envisioned.

The American Library Association, with over 60,000 members, is the world's oldest and largest organization for libraries and librarians. Their annual meeting held every June was scheduled this year for New York City.

Esther planned to attend and bring Sarah with her to make a brief holiday of it. Esther called me and asked if she and Sarah could stay in my apartment while they were in the city.

"It's so good to hear from you, ma'am," I said. "I'd *love* to have you and Sarah stay with me. I have a bedroom that's available, and you two would have a bathroom to yourselves as well."

"Oh, that sounds lovely. It will be so nice to see you, Sammy," Esther said.

"I have to warn you though, ma'am. My father lives with me now."

"We know that, Sammy. That's why you left the Bay Area."

"My father has become quite eccentric in his old age. You may find him offensive."

"Oh, I'm sure it's nothing we can't handle, dear," she said.

"Esther, he blares right-wing hate radio all day long. It's relentless. It never stops. It's anti-Black, anti-gay, anti pretty much everything you and Sarah and I believe in. He won't stop and he doesn't apologize. You're welcome to stay, and I'd really love to see you, but this is the reality you'll be engulfed in."

"Oh dear," Esther sighed. "It sounds as if your dad's an intolerant fellow."

"He's always been to some extent, but it's never been this bad."

Esther chuckled. "So, dear, it appears that you're asking your mistress to choose between a house resonant with right-wing hatred, which happens to have a slave in it whom she loves dearly, or an impersonal, overpriced hotel where everyone will be gawking at the interracial lesbian couple prancing through their lobby."

"I guess I wasn't really thinking about the alternative," I said. "Maybe I can get Emmanuel to turn it down a little bit when we have guests in the house."

Esther's voice took on an impish tone: "You know, Sammy, I'd actually like to meet this father of yours. Just seeing the expression on his face when I mess with him a bit would be priceless."

"He's not nearly as compliant as I am, Mistress," I said. "Even *you'd* have your work cut out for you."

Esther laughed. "Any dominatrix worth her salt needs a challenge now and again."

"All right," I said. "It's set. You'll stay with me. I'll have a car pick you up at the airport. I can't wait to see you both."

"Thank you, dear," Esther said. "You're a love."

———⏝———

The doorman showed Esther and Sarah up to my apartment and carried in their luggage. I thanked him.

Emmanuel had not gotten up to greet the women. He was fiddling with electronic components at the dining room table, a particularly odious anti-Black tirade booming on his radio.

I took Esther and Sarah into the dining room.

"I told you I had two friends coming in from San Francisco," I shouted at Emmanuel to be heard over the radio. "I'd like you to meet them."

When Emmanuel lifted his head to glance in our direction, the look of shock and confusion on his face was farcical. All I had told him was that two friends would be visiting. I made no mention of their gender or race.

Without hesitation, Esther walked directly over to him and extended her hand.

"I'm Esther," she said.

Emmanuel seemed uncertain as to what to do, but he reluctantly stood to shake her hand. Esther was wearing especially high heels and towered over him majestically.

"You have a wonderful boy," Esther said. "I love him dearly."

Emmanuel gazed up at her, but said nothing at first. Finally he tentatively mumbled, "That's nice, I guess."

"This is my life partner, Sarah," Esther continued, motioning across the room. Sarah nodded from where she stood.

"Nice to meet you," Emmanuel stammered in a hoarse whisper.

Esther leaned closer to Emmanuel's face. "Might I ask you a favor," she said sweetly. "I have a medical condition that is exacerbated by loud noise. If I could impose upon you to turn your radio down a bit while we're here, I'd be most grateful."

Emmanuel's mouth opened and he gazed at Esther vacuously. He looked to me and then back to her. "Oh, okay," he finally muttered. He reached down and lowered the volume dramatically.

"Oh, you're such a dear," Esther said. With that she caressed the side of Emmanuel's face with her palm and kissed him on the cheek, leaving a bright-red lipstick mark on his skin.

Emmanuel stood frozen.

"Let me carry your luggage up for you," I said, smiling broadly. I took their bags and accompanied the ladies to their bedroom upstairs. When I came back down the steps, Emmanuel was standing in the hallway.

He was furious. But despite being agitated, Emmanuel kept his voice to an enraged whisper. "What the hell is going on? These are who your friends are? A Schvartze dyke and her white girlfriend? Are you *meshuggah*? You bring these people into *my* home? You're *meshuggah*! San Francisco turned you wacko!"

I ignored him and went into another room to wait for the women to bathe and change.

Esther, Sarah, and I went out for cocktails and dinner. It was late when we got back. Emmanuel was already asleep.

"Come into our room with us," Esther whispered.

Their bedroom was at the end of the hall. The three of us went in. Sarah closed the door behind us and locked it.

"Sarah, see that the boy undresses," Esther said softly. As I took my clothes off, I noticed Esther remove several hunks of rope from her suitcase, and three bandanas.

Esther pointed to a wooden chair in the corner of the room. "Sarah, pull that over here, where we'll be able to see it."

Sarah positioned the chair alongside the bed. Esther motioned to me to sit down.

Working together, the two women bound me securely to the wooden chair.

The two of them began to undress. When they had both stripped to bras and panties, they sat on the edge of the bed and began fondling each other. I watched intently. They kissed on the mouth for a long time. Then Sarah's lips and tongue began to explore Esther's neck and shoulders. Esther tilted her head back as her hands stroked Sarah's thighs and torso.

Both Esther and Sarah were becoming quite aroused.

Sarah reached around to unhook Esther's bra, but Esther stopped her. "I think the boy's seen enough," Esther whispered. With that Esther stood up, took one of the bandanas, and blindfolded me with it. A few moments later I felt fingers squeeze my face, forcing open my mouth, which was summarily stuffed with a wadded bandana. The third bandana was threaded through my lips and tied behind my head.

Esther whispered in my ear: "Sammy dear, having you here all trussed up like this, with Sarah and me being able to glance at you from time to time as we make love, will enhance our experience mightily. You do enjoy enhancing your mistress's lovemaking experience, dear, do you not?"

I nodded compliantly. I felt Esther kiss me softly on the forehead, above the blindfold.

For the next forty minutes I listened to sensual sounds of bodies shifting and rolling on freshly pressed sheets. I heard licking and panting and heavy sighs. And finally there were long, loud, exquisite moans.

When the women were done, there was a period of silence. Then Sarah untied me. I realized, to my disappointment, that they had both put on pajamas before releasing me and removing my blindfold.

I went back to my room, where I masturbated. My orgasm was explosive.

Esther left the house early the next morning for the first session of the library conference. Sarah accompanied her, planning to do sightseeing and shopping until the meeting adjourned and she could join Esther for drinks.

They were already gone when I went down to the kitchen and began cooking scrambled tofu with mushrooms and caramelized onions, one of my favorite breakfasts. When Emmanuel first saw me make it months earlier, he'd have nothing to do with it, insisting that it looked revolting. I discovered, however, that if I included turmeric among the spices I used to season it, the tofu turned the same yellow as scrambled eggs. After that it became Emmanuel's preferred choice for morning fare.

As we ate, Emmanuel said to me, "Did you hear those two dykes making love last night? Goddamn it, I was three doors down and I heard it like it was happening right next to me. For crying out loud! It was disgusting! Did you hear it?"

"Oh yes," I said. "I heard it."

24.
Costa Rica

BARON AND KENNEMAN Antenna Technology rented office space in downtown Manhattan. Jake, a full professor now at CCNY, and recently named department chair, was rarely there. But I met frequently with Paul O'Rourke. He and I also talked often with the engineers with whom we contracted for our installations. Paul had not landed another megaproject like the medical center engagement in the Bay Area, but we had many other, smaller installations going on, most in the greater New York City area, all handled by contracted staff. Our profit margins were excellent.

CCNY was on spring break, so it seemed a fine time to have the three principals, Jake, Paul, and myself, convene to chart strategy for the upcoming months. I arranged a two-hour meeting starting at ten in the morning. I arrived just a few minutes late.

I heard yelling and scuffling before I entered. When I opened the door to the suite, I saw Paul and Jake shouting and gesticulating angrily. Jake was a much bigger man than Paul, but Paul seemed the aggressor.

Before I could say a word, their encounter escalated. Paul pushed Jake. Jake shoved him back, but Paul used Jake's momentum to grab him and throw Jake into a filing cabinet. Jake's back slammed hard against the metal, and he slid to the floor, trembling and cowering as Paul stomped toward him.

I could see Paul was seething.

I ran over and put my arm out to stop Paul's progression. Paul turned and tried to throw a punch at me. I instinctively parried the blow, grabbed Paul's sleeve, and executed a jiu-jitsu throw I had used in sparring sessions hundreds of times, tossing Paul over my hip. He hit the floor with an audible thud. Paul cursed at me and tried to get up, but I held him down with a firmly applied wristlock.

"I'm a fifth-degree black belt now, Paul," I said. "Don't do something foolish."

It took Paul just a few moments to calm down. "Okay, you can let me up, Sammy," he said. "I'm over it; you have my word."

I allowed Paul to stand. I walked over to help Jake, but he held up his hand, signaling that he preferred to remain seated on the floor for now.

I took a couple of steps back and looked from one to the other. "Do either of you want to tell me what the hell is going on?" I asked.

Neither said a word.

"All right," I said. "Let's call it a day. We'll talk about this another time. Paul, go home. Jake, you look a little shaken up. I'll take you home myself and make sure you're OK."

Paul walked out without saying a word.

I turned to Jake. "Let me help you into a chair," I said. I rolled one of the chairs from the conference table over to Jake's side and helped him into it.

"Are you okay?" I asked.

"I'll live, Doc. Nice jiu-jitsu move there. You put that little hoodlum in his place."

"Do you want to tell me what this is about?" I asked.

"I could use a drink, Doc. There's a hotel down the block. Their bar is elegantly appointed and open all day."

"It's ten in the morning, Jake!" I shouted.

"Perfect time for a bloody mary, Dockles."

"First tell me what this is about. Please."

"Rather prosaic, actually. It's about Jill."

"Jill? You told me that you and Jill broke up, *again*, a couple of weeks ago. Didn't you?"

"Yes, Doc, but it wasn't until this morning that I realized she was shacking up with O'Rourke."

"She's living with *Paul*? How does she even know him?"

"We were all at the company Christmas party in December. They must have met there."

"That was months ago, Jake. You think they've been seeing each other all this time?"

"Who knows, Doc. But she sure as hell dropped him off this morning in her car. I was half a block away and watched the whole thing."

"Is there anything more to it, Jake? That looked pretty violent for a woman changing boyfriends."

"Nothing I care to discuss, Doc. Let's go get those bloody marys."

Jake seemed a bit unsteady on his feet when he first arose but after a few steps appeared to be walking fine.

We took the elevator down and headed for the hotel. "I can't drink bloody marys anymore, Jake," I said. "They're not vegetarian."

"What?"

"There's Worcestershire sauce in the mix. That has anchovies in it. Not vegetarian."

"You're becoming anal retentive, Doc. Drink a goddamn mimosa instead."

I had two.

Jake drank three bloody marys. After that, he said he was fine to get home by himself, and that the walk would do him good. We hugged. Jake strolled off.

I suspected that more was going on in this romantic triangle, but neither Jake nor Paul was willing to talk about it.

I returned to the office, but I couldn't work. The violent encounter replayed itself in my mind. Paul manhandling Jake. Jake cowering. My throwing Paul to the floor and holding him there.

I was embarrassed that the thing that kept gnawing at me was not the scuffle, nor the long-term negative effects it might have on my business.

Instead, I was obsessed with the certainty that women who saw Jake and me together always saw Jake as the big man, the athletic man, the man who could protect them. Even though I could flatten Jake in an instant. Even though Jake cowered before Paul O'Rourke and *I* dispatched O'Rourke summarily. Even though I had trained for years to disarm attackers who carried knives and guns.

Women would never see that.

To them I was just a short, slender, unimposing pushover. No matter how many weights I lifted, how many black belts I earned, how many jiu-jitsu sparring tournaments I won, that perception of me would never change.

Emmanuel's electronics components completely blanketed my dining room table. He and I now used the smaller table in the kitchen for meals.

The components were alluring. There was a project I had ruminated on for some time, and I was eager to tinker. But the right-wing hate radio was intolerable. I asked Emmanuel if he'd consider listening through headphones when I was working there with him. He said he didn't mind headphones themselves, but he didn't want to be tethered to radios. So I proposed a project we could work on jointly.

Together, over the next few days, we designed and built tiny transmitters. We hooked them up to each shortwave radio such that flipping a switch diverted the radio's output from the loudspeaker to the transmitter, which sent the signal out on a local frequency. We then fitted the headphones with a tiny complementary receiver that converted that frequency back into sound.

They worked amazingly well. The brief project also gave Emmanuel and me something we could pursue together and not fight about.

I did, however, make certain that the transmitted signal was not powerful enough to seep beyond my apartment. I did not want anyone in the building or beyond to even *possibly* associate that hateful rhetoric with me.

With some quiet in the house, I began spending time at the dining room table, tinkering with components. The premise for my experiment was enticing. I knew that I could amplify radio or television waves. I also knew, from incidents in my life, that I had on occasion sent psychic suggestions to other people. If psychic transmissions were conveyed by some sort of wave, was it possible to build a mechanism that could capture, amplify, and transmit psychic waves more powerfully than I could innately?

It seemed fanciful, but the possibility still intrigued me.

At one point, about a week after I started, Emmanuel took off his headphones and asked me what the hell I was working on. I explained the premise to him.

"That's not science!" he screamed. "That's idiocy! San Francisco turned you into a dyke-loving wacko *mashugana*! Build a goddamn radio like a normal person!"

He rolled his eyes and slipped his headphones back on.

———※———

Four days had passed since the office scuffle. I had not heard from Paul. I tried calling him at home, but I got a message saying his phone was disconnected.

That aroused my concern.

I employed a part-time bookkeeper who came in twice a week. She was due in this afternoon—I was anxious to talk to her. Jake, Paul, and I all had private holding accounts associated with the business, separate from the enterprise's main income and expenditure ledger. I was very curious to know whether Paul had emptied his.

When the bookkeeper looked into it, my suspicions were confirmed. Paul had drained his account. That didn't surprise me. What did surprise me was the bookkeeper's discovery that Jake's account was zeroed out as well.

Jake was teaching a class, but I left a message with his assistant to please have him call me back as soon as he could. When he did, a couple of hours later, I asked him if he had any funds in his holding account.

"I have a shitload in there, Doc. Why?"

"It's gone," I said. "The bookkeeper just confirmed that. I suspect O'Rourke stole it."

"I had over $50,000 in there, Doc!" Jake screamed. "It's all gone?"

"You had over $50,000? Why on earth so much? Those are meant to be temporary holding stages until you transfer the money to your own private investments. Why did you have so much in there, Jake?"

"I hadn't gotten to it! What's the difference? That felon stole my money. Where the fuck is he?"

"I have no idea," I said.

"Are you going to call the police?"

"I don't want to do that, Jake. It would focus too much attention on a potentially embarrassing situation for the business. I have an idea about how to deal with it ourselves."

"I need my goddamn money, Doc. I depend on that."

"All right. Listen, Jake. I'll reimburse you the money."

"I can't take it from you, Doc. That's not right."

"I can afford it. Just take the money, Jake. If we're able to recover it from Paul, you can pay me back then."

"I don't know, Doc."

"I insist," I said.

———※———

Gus Taylor, the large, imposing African American man Jake and I would later use as a driver in the city, had been a New York City police officer for many years, and was recently promoted to sergeant.

Gus and I grew close during the years I ran the chain of television and electronics stores. I had security guards in every store, and supervisors who oversaw them, but it was Gus, acting in an advisory capacity, who designed our approach to overall security. He had been incredibly successful at keeping our customers and staff safe, and our inventory free from theft or vandalism.

This sort of "moonlighting" was common among police officers—many served as bouncers or private guards during off hours. But the engagement I now proposed to Gus was a different thing altogether. I explained to him that for several months, I had a private detective investigating the whereabouts of Paul O'Rourke. The detective had finally tracked him to a small town in Costa Rica, where O'Rourke and Jill Swenson had purchased a bed-and-breakfast inn and were now the proprietors.

Gus sat across from me in the meeting room of my downtown office as I detailed my request.

"I have a score to settle with O'Rourke," I said. "I'm going to hire a private jet and fly down to Costa Rica. I'd like you to take a few days off and come with me. I'll need a driver-slash-bodyguard."

"And you're going to confront him?" Gus asked.

"That's right."

"To what end, Baron? You expect him to give you the money back?"

"I don't know," I said. "Maybe."

Gus looked annoyed. He was not a man to mince words. "Baron, you're a smart guy," he said. "But you're not thinking straight. You're still angry. Look at the money you already spent on the PI. Add in the money for the private jet, and the car, and whatever it is you intend to pay *me*—"

"Which would be a lot," I said.

"Which would be a lot," Gus repeated with a smirk. "You already spent a whole lot more than the $50,000 O'Rourke stole. And he put that money into buying the B-and-B, so you're not going to see that either, Baron. What the fuck are you thinking?"

"It's not about money anymore, Gus."

"So, it's personal. Between you and O'Rourke, huh? And what are you going to do when you see him? Have it out? It's not making sense to me, Baron."

"I've known Paul O'Rourke since we were both kids in Co-Op City.

We've been friends all these years. He stole money from me, Gus. I can't just let that go and walk away."

"He didn't steal the money from *you*, Baron. He stole it from Kenneman."

"It's *my* business!"

Gus looked down and squeezed his forehead over and over with his thumb and forefinger. He pondered silently for nearly a minute.

He finally looked up. "You've had months to cool off, and you haven't. You're gonna go down there and do whatever bonehead thing you're gonna do whether I go down there with you or not. Am I right, Baron?"

"I'm afraid so, Gus."

He sighed. "All right, Baron. I'll go with you. It's a stupid idea, but at least I'll keep you from getting into something you can't get out of." He paused. "And I can use the extra cash right now."

We wound up hiring not just a car but a driver as well. I was dumbfounded to learn that buildings in Costa Rica had no addresses and most small streets had no names. Locations were described by such phrases as "across from the post office" or "twenty meters past the hamburger joint." Gus and I agreed that if we intended to find the bed-and-breakfast, and be able to get away quickly, we had to hire a driver familiar with the area.

We found a driver who spoke good English. He told us that the bed-and-breakfast had been there for many years and attracted a lot of American tourists, and that the place had recently changed owners.

It was up a small, deserted dirt road. The house itself was quite pretty. There were a few cars parked in the gravel lot alongside the building. I got out of the car.

"I'm coming in with you," Gus said.

"I think it's better if I do this on my own," I said.

"All right, Baron, but I'll be waiting right outside the door. If I hear anything bad goin' on, I'm coming in."

"OK, Gus. Thanks," I said, and headed for the front door.

Paul glanced up and noticed me when I entered. He was behind the counter, talking to an American couple. The lobby was filled with upholstered chairs and wooden tables. He appeared to be giving the couple directions to the beach. They walked past me as they left.

Paul came out from behind the counter and stood a few feet from me.

"I figured you'd find me sooner or later, Sammy," he said. "I guess you're here about Kenneman's money."

"How the fuck could you do it, Paul?" I asked. "We were friends. We go back years. How could you do this to me?"

"It had nothing to do with you, Sammy. It was between me and Kenneman."

"It was our *business*, goddamnit. You destroyed the business and took money that didn't belong to you. I don't give a shit *what* was going on between you and Kenneman. I want the fucking money back."

"That's not going to happen, Sammy. And if you're going to talk to me like that, I want you to get out."

"I'm not leaving without the money."

Paul came toward me and shoved me hard. "Get the fuck out of my place. Go back to your bitch Kenneman and don't come back."

"Fuck you," I screamed. "I'm not leaving. I want the money!"

Paul tried to push me again. As he came toward me, I turned and used his momentum to throw him over my shoulder. I executed the throw impeccably. He landed hard on the ground.

Paul jumped up immediately and charged at me. He reached for my neck as if to apply a choke hold.

He was wearing a loose white shirt. With both hands I grabbed at the material of his shirt as if they were lapels of a coat. I rolled backward as I did, curling my legs up and wedging the sole of my right foot into Paul's abdomen as I thrust the leg upward explosively. Paul flew high into the air over my head and fell onto a wooden table. The table smashed under his weight—he and the wood fragments collapsed in a pile on the floor. I leaped up and backed away a couple of steps to gird myself, ready for his next onslaught. We were about ten feet apart.

Paul arose slowly. But he gathered himself and screamed as he ran toward me again.

He didn't reach me, though.

The gunshot was loud and jarring. Paul stopped dead in his tracks. I felt the air current as the bullet whirred over my head and buried itself in the stucco wall behind me. Paul and I both turned toward the sound of the discharge. There was Jill, holding a small pistol with both hands.

She screamed at me: "You touch Paul again and I swear I will shoot you dead, Sammy. Don't you move."

I remained still, considering what to do.

At that moment the door burst open, and Gus, with gun drawn, took one step in and bellowed at Jill in a fearsome reverberating baritone. "Police officer. Put the gun down, ma'am."

Gus's position was off to Jill's side and somewhat behind her. She kept her pistol pointed at me but turned her head to look at Gus. His gun was enormous, his expression terrifying.

"My gun is pointed at your head, ma'am," he shouted. "Put your gun down immediately and step away. Do it now, or I *will* shoot you."

Trembling, she bent her knees and laid the pistol gently on the floor.

"That's good, ma'am," Gus said. "Now step away. Take five steps back."

Jill did as Gus commanded.

Gus walked toward her and picked up her pistol. He emptied it, letting the bullets fall to the floor. He tossed the empty pistol across the room, where it landed behind a couch.

"Baron," he yelled. "Get back to the car. Do it!"

Gus pointed his gun alternately at Jill and Paul as I ran from the building. A moment later Gus joined me in the automobile. He shouted at the driver, "Get us to the airport! Now! No stops. Go fast."

———————

A week after returning from Costa Rica, I was perhaps even more furious than when I had left.

I tried to get back to our business. A couple times a week I checked in with our lead engineers to get implementation updates on current projects. But the conversations were perfunctory. I could barely focus on them.

Instead, I spent hours each day at the dining room table with Emmanuel. As my father sat with headphones blaring hate speech into his ears, building new shortwave radios to increase his access to right-wing propaganda, I sat at the other end of the table, testing configurations for my telepathic wave amplifier.

I remained obsessed with Paul and Jill. I wanted to hurt them. I wanted to break their bones and leave the two of them lying battered and broken in that lobby where Jill had fired a bullet over my head.

My thoughts kept returning to Alderman Jarielski in Chicago, and the broken arm he suffered at the very moment I imagined myself inflicting that same injury upon him. What if I really had caused it? With this machine amplifying my psychic transmissions, I could wreak havoc upon the bodies of Paul and Jill, and yet remain unscathed and blameless, miles away.

I continued to fine-tune the electronic apparatus. I swapped parts in and out manically, trying various frequencies and amplification patterns. Each time I reset the configuration, I tested it by attempting to send a psychic call to Emmanuel across the room.

I had made hundreds of such trials, telepathically yelling, "Emmanuel, look at me!" Over and over, it had elicited no response from him whatsoever.

Then one day, to my great shock, I sent the transmission, and Emmanuel turned in my direction, pulled his headphones from his ears, and asked, "Did you call me?"

"No," I said. "Go back to what you were doing."

But the proof was now there. I could amplify my thoughts and attack Paul and Jill mercilessly, inflicting upon them every degree of pain and injury I desired.

I closed my eyes and imagined the two of them. I pictured the small building that housed the bed-and-breakfast inn. I tried to see them clearly, there in that building. I wanted them as vivid in my mind as possible before launching my onslaught.

My mind was focused.

I was ready to attack.

But just as I was about to begin the assault, a tsunami of self-hatred engulfed me. It staggered me. I felt barely able to keep my balance on the chair where I sat. I bowed my head and closed my eyes. A pain crept through my solar plexus and down to my hips.

The loathing I felt for myself was the most overwhelming emotion I had ever experienced.

What have I become? How can I do this? I loved these people once. Now I want to break and batter them over money? Money I could easily afford to lose? Who am I?

I straightened up and switched off the machine, then slouched in the chair and leaned my head back. I felt drained and exhausted.

For the first time in my life, I contemplated suicide. My thoughts were not concrete. It was not as if I wanted to kill myself then and there and was looking for a way to do it. Instead, it was a vague consideration—but something possible, something I might make real if I thought about it further.

These notions terrified me. My mind began screaming silently as I sat motionless on the chair.

I need help. I cannot rescue myself from what I have become. Please, something, help me. I don't want to be this creature. I can't survive as this creature.

It was at that moment that my mystical breakthrough occurred. Spontaneously.

After all the meditation sessions where I felt close but not quite there, the spiritual sensibility I sought for so long now rushed into me and filled every crevice of my mind and body with a consciousness that was overpowering, yet comforting and safe.

I felt protected. Redeemed.

I realized palpably that I was a tiny part of something universal, magnificent, and unfathomable.

Wordlessly, nonrationally, the consciousness wiped away the duality of every moral dilemma I had ever pondered. Good and evil, love and hate, all seamlessly wove themselves into a unified tapestry that made immaculate sense.

Time seemed inconsequential. This universal sensibility was not just ubiquitous and eternal—it was all and everywhere at the same instant. All things past, present, and future entwined together without creases, without corrugation, without rational shape or definition.

I felt boundless love for every creature on the earth, humans and animals, without differentiation. It was more than love. I had become a part of them, a tiny part, a cog in a massive network of amorphous consciousness shared by each of them.

That sense of love now extended itself to every plant and rock on earth, every planet and star and dust particle in the universe. They were my family now—I was an intimate part of all of them. They accepted me as their own.

Most of all, I felt joy. Unfettered and unmitigated joy. Not a sort of momentary happiness over an incident or an accomplishment. This was a penetrating, engulfing, pervasive joy that seemed infinite and impervious.

I knew that I would never again be what I had been. Everything had changed.

My life would begin afresh.

———⌣———

I dismantled the telepathic amplification machine. I never again attempted to consciously send psychic messages to others, with or without electronic assistance.

Emmanuel's heart continued to weaken. Over the next few months, he had several small heart attacks and a ministroke. He slept a great deal each day.

I noticed that he rarely got angry anymore. Perhaps he had gained sufficient wisdom to finally transcend such outbursts, or perhaps they had just become too physically taxing for his weakened anatomy. I asked him once if he knew which one it was. He just laughed softly.

He died peacefully in his sleep shortly after that.

I met Jake for lunch a week after Emmanuel's funeral. I told Jake that I thought we should sell our business. Two of our senior engineers were interested in buying it. Jake had no objection.

I also shared with Jake that I planned to buy a house in San Francisco. I would keep my New York apartment, and split time between the two. I assured him we'd still see lots of each other. He said he was happy for me.

"And I want to get a dog, Jake," I said. "I've always wanted a dog."

"Dogs are good, Doc," he said.

Through a realtor, I secured a flat in San Francisco to use as a base to look for a house. I scheduled a charter flight from New York to the Bay Area and arranged with my doorman to check on my New York apartment now and then, and to check that my housekeeper continued to clean each week while I was gone.

I was looking forward to phoning Esther, to let her know about my decision. On the day I planned to call, I was surprised to see an envelope in the mail from her. She had never sent me a letter. Esther always called when she wanted to talk.

I opened the letter. It was handwritten:

Dearest Sammy,

If you are reading this letter, then I am dead.

I had been experiencing pain, but I ignored it for some time, hoping it would go away. When I finally went to the doctor and had the tests, the diagnosis was liver cancer. I had only a few weeks left at that point.

I did not want to burden my friends and family with my suffering. Sarah kept my secret and took care of me for the time remaining.

I wrote a few letters such as this one near the end, and asked Sarah to mail them after I passed.

Sammy, I want you to know how dear you were to me, and how much I loved you. There were few things in my life that made me happier than when we were able, after so many years, to reconnect, and experience the secret joys that we could share only through stares and innuendo years earlier in the Bronx. The moments we spent together were among my happiest.

I wish you good health and a long life, Sammy. But life, no matter how long, is but an instant in time. So I have no doubt that I will see you soon, and be able to enjoy your company again.

All my love,

Esther Johnson

For months, I thought of Esther intermittently throughout each day, and cried uncontrollably when I did.

———⌣———

It took me a few months to find the house I wanted in San Francisco—a modest and comfortable home just a few blocks from the entrance to the Rose Garden in Golden Gate Park.

The other San Francisco house I owned was still used for play parties by the BDSM group I had originally joined. After that first party, at which Esther and I reunited, I had always attended parties there as her slave. Esther never mentioned it, but she seemed to take pride in being not only the only African American dominatrix in the community, but also the only woman who regularly brought both a male and female slave to parties.

With my permission, additional groups in the Bay Area BDSM community had begun scheduling parties at that house as well. The groups had formed a board with one representative from each association to oversee its upkeep.

I decided to donate that house to the BDSM community, with the stipulation that it be called, in perpetuity, the Esther Memorial House. I was given an open invitation to visit the house for any future parties I might wish to take part in. I was appreciative, but never attended one.

Without Esther, the prospect of public play now seemed somehow hollow and gratuitous.

But my private fantasy life remained rich. I concocted rousing scenarios, some with Esther, others with Stephanie. On rare occasions, I envisioned encounters with the two of them together. I found these more difficult to orchestrate realistically, but when I was able to, my physical response was delectably volatile.

Sarah asked her law firm to transfer her to their Chicago office. Her family was there. She and I corresponded through letters for about a year but lost touch after that.

I began undertaking occasional bouts of private consulting work, much of it pro bono for nonprofit organizations and charitable foundations. One of my favorite stints was at the C. G. Jung Institute of San Francisco.

After a couple of years, I finally fulfilled my dream of adopting a dog. I visited the shelter and viewed many canine candidates. One, however, riveted my attention. She lay motionless in the back of her cage, as far from the human onlookers as she could get. She didn't move or respond to my calls. But there was an energy about her I found beguiling.

The placard on the cage said she was two years old, a cattle dog and corgi mix. Her name was Sapphire.

I expressed my interest to a shelter representative.

I was led to a small outdoor enclosure with benches and grass, surrounded by a wooden fence that reached about to my chest. I was asked to sit and wait. They'd bring Sapphire to me so the two of us could spend some time together, and I could see if this was indeed the dog I wanted.

I waited there a long time. When a young fellow finally brought Sapphire in, it was clear he'd had difficulty coaxing her to make the trip. He had to practically drag her into the enclosure.

I was on the bench. He positioned Sapphire near my feet.

Sapphire immediately plunged down on her belly, buried her paws and tail tightly beneath her, and pressed her head hard against the grass. No matter what he or I did, the dog would not budge. She allowed me to pet her, but displayed no reaction whatever, and remained so still and rigid that she appeared genuinely catatonic.

"Six other families looked at her," the young man said. "She was like this with everyone."

"Do you think she's suffered some sort of trauma?" I asked.

"Most likely," he said. "She was picked up wandering the streets of San Jose. No identification. No clues other than a huge scar running almost all the way down one of her back legs. It must have been a painful injury. We can tell it was never treated because the scar is jagged. But that's all we know. I wish these animals could tell us what happened to them. But they can't, no matter how much we ask."

He and I tried for another ten or fifteen minutes to get some response out of her, but she remained motionless and utterly impassive.

The young man seemed flabbergasted when I said, "I like this dog. I'll take her home."

As we filled out the paperwork in the shelter's office, the young fellow appeared fearful that I would soon become frustrated and bring the dog back.

"You'll need to be patient with her, sir," he said. "It could take six months or more before she comes around. A dog psychologist might be a good idea, if you can afford it."

He didn't say that if I decided not to take her, or if I brought her back, she'd likely be euthanized to make room for a more adoptable dog. It was obvious. But that wasn't why I chose her. I sensed a singular spirit buried under her fear. She was sad and alone, but seemed extraordinarily intelligent, and capable of great love and loyalty. And perhaps even zest for life.

The first couple of days were hard. I could barely get Sapphire out of the house for walks. She'd skulk along slowly, low to the ground, her tail held tightly between her legs. I'd only be able to drag her a quarter of a block; then she'd become so frightened we'd have to turn around and go back.

But love, good food, and lots of physical contact soon rendered the six-month diagnosis moot. In two weeks we were taking longer walks. By six weeks, she was prancing about the neighborhood as if it was hers, her tail wagging proudly. She'd allot her urine carefully, marking her new territory constantly in small squirts, but she was smart enough to realize that when we neared the house on our return, it was time to stop and empty her bladder of her remaining store.

I began taking her on long morning hikes, where she could roam off leash. She took to it immediately. The only clue to her past that I ever picked up on was her distinct fear of large men with beards. She'd run from anyone fitting that description if we encountered them on the trail. That phobia faded within our first year together, but it suggested to me at least some aspect of what her story might have been.

25.
Cat's Whisker

VIRGINIA FERGUSON TOOK ME UP on my dinner invitation while her husband was out of town, attending an insurance convention in the Midwest. We made a day of it.

Following our afternoon tai chi session in Golden Gate Park, we drove across town to Rainbow Grocery, a huge vegetarian co-op. We bought vegetables, fruit, grains, and tofu. We also purchased a slab of a deliciously pungent fermented soy product called tempeh. Virginia and I had chatted during the drive over and were surprised to discover we both loved tempeh. We decided to make it the star of our main dish.

Virginia also introduced me that afternoon to sea vegetables, with which I had never experimented. She bought wakame, kombu strips, kelp flakes, and a small block of agar.

On the way back to my house, we stopped to pick up her dog, Kata.

It was the first time Kata had visited my home, but Sapphire knew him well. Kata sniffed around a bit, with Sapphire shadowing close behind him. Then Kata wanted to play. But Sapphire would have none of it, and plopped down by the fireplace. Kata tried futilely to lure Sapphy into chasing him. He finally gave up and lay down next to her, their bodies pressing lightly against each other.

Virginia and I spent the rest of the afternoon preparing the multicourse vegan feast that we had designed while driving to the market.

Our appetizer was two small whole wheat bruschetta toasts, with a mock tuna salad topping. The tuna fish mouthfeel was impersonated by chopped chickpeas and artichoke hearts. It was flavored, as one might expect, with minced onion and celery, and vegan mayonnaise. But it was a combination of nutritional yeast for a fleshy underpinning and flaked kelp for a fishy tang that made the amalgam eerily authentic.

A small cup of light soup followed. It was a favorite of Virginia's, a classic Japanese miso soup with small cubes of tofu floating in it. Japanese dashi (or broth) is traditionally prepared with dried bonito flakes produced from a medium-sized fish related to mackerel and tuna. But Virginia again used seaweed, in this case kombu strips, to evoke a fishy flavor, and made a delicious stock. She also added a few enoki mushrooms and a pinch of the sea vegetable wakame, which inflated and burst as it cooked, flecking the soup with delicious, salty green shards.

A small salad of avocado, heirloom tomato, black olives, red onion, and pine nuts followed. We dressed it with olive oil and balsamic vinegar, and sprinkled on top of it tiny pinches of a brie-like vegan cheese, made of cultured cashew milk.

Our main course was marinated tempeh over a bed of quinoa. The tempeh was first simmered in red wine with vegetable stock and herbs, then seared in olive oil to crisp the surface. We topped it with a sauce of macerated fresh figs cooked in stock with onion, garlic, vinegar, and rosemary, then sprinkled toasted pistachios onto the plate just prior to serving.

For dessert, Virginia showed me how to use the seaweed agar as a gelling agent. We made a vegan cherry gelatin, sweetened with maple syrup.

I drank wine with dinner. Virginia did not, pointing out that the Rosicrucian Order advised against alcohol as well as flesh foods. She said *cooking* with wine was all right, as long as the alcohol burned off.

I mentioned that while Eastern religions eschew alcohol, and characterize it as an impediment to spiritual enlightenment, Western religions such as Judaism and Christianity incorporate wine into their ceremonies. Since Rosicrucians investigate the religious practices of *all* religions, there might be some ambiguity there.

But we pursued it no further. Had I been talking with Jake, we'd have debated the point through at least two rounds of cocktails.

After dinner we took the dogs out for a short walk. The neighborhood was new for Kata, so he did lots of marking, spraying small parcels of his urine on the sidewalk and the bottoms of trees.

"Sapphire doesn't mark her territory anymore," I said. "She used to, a great deal."

"Why do you think, Sammy?"

"Maybe physically the muscles there just don't hold as well now," I said. "But I actually think it has more to do with confidence. Sapphire can't hear now, she doesn't see well, she can't run. I believe she's aware of all that on some level. She doesn't feel deserving of marking the territory."

"Do you really think so?"

"I do. Sapphire was very fearful and timid when I first got her. It was completely attributable to what was going on in her life at the time. So, I see no reason why she couldn't return to that sensibility, if she interpreted her place in her environment as uncertain. She's extraordinarily aware."

When we returned home I poured myself another glass of wine. We sat with the dogs in the living room. Virginia sipped on chamomile tea. A log burned in the fireplace.

"You seem happy with your life," Virginia said.

"I think I crossed a hurdle recently," I replied. "The deaths of my mother and my brother haunted me for many decades. Both their deaths could, in some way, be attributed to me, to things I did. In my brother's case, it was straightforward. I introduced him to drugs. When I realized he was taking it too far, I tried to intervene. But I couldn't stop him—it was too late by then. With my mother it was much more nuanced. I was angry at her for a long time. Our relationship was awful. I wished her dead. And then she died. I do have some psychic talents, Virginia. I'm a bit of a sender. I could have caused it. Or not. It's impossible to know. But both deaths haunted me for a very long time. Only the nonrational power of mystical consciousness has cleansed me of it now, without my needing to know if I was indeed responsible for either one."

"Sammy, I'm glad you've gotten past all that. But you need to know, neither of those were your responsibility. You didn't directly cause either of them. Lots of us experimented with drugs back then. Almost all of us got through it. If your brother didn't, especially if you tried to help him, that's on *him*, Sammy.

"And as for your mother, the idea that *you*, at that very young age, could possibly have had the psychic power to cause another person's death is absurd. Exalted masters who have practiced meditation for their entire lifetimes can't do that. Believe me, if people could kill other people just by thinking about it, the Pentagon and CIA would be all over it. In fact, Sammy, the only being that I know of that you've *truly* been responsible for is Sapphire. And nobody could be more nurturing and loving than you are to her."

"Thank you, Virginia. That's very kind."

"She's a special girl, isn't she?"

"I don't just say this as a proud parent—many others have corroborated it: Sapphire is the smartest dog any of us have known."

"There's something else I've been thinking about, Sammy—your lifelong interest in the Rosicrucian Order. It's occurred to me that you could be thought of as an honorary member of sorts. Your whole life has been a journey of examining spiritual paths and artifacts. In a way, you've mimicked what the Rosicrucian Order has done for centuries. You've fashioned your own personal Rosicrucian-type journey."

"I trust my own path now, Virginia. It took me this long not just to *find* it, but to convince myself that I had examined other options thoroughly enough to *embrace* mine without doubt or fear."

"Most people can't do it themselves, Sammy. They need an organization to be part of. It's somewhat remarkable that you did it completely on your own."

I laughed softly. "Virginia, I had no choice. I could *only* do it alone. Not because I'm better or smarter. Because I'm innately *incapable of joining an organization*."

"Well, I run our neighborhood's small Rosicrucian lodge, Sammy, so in a way, it's mine. And I'll have you. Even if only as an honorary member in my own mind. Consider yourself an honorary Rosicrucian, Sammy." She giggled girlishly. "But keep it just between you and me."

"Agreed," I said. "Thank you."

"I just got a great idea!" she exclaimed. "We have a meeting in three weeks, and I haven't been able to find a presenter yet. Why don't *you* be the speaker? You can describe your spiritual path, how you came to practice walking meditation. I think it would be well received, Sammy."

"Are you sure?" I asked.

"Sammy, you'd be helping me out. I need a presenter."

"Well, if it would really help you . . ."

———⟨⟩———

Virginia introduced me.

"Our presenter today is a very interesting man. He is a spiritual seeker, like us. But his innate and encompassing introversion prevents him from joining a society such as ours. So, from the beginning, he was forced to go it alone. Even so, he followed a path very close to ours, examining mystical artifacts wherever he could find them. He culled out those that suited him personally, but also was driven to make his spiritual beliefs completely compatible with science. I'm proud to call him a friend. He has, at times, been an engineer, an inventor, an entrepreneur, and a jiu-jitsu master. But he has *always* been a seeker. Please welcome Samuel Baron."

It was a small group. There was light applause.

I walked to the podium.

"After listening to so many talks here," I said, "being asked to speak is a true honor. And humbling. I'd like to start by thanking many of you in the audience who have accepted and befriended me, despite my less-than-orthodox association with the Rosicrucian Order.

"Please let me emphasize at the beginning that what I'll be talking about today is my own personal journey. It may correspond in ways to yours, or may not. All our paths are valid. I'm just sharing mine.

"Virginia touched on the crux of what I want to talk about—science and spirituality. I find it sad that so many people feel they need to choose between the two. We all know of people who feel they must reject Darwin's theory of evolution, or the big bang theory of the creation of the universe, or other aspects of science. Their rejection stems from their belief that these scientific perspectives clash with their religion. Here, in the twenty-first century, these poor people miss out on the incredible beauty and wonder of science.

"But I'm sure we all know people too who have become atheists, who steadfastly believe in nothing. Because, if they dared to believe, they'd be contradicting the tenets of science; they'd be basing their ideology on faith rather than facts. Don't these people *also* miss out on something just as vital and important? Since the earliest days of humankind, every tribe has developed rituals to fuse their corporeal existences with the mystical reality they sensed as extant in the cosmos. It is a yearning as innate to us as is our quest for factual knowledge.

"But are science and spirituality really so different? Or are they, as they seem to me, two distinct aspects of the very same reality?

"A palpable excitement wells up in me when I read an article, or view a documentary, on animal intelligence or evolution. I get chills and feel my spiritual self reignite viscerally as I learn how in our amazing world, over millions of years, living things have adapted, changed, evolved, and thrived. Are these millions of metamorphoses any less spectacular than the story of Genesis in the Bible? To me, they are in a way *more* spectacular.

"My personal scientific journey began with electronics. Radio, to be precise. Invisible electronic waves that transmit sounds that have been broadcast. The scientific challenge of radio is to find a way to capture those waves, and convert them back into a form that humans can hear and understand.

"Is this act so different from what all of us in this room do when we try to tap into the essence of universal consciousness through meditation? Are we not like an antenna trying to pick up a radio signal? Are we not like electronic components attempting to parse, amplify, and make that signal understandable? Of course, we try to comprehend something far more magnificent and vast than simple sounds. We try to experience something that cannot be rationally fathomed or understood.

"That's important to me. That cosmic consciousness cannot be *rationally* fathomed or understood. It can only be experienced. That, I think, is the greatest mistake we humans have made through the centuries. We've been so arrogant as to believe that we can *rationally* understand cosmic consciousness, corral it, and codify it in laws and admonitions.

"In my opinion, we should instead humbly accept that we can experience it only *nonrationally*. We can go back to it over and over, and take from it whatever wisdom and compassion we can bring back to our material lives. But that, really, is all we can do.

"We all seek to receive signals as best we can. Sound is a perfect example. As an inventor who started by building radios, sound has become, for me, a sort of symbol for anything we seek to corral.

"It's interesting, I think, that when humans process sound, science and mathematics become intimately bound up with emotion and spirit, with respect to what we hear. The frequency of sound waves is interpreted by the human ear and brain as *pitch*. If you stretch a string, and pluck it, the vibrations produce waves in the air that we hear as sound. But if you delve just a bit deeper, remarkable truths emerge. Pressing a guitar string at the fret that divides the string exactly in half results in precisely doubling the frequency of the sound wave. Our ears and brains interpret this doubling as a perfect octave, which for whatever reason sounds to us as if the pitch has come exactly full circle. The tone has completed, rectified, and resolved itself and begun a new cycle. We hear it as the same note.

"So there is a connection between how we as humans hear sound, and what scientifically produces sound. Similarly, we can interpret music as beautiful or even mystical.

"The music of Bach has been called by some the most spiritually moving music in the history of Christian-inspired compositions. But scientists often describe Bach's music as *mathematically* pure. I don't personally meditate to music, but I know people who do, and many of them have told me that Bach's works are the best for that purpose. I *do* practice yoga with music, and always play Bach during my sessions.

"So, *meditation* is sort of our mystical *radio*. It is the means we use to capture those invisible signals and convert them into something we can, as human beings, experience palpably.

"As is probably true for most of you, I've had a long history with meditation. I studied jiu-jitsu for many years. Meditation has always been a constituent of martial arts. For me, though, the meditation I practiced there focused me for training and sparring, but it didn't take me to the ultimate spiritual destination I wished for.

"Years ago, I went to a meditation retreat. It was in many ways a humbling experience, but it ultimately spurred me to meditate daily. And perhaps even more importantly, it inspired me to become a vegetarian. That dietary path, remarkably, changed the whole fabric of spiritual receptivity for me. And that was a surprise to me. I never would have rationally made that connection between diet and mystical receptivity.

"Then there was my breakthrough moment. All of us have sought the breakthrough. The mystical breakthrough I ultimately experienced was extraordinarily powerful and magnificent and life altering. However, it was by no means an end in itself. I at first imagined it *would* be. I thought I'd live blissfully ever after. But as we all know, that is not the case. There is so much more work to be done. It's really only a beginning.

"The sensibility the breakthrough engendered remained integrated in me for about three months. Then it started to fade away, and I had to rely on meditation to get back to it every day. I was usually able to return to the state, but it often dissipated shortly after I finished meditating. The most disturbing thing for me was that it often seemed like a parlor trick, being able to conjure up the state the way a magician would pull a ball out of the air. I wanted it to be *more* than that. I wanted it to be *part* of me. But many times it wasn't. The state would reappear, but then it would disappear very quickly—and I'd remain intrinsically unchanged.

"That became my biggest frustration.

"It was that frustration that eventually led me to *walking* meditation. Meditating while I'm hiking each morning, while I'm keeping an eye on my dog, while I'm happily undertaking sporadic chats with my many trail acquaintances, while I'm occasionally spotting a blue heron soaring, or an owl perched high on a branch. All of that creates a meditation state that is vibrantly in the moment. It may be somewhat less intense than a seated, silent meditation state, but for me it is much more real, much more integrated into my corporeal being. And most importantly, it tends to stay with me for the entire day. It fuses into my being. It becomes who I am. And that is what I always sought—to integrate that sensibility into my day-to-day being.

"I practiced walking meditation for a long time before discovering a new twist on it. It's probably not an ideal way to try to start if you're new at it, but once the illuminated state of being becomes a familiar one, you can move on to this variation. Rather than working from the outset at stilling the mind, letting thoughts drift away and dissipate, this variation encourages you to allow yourself to think, to ponder issues that concern you, but only after first programming the mind to stop when it's ready, and still itself then. I find now that often one effort leads to the other—the issues I ponder set the stage rationally for the leap into the nonrational mystical experience that follows.

"But no matter how long I've been meditating, it never becomes a perfect science. Every day is a bit different, as I try to tune in to the mystical energy as clearly and fully as I can. So for me it comes full circle, back to my analogy of picking up radio waves.

"My father built radios all his life. It was he who introduced me to radio. But of all the radios we built together, the most amazing was the most basic. It relied on something called a cat's whisker. There was an antenna and a ground and a pair of headphones. But the magic of turning electronic waves back into sound depended on a primitive semiconductor called a cat's whisker, which we concocted out of a tarnished kitchen knife, a bit of graphite from a pencil, and some wire. But you had to fiddle with it. Every time you hooked it up, you had to patiently move the graphite to various spots on the tarnished knife, and constantly adjust the pressure that the graphite's point exerted on the metal. These seemingly innumerable tweaks were necessary to tune the signal. No matter how many times you used the cat's whisker, you could not evade that persistent recalibration.

"Meditation, at least for me, never becomes automatic or precisely repeatable. It's like that cat's whisker I built as a boy with my father. Just like the radio waves, the reality I seek to touch is out there, hovering invisibly, around me and within me. But I need to keep readjusting the elements in play—keep jiggling the stylus to find precisely the spot on the tarnished knife, to receive the transmission. And like electronic amplification, I continually filter out the stray thoughts, and amplify that which is eternal and immutable."

———————

I flew to New York for the twentieth anniversary of Emmanuel's death.

Virginia Ferguson had offered to watch Sapphire. She thought Sapphy was too old and frail to make the trip. But I told Virginia that now, more than ever, Sapphire and I needed to stay together.

I chartered the same jet we had used so many times. Sapphire knew the cabin well, and slept most of the flight.

We stayed at my apartment off Central Park the night we arrived. When we visited the cemetery late the next afternoon, it was snowing lightly. An inch or two of snow covered the grass and paths.

Sapphire had always loved snow.

We hiked up the hill to Emmanuel's grave. My mother's tombstone and David's were alongside his. Sapphire and I stood silently in the snow for a long time.

I noticed a woman in a black coat walking toward us. The snow made it difficult to identify who she was. It wasn't until she was quite close that I could make out her features.

I was stunned.

It was Stephanie.

Her hair was a bit shorter. There were lines on her face that I did not recall. Her eyes seemed wiser—the skin around them bore witness to years of life. Her face was a bit thinner, its skin more taut.

She looked beautiful.

"Hello, Sammy," she said softly.

"Stephanie! It's so good to see you. You look wonderful."

"Thank you, Sammy. You look great too."

I turned and faced her fully. "What are you doing here?" I asked.

"It's Emmanuel's twentieth. I couldn't very well miss that. And I could have sworn you were calling to me. You've been in my dreams for weeks."

"Calling to you?"

"You always were a sender, Sammy. Were you sending a psychic message to me?"

I thought for a moment. "Perhaps. I honestly don't know, Steph." I smiled. "I learned a long time ago to leave all that sort of thing to my subconscious. I never mess with psychic transmissions consciously anymore. It works out a whole lot better when I keep myself out of it. I can't be trusted with that kind of power."

Stephanie looked probingly into my eyes.

"You've changed, Sammy," she said. "You're gentler. You've let go of so much."

"I have," I said.

I paused a moment to formulate what I wanted to express. "Listen, Steph, I'm so sorry for everything that happened. I was so wrong—"

She held the finger of her gloved hand up to my lips, but didn't quite touch them.

"Stop," she said. "There's more than enough blame to go around. I never told you this, Sammy. But I intentionally let things slide with the Chicago project. I thought if it had problems, you'd come out to Chicago, and I'd be able to spend more time with you. But it kept you away, didn't it?"

"My God, Steph, why didn't we just talk to each other?"

Sapphire had been sniffing Stephanie's tall leather boots. Now Sapphy lay down in the snow, resting her snout near Stephanie's right instep.

"Is Sapphire okay near your foot like that?" I asked.

"It's fine," she said. "She adorable. How old is she?"

"She's eighteen now."

"Eighteen? My goodness."

I gazed at Stephanie's face and smiled. "So, how have *you* been, Steph? Are you still living in Chicago?"

"Actually, I live right out here on Long Island. Just about twenty minutes away."

"Really? I heard you got married."

"Sammy, I got divorced a long time ago. We were okay for a few years. But the more he drank, the more violent he got. The first time he hit me I forgave him. The second time I left."

"He didn't hurt you, did he?" I asked.

"Nothing I couldn't recover from. But I did have to put out a restraining order on him."

"Did he honor it?"

"Not really. That's why I left Chicago, and moved back to New York."

"Well," I said, "at least you're rid of him now."

"I don't know," she said. "I could swear I see him sitting in a car in front of my house once or twice a year."

I leaned my head toward her. "Do you think it would help," I asked, "if you were seen regularly in the company of a man who was once a jiu-jitsu master?"

Stephanie laughed softly and took a step closer.

"Being seen in your company would help in a whole lot of ways, Sammy."

It started snowing harder. The wind picked up. Snowflakes swirled into our faces.

"Why don't you and Sapphire come home with me?" she asked. "Spend the night at my house. It's much closer. I'll make dinner. And my neighbor has a dog—I'll borrow some dog food for Sapphire."

"I have a driver here," I said.

"Send him home."

I looked away, then back toward her. "I'm a bit of a pain to cook for these days, Steph. I'm a vegan now."

Stephanie smiled. "Oh God, not you too! I have two nieces who turned vegan. Well, thank goodness I got to practice on them. I actually make a vegan lasagna that even *I* like."

"Really? What do you use in place of cheese?"

"Oh, I blend up raw cashews, chickpeas, and tofu. It sounds weird, but it's surprisingly good once I season it up and throw in a bunch of nutritional yeast."

"It sounds delightful," I said. "We'd love to join you."

The three of us started back to the cars. Emmanuel's plot was a good ways in—it would take us several minutes to get down to the parking lot. Stephanie slipped her hand inside my upper arm as she walked beside me.

"I'll need to make a quick stop at the hardware store on the way home," she whispered. "I need a hunk of rope and some clothespins."

The glare of the setting sun reflected off the fallen snow. I was sure it rendered Sapphire nearly sightless. I watched her nuzzle between Stephanie and me as she walked. Her fur gently brushed each of our calves.

I knew she felt safe there.

The End